THE WAVES OF DISSONANCE

A Dystopian Novel

ISBN 9798694618182

To my hero, Captain Steven Clark, who shows me every day that TODAY is the best day ever.

In 1997, this story first came to life in a tiny upstairs dormer "closet-office" inside a drafty old Quantico, MD farmhouse. Since then, many friends and readers have lent me their encouragement, opinions, and editorial skills, and I owe them more thanks than this page can express. Thank you so much to Jacki Prevenas (editor extraordinaire!), and to Linda Bush, Tina Whittle, Marge McLaughlin, Bob deLaar, Nicole Gillen, Cal Milsap, Maria Mellis, Rick Pieece, Tim Kenney, and, of course, my rock, Steven Clark. Thank you all so much!

DAY ONE

The Dragon

"A great and wondrous sign appeared in heaven: a woman… was pregnant and cried out in pain as she was about to give birth.

"Then another sign appeared in heaven: an enormous red dragon… stood in front of the woman… so that he might devour her child the moment it was born. She gave birth to a son, a male child who will rule all the nations…

"And there was a war in heaven."

--Revelations 12:1-6
The Bible, New International Version

DEPOSITION #20561110.001

Even in a society made up almost entirely of women, Katherine Buford made heads turn. I should know; she turned my head first. You might ask, then, how I could give her up. All I can say is that at the time, I told myself she would be better off without me, that it was all for the best, and I had no other alternative. Truth is, though, there is always a choice. Back then, I just tended to make bad ones… and selfish ones. I knew a daughter would only hold me back.

It wasn't until two years later, when I first saw Katherine's face over live TV, that I realized my mistake. I couldn't look away. I knew she was mine, of course; but by then, Senator Pat Buford had already adopted her, turning the girl into a miniature version of herself, and nothing short of a political upheaval could have wrenched my daughter out from under that old crone's powerful control.

I spent the next sixteen years chasing other dreams… or so I believed. Now, I realize my subconscious had lured me into a close, working relationship with the very person I detested. The benefits, however, were clear: I had full access to Katherine every Sunday night, thanks to Pat's reality show, *Family Hour with the Bufords*, and from there, I got to watch my daughter grow up amid lights, cameras, and charismatic sermons.

By the time Katherine turned eighteen, I thought I knew everything about her. I knew, for instance, she was always smiling, even when she had worn braces in the sixth grade, and that her bouncy, brown bangs hung constantly in her eyes. I knew she fidgeted in church, got tongue-tied in public, and tended to talk to herself when she thought no one was watching.

It's what I didn't know that hurt her.

The day I decided to publicly proclaim her as my own, the timing seemed perfect. At eighteen, she was finally a woman. With her popular face and influence, she would be ideal to rule by my side. If only I had known what she was planning, I would have intervened much earlier. I would have told her the truth, said that I'm sorry, and protected her from the evils of the other side. Now, it appears, I have missed my chance.

Every time I close my eyes, I will forever relive the moment I last saw my daughter's face. What I witnessed that day, no parent should ever have to see.

ONE

Waverly Nelson leaned back against the hard, muscular leg of the only man she had lain with in over eighteen years, and smiled absently at his head, lying forty feet away. In the pre-dawn shadows beside the glassy Potomac River, she could see the man's cavernous mouth—gaped open in a perpetual, frozen scream—and his wide, unseeing eyes staring upward, as though beseeching the heavens for mercy.

Only, Heaven wasn't listening.

Like a colossal, mythological figure caught midway between purgatory and hell, the bearded statue before her, called *the Awakening,* lay frozen on its back. One massive, gunmetal arm stretched upward toward freedom, its gnarled fist frozen seventeen feet in the air, and the other hand rose to nearly ten-feet tall, trapped firmly by the ground at the wrist. A lone foot, behind her, and the protruding bent knee at her back were the only other body parts above ground.

Just as it should be, she thought.

Thanks to Waverly's generous donations over the years, this National Harbor landmark was one of the few works of art to withstand the many years of neglect following the 2020 Plague. When she had first visited it as a child, most historic buildings and memorials in the infamous "D.C. Ghost Town" (New America's former Capital) were already covered in vines. *The Awakening* had been no exception.

That day, she had cowered under the statue's massive, open palm, certain the disembodied giant would spring to life at any moment and squash her tiny body. She had bravely bared her teeth for her father's camera—"Just one more shot, Sweetheart!"—but all the while, she had sensed the sculpture's cold, metallic fingers overhead, closing in.

"Powerful, isn't he?" her father had later boasted as they explored the man's Zeus-like face, pulling off weeds and rapping their knuckles against his beard and each sunken, hollow eye. "He survived the Plague, just like your ma and me, and he's still struggling, too. This sculpture represents man's unyielding determination... his spirit! By rising up and freeing himself from the bondage of hell and earth, he reminds us to never give up hope." He saw her skeptical expression and laughed. "Trust me, little Wave, you have nothing to fear from him."

Waverly had eyed the statue with continued misgiving. Even at that young age, she had known her father was mistaken. To her, the man wasn't rising toward Heaven; he was falling from it. And in his desperate, flailing attempt to save himself, she knew he was liable to grab onto anything, or anyone, to keep from sinking further. To her, the statue represented man's weakness. It showcased his defeat.

Now, thirty years later, as she mindlessly fingered a ladybug-shaped pendant hanging from a chain around her neck, she couldn't stop smiling.

"Looks like I was right, Pops," she said to herself, aloud. "After all, your man is still lying here, frozen and helpless in the sand, and in three days' time, all men, including Senator Marshall Danforth, will be in virtually the same position."

She could hardly wait.

***

Waverly Nelson and Senator Danforth went way back—back to the days he was a thin, eager young pastor at First Calvary Baptist Church in Boston, and she was a pregnant teen in labor. Danforth's pretty wife, Marisa, had also been in labor at the time. They were still wheeling young Waverly in when her baby had started to crown. Over the pain of her contractions, she had heard a male voice declare, "Remove that whore from my wife's room at once!" and had known the man meant her.

No one listened, however. With the hospital severely short-staffed and both women in active labor, an intern had wheeled Waverly's stretcher right next to Marisa's so the doctor could take care of them both. The

5

deliveries were nearly simultaneous. At one point in the final birthing moments, Waverly could have sworn the two women had even held hands.

Later, in Recovery, Waverly had awakened to find a man lurking by her bed. His wrinkled suit and shirt suggested a long previous night, but his eyes appeared strangely animated. She recognized his voice in an instant. It was the same man from in the delivery room.

"Young lady," he announced, as though delivering a prepared speech. "You have been living in a cesspool, both physically and spiritually. It is time for you to atone."

Sheets rustled as other patients stirred to watch.

"I was there when your pimp dropped you off," he continued. "Fat into labor, yet there you were… in fishnet stockings, a purple boa, and peacock-feather eyelashes. Ridiculous! You might as well have had the word WHORE tattooed across your forehead. And don't even get me started about your scars! No doubt you're a junkie and burned off your hair freebasing!"

Waverly sank into her pillow and pulled the top sheet up to her chin. The sheets smelled like bleach, but they did not make her feel clean. She squinted at the man in confusion and exhaustion. *Why is he saying these things?*

"I heard you tell the Hospital Advocate you are homeless and alone," he continued. "What are you; sixteen? What kind of life can you offer a child? My church offers financial and emotional support for people like you. We'll pay your medical expenses and provide you a generous check to help make a fresh start. In return, all you have to do is sign these papers relinquishing all parental rights."

He pulled out a thick, manila envelope from inside his left breast pocket and placed it on her nightstand. "These papers explain everything. In the meantime, I'm to deliver your daughter to Child Protective Services."

He spat when he spoke, and the shock of it, cold against her check, inflamed her.

"What? No!" she cried, bringing out both elbows from underneath the sheet. He flinched for an instant, as though she were about to attack him, then relaxed as she merely wiped away his spittle and her tears. "No!" she said, again. "You can't!"

That was the first time they made eye contact. The man seemed to consider her words, then he bent over and whispered in her face, "I can do whatever I want."

His breath, she recalled later, smelled strangely of chocolate. He straightened again and continued.

"Listen, kid, I am doing you a favor here, so take the money and be grateful. I promise to personally find your baby a good, Christian home, but if you fight me, I'll see to it you are charged with Child Endangerment... and Prostitution. You will go to jail, and will lose your baby, either way, so I suggest you take my offer. Contact my office when you're ready."

He flicked a business card onto the bed. With an air of satisfaction, he nodded as though concluding a transaction and strode with purpose toward the adjoining nursery. He emerged a few minutes later carrying a tightly-wrapped pink bundle.

"No... please!" she sobbed, but the man never looked back. He walked out the door, taking her infant with him. She never even got to see her baby's face.

No one came to console her. The other women in Recovery turned their backs on her once Danforth left, and even the nurses avoided her. Later that night, Waverly curled into a fetal position and cried herself to sleep.

The next morning, she saw the name on the discarded card, "Reverend Marshall Danforth," and finally began to hate. She shook with rage and frustration that this man could judge her without cause and then leave her with no recourse. That was the moment she pledged to ruin him.

***

Waverly sighed and blinked the memory away. The sun had risen slightly and now outlined *the Awakening's* face, carving deep shadows below the nose, the mouth, and eye crevasses. The sharp contrast made him look more like an evil spirit than the Greek god from which he had been modeled. Waverly barely recognized the change. To her, he had always been a demon.

Without thinking, she ran a hand over her bald head, feeling the still-tender scars, and flicked open her ladybug pendant wings. She double tapped the tiny keypad inside. Instantly, a virtual computer screen blinked to life, midair. With Lite-Brite audacity, its sharp pixels glowed an eerie green against the harbor's rising dawn.

Her company, Cis-Star Technologies, had first patented this VEE technology—and a long line of Virtual Energy Emission devices that followed—thirteen years ago. VEE-6 had been the first to use patterned interference to produce holographic images. Back then, it was expensive and clunky. Newer models were substantially cheaper... in every way. Critics had complained about the VEE's grainy holographic quality at first, but the free press had only helped spread the word. By the time VEE-7 came out, its Holo-lite™ technology was so lightweight she could produce it at half the cost. Sales skyrocketed. Before long, it was, quite literally, the latest public addiction. Today, practically everyone in New America (males and females alike) owned a VEE.

Waverly's own personal pendant was still in the prototype stage. In addition to the upgraded holographic capabilities, its patent-pending Touch-Lite feature allowed users to move data around in midair as easily as touching a traditional hard-slate screen. It was ideal for today's special programming.

With sudden eagerness, she plucked at the projected lights, interrupting the pixel sensors, and pulled up her encrypted file. There, in bright green text, were the commands she had previously written:
> "START MESSAGE:
> *'FOLLOW ME. FOLLOW ME.*
> *FREEDOM AND POWER TO THOSE WHO FOLLOW*
> *ME.'*
> END MESSAGE."

The next word, "RECIPIENT?" blinked the question she had been pondering for weeks. With a deep breath, meant to acknowledge the finality of her decision and all the preparation leading up to this moment, she spoke the name she had selected.

"Paul Brown."

As though mirroring Waverly's excitement at having finally chosen a name, the tiny pendant hummed and displayed the confirming words, "PAUL BROWN."

"EXECUTE?" the green letters asked her.

Waverly's lips twitched slightly.

"Yes," she said. "Execute."

The device whirled again. When it went quiet this time, she nodded and closed the ladybug wings. The VEE fell back hot, but not burning, against her sweater.

It's over, she sighed.

That wasn't exactly true, she knew. She still had one more missing puzzle piece to input, but she had narrowed the list of contenders and would make that decision before noon. Plenty of time. Until then, she would concentrate on the election. Double-checking the time on her VEE-4 (the wrist model, still sold on-line) she noted the polls hadn't even opened out west, but already her program was hard at work, compelling both sides to vote against Danforth.

A knowing smile tugged again at her lips. *Poor Danforth,* she thought. *He has no idea who I am and what's coming.* It almost made her feel sorry for him.

Almost.

She shifted again, and the massive leg's cold hardness behind her spread a delicious tingle down her outstretched legs. She closed her eyes to savor the feeling. She imagined her nemesis—no doubt tucked away in his penthouse office suite soaking in today's mental suggestions she had created just for him—blissfully unaware she had just sealed his fate.

She wondered when she should tell him. Tonight, perhaps? Right after the election results? Or tomorrow, after Buford was sworn in? After so many years spent orchestrating his defeat, it was hard to know what would offer her the most satisfaction.

TWO

Paul Brown wiped his brow with the back of a leathery hand and slipped his Craftsone hammer into its worn, canvas belt. Even with the sun barely above the horizon, he felt the humidity pressing on him with physical weight. His orange T-shirt clung to his back like a wet tissue.

"Whew!" he said, to no one in particular. "I'm sweating like a whore in church! Autumn used to mean bonfires, pumpkin pies, and hayrides. Who turned on the heat?"

"What's wrong, Old Timer?" asked a rookie to his right. "Can't handle the smell of hot tar and crotch rot?"

Paul ignored the comment and the accompanying snickers from behind him. His lungs did hurt from breathing in the last few days of bituminous fumes, but he would never admit it. Especially not to that young pup, whom Paul had nicknamed Green-Bean. Nothing seemed to bother that kid.

Paul reached for his hip-holstered canteen and surveyed the skeletal roof below him. *Not bad for a bunch of convicts,* he thought. He was glad they had finished the flat roof yesterday and had moved on to the tower's upper pitch this morning. Nothing but plywood, felt, and shingles to install from here out.

In a moment of defiance, he glanced over his shoulder—*Good! No women around!*—and peeled off his wet shirt. *Ah, much better!* His team took their cue and grabbed for their own water bottles. Paul noted that Green-Bean actually sat on the blistering roof and let his feet swing over the sloped edge.

Youth! Paul scowled. *Totally wasted on the young.*

From this vantage point, high atop Rock Island Prison's future Observation Tower complex, Paul could see the entire island, below him, and the surrounding Mississippi River, which stretch off north and south, beyond. Without thinking, he flexed his aching hands and frowned toward the western skyline. There along the banks lay the St. Louis Gateway arch, still in ruins, and New Canaan's shinning glass obelisk, the Info-Swirl, behind it. From this distance, he thought the Swirl's spiraling glass exterior looked more like a soft-serve ice-cream cone than a government building.

"Hey, Old Timer!" called Green-Bean. "Arthritis bothering you again?"

Paul whirled on the younger man. "Stop calling me Old Timer!" he said. "When you're forty-five, you'll wish you looked this good."

"Forty-five?" said Green-Bean. "Really?" A worker standing behind the rookie cleared his throat in warning, but Green-Bean looked confused. "What? Look at him; he's younger than my dad, but he looks twenty years older. Dude! Ever heard of sunscreen? And check out those knuckles. Last time I saw something that swollen, I was alone in my cell!"

Laughter came from all around, and Paul frowned. "There's nothing wrong with my hands, you little turd. I just gotta rest 'em awhile so I can hold my date tonight."

He waited for the rewarding chuckles, but Green-Bean was too quick.

"Hell, in that case," said the boy, "why not bring those soft hands over to my cell tonight, and we'll make it a double date?"

Paul reached for his hammer but then abandoned the idea. He needed to teach this recruit a lesson, but not today. It was just too damn hot.

Instead, he addressed the only man here at the Rock older than himself.

"Leonard, can you believe that shit? You and me, we're too old to be up here laying shingles in this heat. At our age, we ought to be kicked back, drinking beer, and watching football!"

Leonard mumbled something under his breath that sounded like "Got that right!" then he blew out one nostril. Mucus landed on the roof with a satisfying sizzle.

Paul faced west again.

His last visit to St. Louis had been twenty years ago. Back then, the Swirl was still under construction, and he was a high-priced defense attorney from Jackson, Mississippi. While on a break from that year's ABA convention, he and a few coworkers had toured the facility. Critics were calling it the "most innovative architecture of our time!" but Paul had been unimpressed.

What had aroused him, however, was the woman architect running the show and the all-female construction crew. Now, that had been worth the trip! He could have watched them all day. He jokingly bet a round of beers that he'd score some digits before the tour was over. His companions agreed to pay double if he got the architect's number. So, for the tour's final half-hour, Paul had used all his best material and his most dashing smile, but by the time the visit was over, it was clear he had lost the bet.

One leggy, blonde reporter named Honey Campbell, who had been doing an article on the Swirl for the *Associated Press*, actually seemed repulsed by his advances. He swore she had sneered when she'd replied he was not "her type."

That night at the bar, Paul laughingly admitted defeat. He bought the beers and endured his colleagues' good-natured ribbing, and that was the end of it—as far as anyone there was concerned. They all went back to the convention the next day and forgot the whole affair.

All, except, for Paul. He returned to the Swirl the next evening and taught Honey a lesson behind one of the job trailers—a lesson he went on to teach many other women over the years: never, ever rebuff Paul Brown!

He shifted his stance on the sloped roof, now, and looked east (opposite the Swirl and New Canaan) to the land across the Mississippi where Honey had undoubtedly moved.

Her and the rest of her lesbian MA'AM friends, he scoffed.

MA'AM (the Movement Against Aggressive Men) had started in Salem, Massachusetts the year prior to his St Louis trip. At first, the small group of feminists had concentrated on companies employing known sex offenders. They boycotted those businesses' products and picketed their buildings until the men in question were either fired or the company went bankrupt. As the group's popularity grew, they expanded their reach to include sexual harassment and discrimination. The movement spread until no self-respecting woman would even hire a man, much less sleep with one. Soon, males in upper-management positions found themselves considered a liability. In disgust, male-owned businesses moved west—to places like Texas, Alabama, and Missouri—and dared the East to survive without them.

"It won't last long," Paul had predicted. "After all, it's not like they can reproduce without us!"

He and his friends had laughed, but they had been wrong.

Left virtually barren, MA'AM teamed up with women from around the world who believed in their cause. They ran ads for special fertility clinics they called Partho-labs, which utilized a new method of in-vitro fertilization. The first ad, Paul remembered, had featured a beautiful dark-skinned woman wearing a white lab coat and glasses. He kept waiting for her to take off her glasses and let her hair down, but it wasn't that kind of ad. Instead, she had spoken in a low, clinical tone.

"We can now genetically engineer human reproduction without using male sperm," she proclaimed. "In Salem, we are using Parthenogenesis (something happening naturally in select animals, anyway) to create the first exclusively all-female society, called the Lytoky."

The ad had skipped to a playground filled with frolicking little girls who sang a catchy rhyme.

> "If you're tired of saying to men
> 'Don't lie to me,'
> come join us in
> the Lytoky!"

Geez! Even now, the jingle made his head hurt.

The campaign had worked, though. Within a year, people started calling everything east of the Mississippi 'the Lytoky.' After that, the term evolved to mean more than merely a manless society or a region; it became a lifestyle choice with its own political party. Salem had been the first city to fall, but the other New England states quickly followed, and the movement spread. Now, eighteen years later, the Mississippi River border was the only thing standing between the Lytoky and New Canaan—the resulting land (with its own political party) sandwiched between the Mississippi and the Rockies.

Paul still couldn't believe it had happened.

At least I got to enjoy myself before they kicked the men out, he spat. The foamy spittle landed on his left steel-toed boot, and it dried almost instantly. The corners of his cracked lips tightened as his thoughts turned again to Honey and her look of surprise when he had approached her that night. *Bet that's the same look she'll have when I see her again!*

"She's still out there, Leonard!" he called to his friend, who was now squatting twenty feet away with a wet towel over his face. "I can feel it!" Leonard lifted the towel and gave him a quizzical look. "My Honey!" Paul explained, as though he hadn't mentioned her name a hundred times before. Leonard nodded and dropped the towel again.

Paul grinned and blinked slowly, like an old crocodile. His skin, leathered from the last thirteen years performing hard, manual labor in the sun, did make him look much older than his age, he knew, regardless of his boasting, but he didn't care.

"I know she's thinking about me right now," he said, more to himself than to Leonard. "And one day we'll meet again; just wait and see!"

"Right," came a sarcastic voice. "How long have you been stuck here at the Rock—the Lytoky's version of Alcatraz? Face it, Old Timer; no one out there is thinking about you."

On impulse, Paul heaved his water bottle. It connected with Green-Bean's back, and the kid's own water bottle went flying off the edge as the startled young man scrambled to keep from following. Paul watched with disinterest. Other workers' heads popped up from their break, like prairie dogs sensing excitement, but no one moved to help him.

"Consider that Lesson Number One," Paul said, once Green-Bean finished flailing. "Never call me Old Timer again. And here's Lesson Number Two: Don't mess with me."

Prior to his encounter with Honey, Paul had been widely known for representing the most notorious and richest criminals of the era. He smirked now, remembering his prowess in the courtroom and the old headline from the *Clarion Ledger*. "PLAGUE TERRORIST BUYS JUSTICE FOR THE PRICE OF PAUL BROWN'S SOUL." The article was not particularly flattering, he admitted, but what did he care? He was a winner. He got things done. He got them done his way.

Then MA'AM put him on their hit list. At first, they had picketed his office. When that didn't work, they had resorted to one of his old techniques: they framed him.

"How else can you explain it?" he had asked his lawyer at the time. "This trial is a sham, I tell you; I'm the victim here!" How was he to know the firm's lovely new mail clerk was only sixteen, for Heaven's sake? Or that her mother was the local MA'AM representative? "Virgin or no, the little slut set me up!"

No one, however, believed his accusations of conspiracy. They all wanted him to pay.

"Damn feminists!" he spat again, remembering the public outrage at his trial.

Although he had defended many other men against similar charges, he was forbidden to represent himself in court. Therefore, since none of his partners or colleagues dared touch the case for fear of publicity, he was forced to go with the public defender. It had been no surprise, then, that after only one afternoon of jury deliberations, the verdict came in: Guilty, as charged. The one break he got in the trial was at his sentencing. Since the alleged crime took place seven days before Mississippi ratified the new Victim's Protection Act, the maximum sentence was Life, without parole.

"If Mr. Brown had lured the girl into his phallic-red Corvette one week later," claimed one biased reporter, "he would have received mandatory castration… an appropriate punishment. Not that castration would have stopped him. Predators like him find other ways to violate their victims."

Paul shook his head in disgust. What did they know about appropriate punishment? After all these years here on the Rock, being bossed around by a gaggle of butch lady-jailors, surely anyone could see that for him, life like this was Cruel and Unusual.

***

"Brown! Back to work!"

The gruff voice, thirty feet beneath him, broke his reverie. It was the foreman… or FOREONE, they liked to be called now. She held a bullhorn in one hand and his empty water bottle in the other. Even from this height, Paul could see the stenciled word, BROWN, on its side.

Foreone; what a joke! he thought, remembering the trial that had outlawed masculine labels in the east.

"The Constitution states, 'All men are created equal,'" the opposing lawyer had begun. "But smart, brave women were imprisoned and tortured simply for the audacity to want to vote!"

Paul had gotten distracted watching her legs during her opening statement, but he had caught the end, just before she wrapped up.

"So, you see, words like Man and Men are not the all-inclusive, innocent terms the Defense's patronizing Special Counsel, Mr. Brown, would like you to believe. Gender-specific terms (such as Chairman, Policeman, and Fireman, for example) promote subtle, yet effective, sex discrimination by implying certain roles are only meant for males."

Got that right, Sweetheart! he had thought. *I wouldn't trust you to carry my two-hundred-pound, deadweight ass down a burning staircase; that's for sure!*

In the end, however, Paul had lost the case, and with it went his indisputable reputation and power. It had only been another six months before his brilliant career was over and his sentence here at the Rock had begun.

He had taken solace in one, small victory at the trial. Because of his argument, the court had agreed to preserve words like Man, Male, Woman, and Female since those terms each described an individual state of being. If it had been up to his opponent, everyone would be described as gender neutral.

"I said, 'Back to work!'" the foreone called up again. "Now! And for MA'AM's sake, put your goddamned shirt back on!"

She handed his water bottle to her assistant and unsnapped her holstered revolver. She didn't like repeating herself. The yard, below, fell silent. Leonard started backing away, sidling sideways along the roof like a soft-shelled crab, and it seemed to Paul that everyone (guards and prisoners alike) expected a confrontation. He could sense they wanted Paul to throw something or be shot dead. Sweat trickled through one gritty eyebrow and into his left eye. It stung, instantly, and he wiped at it without thinking. That's when he heard a bemused 'huff' from his right.

A sudden flash of anger sliced through him. *Does Green Bean think I'm crying?* he thought. *Why, that little shit! I'll teach him…"*

"Drop it!" The foreone's tone had changed. He looked down and saw that her legs were spread in a shooter's stance and she was now pointing the gun at his chest with both hands. "This is your last warning, Brown!"

Paul looked up in surprise at the Craftsone 22-ounce straight claw in his hand. He hadn't even remembered drawing it out. Slow and deliberate, so as not to further rile Little-Miss-Trigger-Finger down there, he holstered the hammer. He forced on a tight-lipped smile and gave an amicable, two-handed wave to show her there were no hard feelings.

Just like a woman to spoil a perfectly good break, he scowled, as he shrugged back on his shirt then pulled some roofing nails from his belt. Heat radiated off his face when he bent over.

Tap tap, he hammered. His left eye still stung, but he didn't dare rub at it again.

Tap tap.

He glanced back to where the foreone had been. The coast was clear. *She must have already stomped off to catch another slacker!*

His team fell in, and someone handed him a new shingle. His knuckles scratched on asphalt, and he grimaced around a mouthful of rough-cut nails as he set the shingle in place. The iron nails tasted like blood. Like Honey's blood, he imagined, or the foreone's.

You'll see, he smiled anew as he imagined the foreone's face. *One day I'll break out of here, just like Sampson in the Bible. And when I do, all you Delilahs better watch out for me!*

THREE

When Katherine Buford's face appeared live on the WLBC (the Lytoky's Broadcasting Channel) special broadcast, women all across the Lytoky paused, with cereal spoons suspended halfway to their mouths, and smiled. They couldn't help themselves. The teen's impish, child-like grin had always been contagious. As usual, her big green eyes, which had earned her the nickname "Kat" when she was only four years old, were wide and expressive. As the on-screen scene expanded, however, the viewers stirred and moved closer to their screens to get a better look. Kat's familiar, messy curls had been styled into a sophisticated up-do, and her cheeks and lips had been blushed Maybelline-pink. Even her skin, usually pale, was now noticeably tan against her white cotton gown.

Our little girl is growing up, the viewers at home sighed in unison.

They watched her gliding down the aisle, keeping time with the organ's music, and nodding from side to side as though to welcome favored guests. The camera's angle widened even further to reveal the cathedral's dark, curving ribs above her, stretched upward like interlacing fingers. Other girls in matching white gowns came into view. Each, in turn, followed Kat down the aisle and knelt alongside her at the padded altar rail. Soon, the entire chancel was filled with young girls of all colors in white.

"And now," whispered an off-screen commentator. "Here comes Kat's mother!"

Onlookers collectively caught their breaths as an older dark-skinned woman stepped into view. At four-foot-eleven, Senator Pat Buford was not that much taller than her daughter's bowed head, yet her presence filled the screen. Her dark, intense eyes and splendid white hair contrasted dramatically with her black velvet robe and made her look more like a bird of prey than the Lytoky's beloved leader.

As she passed the altar rail she paused, as everyone suspected she would, and Kat looked up. Pat smiled at her daughter, causing the girl to break into one of her trademark grins. On-screen, both momentarily seemed to forget the crowds and the cameras. Those in attendance bumped elbows and pointed. Those watching from home sat back and smiled. All felt privileged to be witnessing this tender, private moment between mother and daughter.

Then Buford winked, and stepped briefly out of sight as the camera focused on Kat's face. The next thing the viewers knew, the senator had already climbed into the overhead wooden pulpit and was staring down from her lofty perch.

"My friends," she started, looking directly into the camera. "We are gathered here this morning to celebrate the Lytoky's first high-school graduation class, and to acknowledge our daughters' accomplishments and bright futures. It is not a time to discuss politics or today's upcoming election. This morning, we have put aside our concerns about any outside turmoil and have come to honor these young women as they are propelled into life's next journey.

"As you know, these lucky girls have lived in peace their entire lives. They have never been exposed to men, or to boys. This charter class, which began twelve years ago and today achieved 100% graduation, marks a true milestone in our proud history."

As always, Buford stood perfectly erect when she spoke. Although she occasionally emphasized key points using her hands, she contained herself within the podium's confines, and rarely raised her voice. This calm demeanor was what fueled her critics when they challenged her as "cold" and "impassionate," but what her supporters praised as "no nonsense" and "genuine."

"Our candidate doesn't slouch over the pulpit, arm-wave, or fist-pound like some *other* televangelists," her followers had been quick to point out, referring to her opponent, Senator Danforth. "She doesn't have to yell to show passion. Her poise exudes confidence, dignity, and integrity!"

19

"I, like you," Buford continued, holding out her hands and then crossing them over her heart, "feel mixed emotions today. On the one hand, I am proud. Proud of our daughters, who at the age of eighteen are now the newest members of the Lytoky. Proud that this generation has never experienced sex-discrimination or harassment. Has never experienced fear walking alone at night, or worried about an unplanned pregnancy. Getting pregnant is now a choice—one for which they must apply! It is not something to be entered into lightly, without a permit.

"When we first created our thelytoky, no one thought it would last. The word thelytoky was unfamiliar back then, and a society giving rise solely to female offspring was untested in humans. No one in New Canaan thought we could be sustainable without men. They expected "our little experiment" to fail. But it didn't. Just look at these girls! This graduation class proves that peace and harmony are achievable as long as women are in charge!"

The cathedral's congregation erupted into applause, and every female spectator at home nodded agreement. After a few moments, Buford smiled, then motioned for silence.

"As a mother, I cannot tell you how proud that makes me. I must admit, though, that as a mother I am also concerned. Concerned for my daughter's future, and for women everywhere if we don't win today's election...."

***

Katherine's legs were going numb, her feet ached, and her cheeks hurt from too much smiling. Would this ceremony ever end? she wondered. Heat from an overhead spot warmed her face. To the cameras, she offered her best, well-rehearsed smile; but inside she didn't feel much like smiling. She wiggled her toes in frustration.

These new shoes are killing me, she thought, grinding her teeth. *I should have known Mom would pull something like this! Who does she think she's fooling with that 'this is not a time to discuss politics' crap? That was probably her intention, all along—to turn my graduation into one last campaign speech!*

"Now, now," came a voice inside her head. *"Give your mom a break. The polls open in a few minutes and she should probably be out there."* Katherine tried hard not to roll her eyes.

Not now, Jordan, she thought, being careful not to speak aloud. *I'm on camera; go away.*

"Well, I'm just saying, she's making a sacrifice to be there with you. It couldn't have been easy with her schedule." When Kat pretended to ignore him, he added, *"Hey, you know what I think?"*

Duh, she shot back. It was an old joke. OF COURSE she knew what he was thinking! She and Jordan had been telepathically connected for years—for as long as either of them could remember.

"I think you're being too hard on her," Jordan continued. *"She could have been a no-show, you know."*

Stop it, Jordan. And thanks for taking HER side, she thought and pursed lips. *As always.*

"Well, it's election day, and-"

Just quit it, Jordan. I mean it. I don't want to hear this right now. Go away!

"But-"

"No!"

Oops! Had she really said that last word out loud?

The sound of rustling gowns, as her classmates at the railing craned their necks for a knowing look, sent hot pinpricks to her checks. Katherine cut her eyes toward the rafters. The cameras weren't on her— *Good!*—so at least the people at home had missed her outburst. She chanced a glace behind her, but everyone seemed engrossed in her mother's speech and must not have heard. Luckily, it appeared no one in the cathedral, besides the few smug girls at her elbows, had noticed. Even so, she plastered on a thoughtful face, just in case, and tried to pay attention.

In the background, she could sense Jordan's amusement. Since their telepathic abilities were usually limited to words and to sounds, she couldn't actually 'hear' him unless he made a noise, but after all these years together, she could tell when he was laughing.

It was an odd sensation, hearing someone else's voice inside her brain.

At first, it had been frustrating to communicate. Abstract thoughts and feelings were nearly impossible to translate without an agreed language, and their early, undeveloped minds couldn't form proper words. They couldn't rely on body language or visual clues to interpret what they heard. Unlike twins, who reportedly sense each other's emotions, and often postpone their language-development skills for years because of it, Kat and Jordan didn't have that luxury. They needed to hear something (either a formed thought, in words, or an actual noise from the other side) for it to work.

It wasn't until age six, when a child psychiatrist had reproached her for being "too old for an imaginary friend," that Kat had first realized she was different. Apparently, no one else heard voices in their heads. She wondered, often, how people stood it, being so alone. By now, hearing Jordan's thoughts alongside her own was as second-nature to her as watching TV while surfing the web.

Overhead, her mother's words continued. "Twenty-one years ago, when the MA'AM Revolution first began…"

Kat and Jordan groaned simultaneously. They had heard this speech before. Too many times. He couldn't actually hear her mother, of course, but since Kat heard the sound (even when she wasn't listening), it registered in his brain, too.

"Four score and seven years ago…" Jordan said, poking fun. His reference to the Gettysburg address (something she had never learned in her own school) made her smile, and she instantly forgave him for earlier. She knew he hated his mother's speech, no matter how much he defended the woman.

In an attempt to distract them both, she glanced behind her again. *Still no sign of Aunt Waverly,* she noted. Waverly Nelson, her mother's best friend and work associate, had been part of the family for as long as Kat and Jordan could remember. It wasn't like her to be this late.

I wonder where she is, she thought. *I wanted to say good-bye.*

"You're not afraid, are you?" Jordan asked, suddenly.

Of course not! Kat answered, too quickly. And then, *Why? Are you?* Jordan didn't answer.

Kat chewed her lower lip, and they both fell silent. Of course he was afraid, she knew; they both were! In a few hours, he was going to sneak

22

across the Mississippi River border using a false ID. Assuming that went well, they would each then travel to some covert, top-secret government island off the Florida panhandle where they were finally going to meet.

"Meet" was a strange term, Kat had decided. She and Jordan had been sharing each other's thoughts for years, no matter how intimate, but they had never shared any of the things most friends—*Lovers?*—took for granted. She had never seen his face, for instance, or heard his real voice. They had they never held hands nor exchanged numbers. In fact, she had no physical evidence that he was even real. In a world divided by differences, they were bound by a mental thread of consciousness neither understood nor could fully explain. He had just always been there... this other "voice" inside her head, saying things no one else could hear and no one else believed.

Like in kindergarten, for instance, when Jordan had helped Kat report on where baby cows came from. She had barely gotten to the part where the bull mounts the cow when a blushing teacher had yanked her off the stage.

"Male and female cows mating?" the teacher had scoffed, dragging Kat by the ear to the principal's office. "What nonsense."

A year later, when Jordan helped her recite *the Lord's Prayer* for her fourth-grade poetry reading assignment, the same teacher, Ms. Donovan, had been horrified.

"'Our Father,' indeed!" she had scolded. "Bet your mom won't laugh it off this time, young lady."

And sure enough, when her mother had picked her up from school that Friday, the result had not been pleasant.

"Where do you keep hearing such patriarchal dogma?" her mother had demanded. "And don't you dare say it's your 'Imaginary Friend!' No daughter of mine is going to grow up a miscreant, or a liar. Tell me the truth or there'll be no ice cream for you tonight."

In the end, when Kat insisted that Jordan had discovered the text in a book he called the *King James Bible*, her mom had sent her to bed without supper as well as no dessert.

"Remember when we won the spelling bee?" Jordan asked now, trying to change the subject.

You mean when you helped me CHEAT on my spelling bee? she corrected.

"Well, we won, didn't we?"

That made her smile. They had done that in the fourth grade, as well, to get back at Ms. Donovan, who had wanted another student to win.

Suddenly, something at the pulpit caught Kat's attention, and her smile faltered.

You gotta be kidding me, she thought.

"What? What happened?" Jordan asked her.

Her mother's image had flickered for an instant. Most people probably didn't even notice the change, Kat suspected, and those that did shrugged it off as a blip of bad lighting. But Kat knew better.

Mom's not here! That's a pre-recorded Holo up there. She must have slipped out when she went behind the pulpit.

Kat knew her mom used Holos. ("I can't be expected to visit every small town on the campaign trail, after all," the woman had explained once.) But this Holo was different. More realistic. It had even fooled Kat at first.

I should have known, she thought, renewing her earlier irritation. *All she cares about is the election. Why did she even adopt me? Was that a publicity stunt, too? Is that all I've ever been to her?*

She drilled imaginary holes into her mother's projected face with her eyes, and sensed Jordan refraining from comment. Her mother looked slightly younger on the Holo than in real life, she noted, but not blatantly so. The woman's dark skin was wrinkle-free and clear, and even her neck was smooth and taut, thanks to being surgically tucked the previous summer.

Not bad for sixty-six, Kat grudgingly admitted.

"We are all in mourning, of course, over President Sotomayor's sudden passing last month," the holographic image continued. "Yet at the same time, we must recognize the opportunity this vacancy affords us. This is the first real Presidential election in thirty-six years. It is time for New America to end its long reign of Moderatism, and to finally advance women's rights west, across the border into New Canaan!"

24

Her sweeping gaze covered the congregation, the cameras, and every graduate in attendance, including her daughter's. No one, besides Kat, suspected the eye contact wasn't real.

"By our votes today, we send a clear message to men everywhere. 'We will no longer tolerate your greed, your violence, or your injustice!' Together, we will stamp out sexism once and for all, and, if necessary, every last man along with it!" Cheers rose throughout the crowd. Keeping her elbows close to her body, her mother spread out her palms, imploring the crowd. "Help me save our sisters in New Canaan."

Kat drummed her fingers on the railing. She knew why her mother's gestures were so constrained. She had to stay within the Holo's recording confines. Over the years, she supposed, it had become habit for her mother to use small motions and stand so rigid.

The speech continued.

"Before the Plague, the old, male-dominated Supreme Court outlawed abortion by claiming it was for a woman's own good. Sound familiar? They wanted to 'protect' us from making decisions we might later regret, so instead of going after the rapists and enforcing tougher laws against aggressive male behavior, they went after the women! They essentially instituted sex trafficking by regulating what women could do with their own bodies! They forced women to perform acts against their own will, based solely upon their sex, and made them carry unwanted pregnancies to term—essentially enslaving them for nine months at a time!

"That still goes on in New Canaan. Over there, men also claim that higher education is too disruptive for women, so they banned them from universities for their own good. They said women working long hours is too stressful, so they deny their women higher-paying jobs."

Soft boos rumbled from the pews behind Kat.

"They claim women don't understand complicated political issues, so they spare them the confusion of running for office. Too frail for competitive sports, so they prohibit them from forming teams and discovering their body's potential. Now, they want to prohibit the Lytoky from self-propagation. They want us to reproduce by only using male sperm… and they have the nerve to claim it's for our own good!"

Murmurs filled the cathedral, and Buford leaned slightly forward, as though confiding in a friend. Her voice turned sharper, however, and got louder as she spoke.

"But we know better. We know that when they say, 'it's for your own good,' what they mean (and what they have always meant) is that it is for MAN'S own good. For generations, they have kept women down, afraid we will realize we don't need them. Well, no more! It is time to admit they've been right all along! WE DON'T NEED THEM!"

Predictable cheers erupted from the pews and along the railing beside Kat. Her classmates pounded the railing with open palms and began chanting "We don't need them!"

After an acceptable pause, her mother shifted her glasses and the chanting trailed off. She started again in a lower tone.

"Experts report that eighty-three percent of women living in New Canaan have experienced some sort of sexual harassment. One in four will be sexually abused by the time they turn twenty, and chances are it will be by someone they know. That is unacceptable. It must stop! Help further our cause and vote for Pat Buford for President by logging onto the Lytoky's homepage at…"

Kat stopped listening. She hated the anger, the martyrdom, and the self-righteous posturing. And she knew Jordan hated it too; he was male, after all. She searched her mind as one might hunt a lost memory, but he had conveniently disappeared… or, as close to "disappeared" as he could get. He and his brothers were playing a raucous game of rugby.

Kat had a hard time fully appreciating Jordan's lifestyle. The girls in her school played the same sports, of course, but Jordan's brothers seemed to care more about beating each other up than about playing the actual game.

From age eight, it seemed, Kat's and Jordan's lives had spiraled in drastically different directions. For instance, life in the Lytoky was slow-paced and nurturing; life in New Canaan seemed reckless to her. She was an only child; he was the oldest of six. She had never seen the opposite sex; he couldn't stop thinking about them. She had grown up inside a gated, all-female community and rarely left the school's compound except on weekends. Jordan lived on his father's estate in Grant's Park, Missouri. He had an outdoor pool, a tennis court, and a full staff. He lived there with his family and a half-blind yellow lab named Ruthie. Jordan could come and go as he pleased, and he worked part-time at a veterinary clinic in town. He had used the money to buy his own car, and he usually took Ruthie with him when he went to work after school since his brothers were prone to using the poor creature as target practice when Jordan's back was turned.

Kat sighed. Too bad Jordan wasn't female, she thought—not for the first time. If only he were, they could have met like ordinary people years ago and not have to plan to sneak around like this today. They could even get married, now that they were old enough, and live together. Instead, marriage to Jordan was unthinkable. It was going to be hard enough just to hide her revulsion when she saw him.

She flinched, and mentally checked in on Jordan. Luckily, his thoughts were still engrossed in his game and he had not been listening.

She knew it hurt him whenever she worried about his looks, but what choice did she have? How could she dismiss everything she had been taught just because he said they were all lies? Kat had never seen a man, but she had heard about them in school. She knew how big and ugly they were, with bulging muscles and wiry whiskers—*Like pubic hair?*—on their faces and on their backs. *Yuck!*

Over the years, she had researched every word about Men she could find, but there wasn't much to read. The whole subject was as elusive as her missing adoption records. Inside her school computers' firewalls, articles referenced men and males only in broad terms such as "those people" or "the others." No photos existed, and the few graphics available made them look more like early Neanderthal women than human.

"Why don't we study Man's history?" she once asked a kindly teacher, staying late after class so she could pose the question in private.

"Man's early work was important, sure," the older woman had admitted, squeezing into the desk beside Kat to explain. "But we don't need to know every detail of their lives. For instance, we don't study individual cave dwellers, do we? One created fire; another, the wheel. Later generations created government, then they created wars. We need to know about the past, of course, so that we don't repeat it, but we don't need to know each individual behind every invention. That is personality,

Kat, not history. Without knowing who first discovered the law of gravity, for instance, we can still study the science."

The teacher had patted Kat's arm, seeming to sympathize with her student's puzzled expression.

"Remember when I told you how the early Americans fought for freedom in the original Revolutionary War? Now THAT is worth studying because it is relevant today. Only, instead of a repressed society fighting for freedom and for the right to bear arms, if needed, for a potential Militia, the Lytoky is fighting for our right to bear ONLY female offspring. We are making history here, Kat! For the first time ever, humans no longer need male sperm to survive. It's going to be amazing, Kat, so keep your eyes and ears open, and don't listen to what some old fat, hairy, bald guy had to say a hundred years ago."

Kat shuddered. Did people always have to describe men as so grotesque?

Even Jordan had admitted that most men need to shave every day, and some, like his dad, had hair inside his nostrils and his ears.

Does that mean Jordan will be hairy like that, too, when he gets older? she wondered. *No!* she thought and shook her head to remain focused. *It doesn't matter what he looks like; I love him!*

She loved that voice inside her head—the one without a face who talked into the night about homework, philosophy, and love; and whose sense of humor, sensitivity, and gentle nature made it easy to forget he was a man.

Ironically, after today Kat could finally apply to learn more about men. Only citizens (those over eighteen and with a high school diploma) could access the Lytoky's Info-Net to get unfiltered information. But now there wasn't time. Jordan had to get across the border while both sides were distracted with the election. *It is now or never,* they had both agreed last week.

Doesn't matter, she thought, focusing her attention once again toward her mother's on-screen image. *Jordan is nothing like the monsters you describe, and I'll prove it.*

After today, her mother would finally see that Jordan was real, and the public would recognize her as more than simply Pat Buford's adopted daughter. She imagined the headlines her upcoming tryst was likely to produce: "KAT BUFORD SNUBS MOTHER'S CELEBRATION" and, later, "SHE SNUCK OFF TO MEET A BOY!"

Then we'll see how proud you are of me, she thought, and her smile turned genuine at last.

FOUR

Senator Marshall Danforth stood alone on his penthouse office balcony, hands on his hips, and stared east, across the Mississippi River, at East St. Louis, Illinois. From this height, nearly 630 feet above St. Louis, Missouri, he could see for over thirty miles. Below him, the St. Louis Gateway Arch lay in ruins. Its broken halves crisscrossed 200 feet in the air and resembled two enormous praying hands. The expansive view made him feel strong, invincible, immortal. It made him feel like God.

His enormous frame, as oversized as the view, itself, helped enhance this image of godliness. At six foot four and nearly 370 pounds, his campaign ads often described him as a modern-day Buddha. "...Only, Christian, Caucasian, and considerably better dressed."

That phrase always pleased him. They didn't call him the Rainbow Candidate for nothing. He had come up with that title, himself, since he had been arranging his wardrobe, and his calendar, in the order of the seven rainbow colors years. On Sundays, for instance, he always wore red. Mondays were orange. The rest of the days followed suit. Saturdays were his favorite, since Waverly had once told him he looked particularly handsome in violet. Today being Election Day, a Tuesday, he had chosen his lucky Armani yellow suit, and a matching paisley tie.

Earlier in the campaign, one of his detractors from the third-party Gamma Group, west of the Rockies, had tried to discredit him by complaining he had usurped their Rainbow theme. They claimed it stood for alternative-gender acceptance and sexual inclusion, and tried to shame Danforth for not standing for either of those things.

"Senator Danforth's narrow-minded bigotry is even more egregious," one of their ads had proclaimed, "because as a former Reverend, he should have more tolerance for others."

"Nonsense!" Danforth had tweeted. "I tolerate both males and females equally in New Canaan. You can't get more sexually inclusive than that. In fact, the more women in my bed, the better!"

He had taken a hit in the polls after that one. He had even been forced to hold a press conference for his wife to explain it was merely a tasteless joke, nothing more.

A strong breeze touched the back of Danforth's neck. Instinctively, he reached out and retrieved his WORLD'S BEST DAD coffee mug from its precarious perch on the balcony's top railing. One of his sons (he forgot which one) had made it for him years ago in Bible camp. At the time, Danforth had called the misshapen pottery "atrocious," but when he went to throw it out, he realized the concave base might actually serve a purpose. Sure enough, when he took it to work, it fit the rounded railing perfectly.

He tested the mug to lips just as another gust, stronger this time, sloshed coffee against his chin.

"Dammit!" he spat and dabbed at his chest. This was the third time this week he had ruined a tie.

He swore the building moved just to irritate him. Due to its excessive height, so he had been told, the Info-Swirl could sway like a metronome as much as eighteen inches during an earthquake. In gale-force winds, however, it was supposed to only shift a quarter inch off center. That small distance was supposedly imperceptible to the human brain, but Danforth swore he felt it all the time. He was certain others had experienced it, too. Unfortunately, none of them were still alive to corroborate his theory.

Because its glass exterior resembled a giant waterworks slide, the Swirl attracted its share of thrill-seekers. Every few years, some fool invariably scaled the building, climbed onto his balcony (the slide's unofficial start), and attempted to surf its continuous wave. Everyone who had ever tried it, however, ended up getting too close to the edge and going down. *Straight down. Game over.*

Danforth was certain it was because the building moved out from underneath them, but regardless the cause, the incidents meant more than the loss of an unfortunate soul. With body parts strewn over multiple glass-bottomed tiers, it also meant the loss of productivity in the offices immediately below the landing sites. Last time, it happened in mid-April. Two tax attorneys had arrived early one Monday and had noted a surreal sunrise-color filtering down through an outer Conference Room glass ceiling. Per the report, it had taken them a full twenty seconds to comprehend what they were seeing, and another ten to understand why the disembodied face, staring down at them from a pool of blackish-red, was moving. Then it dawned on them: Vultures. Danforth could almost picture the grizzled cheek as it smeared blood across the glass in stiff, jerky fits.

It had taken a week to return things to normal. Due to bad timing (it was tax season, after all), he had been forced to hire a special recovery team to collect the man's remains, as well as additional cleaners to wash the building down.

Damn window-washers! he thought now.

He still didn't see how hanging scaffold could be so expensive to relocate. He pounded his fist on the balcony rail. When he did, it made the outward-sloping glass section vibrate disconcertingly. With a huff, he turned and walked inside his office suite. He had just enough time to change his tie and check out the new voting instructions before leaving for the polls. A few minutes later, his carbon-fiber office chair creaked as he turned toward his monitor and focused on the START command.

"One Mississippi, two Mississippi..." he counted out loud.

When the Info-net security screen came up and he studied a small icon—this one shaped like a key—he started counting again.

"One Mississippi, two Mississippi..."

The screen flashed repeatedly as its Video Imaging Sensors and Optical Receivers (a.k.a. VISOR) technology synched with his brainwaves. His eyes felt scratchy and dry, but he dared not blink. He needed a secure line. The VISOR received user input via focused light energy. Its inventor, Waverly Nelson, had once explained to him that this energy passed directly through the pupils and into his brain.

"This link between human and machine utilizes amplitude-coded light modulation in resonance with the brain's own electrical impulses," she had told him in confidence. Danforth didn't know what the heck that meant, so he had leaned over and winked.

"I know all about impulses," he had drawled. "Just not the electronic kind."

As usual, his flirting went unnoticed.

I keep forgetting she has no sense of humor, he had consoled himself. *At least she has great legs.*

Waverly Nelson was not only the VISOR's inventor and CEO of Cis-Star Technologies, she was also his campaign manager. Although she supported Senator Buford in public, she had been secretly advising him for the last ten years and served as his mole inside the Buford camp. He trusted her loyalty and her technology, even though he didn't fully understand it.

"The VISOR works similar to an auto-refractor," she had once explained. "You know, like at the optometrist's office when you focus on an object and the machine tracks your depth perception?"

"All I care about is that it takes forever to approve my security clearance," he had frowned, wanting to avoid another technical discussion that would inevitably make him feel stupid.

"Stop being dramatic, Marshall," she had said, clucking her tongue. "You're imagining things again. Just keep your eyes focused forward and wait, like I've told you before."

Easy for you to say, he thought.

"Six Mississippi, seven Mississippi…"

He still couldn't log on.

Oh this is ridiculous!

In frustration, he looked away, and the screen winked back to dark. He yanked open his bottom desk drawer. There, underneath a stash of stale granola bars, he found this week's security code. He knew Waverly would chastise him if she ever found out he printed it out each week, *But what she doesn't know won't hurt me,* he smiled.

He took a long look then tucked the paper away again and spoke the password aloud. Three seconds later, his own Danforth-friendly menu appeared—this one equipped with colorful icons Waverly had developed just for him, such as SERMON NOTES, BIBLE CONCORDANCE, and NCXS News—all the files he frequented daily.

Without keyboard or mouse, Danforth toggled through the New Canaan Broadcasting Station's news as his VISOR screen, now fully activated, traced his eyes' every movement. Hundreds of headlines filled the screen. Everything from, "FIRST CONTESTED PRESIDENTIAL ELECTION IN DECADES!" to "LYTOKY VS NEW CANAAN - YOU DECIDE!" caught his eye.

Yes, yes. But what about the voting instructions?

Most people had been voting from home for years using their tax ID numbers, he knew, but since this was a special election, and City Hall had bought new polling devices, he wanted to know how to vote in person at his scheduled photo op. Thinking he must have missed the tutorial link, he scanned the headlines again. His lips pursed as he focused on the NEXT command. The screen immediately refreshed.

More headlines appeared, but still not what he wanted.

A dark scowl spread across his face as his eyes slipped into a steady rhythm. NEXT, scan, NEXT, scan, NEXT. The VISOR flashed each screen so rapidly it was almost as though it were reading his mind. Sometimes, he swore, it nearly got ahead of him.

In frustration, he closed his eyes.

What the hell is going on? he thought. *No doubt, this is all Buford's fault. She somehow sabotaged the news to prevent me from voting! I can't believe her audacity. Hell, at Katherine's graduation this morning, she practically declared war on me!*

He had warned his followers she would try something like this.

"She's the one who's corrupt!" he had tweeted. "It's a classic example of the fire calling the frying pan black."

His own wife was the first to point out he had messed up the cliché, but Danforth had only shrugged.

"The Lytoky women love my quirky remarks," he told her. "They find my foibles endearing. Waverly told me so, herself, and why would she lie?"

***

The day he first met Waverly Nelson, ten years ago, the woman had been teetering on the edge of insanity—or brilliance; Danforth couldn't tell which. Not that it mattered. Brilliant or not, her visit that day had changed his life. He had just finished preparing that week's sermon when he looked up and saw her entering his study. His first thought was that she was much too young, and far too sexy, to be the CEO of a multi-million-dollar tech organization. The *Times* interview he had read, in preparation for their meeting, claimed she was the hottest young entrepreneur in the business.

But they never said she was HOT in every sense, he had chuckled.

That day, in her revealing, off-white business suit, she had been a vision. She wore her hair long, back then, and her skirt short. His eyes kept straying to her cleavage.

When she introduced herself and politely took a seat, he had been thrilled and slightly intrigued. Her people had been vague as to the purpose of this meeting, and had required he undergo a polygraph, iris scan, and extensive background investigation before final confirmation.

"Sorry for all the security," Waverly began, after the introductions. She spoke in a calm, slow voice that exposed more intelligence than he had expected from someone so attractive. He opened his mouth to say something gracious, but she held up a hand. "It's just that my company has a strict policy when it comes to sharing top secret information."

More fascinated than ever, Danforth remained uncharacteristically silent.

"I am sure you are familiar with my company, Cis-Star Technologies?" she continued.

"Of course," he nodded. *Who isn't?*

Cis-Star was the world leader in computer technology. They had developed everything from the simple INVITE program (which integrated all calendar software packages to coordinate meeting schedules) to the now-common VISOR eye-movement tracker program.

They also produced Adrays: a platform for pre-set physical sensations in movies that transmitted alongside the movie's soundtrack. The previous week, for example, he had attended the new *Titanic* remake and had felt the ice-cold water sting his skin. Unlike theme park 4-D movies, however, which utilized nozzles to splash unsuspecting viewers, Adrays left the viewer physically warm and dry. It was only his stimulated brain tricking him into feeling wet, or cold, or both.

He loved watching movies with Adrays. Every time a bad guy fell off a cliff or rolled a muscle car, Danforth's own stomach plummeted. It was the ultimate vicarious rush. Now, nearly all films exploited that technology. They even sold an app, which worked on most TVs at home—as long as they were equipped with the latest teleVISOR technology, that is. Adrays had revitalized the entire industry.

Waverly got right to the point. "I'm here about an important ethical dilemma. You were once my family pastor when I was a child, so I chose you as a sounding board."

Danforth nodded again. *I knew she looked familiar!* he thought.

The Info-Net had been surprisingly unhelpful in researching Waverly's personal life, so Danforth had been curious why a successful businesswoman in the Lytoky would want to talk to him here in New Canaan. Now, it all made sense. He bet many young women who had moved east with their mothers still remembered him fondly from their youth.

Must be my charisma.

"I've developed a new technology," Waverly continued, "but everything I tell you here is highly confidential and cannot leave this room."

"I see," he said, without explicitly agreeing. He slowly stroked the well-groomed beard he had worn at the time and gave her a meaningful frown. "How may I be of assistance?"

"We are on the cusp of a tremendous breakthrough," she whispered. "One that could potentially be extremely dangerous. We've developed an Adrays-derivative. It's still in the prototype stages, of course, but if successful, it has the power to overthrow entire nations. It wouldn't even be necessary to fight or to interrogate the enemy. The current Adrays only make people feel like they are drowning, or whatever sensation we project, but we can do more than that now. With this new technology, we can control the enemy's core belief system, not just their physical sensations. It can create an 'original' thought in someone's head. Our

Government could simply go in, armed with nothing but a handheld device, and force everyone within range to agree with whatever point of view we project. When in an interrogation, for example, we could make a suspect want to give up information."

"You can do that?" he asked, leaning forward in his chair. "I thought you could only transmit physical feelings, not emotions, or ideas."

"Until now, that was true. The Adrays' wavelengths were limited to transmitting the physical—like pain and pleasure, hot and cold—but this new development has the ability to virtually brainwash entire societies with, quite literally, the flip of a switch. I have to admit, it scares me."

"I see. You're afraid it could fall into the wrong hands, you mean."

"No, Reverend. It's too dangerous even in the right hands. These new frequencies can change what people think, and that might have long-lasting repercussions. It may be merely a synthetic feeling, and not reality, but most people won't recognize the difference. It can make people hate something they previously loved, or worship someone they previously detested. It can make them feel angry, or sad, or feel nothing at all. It can even make them believe."

She paused, and the room grew quiet. A bead of perspiration gathered on Danforth's upper lip as he suddenly understood the power and potential of a new age: The Age of Morality.

"Now do you understand, Reverend?" she continued. "I'm worried my invention is too powerful. I can't sleep at night worrying what will happen if this technology goes forward. Society would never be the same. You can't undo a belief. Once the public is convinced that something is true, and they accept it as common knowledge, it is nearly impossible for them to change their collective minds again. It would be like asking grownups to re-believe in Santa Claus. Their brains would simply revolt. They'd fight against it and refuse to adapt. You know this is true; we've seen it before, even without Adrays."

She paused, letting the impact of her words sink in, and stared up at him as though carefully watching his reaction. He noticed his own breathing had become quick and shallow.

"So, Reverend," she concluded. "Now that you understand my guilt in creating such an abomination, what do you think I should do with it?" She leaned forward, still searching his face.

"I think you should give it to me," he said, without thinking twice. "Together, we can help people find God. This device could lead to world Salvation."

"Or Damnation."

Waverly's dark, quiet words startled him. He clenched his fists and stood. His forearms bulged as he cleared his throat and found his Preacher Voice, at last.

"No, my child. This is God's work at hand, don't you see? You're smart, of course, but you couldn't have invented this without Divine Intervention! God worked through you, then He directed you to me. This is what St. John promised when he wrote the book of Revelations! For centuries, the Bible has been questioned or, worse yet, utterly ignored! Even before the MA'AM revolution, that tolerance-propaganda had practically tolerated our country straight to Hell. Well, no more!"

For the next fifteen minutes he performed the sermon of a lifetime, inspired by what he would later report was "the Word of God." When he finished, he knelt before Waverly and took her hands in his.

"Let me help you," he offered. "What better way to ensure against this technology getting into the wrong hands than to entrust it to the church… to me? We could work together. Wouldn't you feel better knowing your invention was being used for good instead of evil?"

She had looked torn and undecided.

"Miss Nelson, I implore you; let me help!"

He had searched her eyes and been startled at how blue and intense they were.

How had I missed noticing that before?

Since then, Cis-Star's technology had continued to advance, and Waverly was still by his side. She had been instrumental in helping him win his Senate seat, three years ago, and in his current bid for President. Once he won today, he would finally have enough power to squelch the Lytoky's advances and to spread the Good News east again. He could hardly wait.

FIVE

At a corner drugstore in downtown East St. Louis, Illinois, a young clerk stood processing a prescription for a local banker and her wife. Edna Gingham, the banker, wearing a dark gray suit and an even darker scowl, drummed her fingers on the counter.

"Oh for MA'AM's sake, Sarah!" she said to her wife. "Hold your eyes still, like the girl said. I need to get back to work."

"I can't help it!" Sarah said and looked up from the scanner once again, breaking the connection. "The lines were incredible!" she told the clerk. "We usually vote on-line, of course, but I wanted to do it in person this time, you know?"

The clerk smiled back. "I know. I'm going this afternoon."

"Yes, yes," Edna muttered, twirling a finger. "Let's wrap this up."

"Sorry," said the clerk. "I captured an image, but the I-Net's been having trouble all morning. Must be the election. Big turn-out, and all."

Just then, the bells over the storefront doors jingled and an early-thirties woman with straight black hair rushed in. Dressed in checkered sweatpants and a white T-shirt, she looked as though she had just gotten out of bed. She didn't look up when she entered the store, but headed straight for the back, toward the feminine hygiene department. When she paused at the PREGNANCY TESTS aisle, all eyebrows at the counter went up.

Gloria Chiang paid no attention. As the only woman in town openly married to a man, she was used to people's stares. Although she and her husband, Dale, never flaunted their relationship—Dale lived across the border in St. Louis and rarely visited the Lytoky—her neighbors in East St. Louis deemed her lifestyle-choice appalling.

Five years ago, when news about their marriage had first gotten out, a group of concerned citizens (instigated by Edna Gingham) had petitioned the town council to revoke Gloria's council seat.

"She is living a life of sin," the banker had argued. "By residing here in the Lytoky she pretends to be one of us, but every weekend she goes to New Canaan and shacks up with her husband… a man. It's unconscionable! How can we allow heterosexuals to live next door to our children? What kind of message does that send?"

The other council members had agreed with her. Later, as Gloria was turning in her town council credentials, Edna had approached her.

"Consider yourself lucky you work at Cis-Star," she had said. "If your CEO hadn't vouched for you, I could have run you out of town, as well."

Not that men, or heterosexuals for that matter, were illegal in the Lytoky—*That would be unconstitutional.*—but since the number of governmental leaders (both federal and local) had been severely reduced by the Plague, it had forever changed how the country's laws were enforced.

Unlike Ebola outbreaks from decades past, this genetically-mutated virus spread via direct contact with bodily fluids. People didn't know that at first, since those infected were contagious long before their symptoms began, so people stopped gathering in public. They thought it was airborne. Political rallies, athletic events, and church assemblies (any group activity larger than with one's own family) all halted. It was simply too risky. Once they realized it was a biological terrorist attack targeting specific, prominent figureheads, including those in sports and entertainment, the general population breathed easier. People still avoided entering the limelight, however, since doing so had proven to make those who did a target.

"Don't stand out!" became the new slogan for how to stay safe.

That made it difficult to find people willing to report the news or run for public office. Out of desperation, a band of private organizations stepped in to organize aid, restore order, and appoint new Government personnel to rule in secret. With reliable news sources cut off, they created their own website, the Info-Net, where citizens were encouraged to muster and to reconnect with loved ones.

Once the Plague ended, this group, by then referred to as the "Secret Congress," helped establish local elections and fund ads for the incumbents. Early election turnouts were sparse and unreliable, however, so as an incentive to run, the Secret Congress declared a moratorium on term limits. That meant all political positions could now be held for life, assuming they continued to win in future elections. Because of that, and because of President Sotomayor's popularity among the moderates, most young adults in New America had only ever known the one President.

Sotomayor's first act in office, back then, had been to readopt the Constitution. Next came the Amendments. Most were reinstated, with one notable exception: the former Twelfth Amendment. This made the Secret Congress' abolishment of term limits for Presidential and Vice-Presidential positions official.

Years later, due to a bill proposed by Senator Buford, three new geographical regions (the Lytoky, New Canaan, and the Gamma Group states) were formally recognized as independent nations under the New American umbrella. Much like the former United States had once recognized Native American lands as sovereign, these regions were now self-governing and could enforce their own laws—as long as they didn't conflict with the Constitution, of course, or any of Sotomayor's rare Executive Orders.

When Lytoky towns began springing up in the east, they adopted the usual Homeowners Associations, with ordinances that standardized things like roof styles, exterior paint colors, and yard maintenance requirements, but they added a few "extras." One such ordinance required all homeowners be proven "safe" to reside near women. The definition evolved over the years. At first, "safe" generally meant anyone female, gay, or transgender cis-males (those who were born male but self-identified as female).

Heterosexual men, therefore, had only two options: undergo voluntary ED surgery to ensure permanent erectile dysfunction, or move. Most chose to move. Those with sons gravitated west, to either New Canaan or the Gamma Group states, where boys had more opportunities. Those with daughters were more reluctant to move. During the transition's early days, such men relocated outside town limits into designated male-friendly colonies. The Lytoky tended to understand about these stragglers and didn't harass them, at first. Over the years, however, as their children grew and MA'AM expanded, those men slowly moved west, too. Or disappeared. MA'AM blamed their disappearances on the men who lied.

When word got out that certain doctors were selling fake "Safety" cards (medical records documenting ED surgery), the resulting scandal turned every male into an instant suspect, aka target.

"No man can be trusted now!" the ads went up. "Not even card-carrying 'safe' ones!"

Another Lytoky ordinance required women to conceive using artificial implantation. It was mostly a moot point, anyway, since most men had moved west already, but if a woman were convicted of getting pregnant the old-fashioned way (through voluntary sexual intercourse with a man), she could be forced to sell her home. This rule was in reaction to an old 2017 Missouri bill that had allowed women to be evicted from their homes for having an abortion, using birth control, or getting pregnant out of wedlock.

Still, as head of her local Uni-Lifer chapter (an organization who believed all life should be only one gender: female), Edna Gingham had to be careful. She couldn't go around accusing citizens, those over eighteen, of breaking the law without proof. Having a reputation (i.e., married to a man) wasn't enough to guarantee a conviction, her group had learned the hard way.

"No one looks behind bedroom doors here in the Lytoky," was a commonly-repeated phrase when it came to regulating sexual orientation. The only way to expose and successfully deport a practicing heterosexual, therefore, was for the woman to slip up and birth a son.

***

Unaware that the very person responsible for her losing her Town Council seat was waiting at the counter, Gloria seized an item off the top shelf and headed for the front. She paused when she rounded the corner, but it was too late. Edna Gingham had already seen the pink carton in her hand.

"A pregnancy test?" Edna exclaimed in exaggerated disbelief. "MA'AM help us! Don't you heteros ever learn?"

Gloria's jaw dropped instantly. Home Pregnancy kits were common in the Lytoky. Women too eager to wait for their follow-up in-vitro appointments (usually scheduled for two weeks after AI—Artificial Implantation) regularly checked their own hCG levels.

In a pitiful attempt to make up for her wife's outburst, Sarah Gingham stepped forward. "Oh, Gloria," she offered. "Edna and I were so sorry to hear about your miscarriage last spring."

Gloria winced and brought the carton down to her side.

Six months ago, when she and Dale had gone for official confirmation on their first pregnancy, the doctor had called the Lytoky Police. Since Gloria had no AI documentation, they arrested Dale on the spot. When he did not confess to rape, the interrogation got messy. With Gloria screaming his innocence in the adjoining room at the station, the LPs virtually broke three of Dale's ribs and seared his left testicle. The brain-stimulating program allowed him to feel all the pain but left no physical evidence. They eventually let him go since Gloria had refused to press charges, but at some point during that awful night she had lost their baby. With the pregnancy naturally terminated and the fetus confirmed female, no one could accuse her of indecent fertilization, so she had been able to retain her Lytoky citizenship and continue working at Cis-Star.

"I hope you have better luck this time," Sarah added, nodding toward the pregnancy kit.

"Well I don't," said her spouse. "I hope you finally get what you deserve. It's a wonder you don't have some kind of STD, anyway. They still have those in New Canaan, you know!"

"Edna!" Sarah shot her spouse a distressed look.

Just then, the register beeped; Sarah's iris image scan had finally gone through.

"Thank you for shopping," the clerk called out, and filled the awkward silence. "Have a nice day, now!"

Sarah, looking flustered, took her package and turned to go but Edna stayed behind.

"People like you should be shipped to New Canaan where you belong," she whispered. "Cis-Star can't always protect you. Everyone is expendable. You may not have been fired yet for consorting with the enemy but if we can prove you are carrying a man's child this time, even Ms. Nelson will turn on you. Wait and see."

With a huff, she turned and took her wife's elbow.

"Oh, Mses Ginghams?" the clerk called back. "Say 'hi' to Mindy for me at the trial next week, will ya?"

Her words halted the couple in the doorway, mid step. Mindy, the Ginghams' eldest, was being held in Chicago on her third grand larceny offence. If convicted, she would be subjected to the Lytoky's new Three-Strikes Rule.

"I'm sure the trial will be fair," Edna said flatly, before pushing on. "Either way, Sarah and I are prepared to accept whatever verdict the court deems fit."

Gloria watched them go. She knew it was no coincidence the clerk had mentioned the Ginghams' daughter, or that Edna had responded so predictably. Gloria knew if she strained hard enough she would be able to hear the WLBC's running news program on low volume over the store's overhead speakers, and that it was no-doubt broadcasting a segment about the Three-Strikes Rule.

Gloria had approved the Adrays message accompanying this broadcast, herself. It was a simple program—one that transmitted feelings of indignation (for the general public) and acceptance (for the criminal's family). It had been playing all week. The Three-Strikes rule was still relatively new in the Lytoky, but already the public had warmed to the idea. Since there weren't a lot of resources to waste on appeals, and no one favored constructing more prisons, Cis-Star's goal was to soften the public's negative stance on capital punishment and to encourage the public to accept 'a more permanent solution' for those who could not be rehabilitated. That included those repeat offenders convicted of non-violent crimes.

Gloria's role at Cis-Star Technologies was highly classified. She led the Broadcast Division inside the top-secret Adrays Department. The branches under her had many teams spread out on multiple floors. (One branch, alone, took up floors sixty through sixty-seven, and was responsible for the subliminal Public Service announcements. Unlike the Entertainment Division on floors fifty-one through fifty-nine—where text was input by sensory technicians to implant physical sensations over movies—her division's wavelengths controlled people's thoughts. These wavelengths, therefore had to be consistent with the recipients' sense of reality. It took finesse and research.

They couldn't tell a mother, for example, to abandon her child; it wouldn't feel right. But if they planted the notion that her son had somehow been switched at birth and wasn't really her child, it morally freed the mother to send the boy off to his father in New Canaan. It had happened a lot in the early days.

Since the Lytoky couldn't allow boys in their midst to grow into men, the Adrays had compelled women to believe their sons were "surely too different" to be biologically theirs. The Adrays messages hadn't even required specifics. (No child, after all, completely conforms to all one parent's characteristics, so there is always something to arouse suspicion if one is looking hard enough for it.) Besides, people tend to fill ethical gaps in any argument depending on the need. And in this case, the woman's implanted need was to conform to the rules of an all-female society. That implanted need, coupled with the Adrays' other powers of persuasion, gave them the necessary permission they had needed to send their sons packing. Gloria always suspected that without the Adrays, those same women would have fought to the death for those sons.

Before Cis-Star figured out this need for moral dissonance, many men had gone mad at Rock Island Prison—where the Broadcasting Division had initially tested each new subliminal wavelength. Turns out, the prisoners couldn't handle the frustration over the choices they were compelled to make. Since then, Cis-Star had developed multiple levels of wavelength penetration, each based on the specific audience and the acceptable level of moral and ethical risk the participants were willing to take. From this research, Gloria knew, the Uniray Department had been created. They used stronger wavelengths. At a certain prison down south, for instance, called the Oasis, they didn't even bother with the subliminal wavelength. The wavelengths they used bit far deeper into the male prisoner's psyche than her Adrays could ever penetrate.

Still watching the Ginghams as they traveled past the storefront windows, Gloria approached the clerk and placed her purchase on the counter. Sure enough, she heard the faint buzzing of this morning's PSA broadcast from overhead.

"For capital offenses," she heard over the speakers, faintly, "we can try the culprit at once. For non-violent offenses, however, we can take more time."

"Sorry about Edna," the clerk said with a smile as she rang up Gloria's purchase. Then she added, conversationally, "I hope they give Mindy the death penalty, don't you? It would serve Ms. Gingham right!"

SIX

Waverly Nelson believed in the power of Threes. It seemed that everything significant (from celebrity deaths to natural disasters) tended to happen in triplicate. She had noticed the phenomenon with good events, too, and even for things that didn't appear to be all that significant at first. Like today, for instance… three seemingly minor events had been instrumental to her plan.

First, she had finished her programming. *Finally!* Soon, after years of careful planning, every Cis-Star Relay Transmitter in both the Lytoky and New Canaan would start deploying it.

Second, Buford's speech, which Waverly had not only written but had personally programmed the corresponding Adray message to run alongside it, had gone off without a hitch.

And third, Senator Danforth was already way behind in the polls.

It was hard for her not to gloat. Especially now, waiting for him outside his precious Info-Swirl's glass exterior storefront in New Canaan. She had set up this stupid publicity stunt at the polls so she could manually inspect her equipment, which was secretly housed above his office. There, she had installed a Uniray transmitter years ago that she used just for him. He had never realized that the reason she visited him here so often was so she could tweak it regularly.

To annoy him, today she had also installed a device to block all broadcast transmissions in the Info-Swirl's elevator towers and restrooms, including the personal bathroom in his office.

No more toilet-tweeting for him! she had laughed when she flicked the switch less than twenty minutes ago. The more cut-off he was from incoming information today the better.

There was also a powerful Adrays transmitter above his office. With its wide range, it had been surprisingly easy to "encourage" the people in New Canaan (both males and females, alike) to vote for Senator Buford. Most people wanted to be told what to think (her grandmother had taught her that), so her Adrays had merely supplied what they desired.

"Give them a half-truth or even a downright lie delivered with conviction," her grandmother had once said, "and even though someone's head tells them it couldn't possibly be true, most people's need to fit in with the crowd will override anything they see or experience. They yearn to reconcile their perspective of the world. If a group accepts them, especially if it's an exclusive group that was hard to get into, the person will later do anything to justify that group's actions to others. We saw this phenomenon in politics even before the 2020 Plague. People like that hardly ever change their minds; they get too invested. Put them through a hellacious initiation, and you can feed them total nonsense and they'll vehemently retweet it and call everything else fake news. It's called cognitive dissonance, Sweetheart, and don't you ever underestimate it."

Waverly had listened to every word her grandmother had said and had used this concept to her advantage many times over the years in formulating her revenge. She had used the natural tension between the Lytoky and New Canaan to suggest to New Canaan that Danforth was "in bed" with the enemy and that he was funneling money meant for rebuilding New Canaan's infrastructure. Danforth objected to the accusations that followed, of course, but with her help, that only fueled people's indignation.

It hadn't been hard to convince them he was guilty. Danforth had always been a womanizer, and he was wealthy. Having accepted every bribe she had encouraged him to take, he had built a whole compound west of St. Louis and had been seen flaunting his wealth on numerous paid female actors over the years. Now, merely the mention of New Canaan's "struggling economy" (another of her invented narratives) was enough to incense his constituents.

Once a woman won the presidency, it would be the final straw; New Canaan's men would blame Danforth for that, too. Even though these same men would end up voting for Buford, they would turn on Danforth for losing, and then they'd turn on each other. Soon, only the women would be left in New Canaan. Those, she knew, she could turn around to the Lytoky's way of thinking quickly enough.

She could have defeated Danforth much earlier, she knew, but like the Praying Mantis she had once trapped as a child shortly after her mother's suicide, she enjoyed watching him squirm. She had kept the insect in a jelly-jar for weeks back then, opening the lid occasionally to let it climb toward freedom before she closed the lid again. Danforth would soon discover what the insect had also learned—that she had only kept him alive to torture him. False hope was intoxicating to watch, she had discovered, and she relished the anticipation of his defeat.

Ensuring his progression from religion to politics three years ago was all a means to an end: his end. Like her grandmother had always said, "The bigger they are, the harder they fall." Besides, no one could incite more disgust in women. With his silly clichés and pompous rainbow suits, he had even turned off the other gentle voters in the Gamma states.

Below her, a black sedan rounded the Info-Swirl block. Waverly blinked and watched a hoard of "reporters" she had hired for this occasion rush down the Info-Swirl's steps.

She knew it wasn't Danforth. He would never own anything hydrogen fueled.

Even though such vehicles had been on the market for decades, most people in New Canaan still clung to the old technology: preferring the smell of diesel to the efficiency of hydrogen. Not that she blamed them. After the Plague, anything involving biological or chemical reactions made even the staunchest conservationist wary.

Sure enough, the sedan moved on and the "reporters" wound their way back up the stairs to wait. Waverly glanced around. The city had certainly gone downhill since her last visit, she thought. Under Danforth's control, extravagant casinos had appeared in town. Across the street, instead of the park she remembered, red neon "HOT WOMEN!" signs blinked down, even in broad daylight. Litter, and the smell of stale popcorn and urine permeated the air.

She watched the people walking by… especially the women. She would have to work on them, next, she knew. Most had big hair, lipstick, white teeth, and blank faces. She hated them. They were followers. Sheep. Women like Danforth's wife, Marisa, who allowed herself to be controlled, and who self-righteously stood up for him in press conferences.

Serves her right he cheats on her! Waverly thought. *She got to keep and raise her own child; I didn't! What does she have to look so unhappy about on TV?*

Waverly wondered, suddenly, if her own mother had been like Marisa: pampered by her husband and yet still unsatisfied.

***

Waverly's mother, Irene Lancaster, had been a heavy drinker for as long as Waverly could remember. She was an ugly drunk, chastising her husband and daughter over the slightest misstep and leaving the house for days without notice. She never raised a hand to either one, at least, but she never smiled or said, "I love you," either.

Her father more than made up for her mother's shortcomings, however. With his roaring laugh and extravagant gestures, Eric Lancaster filled Waverly's early childhood with sunshine and joy. He took her out for Sunday excursions (sometimes for ice cream at the park, other times farther away, like that time to D.C.), and they'd make a day of it. The people in their Boston community saw how he treated his little girl and called the man "a saint" or "a dear." Waverly had agreed.

It was during one such outing, when Waverly was five years old, that her mother lit a pumpkin-scented candle, drew a hot, soapy bath, and quietly slit her wrists. By the time Waverly and her father returned to the house that evening, Irene had long-ago bled out. Waverly still remembered the splashing sounds her father made when he had pulled the body from the tub, and her mother's parched elbows tearing off the porcelain rim.

Three days later, at the funeral, Waverly had overheard her mother's story.

The Waves of Dissonance

Young Irene had been seventeen when the Plague first broke out. Rumor had it her parents worked for a top-secret government entity and were always away from home. Irene, feeling abandoned, sought attention in other ways. When her high school shut down and instituted on-line training, she never attended a single class. She went through several older boyfriends that year and joined a local gang.

Back then, law enforcement couldn't keep up, and petty crimes and looting were rampant. People were afraid to leave their homes. Even if someone were arrested, no one showed up to court (not even the judges, sometimes), so most criminals went free. Irene had been caught red-handed on more than one occasion but was never arrested.

No one at the wake knew what had happened to Irene's parents or why she had run away, but they knew she had met and seduced the kindly security guard, Eric Lancaster, when he detained her for siphoning gas at a truck stop. Impressed by her beauty and her youth, he offered to marry her and to take all her troubles away.

"It's not the first time a woman's been promised that before," a voice had snickered from inside the funeral parlor's gossip circle. "Too bad she hated being a mother. The little tramp couldn't keep her pants on after the baby came along." The whole group had giggled, then, until someone spotted five-year-old Waverly staring up at them with wide, unblinking eyes. They immediately changed the subject, but the damage had been done. Everywhere she went that day, snippets of conversations stopped as she walked past.

"Only twenty-two years old…"

"…came from money."

"Had been depressed for years…"

"…mentally unstable…"

Later, after the gravesite service, Waverly sat with her father under the big green tent and watched the mourners filing past.

"I'm so sorry," they said to her father. Or, "I know how you must feel."

But no one spoke to Waverly. Unable to meet her gaze, they quickly turned away. Waverly burned with shame, believing they must blame her for her mother's unhappiness and death. That night, alone in her room she cried out in her sleep. Her father rushed in and hugged her tiny body.

51

"You miss mommy?" he asked her.

Too guilty to admit she did not, Waverly cried even harder.

"Daddy misses Mommy, too," he said. "You're too young to understand this, little Wave, but she just wasn't happy here with us."

Waverly nodded that she DID understand, but she didn't say a word. She didn't want him to know it was her fault—that being Waverly's mother was what had driven her to drink. If he found out, she feared he might start hating her, too.

It took four months for her grandmother to track her down, but only twenty minutes on her father's front porch to demand full custody. Still in mourning, with no childcare available and a full-time job to attend in person (he was an 'essential worker,' after all), Eric had let all housekeeping and yardwork slide. He had also picked up his wife's former habit of drinking Aristocrat before noon on the weekends, and straight from the bottle on weekdays after work.

"I came as soon as I learned," Waverly had overhead a woman's voice that Saturday afternoon. "I've been searching for my daughter ever since she ran away, but I never thought I'd find her in the obituaries. I didn't know she was married or had a daughter until last night. It's all been quite a shock."

"Oh?" came her father's drunken reply. "Aren't you the reason she ran away in the first place? I heard you and your husband neglected her. She said you were so self-absorbed you never even came looking for her."

Her grandmother sighed. "That's a long story," she said. "Regardless, I'm here now and ready to take my granddaughter home."

"Home? What do you mean? This is her home!" He staggered a little when he swept his arm to indicate the disorderly living room behind him.

"Oh, please. Look around; your live in a dump, and you're a drunk. You can't possibly take care of a child in your condition."

He tried to slam the door in her face, but Pearl Nelson was not the kind of woman men easily shut out. With a nod, she sent in three women in dark suits to push past him. While they bustled around the house gathering Waverly's things, the older woman took Waverly's hand and introduced herself.

"Want some ice cream?" she asked next.

Waverly liked the woman instantly. The two sped off in Pearl's Thunderbird convertible, and Waverly remembered being so engrossed in conversation that she hadn't even looked back—a fact she later regretted.

At first, she thought the trip to Salem was just for the weekend. But when her father never made contact or came to get her, she came to believe he didn't love her. Just like her mother, he must have started drinking in the first place to get rid of her. And now he had gotten his wish.

She thought that for another eleven years, until her grandmother's assassination. By then, Waverly was sixteen and in the political turmoil surrounding the murder, Waverly fled for Boston. There, she tracked down her father's grave and the old house, which looked as though it had been boarded up for years. Her father's kindly neighbor told her Eric Lancaster had been killed in a car accident shortly after Waverly had gone to live with her grandmother.

"I'm sorry to say, the news claimed he had been driving drunk."

The neighbor suggested a discreet lawyer he knew—to help her probate her father's will and to file for emancipation.

"Until then," he said, "you can stay with me and my family."

That night at dinner, with her mind reeling with confusion and emotional turmoil over both her recent losses, Waverly had met the neighbor's son.

"How you doin'?" asked a handsome boy with gray eyes.

Her most vivid memory living under that roof was the boy's blond, tousled hair rhythmically flapping as they clumsily made love, and the smiling man's face over his shoulder—the one who had watched from a framed portrait on the neighbor's musty basement's wall: the face of Jesus.

Three months later, after she had moved back to her father's house and the boy had moved on to another girl, it was Jesus that Waverly blamed the most.

It's all your fault! she prayed. *I was finally safe, and I believed you approved! Now I'm all alone again!*

Three weeks later, she found out she was pregnant.

The authorities found no cause for the house fire that night. The neighbor's boy, according to the report, had gone to visit his former girlfriend after she had called him in near-hysterics. He had, apparently, been succumbed by the smoke when he had tried to rescue her from an upstairs bedroom. His face was barely recognizable in the ashes. Young Waverly, they noted, had barely made it out alive, and suffered superficial scratches and a burned scalp. Poor girl lost all her hair, though.

Although the boy's distraught father claimed Waverly had set the fire intentionally, no one could ever prove it.

Regardless, Waverly was homeless again. She spent the next eight months off the grid in an abandoned apartment building across town with three other teenage runaways. Angel was her favorite. She gave Waverly her hand-me-down clothes and dressed her up like a living doll. During the evenings, she would rub Aquaphor onto Waverly's tender burns, massage her swollen feet, and practice fun make-up techniques... such as the peacock-feather eyelashes that Waverly had been trying on the day her water broke.

Regardless of what Danforth had seen or read in her chart, Waverly was seventeen when she had given birth, and she was not a whore. After he had taken her child away, her former lawyer had caught up with her in the hospital and revealed he had been trying to reach her for months. Her grandmother's trust had been unearthed, he said, and Waverly was the sole trustee... with no conditions regarding age.

Waverly still found it hard to believe how things had turned around. At age seventeen, she had gone from being homeless, pregnant, and alone, to being one of the wealthiest people in New America.

The power of threes.

Later, after she moved back to Salem, she thought about contacting Kat. It didn't take a genius to figure out where she had gone. It had been all over the news back then how the infamous Massachusetts Senator, Pat Buford, had visited the Danforths immediately following the birth of their first son, and how she had come away with an adopted preemie. On TV, Buford appeared kind, intelligent, and wealthy. She was also an outspoken political feminist, which Waverly knew her own grandmother would have liked.

Hell, they might have even been friends for all I know, she had thought at the time. *At least my daughter is in good hands and in a community without men... men who pretend to love you and then abandon you.*

54

She decided to make a fresh start. The first thing she did was to adopt her grandmother's last name, and to immerse herself into her new role as CEO of Cis-Star Technologies. Initially, her grandmother's company had provided secure networking collaborations to the aerospace and defense industries. Back when she was living with Pearl, Waverly had risen quickly from a mail clerk to the youngest R&D inventor in Cis-Star's history. She had even had her own workbench in the lab, alongside her grandmother's.

Cis-Star's board of trustees never questioned her reappearance or her new name. In the year-long chaos following Pearl's high-profile murder, the company's stock had plummeted. This bright, young inventor was just what they needed to breathe new life into their holdings, they thought.

"I'm taking the name Nelson out of respect," she had addressed the Board at her very first meeting. "I can think of no better way to honor Pearl Nelson's legacy."

But, of course, she had other motives. She was already forming her revenge and didn't want to risk Danforth recognizing her the next time they met. She knew being Cis-Star's new CEO was a far stretch from the homeless youth he had encountered in the hospital back then, and with her new collection of 'hats' he wouldn't recognize her bald head. Still, she had signed a lot of forms that day in the hospital, so the name-change ensured anonymity. Turned out, it was a needless precaution. When she finally did "meet" him in his office years later, he had been too busy noticing her cleavage and legs to even look at her face.

With the Unirays tucked safely in her briefcase by her side, she had sat in his office and had used his notion of God and morality against him. She purposely kept a low profile in politics, after that, and had enjoyed her role behind the scenes. As Head Puppeteer, she was content to control both Danforth and Buford from afar.

Cis-Star's inventions weren't her grandmother's only successes. Turns out, Pearl Nelson had invested heavily in her own company and had diversified wisely—a move for which Waverly, as Pearl's only heir, was profoundly grateful. The woman had also constructed two towers: Cis-Star Technologies Headquarters, in East St. Louis, Illinois, and New Canaan's Info-Swirl, directly across the river from it. Since Pearl had built them under a shell company name, both were totally, and secretly, under Waverly's sole control.

Unlike the showy Info-Swirl, Cis-Star's Headquarters was a plain, rectangular box. Pearl and Waverly had laughed at its appropriate nickname, the Yardstick, for being so understated and inconsequential— just the way her grandmother had intended. Unadorned and windowless, except for the first ten public stories and Waverly's penthouse on the 77th floor, no one ever stopped to comment on it or its bland appearance.

From the Yardstick, Waverly's team secretly controlled both the Lytoky and New Canaan by integrating powerful wavelengths into select transmissions on both sides of the border. Since the new Senate no longer funded FCC monitoring of transmission wavelengths (that role had long ago been outsourced to Cis-Star as a private contractor), she was free to broadcast unregulated subliminal suggestions over once-defunct analog wavelengths. These, she sent without restriction to everyone who owned a VEE, regardless of gender or location—an enormous reach. By partitioning her messages, and therefore providing different (and sometimes purposefully conflicting) information to each opposing segment of society, her implanted suggestions soon controlled all popular and public opinion. Where the fashion industry had once influenced what the common people wore, Waverly now controlled what the public thought.

Danforth had shamed Waverly when he took her child away. He had accused her of living in a moral cesspool. It delighted her to know he would soon feel the sting of similar accusations as she finally exposed him for the beast he had become... in every sense. From the day she had first introduced herself in his office, she had been enjoying her revenge. He had gained two hundred pounds since then, and every time he unquestioningly followed one of her powerful, unethical suggestions, she had sworn he had gained another pound.

Waverly blinked the past away and raised her chin as she noticed the "reporters" running down the Info-Swirl's steps again to surround another vehicle. This time, it was a white limo. She plastered on a smile for her next performance just as Senator Danforth emerged and waved.

***

"Get ready to smile, Risa-O," Danforth said to his wife.

It was his favorite term of endearment. A certain New Canaan article had once likened his family to the historic Kennedy clan. The photographer had staged his boys, handsome and fit, as though at the line of scrimmage, with Danforth as referee. Marisa's photo showed her at the sidelines in a high-necked pink dress and her hair done up under a matching pillbox hat. As intended, the article referenced her beauty and the obvious comparison to the former first lady, Jackie-O. Danforth had saved the article and photo, and he mentioned it nearly every time he introduced her in public.

"She may not look like it now," he routinely said and laughed, "but here's proof she cleans up well when she wants to."

Now, taking a deep breath, Danforth pulled on Marisa's arm. "Ok, here we go!" he said ushering her through the media gauntlet.

"Senator Danforth! Are you nervous about today?" one journalist called.

"Who will you be voting for?" asked another.

"What will you say in your acceptance speech?"

He smiled and tried not to let claustrophobia unnerve him. Waverly had explained it was important to be seen voting on Election Day, but did the reporters have to get so close? Like a quarterback running offense, he steered his wife ahead of him, using her as a prow to part the media wave. She stumbled once and nearly twisted her ankle, but he pushed her through until they reached the top.

"Whew! Got you through that one, didn't I?" he told her and dabbed at his forehead with a yellow handkerchief. Cameras flashed as he and Ms. Nelson shook hands.

"You look good enough to eat," he told her. "If only I weren't married…" He let his voice trail off but looked directly at her chest so she would follow his meaning.

"Good to see you, too, Senator," Waverly smiled. "You too, Marisa. How are the boys?"

He smelled Waverly's perfume as she leaned in to hear his wife's response, but only broken phrases reached his ears, "The twins are with…Daniel broke his…and Jordan is…" He didn't catch the rest. Most of his boys were too young for the grueling campaign trail, and those that were older he kept out of sight, upon Waverly's suggestion.

"You don't want the public recognizing their faces," she had once advised him. "Or they might end up getting more popular than you."

Where would I be without her? he thought.

"Behind every great man, there's always a great woman," he boasted every time he mentioned her. His wife used to look at him funny whenever he said that line, but what right did she have to complain? What had she ever done for him except spend his money and raise his sons?

Waverly, however, was different. Over the years, he had learned to rely on her for everything. She was his sole advisor on the campaign trail, albeit in secret and usually from across the border. She provided the women's point of view. This, she assured him, gave him the inside track against his opponent, Senator Buford.

He reached for Waverly's hand again, crowding Marisa slightly away, and posed for another camera. Today was his day. Soon, he would get what he always deserved; he could feel it.

SEVEN

Gloria Chiang rushed off the elevator and studied the Partho Lab's square "FAMILY PLANNING" sign before her. As she read the business hours, her hand rose instinctively to tap her VEE, then she stopped herself.

Of course they're open, Stupid! she chided herself. *You have an appointment* (one made hastily after seeing the home pregnancy strip turn pink early this morning).

She reached for the door and paused, like a wary rabbit testing the breeze. She had no back-up plan. If caught by anyone on the Town Council, it would surely get back to Edna Gingham. Suddenly, the elevator dinged behind her. With a final deep breath, she opened the mahogany door and bolted inside.

Two women sat huddled by themselves in the clinic's waiting room. To Gloria's relief, they did not look up. They held hands and whispered in confidential tones as she passed. The room, itself, felt cozy and womb-like—with soft, inviting chairs in pink and maroon hues, thick carpeting, and dim lighting. There wasn't a single sharp angle in sight.

The receptionist, whose plastic nametag identified her as WINNIE, looked up with a smile. One look at Gloria, however, and the corners of her mouth sagged slightly. Apparently, Gloria's reputation in town had preceded her.

"The doctor will see you soon, Ms. Chiang. Have a seat." She pushed a rose-colored V-pad, an early-model tablet, across the counter. "Here's a pamphlet to read while you wait."

Gloria found a seat outside the receptionist's line of sight, perpendicular to the other couple, and bounced the tablet on her knee. Its screen had a simple message, "IN VITRO FERTILIZATION: QUESTIONS AND ANSWERS TO ALL-FEMALE PROCREATION."

Gloria looked around impatiently. *What's there to know?* she thought. *Women get pregnant all the time; how hard can it be?*

A few minutes later, with nothing to occupy her time but the sound of Ocean Waves coming from over the clinic's overhead speakers, Gloria got bored and scrolled down the V-pad's slate screen.

Q: What is Parthenogenesis?

A: Parthenogenesis is a means of reproduction that produces only female offspring. People used to call it VIRGIN BIRTH because the eggs are fertilized without using sperm.

Q: How does Natural Parthenogenesis differ from Artificial Parthenogenesis?

A: In nature, Parthenogenesis occurs when an egg contains a full copy of all the mother's DNA, instead of only half. Since sperm is not necessary for reproduction (the female egg is the key to preserving the species), the female replicates the other set of DNA.

Artificial Parthenogenesis occurs when two viable eggs are extracted surgically from two different females. Since each egg carries one-half the required chromosomes, a genetically-complete embryo is formed when the DNA from those two eggs unite in a controlled environment.

Q: In what animals does Natural Parthenogenesis occur?

A: Since the early to mid-1900s, biologists have noted this phenomenon in several smaller species, including insects (black vine weevil, white-fringed beetle, and the Fuller rose beetle), crustaceans (brine shrimp), and reptiles (whiptail lizard). As far back as 2007, female hammerhead sharks were observed reproducing via Parthenogenesis. Honeybees and mosquitoes reproduce their drones this way and, incidentally, their societies are highly organized and well maintained— much like the thelytoky we enjoy today.

Q: What are the drawbacks to Parthenogenesis?

A: In nature, asexual reproduction weakens populations by reducing genetic diversity and making organisms harder to adapt to changing environmental conditions. For example, the emergence of a new disease…

Gloria stopped reading. She wasn't going to undergo the procedure anyway, for goodness sake. She only needed her name on the Partho-lab registry so that no one could question her pregnancy.

And please, she begged the Universe. *Let my baby be a girl!*

***

"I'm sorry, Ms. Chiang," the doctor repeated an hour later, as she arose from behind her desk to signify the interview was over. "You've been denied fertilization. There's nothing I can do."

The interview has lasted less than five minutes. Gloria's white paper gown, the one the nurse had given her before walking her back to the doctor's office, still lay folded in her lap. Slightly damp from her sweaty palms, it mocked her with its crisp, never-to-be-worn appearance. She had not even gotten to the examination stage of her appointment.

"But why? I'm healthy; I'm young. Why can't you put me on the list? Why won't you help me have a baby?"

Dr. Bell glanced toward the closed door and sank back in her chair. *No need to cause a scene,* her body language seemed to say. She glanced at Gloria's file again, still showing on her monitor, but her tone was softer this time when she spoke.

"Ms. Chiang, I wish I could help, but according to our files you're simply not MOTHER material." She met Gloria's gaze and added kindly, "I'm sorry."

"How can you determine that?" Gloria said. She leaned forward and nearly knocked her folded gown to the floor. "You're just saying I'm unfit because of my lifestyle, and that's unfair!" Dr. Bell raised one eyebrow, and Gloria sat back. "I'm sorry," she added. "But please; you have to let me into the program. I know my rights: you can't deny me a child because of my marital status."

Oh yes, we can, the doctor's look seemed to say. Before answering aloud, however, she turned back to Gloria's file and clicked it off the screen. With that simple gesture, Gloria knew she had lost the fight.

"Let me try to explain the clinic's position," Dr. Bell said. "When a new child is formed by artificial fertilization, we have the opportunity— no, the responsibility!—to see that child raised in a stable home environment. By protecting our children's mental and physical well-being, we are ensuring the Lytoky's ongoing stability. The decisions we make here affect our entire community. We cannot afford to take that responsibility lightly."

"But I can offer a stable home environment."

Dr. Bell sighed, then continued in a patronizing tone. "Ok, for the sake of argument, let's forget that your... uh, lifestyle? shall we say? makes you a social outcast. There are other things to consider. For example, you don't have a female spouse to donate the other egg. We need two eggs to complete the fertilization. Despite what you must think," she added with an indulgent smile, "it still takes two to tango."

Gloria's gaze dropped. She noticed the rose-colored V-pad on the desk and spoke up with renewed hope. "Couldn't you use two of my eggs?"

The doctor shook her head.

"They tried that, years ago. Remember your high school biology?"

Gloria's brow creased slightly, causing Dr. Bell to inhale with exaggerated patience.

"Well, it's basic heredity. Each body cell contains two complete sets of gene-carrying chromosomes, like X-X or X-Y. When an egg forms, it automatically takes half its mother's chromosomes with it. Eggs are always an X."

She held up her right forefinger and wiggled it for effect.

"Now, if that first X is fertilized by a Y-chromosome, the outcome, X-Y, is a boy. If fertilized by another X, it will be X-X... a girl."

She held up her other forefinger and moved them together to represent the joining.

"Since another woman's egg can supply the additional X, a complete X-X cell is formed. That's why our Partho-babies are always girls."

"I understand all that," Gloria said, sharply. "Why can't you take two of MY eggs? They would both be X's. Why isn't that possible?"

"I never said it was impossible. Did you read any of the material?" The doctor indicated the V-pad, and Gloria's cheeks turned pink.

"I... I didn't have time."

Dr. Bell sighed again.

"Like I said, it takes two chromosomes to complete a human genome. If we took both X chromosomes from the same source (from you, for example), the baby's genetic code would be identical to yours. She would be a "clone," if you will, like the sheep and other lab animal tests done years before the Plague. They tried it on humans, if you recall, and the results were disastrous. Remember the Doe-Three Epidemic?"

Gloria nodded slowly. She had heard the term before but wasn't sure what it had to do with her. "Isn't that where a bunch of babies got sick and died?"

"That's right. Years ago, after the sudden expulsion of men, we needed to quickly re-populate the east, so we cloned our more promising citizens. The next winter, we lost over two hundred toddlers to flu-like symptoms. At first, people assumed we were under another attack, remember?

"It wasn't until the donor, Jane Doe #3, came down with the flu, as well, that we discovered they were all from the same genetic batch. The host's genetic code, it turned out, was particularly susceptible to that year's strain. By then, of course, it was too late. Jane Doe #3 was strong enough to fight off the virus, having built up a lifetime of immunities, but her clones didn't stand a chance. From that, we learned that despite our medical breakthroughs, there are certain things we can't predict. The Doe-Three Epidemic proved that single-source fertilization is too dangerous. We need diversity. We can't risk some recessive gene wiping out whole segments of our population later, and in this case, we can't risk passing on an already-documented deviant gene."

Gloria looked down at her lap. Her expertise was in programming computers, not biology. She questioned some of the doctor's explanations, but she had heard enough to learn they would never accept her. She suspected all that technical jargon was a decoy, anyway. With people like Edna Gingham out to get her and her "deviant" heterosexual genes, they would probably never allow her to reproduce even if she had a donor egg.

EIGHT

The smooth, oval window felt cool against Kat's forehead. She had never been on a plane before, nor on any other mode of public transportation, for that matter, so she had already devoured a roll of antacids. Luckily, this was a direct flight to the Oasis.

What will Mom say when she finds out? she wondered. *Will she be angry that I left? Upset? Will she care?*

Outside, dark storm clouds billowed for as far as they eye could see. Some swirled upward, tall and regal, while others squatted, low and fat. All were equally ominous and seemed to change each time she looked out the window—much like her mood today.

The plane shuddered and she heard a flight attendant's cart clinking metal against glass.

It's just the turbulence, she told herself, chewing her bottom lip. *That's what's making me feel so uneasy.*

"Liar," said Jordan, in her head.

A brunette, seated three rows up, had projected a VEE Holo onto her lap from the seatback in front of her. Kat recognized the program; it was her graduation from this morning. Even without ear buds, she knew every line in her mother's speech by heart.

In disgust, she turned toward the clouds again. The plane hit more turbulence. She grabbed her armrests with white fingertips and wished (like she'd been wishing ever since take-off) that the pilot would turn the plane around.

I've got a bad feeling about this, she thought.

"It'll be okay," he told her. *"Besides, it's too late."*

She agreed that was true; he had already crossed the border and was being processed in Immigrations.

She touched her fingertips to the glass and traced the clouds' outlines. One, she noted, resembled a dancer with arms and legs outstretched to one side in an old-fashioned jitterbug stance. As she watched, mesmerized, the dancer's arms seemed to lengthen to the right and her legs twisted left. Her hair spiraled slowly into an exaggerated beehive. Kat blinked, and the cloud-lady's arms and legs had transformed into serpents, and her head had stretched to become a tall, medieval castle.

Jordan! she called, needing to hear his 'voice.'

"I know," he answered. *"I can feel it too."* Their futures were closing in.

"Ear buds?"

Kat turned away with a start. In the aisle stood a smiling flight attendant extending a small, plastic package.

"Pardon?" Kat asked her.

"Complementary ear buds," the woman explained. "I noticed you're not watching your VEE."

"No, thank you," Kat replied, shaking her head.

The flight attendant's smile remained fixed.

"But… they're talking about the election. Everyone wants to hear about that." The package crinkled in her outstretched hand and she blinked, uncertain.

"No. Really. I'm fine."

The flight attendant hesitated a moment longer, then shrugged and moved away. "Ear buds?" she asked the woman sitting one row back.

"Why yes, of course!" the woman replied in an exaggerated tone, clearly meant for Kat to overhear. "I am a patriot, after all."

Kat rolled her eyes and twirled a strand of the coarse blonde wig she had taken from her Aunt Waverly's stash, then she adjusted her fake eyeglasses.

At least no one has recognized me, she congratulated herself.

Overhead, the oxygen hissed. The woman behind her rustled her plastic package, taking pains, it seemed, to make noise, but Kat barely noticed. Her attention had been drawn back to Jordan, in Immigrations, nearly a thousand miles away.

***

Having crossed the border thirty minutes prior, Jordan waited, alone, in a small, windowless room for his Entrance Exam to begin. Per his research, all men traveling to the Oasis first went through this Interview process. He was just about to comment on Kat's pushy flight attendant when three Lytoky MP Officers entered the room. Two wore blue uniforms and took seats across the table from him, and the third wore khaki BDUs. Jordan assumed this last one was in charge by the bars on her lapel. She boosted herself up onto a counter along the far wall. He had a hard time telling the two women in blue apart. They were both pale, had dark hair and wore no makeup. The only difference was that one's hair was cut short, in a bob, and the other one had pulled her hair back in a bun.

The questioning began without introduction.

"So, Mr. Brown," said the first one with the bob, reading off Jordan's bogus border pass name on her V-pad. "What brings you across the Mother Road bridge today, and why did you book passage to the Oasis?"

Jordan had swiped the name "Brown" last week while trolling his father's computer. He had been looking for a way to cross the border undetected when he came across a whole list of names his father evidently intended to grant access across the border once he won today's election. Moving fast, Jordan had swapped his own credentials with the first name on the list, Paul Brown, and had used his father's Senate security code to transfer their iris scans. Luckily, his father could never remember passwords, and kept them all hidden in his bottom desk drawer.

That had, effectively, started the clock. He didn't know what would happen if he and the real Paul Brown both tried to cross the border, so time was of the essence. Assuming his father won the election (which Jordan thought was highly unlikely given the talk he had heard from both sides) he wanted to make sure he got across the border first.

Jordan smiled at the officer in blue (whom he thought of as "Bob" because of her hair cut) and recited from memory his well-rehearsed script.

"I'm meeting someone," he said. "A woman."

"Why leave home for that? Don't you have women in New Canaan?"

"Yes, but they are different over there."

"How so?"

"Oh, this should be good!" mumbled the second officer in blue. He decided to think of her as "Bun." She stretched an arm around the back of her chair and eyed him with open dislike.

"Well, to be honest," he said, "I find the women back home to be boring."

"Boring?" asked Bun.

"Yes. They're too predictable. They only say what they think you want to hear, and…"

"Like you're doing now?"

Jordan's cheeks turned red. This was not going the way he and Kat had predicted. He looked from face to face. Only the woman in khaki seemed amused.

"Mr. Brown," Bob suggested, "Why don't we begin again? It says here you want to defect from New Canaan and that you've requested a tour of duty at the Oasis. Tell us why we should admit you."

"Because in the Lytoky women are my equal and…"

Bun scoffed and cut him off again. "What the hell makes you think we'd accept you as an equal?"

In his mind, he heard Kat's quiet gasp. They had prepared his speech together and practiced it many times, but neither had predicted the interview to be hostile.

"What if they deny you passage?" Kat fretted.

They won't! he thought. Then he swallowed, and his eyes moved back and forth as he tried to think fast.

"Are you saying that YOU consider men and women equals, Mr. Brown?" Bob suggested. "Is that what you're trying to say?"

"Well, yes. Of course."

"Don't you believe in the Bible?" This question came from Bun.

"Uh. Yes?" Jordan frowned. He didn't know what that had to do with anything.

Bob bent and produced a worn leather book from a satchel on the floor. She spread it open on the table.

"Do you know what this is?" she asked.

Jordan's brows creased. "I thought Bibles weren't allowed in the Lytoky."

"Answer the question, Mr. Brown," Bun said.

Jordan shrugged at the book and nodded. As Senator Danforth's eldest son, he had been drilled especially hard in his Bible Studies each Sunday.

"Of course I do; it's a Bible."

"Then tell me how any man who believes in this," Bob tapped the tabbed page with her thumb, "can believe a woman is his equal? This document decrees that women must submit to the dominance of man." She bent to read. "'Wives, submit yourselves to your husbands, as unto the Lord.'"

"Yes, but..."

"And what about this one?" She flipped to another tab with another highlighted passage. "'Let your women keep silence in the churches for it is not permitted for them to speak.' Ever hear of that one?"

Jordan only nodded. He had heard them all.

"Then perhaps you are also aware that these passages have encouraged men throughout history to subject their wives to rape, beatings, and slavery. Isn't it true that in your religion only those with a male anatomy are worthy of respect or power?"

"What? No, that's..."

"Then what about this?" She cleared her throat. "Suffer not a woman to teach, nor to usurp authority over the man, but to be in silence. For Adam was first formed, then Eve. And Adam was not deceived, but the woman, being deceived, was in the transgression.'"

Jordan started to speak but Bun chimed in.

"In your Bible," she said, "a father offers up his virgin daughter to a drunken mob so they can rape her instead of hurting a male stranger, and he is PRAISED for it! Let's see; where is that one again?"

She took the book from Bob and turned to another tabbed page.

"Here it is. 'Do with them what seemeth good unto you, but unto THIS MAN do not so vile a thing. And he brought forth the woman and they KNEW her, and ABUSED HER all the night until the morning, and when the day began to spring, they let her go.'"

"Really? It says that?" Kat said in his head.

Not now, Kat! Please, I'm trying to concentrate.

The Waves of Dissonance

"Your Bible honors the father for letting those men abuse his daughter," Bun continued, slamming her fist down on the page. "Hours and hours of gang rape all night long! Your Bible offers no compassion or concern for the woman. None! This attitude against women persists to this day in New Canaan, and we have your Bible here, in large part, to blame for it. You 'religious-types' believe every word of whatever doctrine you are spouting, and you believe it is straight from some 'Big Guy,' himself. It should be no surprise you treat women as less than human… as property."

"As boring," Bob added.

Jordan could hear Kat in the background thinking she should have paid more attention during his Bible Study classes, but she was quiet otherwise.

He considered his options. He had tried interjecting several times already, but they clearly didn't want to hear his rebuttal. If they sent him back to New Canaan now, he would never get away again. His father would put him under house arrest for sure, or worse.

"Agree with them!" Kat suggested. *"What harm could it do?"*

He shifted uncomfortably.

"Well," he began, "I've wondered about some of those passages, myself, but I guess I figured maybe some weren't translated correctly." He looked around, choosing his next words carefully. "I dunno. Maybe you're right. I have to admit there are men on my side who are afraid of women. Maybe throughout history men have always known that one day you wouldn't need them, so they created ways to keep you down."

Bun sat back in her chair.

"All I know," he said, "is that I don't believe women are inferior. I am in love with one and would never do anything to hurt her. Why else would I be here today, humbling myself before you? That should tell you something. The Bible also speaks about love… about honoring your wife and being thoughtful to her needs. Of being humble and gentle, and to 'love her as Christ loved the church.' That's the message I believe."

Bun paused, then started leafing through the Bible again.

"Look," he said, turning to the one on the counter—the one in khaki who had, so far, remained silent. "We can debate the Bible all day long, but at some point, you need to decide if you will let me go to the Oasis or

69

send me back. You have the power here, not me. Why don't we cut to the chase?"

The Blue team turned to the bemused woman in khaki. She appeared to be mid-thirties, but it was hard to judge since they all looked as though they had spent time in the sun. Most women in New Canaan kept their faces protected outdoors, so he suspected these Lytoky women looked older than their years.

"Fine," she said, and hopped down off the counter. "Get his forms in order. I'll transport him tonight."

Without a word, Bob dropped the Bible back into its satchel and followed Bun in pushing back her chair. Apparently, the interview was over. Jordan relaxed as the woman in khaki offered him her hand. Close up, he noticed she had kind, hazel eyes.

"Welcome to the Lytoky, Mr. Brown. I'm your Transport Officer, Lieutenant Winters. Looks like you'll be joining us this evening at the Oasis." She held out a set of handcuffs expectantly. "Sorry about the cuffs," she added. "It's standard operating procedure." She waited until Jordan's wrists were secure then guided him out the door. "By the way, you're familiar with our subway system, right?"

Jordan, still puzzled over his restraints, nodded without looking up.

"Subway? Why are they taking you below ground?"

Kat's anxious words made him flinch and look up. No one used subways anymore. During the Plague, most tunnels had been destroyed to keep people from congregating in stagnant, contaminated air, or from leaving quarantine cities. The only remaining stations were those forgotten or unfinished. He suddenly wondered where they were taking him. He had thought they would fly. He pictured Kat biting her bottom lip.

"Good!" said the lieutenant, seemingly unconcerned. "Some people get claustrophobic in the tunnels, so I always like to ask. No big deal. This particular tunnel was still under construction when the Plague broke out, so it wasn't finished until a couple decades ago. Anyway, we don't leave until tonight, so you'll wait downstairs in Holding with the others. Don't worry; the actual trip underground only takes an hour or so, then we'll get you on the southbound Transport airplane. You'll be there before you know it. Come on."

The Waves of Dissonance

***

Kat listened as Jordan followed Lieutenant Winters onto some sort of platform. Her plane hit a pocket, causing the passenger behind her to gasp and lurch forward, but Kat's eyes remained focused out the window, concentrating on a scene she could not see.

She heard a soft *"Ping!"* in her mind and recognized it as an elevator door opening. Then, she heard footsteps.

"This corridor leads directly to the tunnels," the lieutenant was saying. The woman's voice echoed slightly and was nearly drowned out by what sounded like an approaching train. *"There's an escalator ahead, do you see it?"*

Kat heard Jordan thinking *"Yes,"* but she guessed he only nodded. The background noise was deafening. Luckily, his direct thoughts were always clear.

"Get on the escalator!" the lieutenant shouted. *"I'll meet you at the bottom later!"*

"See you on the other side, Kat," she heard Jordan thinking, as he evidently stepped onto a moving tread.

See you on the other side, Kat repeated and smiled back. It was an old joke. Every time they left someone else, they always said that to each other in jest, because they never left each other.

The lieutenant yelled something else behind him, and Kat deduced she was giving instructions to the officer taking him down. *"Put him with the others in Holding! You, Brown! Watch your step! There ya go. I'll be ba— in about— or so."* Her voice was breaking up. Kat pressed her temples in concentration.

Jordan? she called. *What's going on?*

The answer came back garbled, like a bad Skype connection. *"Hey I can't h— you. Kat! What's—"* And then he was gone.

Silence.

Kat gasped.

For as long as she could remember, she and Jordan had never lost connection. Not even in their sleep. The blood drained from her face.

Jordan? The word fell dead against the meaty part of her brain. She had lost him.

71

Forever?

A cold chill ran down her spine at the thought as the plane dipped and shuddered again. Someone shrieked, and Kat hit her temple on the window frame. She vaguely noted a flight attendant rushing past, but in her mind's eye, she was still descending into the tunnels with Jordan.

Jordan? she called again. *Jordan, where are you?*

When the plane leveled out, the storm clouds outside had shifted again. This time, the castle had contorted to form the shape of a wide, leering dragon.

NINE

"You're what?" Waverly asked, nearly choking on her coffee. "Did you say you're pregnant with Dale's baby?" she managed to cough. "Again?"

She adjusted her pendant to get a better look. The interactive Holo-image stared back in mid-air as Waverly's private Cis-Star helicopter gained altitude. Gloria Chiang nodded but did not meet her employer's gaze. An uncomfortable silence followed as Waverly set her coffee aside and let the news sink in.

"Gloria," she said at last, "this is the last thing I need right now."

"Yes ma'am. I know. I'm sorry."

Waverly glanced out the window. Having just left Danforth in St. Louis, Cis-Star's Headquarters Building, where Gloria now undoubtedly stood, was just below her.

Where did I go wrong with this one? Waverly wondered.

She had expected great things from Gloria. For her age, which Waverly knew was only six years younger than, herself, Gloria had exhibited a real thirst for knowledge and ambition: two things Waverly admired in her employees. Gloria's IQ was off the charts, of course (Cis-Star only hired the best), but unfortunately, like most geniuses, Gloria's common-sense skills were grossly underdeveloped.

Gloria had come to Cis-Star fresh from grad school where she had finished top of her class. She had excelled in the R&D lab, but it was her creative ideas on destructive interference programming in the company's on-line chat room, that had caught Waverly's attention. Over time, she rewarded Gloria with increasingly high-profile, confidential assignments.

The girl had even helped troubleshoot the latest VEE prototype—the very pendant now exposing her discomfort. She was the only other person Waverly had ever trusted to program the Adrays' frequencies.

Waverly could easily grant Gloria diplomatic immunity, she knew. But as a top-ranking Cis-Star director—especially one trusted with such top-secret technology—Gloria's blatant disrespect for the rules was disturbing. After all, this was not the first time the woman had screwed up.

Three years ago, when Waverly sent her to New Canaan on an extended tour of duty, Gloria had met Dale Stevens, the Info-Swirl's Facility Manager. Posing as Cis-Star's Technical Support, Gloria had converted St. Louis' cell towers over to the latest Adrays frequency and had planted listening devices in Senator Danforth's office tower. Unfortunately, she also fell in love.

At first, Waverly decided to indulge the fling.

A little fun never hurt anyone, I guess, she reasoned.

When the assignment had ended and Gloria came back to headquarters, Waverly assumed the affair was over. She was wrong. The following spring, Gloria announced they had gotten married.

That was strike one.

Then, Gloria had gotten pregnant. It was an accident, Gloria had assured her. Still, since Waverly couldn't afford to have her deported to New Canaan, she had "helped them out" by alerting the authorities. She also made sure the LPs taught them both a lesson before letting Dale go free.

Strike two was a bitch.

After that, she had specifically programmed Gloria to be more careful in the future. Sizing up the woman now, Waverly wondered if maybe Gloria was immune to the Adrays programming. Cis-Star employees underwent mandatory pre-hire testing to make sure they were controllable, and Gloria had been no exception.

Over the years, Waverly had determined that a sizable percentage of the human population (nearly five percent) were Adrays "resistant." For ninety percent of that resistant group, the frequencies failed to influence their behavior at all, even days later. She called that group "A-free," as in "free of the Adrays' influence." Waverly didn't worry about them. She still maintained control over them by group-dynamics: a phenomenon resulting in things like peer pressure and mob-mentality.

The other ten percent within that A-free group, however, registered actual words when they encountered the Adrays. When hit with the specialized wavelengths, this small subgroup could tell they were being manipulated. Waverly called them the "A-sensitives." Most A-sensitives either went mad or joined the Gamma Group to move away from the Adrays' broadcasts. (Cis-Star hadn't yet bothered to infiltrate the Gamma states.)

It was because of this A-sensitive phenomenon, she assumed, that some outspoken Gamma citizens had recently started calling themselves "The Rebellion" and had accused both the Lytoky and New Canaan of brainwashing their respective constituents. Waverly considered the group passive enough to render them innocuous. Mainstream media called those people conspiracy theorists, or quacks. Waverly always laughed when she heard their demonstrations denounced. No one realized the quacks were right—not even her Cis-Star employees who helped her send out the Adrays to both sides.

She had learned from her grandmother to silo her secrets. By keeping each Cis-Star department physically separate from the other, it ensured no one fully understood what the other was doing. Even the divisions within each department were kept apart. The building's design had accounted for this. Certain elevator banks only serviced specific floors, and individual lunchrooms had been sprinkled throughout to keep the staff from mingling. The largest of her six Departments, for example (the Adrays Department), had multiple divisions—each with segregated branches. One branch sent messages only to New Canaan. Another, only to the Lytoky. There were still others devoted to broadcasting singular topics, such as keeping the Lytoky women interested sexually in only other women. That branch, alone, took up three floors. No two branch heads knew where or what the other was transmitting, and only a handful knew any program's full content. The Staff Writers were the ones truly in the dark. They had no idea their words became programs. They believed they were writing for potential movie clips.

Waverly personally implanted the appropriate bias into all her employees' brains so that no one questioned their perceived mission. Still, it wasn't impossible for an occasional employee to slip through.

"How long have you known?" she asked Gloria.

The woman paused before answering. "About three months?"

Waverly's eyes narrowed. *Three months… Really?* She couldn't help noticing Gloria had answered with a question. Waverly tried to recall the last time she had seen her employee in person. *It must have been only a few days ago. Had she appeared, or acted, differently then?* Waverly couldn't remember.

"You're the first to know, though!" Gloria added, as though that made a difference.

"I see. Is it a girl?"

"I don't know."

Waverly waited for Gloria's face to betray her. Surely, at three months, Gloria's doctor would know the child's gender.

At three months, it was too late to terminate a pregnancy. Even if a woman were carrying a boy child, a second trimester abortion was highly discouraged unless the mother's health was in danger. Besides, since pregnancies were such deliberate events these days (each requiring permits, artificial implantation appointments, etc.), convenience-abortions were unheard of these days. So, that meant Gloria was either being dishonest about not knowing the gender (because she already knew it was a boy), or she was lying about the three months, and therefore didn't yet know the baby's sex. Either way… Gloria had just lied to her.

Strike three.

The seconds ticked by in silence.

"Let me guess…." Waverly finally spoke. "You're telling me this now because you need my help. Again."

Gloria nodded enthusiastically.

"Yes ma'am; if it's not too much trouble!"

Too much trouble? Waverly wanted to scream. *Of course it was too much trouble! It was too much trouble LAST time, but you didn't seem to appreciate that fact! What was wrong with this hetero couple? Hadn't they ever heard of birth control?*

Waverly took a deep breath.

"Gloria," she said aloud, "you know that if this child is a boy..."
"I'll be deported to New Canaan and lose my job," Gloria cut her off.
"Yes, I know. Dale and I have already discussed it, and we're prepared for that, if it happens."

As if things weren't bad enough.

Waverly tapped her fingers on the armrest, thinking harder now. How could she lose her best employee at a time like this? Worse, how could she risk losing Gloria to the other side? She had invested a lot of time and resources into that woman. If she were deported, it would be natural for Gloria to seek employment at the Info-Swirl. *Of all places!* The senator would be a fool not to hire her. Even though it was highly irregular for New Canaan women to work outside the home, Danforth would jump at the chance to learn Cis-Star Technologies' inside information.

Hell, he might even hire her as a courtesy to me! she thought. *How ironic.*

Waverly could probably negate that using her Unirays on Danforth, but she had not yet planted that seed, so it was a risky proposition and would take a lot of work.

"Gloria," Waverly started again, straining to sound empathetic. "If you get deported, you won't only lose your job, you'll lose your freedom and sense of self-worth, as well. We've discussed this before, remember? Over there, you are property. You can't even go to the store unless your husband gives you permission. Sure, you think Dale is a great guy now, but trust me; in a few years, when the newlywed magic wears off, he'll be like all the others and start taking you for granted. Then where will you be?"

Gloria dropped her gaze but raised her chin resolutely. "I'll do whatever it takes to keep my baby," she said.

Fool! How could you be so careless?

"There are fertilization labs, you know!" Waverly blurted. "I could have pulled some strings and allowed you to use Dale's sperm, if that's so goddamn important to you! Did you ever stop to think how your actions affect others?"

On screen, tears streamed down Gloria's face.

"I'm sorry, Ms. Nelson. I know I let you down, but I love him! I do! And I want to keep this baby!"

The scars on Waverly's head throbbed under her wig. She often regretted accidentally burning off her hair when she had burned down her old house in Boston, but she had never regretted locking her old two-timing boyfriend inside her bedroom before she set the fire. In the end, her hair had been a good cover, though. Because of her injuries, no one but the boy's father had ever suspected her of wrongdoing.

The boy hadn't even wanted to come over that night, she recalled, but she had begged him to see her One Last Time. Her lips twitched at the word choice. That had been the last time she had ever begged anyone for anything.

Until Danforth had taken her baby, of course.

She scratched her scars, gingerly, and frowned back at Gloria.

Perhaps it's time to create a special Unirays message just for her, she thought.

Unirays were different from Adrays in that they targeted specific individuals and, therefore, allowed for precise programming. Unirays stimulated the same neurotransmitters in the brain (the area that reproduces rhythms and supports language), but they needed an individual's dopamine fingerprint to work. Such fingerprints were unique to each individual and could be obtained with a simple iris scan. Unlike Adrays, the Unirays worked on nearly everyone, but to varying degrees.

It would take some work to set up the right program but...

Waverly's eyes suddenly widened. *Of course! Gloria's my missing puzzle piece! Why didn't I think of that before?*

She decided not to be too hard on herself. This morning, when she was finalizing her FOLLOW ME programming at *The Awakening*, she had not considered Gloria because she was too valuable an employee. But now...

If I'm going to lose her anyway, this is better than losing her to the other side! Besides, I've been entirely too lenient about mixed marriages; it's time I send a message.

Her smile came easier now when she addressed Gloria's Holo again.

"Well, ok; I guess there's no use crying over spilled sperm, now, is there?" She watched Gloria's tear-filled eyes soften at the pun, as she had intended. "Look, I'm sure I can think of something," she continued. "Maybe I can get your name on the Partho-lab records, after all, so there won't be any suspicion. I'll touch down in Chicago shortly, then off to

Boston. I'll call you when I get there... say around two? You'll be home?"

Gloria nodded, smiled, and simultaneously sniffled.

"Good," Waverly continued. "I'll call your home phone. You're still at 343 Plumb Street, right?"

Once again, Gloria nodded and wiped away fresh tears... this time of happiness.

"Oh, thank you, Waverly! I mean, Ms. Nelson. I knew you'd come through for me."

"Well, don't thank me yet. If it's a boy, you know, there's nothing I can do."

That was a lie, of course; there was always more she could do if she chose. But there was no point discussing it further. *In a few hours, keeping her baby will be the last thing on Gloria's mind,* she knew.

The instant Gloria's on-screen image disappeared, so did Waverly's smile. She shook her head in frustrated disbelief at Gloria's stupidity, then spent the remaining short flight editing her program's ending.

"UNIRAYS RECEIVER: CONFIRM NAME?" the virtual VEE screen blinked at her.

She nodded at the previously coded name, PAUL BROWN #2067.

"Confirmed," she said.

"OBJECTIVE?"

"Gloria Chiang, 343 Plumb Street, East St. Louis, Illinois."

"TIME?"

"Fourteen hundred."

"EXECUTE?"

"Yes."

"ARE YOU SURE?"

"Yes."

Her stomach dipped, telegraphing the helicopter's descent, and she glanced out the window as she snapped shut the pendant's ladybug wings. O'Hare's Cis-Star helipad was quickly approaching.

"Sorry, Gloria," she whispered. "But you left me no other choice."

As her altitude continued to drop, Waverly steeled herself mentally for what lay ahead, and felt her body tighten with anticipation, as though bracing for impact.

TEN

Prisoner Paul Brown slouched while he ate, with elbows out like a firefighter scarfing down chow before the next emergency. He held his tray steady with one hand so it wouldn't wobble on the graffiti-chiseled wooden table. His own contribution to the table's carvings had been the words BITE Me to the right of his tray. It had taken him nearly a year, painstakingly etching each letter with his thumbnail during meals, but he wasn't happy with the results. He'd been forced to squeeze in the final, lower-case "e" at the end, because the word ME had somehow gotten too close to another word already on the table. Otherwise, it would have appeared as BITE MEN.

Bad planning on his part, he admitted.

"You should'a seen that "N" acomin'," his friend, Leonard, had commented one day from across the table.

"Mind your own business, Fucktard!" had been Paul's only response.

He was certain that the other word, ZEUS (running perpendicular to his BITE Me phrase), hadn't been there when he had started his work. Like a bad game of Scrabble, the "Z" in Zeus ran vertically, totally ruining Paul's artistic expression.

That had been over three years ago. Today, as Paul and his team ate lunch at Table #9, he read the words with only mild disinterest. Like mannequins controlled by unseen strings, each inmate methodically scooped his food, raised his spoon, and opened wide. They had to eat fast or their spoons, made from recycled materials, would disintegrate and turn to mush.

They ate in silence.

Even the guards seemed unusually lethargic today. Several leaned against tables or walls, and some sank low in their chairs. Others tapped out time to the piped-in music while keeping a drowsy eye on the prisoners. Security in the cafeteria was always lacking, but who could blame the guards? There had not been a serious disturbance on the island for more than a decade, and even that had been a fluke. Rumor had it that a riot had broken out before breakfast one day and a guard (who had allegedly been having an affair with a prisoner) got herself killed.

"It was the overhead bell," the story went. "It triggered some kind of post-hypnotic suggestion that made all the inmates go berserk!"

Paul doubted the story was true. He didn't remember such an event, and he had been here nearly thirteen years.

"Hey Leonard," he called, "pass the-"

Suddenly, exquisite pain, like a dentist's pick scraping raw nerve, erupted in Paul's mouth. It made him drop his spoon and cradle his throbbing jaw.

Damn those O-rays! he cringed.

He had heard that some men get ice-cream headaches. They were the lucky ones, he thought. He, on the other hand, felt shooting pain in his right bottom molar every time the warden turned on her machine. Three times a day, after every meal, Paul wished he had that ice-cream-headache-disorder-thing, instead. After all, they rarely got ice cream here on the Rock.

No one else ever seemed affected by the propaganda machine. It was Paul's own private hell.

Usually, the pain only lasted a couple of seconds, followed by whatever Feeling-of-the-Day the warden had selected for their post-dining pleasure. Years ago, after he had passed out from one particularly painful episode, Paul had awakened in Medical and overheard them discussing the O-rays, and their so-called subliminal messages. To Paul, however, the messages weren't subliminal; he heard actual words.

Words intended to turn us all into compliant pussies, no doubt, he thought.

Today at breakfast, for instance, he had heard the repeating phrase, "Work hard and you'll never grow old. Don't be an Old Timer. Work hard...." No telling what it would be now, for lunch. The warden never used the same message twice in one week. She was predictable that way.

During evening meals, she usually played only low-key, simple themes like "I'm tired," or "What a satisfying meal!" (Anything to keep the inmates docile and quiet before sending them off to bed.) It was a mind game, of course—one he always tried to resist.

Today's programming started off differently, though. Along with the initial pain came a loud buzzing sound. It reminded him of static. He listened, curious, and let go of his jaw. Just when it seemed he might get a break today, a blast of words crashed into his brain. He jolted in surprise and covered both ears, but as usual, the words were not coming from outside. They registered deep inside the back of his head. Within seconds, the volume intensified, blocking out all other thought. He squeezed shut his eyes, but the pounding words continued.

"Follow me! Follow me!" a booming voice commanded. *"FREEDOM AND POWER to those who follow me!"*

Over and over, the Voice (it sounded like his own) beckoned for him to follow. After the third repetition, he realized that although the sound was throbbing, it was bearable. In fact, it was becoming oddly pleasurable. Slowly, he lowered his hands again and squinted beneath each reverberation. No one returned his gaze. His neighbors were all sitting up, now, and staring intently at their plates. No one was shoveling food.

Do they hear it, too?

After nine more seconds repeating the same line, the Voice's volume lowered to a more conversational tone, except for when it said his name, which was always punctuated and near-deafening.

"MR. BROWN! Now that I have your attention, listen up. The time has come for you to fight against those who unjustly persecuted and imprisoned you. Follow me and I will set you free."

His eyes searched the room. Could he be losing his mind?

"You, MR. BROWN! You are my chosen one. Judgment Day is coming, and you will lead the way. Follow me. Follow me."

He almost jumped to his feet right then, but the Voice held him back. His heart raced, and a thin line of perspiration beaded on his upper lip as he struggled to retain control. He listened intently to the Voice and memorized each detailed instruction, nodding occasionally despite his suspicion that the Voice's owner was nowhere close and was not watching. Ten minutes later, when the cafeteria bell sounded, he was ready to do his part.

***

The foreone walked through the cafeteria's steel doors an instant before the bell went off.

She did not usually eat with the prisoners—spending all day with them in the sun was torture enough. So today, like most days after bringing in her group, she had retired to the guard's lounge to rest in air-conditioned comfort. While there, she had sensed a strange foreboding, like the proverbial "little voice inside her head" telling her that something was awry. Following this intuition, she impulsively left the guards' lounge and walked directly to the cafeteria.

Through the small wire-reinforced window, she surveyed the scene inside. Everything looked normal. The guards were standing around—or sitting, as in the case of Sal Dotter (the oldest guard in the ward, who constantly complained of aching feet)—and the prisoners were behaving. Their heads were bent, and their spoons were down. They seemed totally engrossed in the music.

All except for one.

Prisoner Brown was staring at her. When their eyes locked, he did not look away. That clue, alone, should have alerted her. If she had studied the other inmates closer, she would have noticed that although their heads were bowed, they were not relaxed as she had at first assumed. They were tense and expectant; each jaw clamped in concentration as they waited and listened... but not to the music.

The instant she pushed the door open, the prisoners jumped to their feet and yelled. Lunch trays and chairs went flying. She reached for her gun, but someone ran toward her and slammed her against the hard doorjamb. Shots were fired, men went down, but the rioting continued.

***

The foreone closed her eyes just before Brown slid past. He paused slightly when he saw her pressed so seductively against the doorjamb, but he forced himself to move on.

Sorry I can't stay and play, he thought.

He turned down the hallway and into the guards' lounge, which someone had neglected to lock. Once there, he found the secret escape hatch labeled, FOR EMERGENCY EXIT ONLY, behind a fake filing cabinet—exactly where the Voice had said it would be. He punched in the code it had given him and watched the door glide soundlessly open.

Outside, a Jeep was waiting, with its engine still running. He wondered how many guards had been suddenly called away for luck like this to continue.

So far so good, he thought.

He threw the gearshift into first and escaped through the open gate. By the time he reached the dock and the awaiting speedboat, only three minutes had passed since the foreone had first opened the cafeteria door.

***

Fifteen minutes later, the other inmates awoke from their trance. They dropped their hostages, chairs, and trays, and settled down onto the floor, feeling disheveled and confused. The riot ended without anyone even knowing why it had begun.

Between the mangled casualties and the flurry of handcuffs, another ten minutes passed before the official head count was taken. Only then did they discover a prisoner had gone missing, along with the warden's prized speedboat.

One guard, Sal Dotter, was found slumped over Table #9, clubbed in the face by her own folding metal chair. Poor Sal would never complain about her aching feet again.

ELEVEN

Fireworks exploded and white doves took flight as the stadium erupted into foot stomping, heart-pounding applause. Friends and campaign workers rushed the confetti-strewn stage to engulf their new leader with hugs and back-pounding congratulations. In the mayhem, Pat could barely breathe, much less see.

Out in front, for a change, her friend Waverly Nelson made the announcement. Over the loudspeaker, her slow voice boomed and reverberated throughout the stands.

"Ladies! Ladies! It's official! The ballots just closed, and the results are in! The new president has already taken the oath. I am, therefore, proud to be the first person to introduce New America's newest President, our very own hometown hero, Pat Buford!"

Pat raised her arms in triumph and walked downstage to shake Waverly's hand. The crowd thundered in response. Their adoration pulsed over her, through her, and in her. The packed stadium writhed, and jewelry glistened. Multiple camera flashes throughout the crowd looked to her like feeding piranha, with sunlight randomly flashing off their silvery scales. It would take several moments for the frenzy to quiet enough for her to speak. In the meantime, she waved and threw kisses as Waverly retreated.

Some women, she noted, wore pantsuits. Others, more feminine skirts and dresses. Most of the "under twenty" crowd, however, were wearing the latest fad: a one-piece wrap-around skaris—a cross between traditional Indian saris and shorts. Katherine had several at home. In fact,

Pat wouldn't be surprised to see her wearing her favorite white one tonight.

On impulse, she searched among the women backstage, but no one was there but her dark-suited Security Detail. No one had seen Katherine since the graduation this morning and she wasn't answering her VEE.

Why didn't they assign her a Security Detail BEFORE the results? she wondered with a frown. *Maybe then, Kat would have gotten here on time.* She glanced again at her Detail. *Then again, maybe not.*

The Secret Service was more for show, these days, than for actual protection. Since the late President Sotomayor had been so beloved, she had cut funding for this "unnecessary" service, so by now, the department was severely understaffed and the officers untrained. Pat bet that both she and Katherine could easily outmaneuver them.

Still, it shouldn't take the Secret Service to get my daughter to attend my celebration! The whole reason I chose Salem was so we could share this memory together!

She shook her head and forced herself back into the moment, to her unprecedented victory. Looking around, she had to admit it felt gratifying to have won by such a landslide. Especially considering everything Danforth had said about her on the campaign trail. She could only imagine how this defeat was affecting him.

The poor bastard.

She had known him for twenty-six years; ever since she was his Professor at Cambridge University and he was an up-and-coming sophomore in her Religious Studies class. Over the years they had kept in touch and she had even officiated at his wedding. After his graduation from seminary they parted ways. Pat moved here to Salem and became a TV evangelist. She joined the MA'AM revolution—an acronym she hated for its archaic connotations, but it got the point across—and Danforth started his own church in Boston. There, he publicly denounced MA'AM and everything it stood for. He had even mentioned Pat, by name, in rather unkindly connotations, she recalled.

Six years later, he had surprised her with a phone call. Seems he had discovered an abandoned newborn who needed a good home and wanted to know if she was still interested in adoption. She had jumped at the chance. She was no fool; she knew a favor like that always came with a price, but she was willing to risk it.

Still, when he came to her eight years later, ranting about Waverly's mind-control device, she thought he had gone mad. Another religious fanatic brainwashing his congregation had little appeal to her.

"By sending these subliminal messages over your weekly program, we can convert thousands to Christianity in one swell foop!" he had explained.

Bemused, she smiled at his misstated cliché but let him keep going. Christianity was not the only religion she promoted on her weekly program. As a former Unitarian Universalist Minister, she was just as likely to highlight Humanism (her own belief), or Buddhism. On the show, her guests discussed everything from spiritual awareness and women's health, to political reform. By connecting himself to her show, she suspected he thought he could persuade her viewers to go back to being housewives. His own livelihood as Pastor at First Calvary Baptist Church in Boston, no doubt, depended on it.

"Don't you see?" he continued, with his feet casually propped on her desk. "These Adrays have the potential to change the world! The public is too naïve to know what's good for them; they need our help resisting evil."

She was already concocting an excuse to let him down easy when he finally said something that interested her.

"It will pay for itself in no time, you know."

Now he had her attention. With more funding, she could hire additional hospital chaplains and increase her show's seminary scholarship program. Back then, even twenty-six years after the Plague, the ministry profession had not fully recovered. The terrorists had targeted outspoken preachers along with the politicians, so it had taken a toll on seminary enrollment. She was adamant about training and funding for all religions.

"I'd use it on my own congregation," he was saying, "but your show has a greater reach, obviously. Can't you picture it? Within six months, we could be broadcasting nationwide in time for Christmas. What do you think?"

Pat studied his face.

He looks so smug, she thought. *Can I really work with this man?*

She could see that it bugged him that she didn't respond right away.

"We could start out simple, at first," he added. "You know, 'Thou shalt not kill,' and 'Love thy neighbor.' That kind of thing."

"As long as they don't take us too literally," she said. "After all, we don't want another Woodstock on our hands."

Seeing Danforth's irritation reminded her how much fun it had always been to mess with him. And how easy. Maybe it would be worth trying this thing out just to needle him some more.

He uncrossed his ankles and brought his feet down to the floor.

"No, of course not," he said, sitting up. "How about something like, 'Treat everyone kindly.'"

"Unless they're being robbed. My viewers can't be sitting ducks in a crisis, you know. And what if some maniac molested a child? Would you want him treated kindly, too? If these rays are as powerful as you claim, we need to be careful, here, Marshall."

As expected, Danforth puckered his lips. She knew he hated it when she called him by his first name.

"Well, these are only suggestions off the top of my head," he said, evenly. "It goes without saying we would study all scenarios before implementing one. I am merely pointing out the possi-"

"Okay, okay," she cut him off. "You sold me. I owe you for Katherine anyway, so let's talk logistics." She sat forward and rested her elbows on the desk. "You say you want to save the world, right? Well, first things first."

She held up her left hand and ticked off her talking points.

"First, we need to lay out our goals and objectives, and our strategy for success. Second, we need to pre-empt any regulatory agency, or government, approvals. That will be your job. Third, we must find a way to mitigate potential information leaks. (You can't imagine the backlash if the public thinks we are trying to brainwash them!)"

She said this last almost to herself, and then shrugged.

"Fourth, we have to verify that these Adrays actually work, and, if so, their broadcasting range."

Next, she held up her thumb.

"Last but not least: cost. I'm guessing your Cis-Star friend didn't offer to finance this little adventure, am I right? Or did you think I would fund it all?"

He looked suddenly uncomfortable, so she gave him a meaningful frown and went on before he could interject.

"Now, I know that is a lot to think about, Marshall, but before we get off the subject, let me suggest our first course of action there, too. You said Cis-Star has a portable unit, right?"

He nodded.

"Then our first priority should be to influence some seed money from my network sponsors. If that fails, you will have wasted as little of my time and money as possible, and we can forget the whole affair. Deal?"

Danforth opened his mouth, but Pat continued.

"First thing tomorrow, contact your friend and set up a meeting so she and I can go over the specifics. While we are doing that, you can outline a list of other potential sponsors. Better yet, give me Ms. Nelson's number. Nothing personal, but my schedule is so full you couldn't possibly plan a time convenient for the both of us."

With that statement, she had flicked her wrist to activate her VEE (it was only a Version three back then) and immediately established herself in control.

Danforth's ire was immediate.

"Nothing personal," he would find a way to fit into random conversations with her, after that. Luckily, once Waverly stepped in as their go-between, she rarely saw the man anymore except for his ads on TV.

An unexpected breeze licked Pat's neck, and she shivered. Her thoughts turned back to her adoring fans. She stretched out her fingertips and watched them reaching back. Some screamed. Some smiled. Others wept openly in emotional release, as though in the presence of a rock star. She swayed her arm back and forth, and they mirrored her, from one side of the stadium to the other. The result was an enormous human wave.

So why aren't I euphoric? she wondered.

As if in answer, she searched the stage wings again.

Where could she be? She's missing it! We should be sharing this victory together; I shouldn't be up here alone!

Look at this crowd! she wanted to say. *This is all for you; for your future! Surely this makes up for the missed birthdays, the recitals, and plays. Now, Kat would finally understand the reason for her sacrifice, right?* A moment's regret crossed Pat's face. *It HAD been worth it, right?*

Without her daughter here to witness the enormity of all she had accomplished and to experience the crowd's emotional swell, she would never understand how much the public believed in her, needed her, and loved her.

More than my own daughter?

She wondered if her daughter knew how much she loved her, and how difficult it had been to be away from her on the campaign trail, or if she had even appreciated the effort it took this morning to attend the graduation ceremony in person.

Probably not. Most likely, she's upset that I slipped out early and delivered my speech via Holo. Maybe when she grows up, she'll realize everything I did for the Lytoky was ultimately for her.

So many precious memories missed while she was stuck alone in hotel rooms. Several times she had decided to give it up. She had gone to Katherine's school, determined to bring her home, but something always got in the way. A crisis here, an urgent matter there. Nothing memorable, it turned out—at least not now—but somehow it had always kept her away.

No wonder Katherine resents me... and the Lytoky, she sighed, and gazed back at her fans. Controlling the public was nothing compared to controlling her own teenage daughter. *Perhaps I should ask Waverly to develop a special Unirays program just for teens,* she mused. *Maybe then, Katherine would understand.*

***

Waverly stood backstage and watched the jubilation. Kat was late, she noted, but that wasn't a concern. *I would be, too, if I were an angry teen,* she thought. Teens and parents had a hard time getting along anyway, even under normal circumstances. And, of course, the Bufords were hardly normal; Waverly had seen to that.

Kat had been nearly eight years old when Waverly first went to Danforth with her "new" invention. He had no way of knowing she had already been using it on him for over four years by then. Waverly had wasted no time influencing her way into the Buford household.

The previous year, Waverly had used the Unirays to encourage Pat, from afar, to send the girl off to boarding school. By the time Waverly arrived, Kat was supposed to feel so abandoned by her adoptive mother that she and Waverly would immediately bond.

That part, however, had not gone according to plan. Waverly made sure Pat was always busy (promoting each new thelytoky community and, more recently, campaigning for President), but Kat never seemed lonely. In fact, on the weekends when "Aunt Waverly" stayed over, the girl usually preferred to be alone in her room, apparently talking on her VEE to her friends.

Waverly, therefore, had been forced to be creative. Once, while she sat on a kitchen barstool, silently watching Kat cook pancakes, she had tested an idea.

"Too bad Pat doesn't have time for you," she had said, intentionally not calling Buford her Mother. "But her work is very important, you know."

The girl had looked back at her sharply. "You're busy, too. You run a multi-million-dollar company, but you still make time for me."

Bingo!

"Well, that's true, Kat, but don't let it bother you. Millions love her, you know. I guess she can only spread herself so far."

From Kat's expression, Waverly knew her message had hit home. *"Your adoptive mother has only so much love to give, and you are not her priority."*

Over the years, she had watched the resentment grow. Even without directly using the Unirays on Kat, Waverly continuously reinforced two central themes: One, Buford does not have time for you (and therefore must not love you), and Two, you can always count on your good-ol' Aunt Waverly for support. Not that she wanted Kat to feel unloved, of course. Not really. But she had to admit it was intoxicating to watch the two pulling farther apart.

Don't expect me to feel sorry for you, Pat, she thought now, watching her President in the spotlights. *Not as long as my daughter keeps calling you Mom!*

Anyway, now that the election was over, and Paul Brown had taught Gloria a lesson, her plot to overthrow New Canna was going to ramp up quickly. After that, it would finally be time to tell Kat the truth.

***

Danforth stared at his wall teleVISOR in slack-jawed disbelief.

Surely the numbers are wrong! he thought.

His eyes began to water from staring at the screen so long. Through the blur, he imagined the digits beneath his name increasing, gaining speed until they spun out of control and outnumbered Senator Buford's tally by a landslide. But that was not to be. The election was over, and Buford had already claimed victory.

He could just imagine the scene. They were probably all popping champagne, smoking dope, and falling into a big lesbian orgy right there in East St. Louis plaza!

Where is Waverly? he thought, suddenly. *Why isn't she answering my calls? She was supposed to be here with me after the election. Something must have gone wrong. She always knows what to say to make me feel better.*

At least she had advised him to leave Marisa home, and to wait for the results alone at the Info-Swirl. It would have been even more embarrassing if he had seen the results in front of a crowd. Waverly had assured him that once he won, she would escort him to his "surprise party" celebration. He wondered now where that surprise had been scheduled, and if Marisa were there. In the back of his mind, though, he wondered if his wife even cared.

As he slumped back, a new worry crossed his slick brow. Now that the election was over, what if Waverly abandoned him? It would be just like Buford to try to win Waverly over, too!

How could things get any worse? he moaned and pulled out a chocolate bar.

The Waves of Dissonance

TWELVE

The Transport shuttle was late leaving Immigrations, but Lieutenant Alex Winters wasn't concerned. With her detainees buckled in, and the high-speed train en route to O'Hare, she knew they could make up the lost time. From her back-row seat, she kept an occasional eye on the passengers as she brought up each one's file. She was almost done. The man in this next file, she noted, had been the last one to lash out when he descended into the tunnel earlier. Happened all the time. This one, however, had diplomatic immunity.

Must be meeting someone special, she thought and flipped through his stats.

ETHNICITY: Caucasian.
HAIR COLOR: Blond.
HEIGHT: Six Foot Two.
BUILD: Muscular.
AGE: 45.

What? No, that can't be right. She frowned and glanced two rows up, but his back was to her. *Hmm.* She shrugged and punched in the code for APPROVED. What did she care? It would take too much effort to interview him and enter a correction, but she didn't feel like spending a lot of time on this today, especially since she still had two more files to go and the shuttle would arrive at the airport shortly. Once there, she would have to herd her brood onto a jet for their final leg to the Oasis.

Ordinarily, she would have checked the passengers out before leaving Immigrations, but she had been running late on a personal errand. She patted the flask in her front jacket pocket, out of habit, and smiled. It had all worked out, though. Since there were so many men seeking passage tonight, the Disposition Officer, Private Saragusa, had helped her out.

Usually, even on a busy night, she only had to process and transfer a handful of Escorts. When she had returned to the station before final departure, however, the Holding Room had been full. Since the train car held only eight, those who didn't make this afternoon's shuttle would be held over until tomorrow.

"Must be the elections," Saragusa had shrugged back at the station. "Must be a bunch of them wanting to jump ship."

Alex tapped her thumbs on her tablet and tried to focus on the next file. This was only the second night of her four-day tour, and she was already exhausted. She couldn't wait to hit the rack and have a drink, but not in that order.

The next name she pulled up was a Regular. Since he had been here before, less than a year ago per his file, she decided to approve him on the spot without reading further.

To hell with procedure.

Only one more file to go.

This last man was seeking formal asylum. That was unusual. It either meant the Oasis was to be his permanent home or only a temporary stop on his way to the Gamma states.

Curious, she read his file. He had been in several fights as a child and was expelled from four different high schools but there was no indication why he would permanently defect from New Canaan. Teachers listed him as quiet and well behaved, and he even got fairly high grades in school… for a boy.

Intrigued, now, she pulled up his high school transcripts and there it was. Next to his sophomore Physical Ed grade, a D, his gym coach had entered only one word: Faggot.

Now she understood.

Men in New Canaan were great believers in the Bible, she knew. They quoted scripture as if they had written it themselves. Seemed to her, though, they always overlooked the most important passage: the one that started "Love thy neighbor."

Poor recruit, she frowned. *It's not his fault he's different.*

She could imagine the insults, the bullies, and the well-meaning lectures meant to change his "evil" ways. On impulse, she shrugged and approved him, too.

What the hell.

So much for background checks tonight. Tomorrow she would deal with the ones left behind back at Immigrations, but now she could sit back and concentrate on more important matters… like verifying her bootleg tequila shipment had arrived at the Oasis on time. With any luck, it would be waiting for her in her cabin when she got home tonight.

THIRTEEN

At St. Elizabeth's Teaching Hospital in East St. Louis, Illinois, Dr. Taylor Bott glanced up from surgery. Several female visitors, wearing blue surgical masks stamped with the word VISITOR in large white letters where their teeth should be, had just entered the O.R.'s Observation deck. The slim doctor frowned. To her, their masks made them look like Halloween disguises.

Damn visitors! she thought. *Why do they have to be in my O.R.?*

"It's bad enough you have us on such a strict schedule," she had argued against their presence just last week in their monthly staff meeting. "But now you're allowing Trick-or-Tweeters to watch over our every move? They're not even related to the patient, for MA'AM's sake! We keep family members in the Waiting Room, but not complete strangers? Unbelievable! They hover overhead and distract the surgeons, and then post everything they see on social media. It puts our patients at increased risk for no reason. Let them watch from the back wall or something, if you have to, but for goodness sake, don't parade them right in front of the window with a tour guide who talks so loudly I can hear every word."

Lou Franklin, the persimmon-faced hospital administrator, had listened without emotion, then had taken off her wire-rimmed glasses and pinched the bridge of her nose.

"Dr. Bott," she said in a bored, I'd-help-you-if-I-could tone that wasn't convincing, "You are exaggerating, as usual. You act as if the visitors are children and that we haven't taken the necessary precautions. These are paying customers who have been screened for sickness and have been provided masks and gloves. You must remember what we're up against

97

here. With the upcoming election, everything must be transparent. New Canaan is scrutinizing our every move, so we must show how much more efficiently we can run a hospital. If allowing open, guided tours is the only way to assure the public we are not cutting corners, then so be it. We must win this election and advance the Lytoky's cause. We all have to do our part."

Her decision had been final. So, every fifteen minutes a new tour shuffled through. Taylor scowled at this newest batch. They squirmed like children in church.

"Now, as you can see," called their tour guide after checking her V-pad program, "this patient came to us with a history of severe uterine cramping, chronic back pain, and apparent infertility. In the past, male doctors would have dismissed her symptoms as PMS, stress, or some OTHER mental problem."

She paused, letting her joke sink in. The visitors nodded and chuckled on cue.

"We've all heard the stories," she continued. "They wouldn't have taken her seriously. They would have told her to go home and relax, but all-the-while a serious, debilitating disease would have silently wiped out her reproductive organs."

The guide pointed to the large-screen monitor above the patient's head.

"By using laparoscopy, however, our doctors have diagnosed her problem as stage-two endometriosis and has used hypercryogenic gene-splicing therapy to alter the disease's progression. After this, a follow-up round of prescription-therapy will ensure the woman's full remission forever. We've used this technique for decades on older, more obvious endometriosis, but now we can actually reverse the genetic damage before it makes her infertile. Like cancer, this disease can now be stopped before it has a chance to spread."

The visitors clapped.

The tour guide turned and seemed to notice, at last, that nothing was happening onscreen. She looked down and made eye contact with Taylor. For the first time, she seemed to notice the doctor's displeasure and that she had purposefully halted the procedure.

"Well, perhaps we'll move on to the next O.R.," the tour guide said, as she turned back to her group. "Over there, a new technique for treating

Crohn's disease is already underway, and THAT surgeon is really amazing."

She clucked her tongue and gave Taylor an ugly glance over her shoulder as she ushered the visitors out. As soon as they were gone, Taylor went back to work. She pushed the needle through her patient's iodine-stained skin to close up the navel.

"I still say you need a vacation," her anesthesiologist resumed their previous conversation as though nothing had happened. "That place I mentioned treats you like a Goddess. They even have MEN there. I know, I know; it sounds racy, but they wait on you hand and foot…" She lowered her voice and moved in closer to Taylor's shoulder. "…and anywhere else you might desire, if you know what I mean."

Taylor frowned at her friend.

"Annie, what would I want with a man?" she said.

"Are you kidding me?" Annie laughed. "Sweetie, I know it's been a few years, but surely you haven't forgotten. I certainly wouldn't mind having a man around now and then to help me scratch a certain itch." She winked, above her mask.

"It's been almost fourteen years," Taylor said, "and No, I haven't forgotten. I remember how big and ugly they are. How could I forget?"

"Oh, you're just remembering what they taught you in school. When was the last time you actually saw one in real life?"

"I don't want to talk about it."

"Your Dad, huh?"

Taylor ignored her, and Annie nodded. "Yeah, I guess a lot of you youngsters still feel abandoned by your fathers."

"I'm not a kid, Annie. I'm thirty-five, for MA'AM's sake!"

"You know what I mean. All you girls born after the Plague seem like youngsters to me. Hey, I know what you need! A bunch of us are going to Cockers tonight after shift. Why don't you come with us?"

Taylor almost missed a stitch.

"Annie!" The thought of going to one of those seedy hetero clubs made Taylor visibly shiver. "What could you possibly want in there?"

Seeing Annie's mischievous grin, Taylor couldn't help but smile.

"But what if you get caught?"

"It's not illegal, my dear, just unpopular. Lighten up! Stop wearing your gonads on the outside and come have some fun with us. Seriously! It will do you some good to get out."

Taylor wrinkled her nose. "No thanks."

"Ha! You look like a beefcake who just got kneed in the groin! Come on; lots of people do it. You'd be surprised at who you see in there."

"Bet you'll never see Pat Buford; she wouldn't be caught dead in a place like that."

"You're right, of course," Annie agreed. "She wouldn't be caught!" Taylor gave her a sideways look, and Annie chuckled.

"Besides," Annie continued, "I hear she has her own private island: a place off-limits to ordinary folks. Somewhere she can mingle openly with men, like in the olden days." Taylor noted a hint of nostalgia coming from her older friend. Then the woman's tone abruptly changed as she moved to another topic. "Speaking of mingling, have you seen the new radiologist downstairs? She's pretty cute and I hear she's available." Her voice practically sang the last word.

"I've told you before, Annie, I'm not ready to date."

"I know, I know. But Rebecca would have wanted you to." The anesthesiologist noticed Taylor's look. "Oh gosh! I'm sorry! I didn't mean… It's just that it's been awhile, and I thought…" For once, the woman fell silent. For the remaining procedure, a total of two minutes, Annie seemed uncharacteristically at a loss for words. She opened her mouth a couple times, but no words came out.

The instant Taylor cut the thread, marking the procedure officially complete, Annie bundled up her equipment and made for the door. Taylor could hear her cursing to herself all the way down the hall. "So stupid! When will I ever learn?"

A technician came and wheeled the patient out to Recovery, but Taylor stayed behind. Three new women wearing green-covered slippers pushed in and got to work. They didn't waste time being cordial. The surgery had taken longer than expected so they immediately plugged in their mops and began guiding the electronic devices across the floor with their GPS joysticks.

Splash-swish.

The Waves of Dissonance

As it did with everything here, the hospital administration closely scrutinized janitorial movements. Taylor speculated Dr. Franklin knew exactly how long it took to clean this room, as did the cleaning staff.

Splash-swish.

As if on cue, motorized scrubbers advanced on Taylor. She slipped off her surgical cap with deliberate slowness, flexed her tired shoulders, and sighed. Her morning schedule had been long, and she didn't feel like going over the operation's play-by-play with her patient's waiting spouse. She wanted to be alone.

This would be a good job if it weren't for the people, she thought, and smiled sadly. That had been a running joke Rebecca used to say.

Rebecca and Taylor had been married only five years when they decided to have a child. Despite what the tour guide had said about modern technology, they had not advanced as far as the visitors were led to believe. Even with weekly pre-natal screenings and checkups, Rebecca had suffered an aneurysm during the first hour of premature labor and had died within minutes. Her doctor wasted precious moments setting up for a caesarian while their baby slowly suffocated.

Taylor had been in surgery at the time, three floors away, but no one had bothered to tell her Rebecca was even in labor, much less in trouble. She had found out later, after she had delivered her own good news to her patient's family.

Splash-swish.

Taylor opened her eyes and turned toward the door. The cleaning crew drones were already halfway across the room and she still had a job to do. With these dark memories mirrored on her face, she let the door close behind her and made for the Waiting Room. Her patient's spouse, sitting alone in the back corner, looked up expectantly when she entered, and searched the doctor's face. Seeing only a furrowed brow, the woman mistook it as bad news. It took several minutes, and Taylor's repeated assurances that her spouse was perfectly fine, to calm the woman down.

In the excitement, Taylor noticed a group of masked visitors peering through the Waiting Room door, watching the show, and filming her with their VEEs.

Looks like they got their treat, after all, she thought.

***

"Dr. Bott, report to ER, STAT!"

At the sound of her name, Taylor turned and sped toward the Emergency Room wing, grateful to get away. The loudspeaker called again as she rounded a corner and almost toppled Lou Franklin, the hospital administrator.

"That's why we have mirrors, Bott!" the older woman called. "Use them! Oh, and don't be late for Thursday's ad hoc staff meeting We're going to discuss the election aftermath."

Yeah, yeah. Can't wait.

She found Franklin's lectures on hospital politics almost as dull as the administrator, herself. She passed through the ER's double swinging doors and saw a young intern tapping furiously on a V-pad.

"Got one of your patients here, Doc," the intern said. "Or, at least I think I do. The triage nurse said you're her GYN, according to her iris scan, but I can't get this damn thing to work."

Taylor wondered who had left the ER in the hands of someone so inexperienced, then remembered it was probably another one of Franklin's money-saving policies. She grabbed the V-Pad away from the intern and pulled up the "Admissions" tab. She was still skimming Nurse Kim's notes as she pushed aside the examining room's plastic curtain. Once inside, she froze.

There, on the cold metal table, sat a bloody woman rocking back and forth wearing a faded hospital gown. Her bare, scratched legs dangled over the edge, exposing bruised inner thighs, already turning purple. Her swollen face was unrecognizable. It looked like she had a broken nose and, possibly, a shattered cheekbone, too.

"What happened here?"

"Possible rape victim," said the intern, who had followed her in. "She hasn't spoken since she got here. I processed her, myself."

Taylor didn't know where to begin. Most emergencies these days were either premature deliveries or the result of disease or an accident, not brutality.

"Any internal bleeding? Broken bones? Concussion?"

The intern glanced at her VEE.

"Undetermined. She's been uncooperative and combative. But I did manage to get a vaginal probe, a sperm sample, and some excellent Digital photos."

Taylor whirled on the intern, ready to chastise her for such lack of compassion, but the expressionless face looking back made her stop. It was useless. The intern was merely following procedures. Franklin would clearly require physical evidence in a case such as this. Taylor turned back to the exam table and vowed to condemn such abhorrent treatment like this at the next staff meeting.

"What's your name, Dear?" she said. She stepped forward and placed a hand on the victim's shoulder. Terror immediately filled the victim's eyes and she flinched and flailed her arms. Still caught between illusion and reality, the battered woman scrambled to the table's far edge and crouched, with both elbows up in a posture of self-defense. Clumps of black, tangled hair, still clotted with blood, lay twisted across her cheeks, making her look crazed, and feral. After several more minutes of gentle coaxing, the woman sat, again, and hugged her knees to her chest. Her split lips quivered, and her eyes filled with tears when Taylor asked her name again.

"Gloria," she answered softly. "My name is Gloria Chiang."

FOURTEEN

Lieutenant Alex Winters scowled at the road in front of her. The two staff members in her Jeep's back seat were prattling way too loudly, and they would not shut up.

It's bad enough Captain Chad grabbed me the minute I touched down and assigned me a Special visitor drop-off tonight, she thought. *But now I'm stuck with Thing One and Thing Two for the drive back? This sucks!*

She had given these two chatterboxes their nicknames (behind their backs, of course), after last year's *Cat in the Hat* remake came out. The reference fit perfectly. As Hospitality Staff (a PC term for housekeepers) their job was to make guest accommodations presentable before each new arrival, but like the movie characters, these two were virtually inseparable. They finished each other's sentences and talked non-stop. Alex swore that between the two, they had never been silent five minutes in a row.

"I imagined her taller," said Thing One to Thing Two.

"I know, right? TV can be so misleading."

"Yeah, maybe it's because her mom is so short, it makes her look tall."

"Good point!"

Alex glanced in her rear-view mirror and caught Thing One smiling back. Apparently, they knew something she didn't.

"Okay, I give. Who are you two talking about?"

The women giggled at her ignorance and leaned forward together.

"That girl you dropped off back there before you picked us up?" started One. "That was Pat Buford's daughter, Kat!"

"She was traveling incognito!" finished Two. "You mean you didn't recognize her under the blonde wig?"

"I would have known her anywhere," nodded One. The pair sat back and continued their bullet-fast dissection of Kat's disguise.

So that's why she looked so familiar! thought Alex.

Now it all made sense. Usually, when Alex made her rounds from Immigrations, she was relieved of duty as soon as the plane touched down and she wasn't expected back on duty until the next morning's reverse Transport. She was never asked to make guest deliveries, too! Captain Chad was a stickler for seniority, though, so in her captain's eyes this assignment tonight was probably a special honor for Alex, since the client was such a celebrity.

To Alex, however, it was just another distraction. The girl's visit would undoubtedly require extra effort—especially if she were the "creative" type who wanted special attention. Last time Sotomayor's granddaughter came here, for instance, Alex was kept busy all week on the other side of the island securing Fantasy Medieval Palace with an ever-increasing list of demands, such as scarves, whips, and champagne. Who knew what President Buford's daughter would be demanding by week's end?

"Just my luck," she muttered sarcastically, under her breath. "Another Deviant."

"Deviant?" said Thing Two, sitting forward and pressing her cheek against the headrest. "That's rich, coming from you, Lieutenant. I hear you have a soft spot for Deviants."

Thing One giggled and followed the other in leaning forward. Now both faces were squeezed between the headrests.

"Yeah, didn't you get caught with an Escort once, a few years back?" she asked.

"'Oh, but that was different!'" Thing Two lilted at the other, pretending to be Alex. "'He didn't need to be brainwashed in order to go to bed with me!'" They both laughed.

"What was his name again?"

"Robert, wasn't it?"

Alex winced and tried to ignore them. She turned her attention back to the road. The Hospitality twins snickered and sat back, where they dropped into a new, rapid-fire argument over which of them was more likely to sleep with an Escort.

Alex tapped her thumbs on the steering wheel. She had met Robert nearly two years ago. *And, yes, he did seem different, dammit! He didn't act hypnotized, or stoned, like the other escorts did; and he didn't repeat the same stupid lines the Infirmary program escorts to say. His eyes were clear, and he actually looked at me when he talked. He even spoke intelligently.*

The Infirmary (affectionately called the Roach Motel by the staff) was "where cockroaches check in, and Mimbos check out!" Alex had laughed the first time she had heard the joke, but not anymore: she had seen too many men altered by that place.

Per the website, the Oasis was a top-secret retreat where government officials went to "get away from it all."

"SORT OF A MODERN-DAY CAMP DAVID" went the ads. "BUT WITH A TWIST!"

It didn't take a genius to figure out the "Twist," Alex thought. She wished they would just admit what it really was: a place for rich women to get laid.

Or worse.

Each part of the island had its own unique theme. Here, for instance, in the Rustic Fantasy section, a guest could take long walks along dense forest paths or on her own secluded beach. The other quadrants were far less pastoral, but all promised to fulfill their guests' every desire. Female patrons paid top dollar for the experience. Males, however, paid a much higher price.

Alex wondered, not for the first time, if she were the only one bothered by what went on here. She wiped at her lips. Her mouth felt chalky and dry: too dry.

When she had first met Robert, she had been assigned to escort him back from his nightly assignment at Fantasy Log Cabin #3—the cabin where she had just dropped off Kat. Somehow, in the Jeep outside his barracks, they had talked for hours. Every night after that, she had taken the long way back. By the end of the second week they had been lovers.

What was I thinking? she scowled now.

The first time Robert had told her he loved her, Alex had laughed in his face. The Motel used O-rays to instruct the Escorts to say that kind of thing, she knew. But over time, she had started to believe him. After all, he told her things she had never heard before. Like, about the Rebellion: a group of men and women in the Gamma states fighting for desegregation. The idea had been fascinating to her, and she had yearned to know more.

On his last night, he had asked her to join him… as his wife. Together, they would find a way to get him off the island and back with the Rebellion. Once there, he would send instructions for her to follow. She still remembered the feeling of excitement the next evening, as she had rushed to the cabin with her idea about how to dismantle the island's security system only to find the cabin empty. So was his bunk back at the barracks. No one, it seemed, had even heard of him. Not even Captain Chad. It appeared there was no record of him having even been admitted to the Oasis. He had disappeared after serving only six weeks of his required six-month commitment.

Fantasy Log Cabin #3 was the last place she had seen her lover, and where they had conceived their child. If little Bobby had been a girl, Alex probably would have been allowed to keep her. But the Uni-Lifers had mobilized quickly after her first sonogram, and had demanded she give her son away. She only hoped they had found him a good home.

Alex studied the two Things in the rear-view mirror. They were still giggling and talking excitedly about Kat, but she knew they would later be talking about her again. She had a sudden urge to slam the Jeep into a tree.

That would wipe the smile off their smug little faces, she thought.

She dropped her gaze back to the road and sighed. Her head was starting to throb, and she desperately needed a drink. With a little luck, the shipment she ordered earlier this afternoon would be waiting for her back in her cabin… a shipment with a little yellow worm in the bottom.

FIFTEEN

The doorknob turned easily. Like a warm knife slicing through butter, the cylinder rolled over and the heavy door swung open. Light from inside spilled through the opening like a serpent's flickering tongue. Kat pushed the door open and stepped cautiously inside.

Jordan? she asked in her head, and then, "Jordan?" out loud.

No answer.

He must still be on his way. The lieutenant who had dropped her off said some new recruits had just arrived. *I bet he's in that batch!*

She entered the log cabin and let her eyes adjust. There wasn't much to see. In the main room, a stone fireplace filled the far corner. The lit fire cut deep shadows in and out between the horizontal, chinked walls. Inside the bedroom was an enormous four-poster bed—its red-checked flannel sheets already turned down. The only other item of interest (besides a tweed sofa and a black, retro-phone on the coffee table), lay at her feet, hugging the heartwood-pine floor. She almost laughed out loud when she saw it.

The giant, bearskin rug looked to be over twenty feet long, finger-to-toe—or, more correctly, paw-to-paw. It was solid black, except for the brown muzzle facing the fire and a speck of tawny beige in its ears.

Off came her sneakers. She sank her travel-weary feet into the coarse-but-luxurious fibers and wiggled her toes in delight, making the fur part between each digit. Her red-lacquered toenails caught the firelight and looked like shiny drops of blood.

She held out her hands to the fire. Sure enough, it was genuine wood.

How decadent! The only thing missing is a moose head and a double-barrel shotgun over the mantel, she giggled. Ordinarily, that kind of thought would have come from Jordan.

Where is he?

Impatiently, she checked the time on her VEE again. Nearly ten hours had passed since Jordan had disappeared below ground. For the first time in memory, she was completely alone. The weight of it made her feel small, and unexpectedly exposed. Without Jordan, everything seemed too loud, too bright, and too conspicuously harsh. She searched her mind constantly, like worrying over a missing tooth. As though on cue, she heard a car door slam outside.

Jordan?

Frozen in place, with her toes still curled deep in the rug, she listened. First, came multiple footsteps on the landing. Then came a voice, indistinct. Her heart raced, but still she could not move. A faint tinkling sound came next that sounded like metal dropping away and then hard footsteps retreated. Finally, the sound of tires on gravel.

She bit her bottom lip and waited. Her face flushed with heat as the doorknob slowly turned.

***

Jordan paused, with his hand on the knob, and glanced behind him as his transport vehicle pulled away. Above him hung a moonless sky. Earlier, two soldiers had roused him from the back seat of a hybrid Jeep and had marched him across what appeared to be a military compound.

"Someone asked to see you," one had explained.

Kat?

It had to be! After all this time, he would finally be able to see her, touch her, and hold her. He wondered if she was as beautiful as he had imagined; if her cheeks were as smooth, her eyes as clear, and her lips as soft.

The soldiers escorted him to the door, one on each arm. Their slow, restrained pace was maddening. Finally, they uncuffed his hands, stood back, and let him walk up the outside steps alone. Standing at the threshold, he pushed the door open slowly.

SIXTEEN

Marisa Danforth pulled out an oversized, downy-fresh shirt from the wicker basket at her feet and held it up to the light. Sure enough, another button was missing. Third from the bottom, as usual. *Right where his fat belly keeps popping it off!* she thought. She shook her head and adjusted her reading glasses, wondering when she had gotten old enough to need them, and reached for her jar of buttons.

"This is the last one!" she said aloud in mock reproach. "If he loses another, he'll have to sew it on himself!"

Right! she chastised herself. *And after that you'll tell him to stop sleeping around or you'll leave him.* Marisa grinned and grimaced simultaneously. She knew she would never say those words to her husband. Not now.

As though in response to her rebellious thoughts, she unfolded a pink smudge on the shirt's inside collar—one that could only be lipstick. It was a new color this time; he hadn't even bothered to hide it. She bit at her own nude lips and absently tucked a stray strand of dark hair into her loose bun. Then she draped the ample cloth across her lap and stabbed the needle into the fabric before yanking it out the other side.

Fool, she scolded herself. *You should have left him when you had the chance.*

Years ago, when she found the first lipstick smear on her husband's shirt collar, she had gotten overly excited. Back then, divorce was still a possibility. Surely, such evidence of infidelity would be her ticket out, she had thought at the time. Jordan was only seven years old and too young to understand, but not too young for her husband to use against her.

As their argument had climaxed that day, and Marisa had stomped toward the door, pulling Jordan's small hand in hers, her husband had barred the way.

"Wait!" he said. "I'll move out. Don't tear him away from his friends mid-year, for Christ's sake. Wait until school lets out. One more month; what harm could that do? I'll leave tonight."

Her husband's argument had seemed logical at the time, but Gus, their groundskeeper, had been unconvinced. The next day, he had given his unsolicited advice while helping her plant tulips along the circular drive between the main house and garage.

"Don't believe him, Missus. He's up to no good. You should file at the courthouse today!"

Sure enough, one week after she had threatened to leave, New Canaan enacted the new Family Protection Act. Thinly disguised as a bill to keep families together, the new FPA required a two-year Partnership before filing for divorce. The new act replaced the one-year separation previously required.

"Once the two parties split up, the marriage is three times more likely to end in divorce," the lawmakers issued in a statement, as justification. "Our goal is to ensure families stay together and that every opportunity has been exhausted before they make rash decisions that they may later regret. We need to look out for our citizens when they are in too much emotional turmoil to look out for themselves."

New Canaan claimed the Act affected both males and females equally, but the Lytoky broadcasts said otherwise. "Once again, New Canaan is forcing morality on its female constituents," they reported. "What a charade!"

Under the new Act, once either party filed for divorce, the couple was required to cohabitate for two years, minimum (or half the marriage length, whichever was greater) and attend weekly Partnering sessions. To discourage extra-marital affairs, neither spouse could leave the residence (except to-and-from work) unaccompanied by the other. It was similar to the conditional permits issued to those claiming work-hardship over a revoked driver's license. Only, in this case, any spouse who refused to follow the rules forfeited all parental rights and any potential financial entitlements.

Marisa did not know how he had done it, but she knew her husband was behind the Act. Even though he claimed it had been in the works for years, she knew better.

Either way, from that point forward, she was stuck. Like most New Canaan homemakers who did not work outside the house, she never filed for divorce; it was too risky. If she had, she would have been a virtual prisoner in her own home and would have lost custody of Jordan the first time she left the estate alone, even to run a household errand. Her husband, on the other hand, could come and go as he pleased. His work as State Senator was highly subjective. She knew he would be free to leave, at will, even for weeks at a time.

Due to the Act, Marisa suddenly went from having a solid place in society to being precariously perched at the edge. Not only did she have to put up with her husband's open philandering, she had to allow him— *no, encourage him!*—to sleep with her, as well. After all, heaven forbid he should tire of her and file for divorce, himself.

For that reason, every time he came home, Marisa brushed out her long brown hair, put on make-up, and forced herself into one of the many negligees he had bought for her. It turned her stomach to watch him sucking his wet lips, but on the days he was able to perform, she suffered his weight, and his taste, in silence. After all, "Obedience Training" resulted in fewer scars for all the boys when he was satisfied with her.

Marisa looked up from her mending and gazed thoughtfully out the Sewing Room window. She wasn't the only one who had sacrificed, she knew. In the early days, she had heard of men in Lytoky towns who had given up more than their dignity to stay with their daughters. Rumor had it, some had undergone voluntary castration.

At the hair salon (one of the few places Marshall encouraged her to go whenever her roots began to show) the others gossiped angrily about the Lytoky injustices. It amazed Marisa how much time they expended being indignant about "those feminists" yet they neglected what was happening right here… to her and to countless others like her. It seemed to her that parents on both sides of the border suffered for their children.

Though Marisa technically had six sons by marriage, Jordan was the only one she could call her own. Marshall had acquired the rest without her, adopting them over the years, seemingly at random. The youngest was only five. Marisa presumed they were all his bastards, but it would have done no good to confront him. He would only have lied.

So far, Marshall had only brought home boys. She often wondered if he had ever sired a girl. New Canaan needed daughters to replenish the reproductive gene pool. Women were scarce here because of the Plague, according to the news. But Marisa suspected it was because so many women had fled to the Lytoky during the MA'AM Revolution. She wished she'd been one of them.

Theoretically, now that Jordan was eighteen, she could finally let go and risk filing for divorce, but how could she abandon the others just because they weren't her biological sons? Didn't they need her protection, too?

What would happen to them if I left? she often wondered. Wasn't her sacrifice small… considering the reward? Besides, with no other relatives and no marketable job skills, she had nowhere else to go. At least not in New Canaan.

Still looking out the window, she remembered a conversation she had overheard a week ago. She had thought Jordan was on his VEE in his father's study.

"Yes," she had heard him say. "I'll leave school early, pick up Ruthie, and then drive to the border. Should reach Immigrations by noon. Cabin 1506. Got it! Now you!"

She heard him pause, as though listening, and then he had continued. "Good; that's it! No, not our real names. What about the ones I found in that "Approved for Release" file? I like the sound of the first one… Paul Brown."

"Jordan?"

Marisa had walked in on him then, but he had been asleep on the sofa. Or at least he had appeared to be.

Must have been talking in his sleep.

Now, she realized, it was nearly sundown and she hadn't seen him come home from school. Nor had she seen the family dog. A strange sinking feeling entered her stomach.

"Oh Jordan," she thought suddenly, sensing a strange sinking enter her stomach. *"Please don't tell me you left without me!"*

A.B. Clark

SEVENTEEN

The sight at the door took Kat's breath away. Over the past few hours, she had tried to steady herself for this moment, but the man at the threshold was not at all what she had envisioned. Halfway between the fire and sofa, she froze and drew one hand, automatically, to her heart. In the dim firelight, the first thing she noticed was his overall proportions. He was taller than she had expected, and had a strangely large, muscular chest that bulged beneath his pink paisley shirt. His blond, thinning hair and leathery skin left no doubt he was well past his teenage years. She glanced behind him. Where was Jordan? Was this man to deliver a message? Did he have the wrong cabin? What was going on?

"Wh- who are you?" she asked.

The door closed behind him. In the silence that followed, he stood watching her. His head ticked back and forth in some kind of nervous twitch, then he cocked it slightly to one side as though in indecision. His face, however, bore no expression.

"What do you want?" she asked him.

The man's face twisted into a devilish grin. Suddenly, he shrugged, and strode forward. The rest seemed to happen in an instant. She screamed, too late, and the man's hungry mouth muffled the sound before she could think to react. His large body spun her around and pinned her against the log wall. She felt the fireplace heat lick her leg. She struggled against him, but his hands held her wrists. Her shin struck a table as he twisted her around again, and she yelped. A lamp crashed to the floor. A moment later, he threw her onto the bearskin rug. His body pressed her down. She tried to scream again, but his wet tongue filled her mouth and his teeth struck hers with a jarring clash of bone-against-bone. Animal scent came from the fur beneath her and from his breath, above.

She struggled and wrenched clear for only an instant. On one knee, she lurched away. In that instant, one thought consumed her—*Mom was right!*—before the man struck out with his massive fist.

***

The door opened, and a blinding light greeted Jordan. He raised his hands to shield the glare, but all he could see was a long table and several dark silhouettes seated around it. A shove came from behind and he heard the door click shut. Someone pressed him onto a metal, three-legged stool facing the inquisition. A subdued voice addressed him from a hidden speaker on the table.

"State your name for the record."

Jordan hesitated. He considered giving them his real name, but Kat was close; he could feel it. So instead, he squinted into the lights and gave them the name on his fake I.D.

"Paul Brown," he lied.

"Where were you this evening, Mr. Brown?"

Jordan tried to pinpoint who was speaking, but the figures at the table were undetectable.

"I was at Immigrations," he said, still shielding his eyes. He looked around in confusion. Behind the outlines and the lights, he thought he spied a mirrored wall.

Is Kat back there? he thought. *Is this some sort of test before they send me to the Oasis?*

Or was he already there? He had definitely been moved since passing out in the tunnel below Immigrations. At some point, they had even changed him into an orange jumpsuit while he slept.

But where am I?

Jordan ran a hand through his hair and winced when he touched a painful knot. *That must have been from when I fell, back at the escalator,* he thought.

The last thing he remembered was Lieutenant Winters standing over him, shaking her head. Her words came back to him in fragments, as if in a dream.

"I warned him about the tunnels. They never listen. First one tonight. Oh well. There will undoubtedly be more. Leave him here; I'll take him over tomorrow."

So, he wasn't at the Oasis, after all.

Does that mean Kat tracked me down here? he thought. *It must! Who else would have asked for me by name? No one else knows I'm here!* But he wondered why the handcuffs, who was hiding behind that two-way mirror, and why everyone was acting so cross. *Maybe it's a rite of passage, like at Immigrations… some form of initiation before they let me pass.*

A voice jolted him to attention.

"Mr. Brown," it said, "stay focused. This is a serious matter. Where were you this afternoon at two o'clock?"

"I told you. Immigrations."

His eyes were starting to adjust. In one corner he saw a video camera's red light. *Are they recording me? Why? Do they do that to everyone?* He wondered if he were expected to give some sort of confession for sneaking across the border. *What is going on?*

He shook his head at the table's silhouettes.

"I arrived at Immigrations this morning before noon and I've been there ever since, as far as I know."

He heard some discussion at the table.

"Mr. Brown," came a different voice, "you have been identified as a Person of Interest in a crime committed earlier this evening. Tomorrow, our witness will identify you, so you might as well confess now. Believe me, it will go much better for you if you do." She sounded bitter, with a note of barely-controlled rage.

For the second time tonight, Jordan felt fear rising in his throat.

***

Paul Brown's time was up. He had known it from the moment he entered the Immigrations subway station and had lost contact with the

Voice. Until then, the Voice had upheld its part of the deal; it had helped him escape from the Rock, told him where to find the Chiang-woman's apartment, and promised him a reward if he only checked into Immigrations. When the Voice disappeared halfway down the escalator, however, he had known he was on his own. His eyes had grown wide and his nostrils had flared. *I've been set up!* he thought.

That instant, the day's events came flooding back as though he had just awakened from a dream. He remembered everything that had happened, but it was as though he had watched it from outside himself instead of participating.

No! he resolved. *I won't go back!*

He considered telling them about "the Voice" but even in his panic he realized "hearing voices in his head" would never hold up in court.

Dammit! he thought. *It isn't fair! I didn't even get to take my time and enjoy myself!*

He wasn't sure if the woman had survived and he didn't really care. He could live vicariously through the memory even if he hadn't been himself at the time.

He had tried jumping the platform, but the guards had been ready. They grabbed him before he got to the edge and stuck him with a sedative. Later, while they had him resting on a cot in a small antechamber, a Lytoky medic had cooed motherly.

"No one is going to hurt you, Jordan. We see by your itinerary you have big plans tonight, so we're not going to hold you back. First, though, you need to calm down. We're simply underground, below Immigrations. It's safe here. Everything's okay. You're just suffering from TRAAP syndrome, what we call Tunnel Reaction - Anxiety and Paranoia."

It took him a moment to realize the medic assumed he had experienced some kind of claustrophobia attack.

"Happens all the time down here," she explained, "especially to the repeat escorts. It's odd for a first-timer, but you're the second one to suffer it tonight."

Is she actually trying to console me? he thought. *Priceless!*

"Listen, the shuttle will be here soon. You're here to meet someone, right?"

"What? Oh, I mean, sure. Right!" The Voice had told him he'd be given a special reward once he got to Immigrations, so when he was filling out the Immigrations form, he checked the box marked, "Special Request." The only other choices were "Repeat Passenger" or "General," and neither of them sounded very special to him. *Maybe the Voice hadn't lied, after all!*

"Good. Get some rest. I'll check up on you before you go, okay?"

"Okay," he grinned. "You bet."

When the medic left, he considered his options. Apparently, no one knew what he had done. They kept calling him "Jordan." Clearly, they had him mixed up with someone else. He could try to escape again, but didn't since he was still in restraints below Immigrations and couldn't expect to get far.

Might as well settle in and enjoy the ride, he decided. *You never know; this could be fun!*

And it was.

First, he had gotten to experience that intensely fast-moving shuttle, then the private jet. *First-class all the way, Baby!* Next, some soldiers had taken him to freshen up. They washed his clothes while he took a hot shower, then they fed him steak and potatoes. He almost asked them for something different to wear, but since the Voice had left the clothes especially for him in the get-away boat, he felt strangely attached. Then, after a bumpy ride down some winding dirt roads they had marched him to this quaint log cabin. When they took off his handcuffs and walked away, Paul had gotten wary again.

Did they finally realize I'm not Jordan? he thought. He wondered if there was a firing squad inside the cabin, or some sort of torture chamber. *Maybe they uncuffed me to make it look like an escape attempt!*

He opened the door cautiously. The young girl standing by the fire was wringing her hands. She was soft and feminine—*just my type!*—and was wearing a white wrap-around skari. *So innocent!* he laughed. *And so easy to get through!* When the door closed behind him, the two stood staring at each other in mutual disbelief. Then he had grinned.

Back in the old days, he had developed a skill for sizing up a situation and making quick decisions. Thirteen years in prison had not dulled that particular talent. As he saw it, there were only two explanations. The first was that the Voice was compensating him for a job well done, and this girl was his reward. The second was that the real Jordan was on his way, and when he arrived, the guards would realize their mistake and haul Paul's ass back to jail. Either way, this moment was a gift he did not intend to waste.

He crossed the room in three strides. Without a word, he scooped up the girl like he'd seen in the movies and bent her backwards to plant an enthusiastic kiss. Instead of reciprocating, she struggled and screamed, and pushed him away. She picked up a lamp, but before she could throw it, he captured both wrists. The lamp fell and shattered. He covered her mouth with his own to muffle her screams. The feeling of déjà vu washed over him. The other woman had struggled just like this, too. It only excited him more.

Still keeping his mouth over hers and ignoring the pain of her teeth scraping his gums, he shifted both her wrists to one hand and grabbed at her breasts. She gasped in muffled horror as he tore the childish skari fabric away and exposed her soft, white bra underneath.

A virgin's bra! he laughed. *How fun!* Her throaty screams continued until he threw her down on the floor. She tried one last time to get away, and he'd been forced to hit her. Her head came down on the coffee table with a surprisingly loud thud.

***

The pain was incredible. Jordan's interrogators had lost patience with his silence and were now using a different interrogation technique. They had stripped him and stretched his arms taut with rubber tubing. Old scars on Jordan's back and legs had startled the guards but did not dissuade them. They were determined to make him talk. They grabbed him by the hair and yanked his sweaty head back.

"Perhaps you did not hear the question, Mr. Brown," one yelled. Spittle spewed onto his face.

"Oh, he heard!" said the other. "I think he heard every word."

"But I'm not Paul Brown! I told you a hundred times already; I'm Jordan Danforth! I'm Senator Danforth's son. Call him if you don't believe me!"

The start of a snarl twisted the guard's upper lip.

"Sure. I'd say that, too, if I were in your position," she said. "Next, you'll tell us you're a woman, I suppose." She laughed and lit a small, pencil-sized butane torch. "That may be true, shortly."

When she lowered it to Jordan's scrotum, the scent of burning hair and flesh immediately filled the room.

Jordan screamed. His testicles were on fire, though the flame was far from his skin. At that moment, he would have told them anything they wanted to know—about Kat, his father, himself—but that's not what they wanted to hear.

"Where did you first see Gloria Chiang?" the closest guard asked again. "When did you decide to rape her?"

Jordan's voice was raw from screaming. He opened his mouth, but only a hoarse whisper came out. Trembling, he hung by straps around his upper arms—his knees having buckled under him long ago. As he stared into the face of his captors, he silently prayed for death.

Just then, a third voice spoke up. It was the voice from behind the lights and video equipment from earlier. It was slow, and calm, and promised a way out of this otherwise-hellish fever.

"All you have to do is confess," she explained. "Confession is good for the soul. Tell us the truth, Mr. Brown, and all this will be merely a bad dream."

In that moment, Jordan saw an end to his misery. He saw the torch, the cameras, and the guards' sneering faces. He watched the black outlines of his captors behind the long table, and gave in. A tear slid down his cheek and he closed his eyes, ashamed of his weakness.

"I did it," he choked.

Remembering the guards' repeated accusations over the last few hours, he gave them what they wanted.

"I raped her," he continued. "I tied her arms and legs together like a rodeo calf and left her there to die."

Silence filled the room. After a moment, the cameras stopped rolling. The guards released Jordan's head, letting it fall limp like a wilted flower, and the lights went out.

"Get the bastard out of here," he heard the intercom-voice say.

And everything went black.

DAY TWO

The Beast

"The dragon gave the beast his power
and his throne and great authority. The
whole world was astonished and followed
the beast... and asked, 'Who is like the
beast? Who can make war against him?'"

--Revelations 13:3-4
The Bible, New International Version

DEPOSITION #20561110.002
(Continued)

When I first heard what had happened, I was sure there must be some kind of mistake. I mean, seriously? Katherine hadn't even seen a man since she was a child for Heaven's sake; it didn't make sense! Besides, who could have done such a thing?

Then they told me.

At the name Paul Brown, my throat tightened. Questions raced through my mind that I dared not ask aloud. Like, *How could he have gotten to the Oasis? Could he have really hurt my daughter?* And of course, *Can anyone trace him back to me?*

EIGHTEEN

WOMAN SEXUALLY ASSAULTED. SUSPECT CONFESSES

Illinois (AP)—Yesterday afternoon, a man sexually assaulted an unidentified woman inside her East St. Louis home. This is the first documented rape on Lytoky soil since the MA'AM Revolution began twenty-one years ago.

Authorities will not reveal the victim's name, or the details, until a press conference later this afternoon, but neighbors at the crime scene, 343 Plumb Street, reported hearing screams at approximately two o'clock Tuesday afternoon. Later, they noticed a paramedic carrying out a woman on a stretcher.

"It looked like my neighbor, Gloria Chiang," an eyewitness reported. "But it was hard to tell from my house."

Neighbors will gather in the town square later this morning outside the Cis-Star Headquarters building (aka the Yardstick) to honor the victim.

Newly elected President Pat Buford issued the following statement. "At times like these, let us give thanks that we live in a community with such loving, compassionate neighbors—the kind who are willing to pray for each other!"

An anonymous source confirmed that an escaped convict from Rock Island Prison already confessed. The source also shared a video from several months ago during a campaign speech where Marshall Danforth, New Canaan's recent presidential hopeful, publicly declared his intention to pardon the assailant, the moment he won the election!

"Apparently, Danforth found a way to set the rapist free in retaliation for losing," speculated the source.

No comment yet from Senator Danforth.

In the pursuit of swift justice, the Three-Strikes Capital Offense trial will begin this afternoon live on WLBC. Check your local listings for pre-trial coverage.

NINETEEN

The Infirmary's road sign materialized in her headlights the instant before she hit it. Lieutenant Alex Winters flinched upon impact, and the Jeep fishtailed.

"Is that the best you've got?" she laughed at the windshield as she steered hard to the left and throttled the engine. The momentum brought the Jeep back-to-center with a head-sloshing jolt that made her whole body grimace.

She shot an accusatory glance in the rear-view mirror. The Infirmary's directional arrow, which had once pointed right, now lay against a tree. Its post, sheared in half, protruded sideways at an awkward angle.

Stupid sign, she thought. *Who needs it, anyway? Everyone knows their way on the island.* A quick frown at her glowing wrist-VEE, made her nearly spin out again.

"Oh for MA'AM's sake!"

Without slowing down, she dropped into 4-wheel drive and heard the gears grind angrily.

"Sorry, ol' Buddy," she spoke to the Jeep, "but it's not my fault the roads are slick the one morning I'm running late."

This was not the first time she had overslept, however, and she knew it. Nor was it her first hangover. Although employees were forbidden alcohol here at the Oasis, Alex had learned, long ago, that everything here had a price.

She made a quick calculation, and at the next curve she swerved off-road (on purpose, this time) onto a narrow animal path. From there, she entered the dark, forest duff. The Jeep shuddered. Too late, she realized she hadn't accounted for last night's storm. As she and the Jeep grappled over slick, fallen limbs, her aching temples throbbed anew. The headlights, bouncing up and down, pushed and pulled her stomach along with it. At one particularly deep ravine, the Jeep gave a shuddering groan.

"I know just how you feel," she sighed, and swallowed hard.

Around another bend, she spied a familiar rhododendron grove and quickly maneuvered back onto the compound's muddy road. From there, she saw a small, wooden sign up ahead announcing "Fantasy Log Cabin #3." It was the only indication she had made the right turn.

Hope Miss High and Mighty doesn't mind me being late! she thought, not remembering her charge's name. It was going to be a long-enough day without some Punctual Princess filing a complaint against her.

Daughters of celebrities were always the worst, she'd found. They acted more entitled than their mothers: the ones who had actually earned their Oasis privileges. This one, she recalled now, was the new President's only daughter.

That means she'll probably want to yak the whole time back, Alex thought and rolled her eyes.

As Chief Transport Officer, Alex escorted guests to and from their Oasis accommodations three consecutive days a week. If this girl turned out to be like all the other first-timers, she would want to talk about her Great Adventure. Alex could almost hear the brat's nonstop chatter now.

"Do you think he likes me?" the girl would ask, breathlessly.

"Oh yes," Alex would dutifully reply with the required, handbook answer. "If he told you he likes you, it's true. He wouldn't say it otherwise."

Donkeyshit.

The men here at the Oasis were directed what to say, what to do, and precisely how to do it. It was all part of the fantasy: to make each woman feel special.

And what better way to feel special than to hear a set of pre-approved, pre-programmed compliments?

Alex wanted to puke.

"Hey! What the-?"

As she turned into the driveway, her first thought was that maybe she had taken the wrong trail, after all. Orange security cones barricaded the last twenty yards, and a half-dozen Military Jeeps had been strategically positioned, beyond them. Their headlights emblazoned the cabin's exterior chink-log walls. At the sight of a SWAT member lying prone on the roof, Alex's stomach cramped. It looked more like a war zone than the cozy, log cabin she had left the previous evening.

Her mind scrambled to remember if she had ever turned back on her VEE's ringer last night after her shipment's arrival. Suddenly, something burned in the back of her throat. She pulled up hard on the emergency brake and barely got the door opened—wincing as the hinges made a loud, grinding squeal—before she vomited in the sand.

Still leaning over, she glimpsed movement from the cabin, where a Hospitality Staff worker, Denise, had just scampered off the front porch and was now striding toward Alex with purpose. Alex wiped her mouth with the back of one hand and steadied herself as she waited.

"What's wrong?" Alex asked, before Denise could pose the same question.

Denise eyed the Jeep's newly-dented hood, and gave her a disapproving look, but Alex resisted the instinct to explain.

"He's holding her hostage," Denise explained.

Alex shook her head. "Hostage? Who? What do you mean?"

"A new recruit has Buford's daughter in there," Denise pointed toward the cabin. "We sent in a team when we couldn't get hold of her. Or you."

Again with the look?

"Where were you?" Denise continued. "Why didn't you answer your VEE? You didn't follow procedure."

Alex closed her eyes. She knew all about PROCEDURE. If a patron failed to check in every morning, the Transport Officer was to assume the worst, per Oasis policy, and secure the situation. For a first-time escort, the initial check-in was at 0700 the following morning. This was supposed to be a safeguard in the unlikely event an escort's programming malfunctioned, but that was a joke, in Alex's opinion. As everyone was well aware, the male escorts here went through rigorous scrutiny. What with prior-approval requirements, pre-boarding background checks at Immigrations, and their required lay-over at the Infirmary, each escort was completely benign. In Alex's experience, every time a client failed to make contact, it turned out to be a simple "misunderstanding" where the guest got caught—*shocker!*—with her pants down.

Literally. Alex suspected they did it on purpose.

As if the thrill of being on a private island with a man who can't say "No" isn't intoxicating enough? she thought. The whole thing made her sick.

Because of these frequent false alarms, Alex had stopped reacting when her patrons didn't check in. In fact, for the last several months she had barely paid attention at all. It hadn't even occurred to her to call the cabin this morning.

Alex pushed off, avoiding the wet vomit, and carefully closed the Jeep's door. Carefully, because her head couldn't handle more trauma and because if she slammed it, she wasn't sure she could get it open again. (The door had a habit of sticking.) At least her stomach had stopped churning. She licked her dry, chapped lips and started for the cabin.

"Who delivered her Escort last night?" she asked, over her shoulder. "How long since he left the Motel?"

"I don't know. Rumor has it she asked for him by name."

Ah. Another "procedure."

If a specific escort was requested by name, it meant they had a prior relationship and the guest did not want the man "altered" at the Infirmary. It was a common occurrence for women to request their favorite "pets."

"The place is a mess!" Denise continued, yapping behind her like a devoted puppy. "Tables overturned, lamp broken, glass on the rug. Looks like she put up quite a fight!" Denise seemed pleased by that thought.

"Have you seen her?" Alex asked.

Denise didn't respond right away, so Alex surmised she was shaking her head. "Nobody has," she finally answered.

The walk to the cabin seemed unbearably long. At the doorway, Alex entered with shoulders hunched, like a student tardy to her first day of class. Inside, she found controlled chaos.

"Where the hell is that ambulance?" someone yelled to her left. At the far wall, a Private stood listening at the bedroom door with a glass tumbler, most likely from the kitchenette, while another knelt, below her, setting up a keyhole surveillance device. Others scrambled about taking fingerprints and photos. Back in the kitchenette, she spied Captain Chad behind the buffet counter.

"I did call her!" Chad was speaking into a virtual 2-D screen. "She's not answering! I'm sorry, Ma'am; I should have called you last night when I first learned who she was, but when I saw the reservation had been made using the family account, I saw no need to question it further."

Chad's head lowered, slightly, as she listened. Alex could hear a muted voice, but since the screen's pixels were one-directional, she couldn't see who was on the other end. Regardless, it was clear her boss was taking a verbal beating.

"Yes, of course now I regret it," Chad responded. "But please understand; the girl is of age. We don't require parental consent once a guest turns eighteen."

After several seconds, the captain visibly winced.

"Yes, I knew she was traveling under an assumed name, but celebrities and their families do that all the time. You never use your real name, either, for example…."

A renewed tirade came from the other end.

"You're right," Chad continued. "I'm sorry. Anyway, I interviewed Kat, myself. She was determined to meet her escort last night and had it all arranged. In deference to you, I approved it."

She paused again and listened.

"Yes. Our Transport Officers check iris scans back at Immigrations. And, as I already explained, she asked for him by name. Well, she actually asked for a different name first, but since we didn't have any passengers by that name, she admitted she was here to meet 'Jordan.'"

She checked her records. "Yes, Jordan Danforth."

Another pause, and the captain wearily shook her head.

"That's correct; no Infirmary first."

The captain seemed to have trouble meeting the gaze of the person on the impromptu screen. She glanced away for an instant, and that's when she spotted Alex.

Did her eyes just narrow? Alex wondered.

Chad motioned for Alex to stay put, then turned her attention back to the unidentified speaker, whom Alex now assumed was the girl's mother, President Buford. After a moment, Chad's posture wilted.

"No Ma'am," she said. "I can't say for certain, but no one's seen evidence of blood so we're hoping for the best."

Alex moved toward the sofa. There, an injured officer sat, bent over, holding an ice pack to her nose with a trembling hand.

That should have been me! Alex thought. As the girl's official Transport Officer, she should have been the first one on the scene.

She knelt to offer her comrade a comforting pat and noticed something dark on the rug by her knee. It could have been spilled coffee, but it looked more like a glob of tar. She touched her fingers to it. The rug's black fur stuck together in a thick, crusty clump, but as she ground her fingers deeper, she could feel that it was moist.

"Yes, Ma'am," she heard the captain saying. "We'll keep it confidential until you arrive, but please hurry. He's made demands."

Alex withdrew her hand and saw her fingertips were now blackish-red.

Blood?

She glanced toward Chad, and their eyes locked again. In that instant, Alex saw her own emotions mirrored back on her captain's face: that of realization, horror, and guilt.

TWENTY

Tucked away in his detention cell, Jordan awoke to the sound of approaching footsteps. For a moment, he forgot where he was. Then the stench hit him.

Is that urine? he thought. *Is it mine?*

Memories from last night made his head jerk upward. Hot streaks stabbed his throbbing temples and he immediately went down again. The coils beneath the thin, dirty mattress bruised his tender hip, and his sides ached from what would later be diagnosed as three broken ribs. Even shifting his legs sent searing pain to his groin and testicles.

The footsteps grew louder until they stopped outside his cell. Metal clanked. Jordan gritted his teeth against the pain and tried to sit up, but instead had to hang his head between his knees to keep from passing out. The heavy bolt clicked, and the bars slid open. Jordan watched two sets of worn combat boots walk in and step aside. Next, came fabric trousers. They swished above a pair of smart leather loafers.

"Hello Mr. Brown," said a voice above him.

Brown?

Oh, right. His fake ID. Why were they still calling him that? Hadn't he told them his real name last night? He couldn't remember. As the throbbing in his temples continued, he concentrated on the loafers and saw one toe tapping the concrete floor. Its owner spoke again.

"I trust you slept well?" she said.

Jordan swallowed and tasted blood. He felt stabbing pain everywhere, including his ribs, chest, and groin, and he was covered in his own urine. He doubted whether this woman really cared how well he had slept.

"I'm Detective Beverly Sparks," the woman continued. "There's someone here to see you. Someone I believe you know?"

Kat?

Jordan forced his head up, too quickly, and braced against the piercing pain.

Above him stood a tall woman with beautiful skin the color of pumpernickel bread. This was the first civilian he had seen since crossing the border. Even though he had been briefed by Kat about women's clothing in the Lytoky, the cultural differences were disconcerting. Back home, women didn't wear traditional male clothing, so the detective's dark gray trousers and white linen shirt would have been considered indecent. He hadn't been as surprised by the Border guards' attire; they were soldiers, after all, and he had known better than to expect them to dress like Amazon warriors.

He squinted beyond the detective. Two escort guards stood alert behind her. Beyond them, the corridor was empty.

But, Jordan thought. *Where's Kat?*

"Expecting someone in particular, Mr. Brown?"

Jordan met the detective's eyes. Even in his fog, her barely-suppressed rage and loathing were nearly palpable.

"Let me assure you," she continued, "no one is going to save you, if that's what you were hoping. You're going to have to pay for what you did."

Jordan's hoarse voice came out as a whisper. "But I didn't do anything wrong!"

"Nothing WRONG?" the detective seemed inflamed at his words and she took a sudden step forward. Jordan flinched involuntarily. "How dare you! I saw your handiwork firsthand, so don't you dare sit there and tell me what you did wasn't wrong!"

"No, you don't understand!" Jordan said, and raised a hand in an attempt to be understood. "I... I mean, I didn't do it! You have to believe me! This is all a mistake!"

Beverly's eyes narrowed to angry slits. Her lips tightened and her fists clenched and unclenched. When she next spoke, her words were slow and deliberate.

"I've read your file. Last night, you admitted everything. You attacked a woman in my city and raped her repeatedly. Now, after having slept on it, you have the audacity to sit there and say it was a mistake? You didn't mean to do it? Is that what you are saying?"

"No! You're not listening! I-"

"Save it for the judge." She turned and addressed the guards. "Get him up. The witness is waiting to ID him, so be quick about it."

When the two sentries pulled him to a standing position, his head reeled backward and the stretching pain in his groin made him swoon. His legs refused to move at first, but before the guards dragged him off his feet he ground his teeth and took one painful, chafing step. Then another. And another.

TWENTY-ONE

Inside Fantasy Log Cabin #3, Paul Brown knelt beside the bed. His knee ached from where he had driven it into glass last night trying to separate the young girl's thighs. He shifted his weight to the other knee and winced. He glanced behind him to the bed, and to the mound of blankets that hadn't moved all morning.

Last night still pissed him off. Without thinking, he licked his swollen lip, where she had bitten him. It still stung. Even though she had fought him off at first, playing hard to get (just the way he liked), she had nearly gotten away when he had her pinned down. That's when he had accidently hit her too hard. When her head hit the glass coffee table and she went down, she immediately stopped moving. After that, she had been no fun at all. Still, he had hoped she was faking it, so he had carried her to the bedroom. The cut on her head made such a mess that both he and the girl were covered in blood by the time he finally got her there.

When she didn't wake up, he tied her up with the bloody strips he tore from his long-sleeve shirt and went back out to the sofa to watch TV. The last thing he remembered was watching *Silence of the Lambs* on the teleVISOR's retro channel. When the first guard barged through the front door this morning, he had jumped to his feet, knocked her out cold with the remote, and barricaded himself back inside the tiny bedroom. Squeezed between the door and the bed, he could barely move.

He glanced again at the sleeping girl on the bed. It had been thirty minutes since the guards had arrived, and all through the shouts and the threats afterward she hadn't roused once. Even so, he had been particularly descriptive when telling the guards outside what he would do

135

to her unless they followed his demands. So far, they seemed to believe him, but he knew they eventually would want proof of life.

Through the bedroom door, Paul could hear somebody breathing. He imagined a woman, probably a young private, listening. The thought of her kneeling so close, with her flushed cheek pressed tightly against the door, made him hard. He hoped she was pretty, but it really didn't matter. On impulse, he whispered into the door where he imagined was her ear.

"Open wide," he said slowly, reaching for his zipper. "Nice and easy… Atta girl."

He heard her gasp in response and he closed his eyes in amusement. Just then, an angry voice came through the door from much higher. This one must have been standing.

"Jordan, I'm warning you! Do not harm that girl! Do you hear me? I don't care whose son you are; if you touch her, I swear to MA'AM I will kill you, myself!"

Paul laughed. This voice sounded like Lieutenant Winters, his Transport Officer from last night. He hadn't seen her since arriving on the island, before he had been taken to freshen up. He had wondered what had happened to her.

"Look, Lady," he said to the door. "I don't have much to lose at this point, so you'd better start negotiating before I get bored. If I'm simply going back to the Rock anyway, I'm going to have to entertain myself enough in here to last me, you know?"

"You're not going back to the Rock, you dick," said the woman through the door. "Rape is punishable by death, or didn't you know? Our courts move quickly over here. By this time tomorrow you'll be-"

"Then I might as well kill her right now!" he yelled.

"No!" came another voice. He heard a slight tussling at the door and inferred his lieutenant had been pushed away. This female voice sounded older, and more composed. "Jordan," she said. "This is Captain Chad. I'm in charge, and I promise you that no one is going to harm you. President Buford is on her way. You still have a chance to negotiate, here, so be smart. If you harm her daughter again, in any way, it's over for you. Don't be stupid."

He glanced at the bed again and frowned. He couldn't believe his luck. Kat Buford, the new president's only daughter, could be his ticket free...

or his one-way ticket to the electric chair. The blankets still weren't moving, and the only visible evidence of his hostage was her coarse, blonde hair. He sank back against the door and winced.

She'd better not be dead, he thought. *I can't hold them off forever. At some point, I'll need her to talk!*

TWENTY-TWO

"Ms. Chiang," a voice urged kindly. "Please look at the lineup. That's a one-way glass. He can't see you or hurt you; I promise."

Gloria sat on her hands and rocked back and forth. Behind dark sunglasses, meant to hide her blackened eyes, she continued looking down as Detective Beverly Sparks repeated the instructions.

"This is the last thing we'll ask of you; I promise."

Gloria's mind revolted. *The last thing?* she thought, angrily. *Somehow, I doubt it!*

Fingerprints, eye-scans, vaginal probes, psychological tests… she had endured them all. Last night, as if the rape were not bad enough, she had been prodded, poked, and questioned. They had even cut off her underpants! With each culture scrape and humiliating photograph, she had relived the assault in her mind. The last straw had been when the nurse had rudely parted her legs on the examining table to clip off a chunk of matted pubic hair. She had fought the woman with renewed strength and vigor.

"Well, at least I got enough for a spectrometer analysis," the nurse had shrugged, obviously disappointed. "I'll test it for DNA and seminal fluid. Gotta do it quickly; sperm starts to deteriorate within an hour. I'll be right back!"

Ten minutes later, the gynecologist had arrived and Gloria was finally offered a warm blanket and kind words.

Now this.

A hand on her shoulder roused her back to the present. The digital clock on the station wall said it 7:16 a.m.—nearly twelve hours since her nightmare had begun. Twelve hours in a shock- (and then a drug-) induced stupor where, in her mind, the attack was still going on.

"Point out the man who hurt you," the detective said softly. "Come on, you can do it."

Gloria couldn't look up. She still saw his face every time she closed her eyes; she didn't want to see him again in person. It didn't matter if a glass wall was between them. She was preparing to stand up and refuse again when a Voice thundered from inside her head.

"TESTIFY AGAINST PAUL BROWN!"

Her eyes widened and she looked around with a start.

"What did you say?" she asked the detective.

"I said you can do this. He won't hurt you."

"No, I mean- Didn't you hear that Voice?"

"What voice?"

Gloria turned to the others in the room. From their exchanged glances, they must have thought she had gone mad. Beverly knelt beside her and gently took her hands.

"Gloria, look at me," she said. Gloria turned obediently. "Believe me when I tell you, we are going to punish the man who did this to you. But first, we need your cooperation. You have to point him out so that he can never hurt anyone again. Think about how you would feel if we let him go and he did this to somebody else. To someone else's daughter."

Gloria looked down and frowned. The detective seemed sincere enough, but the speech hadn't changed her mind. She started to get up, then came the Voice hit her again, only this time it was more insistent.

"TESTIFY AGAINST PAUL BROWN. THAT'S THE ONLY WAY TO KEEP YOUR BABY."

She gasped. *No!* she thought. *Dr. Bott promised to keep the pregnancy test results a secret! Once news leaks out that I'm pregnant, the Uni-Lifers will never let me keep Dale's baby, even with Waverly's help!* For all she knew, the nurse back at the hospital may have already given her drugs to abort the baby, anyway.

The Voice repeated in her mind and grew stronger. Gloria tried to snatch her hands away and cover her ears, but the detective held tight. The Voice seemed so urgent, so confident, so sure. It intensified, but still Gloria said nothing.

"TESTIFY AGAINST PAUL BROWN."
"Look at the glass," Beverly repeated, indicating the two-way mirror and the row of men behind it. "Go on."
"THAT'S THE ONLY WAY TO KEEP YOUR BABY."
Gloria sighed. No one was watching her; they were too busy staring at the lineup, themselves, and collectively holding their breaths for her response. Behind her heavy sunglasses, she squeezed her eyes shut and clenched her jaw.
"Tell us which one he is," Beverly prompted.
"TESTIFY AGAINST PAUL BROWN."
"Then you can go home."
"THAT'S THE ONLY WAY TO KEEP YOUR BABY."
What did she have to lose? Testifying against the man in front of her was easy. She had heard the officers use his name, and had heard him described as tall, blond, and muscular. It had to be him.
"Gloria," Beverly asked, as though from a distance, barely discernible over the Voice. "Do you see the man who attacked you?"
Gloria nodded truthfully that she did. Even behind the protective glass, sunglasses, and closed eyelids, she saw his stringy hair (slightly bald on top), and his middle-aged, weather-beaten face. She saw his humorless eyes and his small, hard lips. She imagined him standing in the lineup with that ugly smirk. She would see that face every night for the rest of her life.
"I see him," she whispered.
"Which one is he?"
Gloria pointed straight ahead. "That one."
Her accusing aim landed on the man labeled Suspect Number Five.

***

Suspect Number Five was a volunteer from the Border Control office in St. Louis. He had a solid alibi for yesterday afternoon and did not even fit the general description. The man whose eye scan showed PAUL BROWN was Suspect Number Three, two men to his right.
Still kneeling, Beverly peered up, around Gloria's sunglasses.
Eyes closed. Who can blame her?

Beverly had been a Lytoky Detective for two years now. Before that, she had been in Special Forces where she had studied Micro-Expressions and earned a reputation for being able to tell when people were lying. Of course, since most of her cases had involved theft, not violence (and she had never before had a sexual assault case), she had also found that good old-fashioned common sense and investigative legwork worked well, too.

Per the report, this Brown-character had instigated a prison riot yesterday, apparently as a distraction. One guard had died during the event, so they might charge him with murder, too.

She had also read about Gloria. Her attending physician, Dr. Taylor Bott, had refused to provide information she considered "not pertinent to the case." That only made Beverly more curious. She researched further and discovered that Gloria had bought a home pregnancy test that very morning at a Rite Aid near her home, and then she had visited a Partho-Lab ninety minutes later. Winnie, the Partho-lab receptionist, claimed Gloria had been nearly hysterical when the doctor refused to take her as a client. On top of that, Gloria was married to a man.

It didn't take a body-language expert to determine Gloria was trying to hide an illegal pregnancy. But would she invent a rape just to save her unborn child?

Too bad the Lytoky has such strict rules requiring virgin births, she thought. *If only Gloria had known where to go for help, her name wouldn't have been flagged at the lab.* As an outreach member of the Rebellion, Beverly had friends who could circumvent the official Partho lab registry. Perhaps her group needed to do a better job of getting out the word. Hetero women needed to know there were options when the Uni-Lifers tried to force non-Partho termination.

One look at Gloria, however, and Beverly was convinced the woman was telling the truth. Gloria's bruises were incriminating enough, but the way she cowered when anyone tried to touch her and the wild look in her eyes left little doubt her fear was genuine. When Beverly had asked her how she would feel if her rapist did this to someone else, Gloria exhibited a visceral reaction. Clearly, the thought touched a nerve. Her emotions were real.

Why put the poor woman through any more pain? Beverly decided.

With the suspect still in lineup, Beverly lowered her eyes and knocked three times on the glass to indicate Suspect Number Three.

TWENTY-THREE

Waverly rubbed her temples as she studied her pendant VEE's bright screen. Last night's celebration had continued until early this morning, so she was slow in taking in Buford's Snapchat recording.

"Danforth's son, Jordan, is holding Kat hostage at the Oasis!" Pat's Holo was saying, looking frantic. "I'm on my way there now! Call me when you get this!"

What? No, that can't be right, Waverly thought. She hadn't seen Kat at the party last night, but she hadn't been concerned. *What in the world is going on?*

Buford looked terrible in her message, as though she'd been crying. Waverly automatically checked the current time. The chat had come in thirty minutes ago.

Waverly remembered meeting Jordan years ago. She had read his bio in preparation for Danforth's campaign. He seemed like a good kid. Whatever was going on (and in the back of her mind she believed it was nothing more than a rumor started by Senator Danforth), she was certain the boy posed no threat.

Still.... With a sigh, she brought up her personal file on him. *Good looking kid,* she thought. *Doesn't resemble Danforth, though.* Then again, the senator had put on so much weight it was hard to recall what he really looked like.

Next, she clicked the IMMIGRATIONS IRIS ACTIVITY program, which would have tracked any movement over the border for the last twenty-four hours. Sure enough, Jordan's name had been scanned into the

Transport System around 1600 and given a special Lytoky Pass. No picture attached, though.

Odd, she thought. *Well, at least that explains how he got to the Oasis.*

Her head itched. Something was wrong. She pulled up his Transport File and noted a manual entry had logged him in. "JORDAN DANFORTH," it read, but the stats didn't look right. She delved deeper. Poring over his previous on-line movement, she found some minor discrepancies and one glaring error. The clock entries indicated yesterday morning around 0930 he had paid a bill at a St. Louis veterinarian clinic. Two hours later, he had checked in for lunch at Rock Island prison.

Rock Island?

The burn mark on her scalp started to throb.

"Computer! Call the Oasis!"

She connected with the island's headquarters a few minutes later and was transferred to the Officer-in-Charge, Captain Chad, who was waiting outside for Buford to arrive by jet. After a quick introduction, Waverly pumped the woman for info.

"Captain, what was Kat Buford's attacker wearing last night when he came in?" she demanded.

"I didn't see him, myself, Ma'am. Let me check." She asked someone off-screen and then responded, "Work khakis and a pink paisley shirt."

Waverly's mind raced. *No! It can't be!*

"Age?" she snapped.

"One sec."

Waverly watched her question repeated. She couldn't hear the response.

"Forty-five, according to his file," Chad reported. "But my lieutenant says he looked much older."

"MA'AM help us!" Waverly cried. "That's not Jordan!"

***

Waverly opened the OASIS ADMISSIONS file. Sure enough, the scan listed as "JORDAN DANFORTH"—the one some fool had approved last night—showed Paul Brown's photo (taken in Immigrations, no doubt) and his statistics. Somehow, he had switched his iris signature with Danforth's son.

Feeling uneasy, she brought up her Unirays program from yesterday. Its running log displayed the preset time of every word transmitted, including the last-minute additions she had orchestrated last night. Waverly scanned the entries.

"12:15 p.m. FOLLOW ME. FOLLOW ME. POWER AND RICHES TO THOSE WHO FOLLOW ME.

"12:35 p.m. …TURN LEFT. THIRD DOOR ON RIGHT (STAFF LOUNGE). OPEN LAUNDRY CHUTE DOOR BEHIND FAKE FILING CABINET IN THE CORNER. SECURITY CODE #2067…"

Blah. blah. blah.

Impatient fingers drummed the desk as she skipped to the end. Everything looked fine on the Unirays' end, she confirmed.

Her instructions had been to go to Immigrations the minute he left his target so that he could receive his reward. Little did he know she had scheduled an automatic arrest-notice to hit his iris scan thirty-minutes after he left Gloria's, and that his "reward" was a set of handcuffs. Even if he had arrived at Immigrations early, it would still pop up in the system and alert the Transport Officer on duty and at that point, she would arrest him. As a fail-safe, Waverly had even placed an anonymous call to alert the station they had a criminal on their hands.

So, what happened? she wondered.

Her Unirays programming had evolved since she had first used it on Danforth, years ago. Now, instead of only projecting messages one way, it also logged every transmission as it bounced back from the intended recipient. In the early days, it had helped her to see how test subject's brainwaves interpreted instructions. Quickly now, she pulled up Brown's Return Frequency report to see what sounds were currently bouncing back from his DNA-receiver.

Nothing. The line was dead. A sinking feeling crept into her stomach as she read the last entry her Unirays had recorded.

"Here you go. Follow the guards into the tunnel. Escalator is straight ahead. Ride d—wn the esc—la—or. Take subw— on your —eft." The transmission ended abruptly. No more messages had bounced back after that. She checked the transmission's time: 1645 yesterday.

No! she thought, realization crashing in. *He was never supposed to enter the tunnels or the Transport system! Why wasn't he arrested? I was told he had been interrogated and confessed! How could he be at the Oasis?*

Evidently, Brown had followed directions and had gone to Immigrations, but someone must have put him on the express shuttle to O'Hare and then on to the Oasis. *Idiot!* And on top of that, something had happened with the transmission connection, and he was no longer under her control.

Waverly sat in stunned silence. How could this have happened? Fear spread slowly down her tightening spine. *It must be the tunnels!* she thought. She had never transmitted Unirays underground before; there had never been a need. Only a few old subways were even operational.

But how could that have caused a problem? Even if it did, Brown had obviously resurfaced aboveground at the Oasis, yet no transmission-link had re-established. That meant he had somehow escaped the Unirays' control once there, too. Immediately, she started inputting a new program, hoping to generate a connection. As she did, her mind whirled.

Exactly *how* out of control is this Paul Brown? she wondered. And more importantly… *What the hell has he done to my daughter?*

TWENTY-FOUR

Dr. Taylor Bott waited patiently in the staff lounge for Nurse Kim to get off her call. Taylor had finished her rounds and wanted to talk about Gloria Chiang, last night's patient. She listened in as Lou Franklin, the hospital administrator, admonished Nurse Kim via Screen Chat.

"I don't care what the excuse," Franklin was saying. "We are not in the business of breaking the law. Assault cases have strict protocol, period. End of discussion."

Sitting in the corner, out of Franklin's sight, Taylor made a face. No way would this be the end of the discussion, she knew. Franklin would chastise Nurse Kim for days, maybe weeks, even, for failing to perform a DNC on Gloria last night. And, as soon as she was finished yelling at Nurse Kim, she would probably come looking for Taylor.

Suddenly, an announcement came over the Staff Lounge's speaker.

"Dr. Bott, report to the visitor's lounge."

Now what?

With a sympathetic grimace in Nurse Kim's direction, Taylor headed for the door. Kim watched her go and gave a wistful smile, clearly wishing she could go as well.

Taylor rounded a corner and wondered who was asking for her this time. After treating Gloria last night, numerous officers had questioned her about the victim's condition. Everyone, it seemed, wanted individual updates.

"Are you the doctor handling the Chiang case?" each had wanted to know. The questions that followed were always the same.

"Was there evidence of forced penetration?"

"Can you prove that in court?"

"What did the semen analysis report indicate?"

She had answered their questions as best she could without divulging her patient's secrets, and had hoped that was the end of it. Now, reentering the tiny lounge, she recognized the dark-skinned detective waiting for her beside the water cooler as the one who had interviewed her before. A slight blush heated Taylor's cheeks and she unconsciously tidied her ponytail.

"Did you forget something, Detective?" she asked.

Detective Beverly Sparks turned and smiled. As they shook hands, Taylor momentarily lost her train of thought.

How could anyone have eyes so blue? she wondered.

"Pardon my intrusion, Doctor," said the detective, "but I was curious about a few missing details in your report. For example, how far along is the victim?"

"Um. You didn't read that in my report."

The detective shrugged sheepishly. "Can't blame me for trying, right?" she said, and handed Taylor an official-looking plastic card. When their fingers touched, Taylor snatched back her hand with a start. To hide her embarrassment, she turned over the plastic card. It was light gray, with the words "Property of ESLPD" on the front and a UPC barcode on back. Taylor turned up her nose as if the detective had just sneezed in her hand.

"What does the East St. Louis Police Department want with me?" she asked.

The detective grimaced slightly. Taylor couldn't help but notice the expression was similar to the one she, herself, had offered Nurse Kim.

"Sorry."

Taylor pulled out her VEE and scanned the card's bar code.

"A summons?" she said. "Are you serious?"

"Grand jury expects to hear your testimony at two o'clock today at the courthouse downtown. I suggest you be there by one."

"But my shift goes until five. Couldn't I come after that?"

"Sorry, but no. We need your testimony. You'll be the star witness if they can't get Ms. Chiang to testify. I'm curious, though, why you didn't tell anyone she was pregnant. It only strengthens the case against him, you know."

Taylor drew her chin upward. "Detective Sparks, I'm not here to help the prosecution. My concern is for my patient. Assuming she were pregnant, which I'm not confirming, one way or the other, she would be forced now to terminate the pregnancy, and that would be detrimental to my patient's recovery. Don't you have any compassion, Detective?"

The detective's face relaxed into a smile.

"Call me Beverly. I'm sorry if I offended you. Of course, I realize your job is to protect your patient. Tell you what… I promise not to tell anyone she's pregnant, and you agree to testify, okay?"

Taylor sighed. "It's not like I have a choice, right?"

"Thank you," the detective said with a grin, and held out her hand, again.

Taylor begrudgingly smiled despite her irritation. "I'd like to say it's my pleasure," Taylor answered, matching the detective's grip, "but you don't know my boss. She won't be happy. I'll have to reschedule some procedures."

Beverly motioned for Taylor to sit, and politely held the chair for her.

"Are you referring to Dr. Franklin?" she asked, taking a seat across the table. "She's a real pain in the ass, that one."

"Oh, you have no idea."

"Yes, well, I talked to Franklin already, and she said the hospital would fall apart if she let everyone take off whenever they chose. She said I didn't have the right to mess with her schedule."

Taylor laughed and nodded. "That sounds like her."

"But she finally agreed when I assured her you would make up for any lost time."

"Oh thanks," Taylor said sarcastically. "You know she'll hold me to it."

"I hope so. In fact, I'm counting on it." When Taylor gave her a sideways look, Beverly explained with a grin. "Franklin agreed to let you make it up by doing a few hours of community service."

"Community Service? I'm being punished for testifying?"

A dimple appeared in Beverly's left cheek. Taylor hadn't noticed it before.

"Not exactly. I was thinking more along the lines of… dinner? With me? We could go to Luciana's tonight after the trial."

Taylor instinctively glanced at the detective's left ring finger. It was bare.

"Why, Detective, are you asking me out on a date?"

The dimple got deeper. "I'm trying to."

Taylor looked away. She had not been on a date in years—not since Rebecca.

"I haven't offended you again, have I?" Beverly asked her.

"No, no. It's not that."

"Well, of course, you're under no obligation. I realize this is probably bad timing and I'm being terribly unprofessional…"

"It's okay," Taylor said and looked into Beverly's eyes. Finally, she nodded. "I'd love to go to dinner with you tonight, Detective."

Later, as Beverly was walking away, Taylor turned the summons over again and thought about Annie, her anesthesiologist friend, and how pleased she would be to know that Taylor had just accepted a first date.

TWENTY-FIVE

Now officially charged with assault, battery, and rape, Jordan lay on his cot with one elbow bent across his swollen eyes, and tried to block out his surroundings. He heard the slap of cards from a cell to his right, an occasional wheezy cough from down the hall, and the occasional belching woosh from the overhead supply air, but no hint of Kat. It was as if she had never existed.

Why can't I hear her? he wondered. *And why hasn't she come to vouch for me?*

It felt so strange to be without her. For as long as he could remember they had shared every thought, even the shameful ones he had tried, at first, to hide from her.

"What are you doing?" he remembered her asking him once when they were still pre-adolescent.

Nothing! he had replied. *Mind your own business for once, will you?*

But, of course, that hadn't been the truth. He had awakened from a strange, sensual dream and had experienced a tight, almost painful yearning. Usually, Kat slept soundly through the night, but her sudden inquiry had startled him, and he hadn't known what to do. So, like the child that he was, he lied and got angry. Over the next few months, his urges grew more painful and more difficult to hide. Finally, in intense embarrassment he had told her what was happening. To his amazement, she hadn't laughed, but had said she wanted to know more. They experimented then, sharing the excitement of mutual discoveries. Who could have guessed those innocent days would have led him to this?

How ironic, he thought, to be accused of rape while he was still technically a virgin. And how equally absurd that while lying here in jail with broken ribs and burnt testicles, he could possibly be thinking of sex.

By age sixteen, Jordan knew he could have any girl he wanted. As Senator Danforth's eldest son, he was a minor celebrity in Missouri. Several of his younger brothers were already sexually active, he knew, regardless of what their father preached, but Jordan couldn't bring himself to be with another girl. The thought of Kat listening was unimaginable to him. He would rather cut off an arm than to hurt her.

His brothers and friends talked a lot about sex, but no one talked much about love. Not in New Canaan. Jordan didn't know if what he felt was love or an obsession, but over the years his urges grew more intense. He needed more from Kat than her thoughts. He wanted to touch her and to feel her body next to his. Finally, he had insisted that they meet.

And look what that insistence cost me! he thought. In frustration, Jordan pounded his free fist on his cell's concrete wall.

He heard a door open down the hall and footsteps approach. He winced and sat up. The musty cot's metal springs protested, also. The olive-skinned woman who stopped outside his cell was wearing a three-piece pinstriped suit that accentuated her curves, and her hair had been pulled back in a sleek, tight bun. He was getting used to the Lytoky look, but he had to admit he didn't like it; it was too manly. The thought surprised him; it sounded like his father.

"Hello Mr. Brown," the woman said, revealing a slight accent. "Or should I call you Mr. Danforth? I'm Myrna Garcia, the Lytoky's District Attorney. You really should have told us earlier who you were. It could have saved us all a lot of trouble."

When he started to correct her, to explain that he had told them last night several times (and again during the lineup this morning), she disregarded him with a wave of her hand.

"No matter. Now that we know, it will speed things up."

A guard carried in a padded metal chair and set it down outside the bars.

"Thank you, Sue," Myrna said with a wink, and waved the guard away. She waited until they were alone before she spoke again. "Anyway, things are different now." In her accent, the word came out "DEEfrint."

Jordan read between the lines. His case was now political.

"Why? What did my father say?"

"Oh, we haven't contacted him yet."

"Don't bother. He won't help."

"Oh, on the contrary. He will be quite helpful, whether he wants to be or not. Once news gets out that you are his son, he will be calling us to make a deal. Don't worry. You'll be out of here in a jiffy."

It sounded like, "JEEfy."

The fluorescent lighting danced in the D.A.'s eyes. She made it seem as though any concerns Jordan might have were preposterous.

"So, what do you want from me?"

"I'm so glad you asked."

She pointed her V-Pad's camera feature toward him and looked up hopefully. "We need a statement."

"A what?"

"The press requested a confession for the twelve o'clock news." She repositioned the camera and paused expectantly.

Jordan blinked and shook his head.

"You don't understand. I'm innocent…"

"Oh, right," Myrna huffed and lowered her arm. "I forgot you changed your plea. Let's see… what did you say last? Here it is. 'It's not me! They tortured me to confess! I didn't mean what I said!" She paused and raised one eyebrow, as though expecting Jordan to interject. When he didn't, she continued. "Look, I've heard it all before, young Danforth. Save it for the jury. We've got a lot of work to do and if you play your cards right, you'll be back in New Canaan before supper."

Jordan stared at her in astonishment as she readjusted her V-Pad.

"You mean you don't even want to hear my side?" he said.

"Doesn't matter," she said, with an air of impatience. "This is your first offense. Well, second, if they count illegal immigration, which they undoubtedly will…" She said this last almost to herself. "But still, as Senator Danforth's son you will likely be extradited back to New Canaan. All you have to do is confess."

"But I'm charged with rape!"

"Yes; this is true." Myrna did not even look up.

Jordan studied her face. She kept playing with her V-Pad, aiming it at him, but she had not yet looked him in the eye.

"They're going to kill me, aren't they?" he asked her.

"What? Oh, no, of course not. Your father will likely claim no crime was committed, and then we'll…"

"How's that?"

Myrna looked at him, at last, in confusion. "You know… since New Canaan goes strictly by the book (by the Bible that is), your crime isn't illegal over there, so he'll probably claim diplomatic immunity for you."

Holding his left side with his good hand, Jordan stood and walked toward the bars.

"Rape isn't a crime in New Canaan?"

"Well, no. Not according to your laws. Don't you know this?" She looked up at him at last, and Jordan wrinkled his brow. "Well," Myrna said, seeming pleased to share her knowledge of New Canaan law, "if she were pregnant and had lost the child, you would have to pay her restitution. The amount can vary from case to case, but I think the going rate is about a year's salary… assuming you were working."

"Killing an unborn baby isn't murder?"

"You seriously don't know this? It's YOUR Bible. Anyway, killing Ms. Chiang would have been punishable by death, of course, but since you merely raped her…"

"I didn't rape her!" Jordan smacked the bars with the palm of his good hand.

Myrna flinched, then started over.

"As I was saying, since you are only ACCUSED of rape…" she raised an 'unlikely' eyebrow, "…you can only be punished 'wound for wound.' That means that if you confess, depending on the severity of her condition, the most you could get for that offense is permanent castration. But even then, that would only be if you permanently damaged her child-bearing capabilities."

"What if I don't confess?"

Myrna gave him another sharp look. "Everyone confesses. Besides, you already did once. This is only a formality."

"No. I refuse to confess."

"But even if-"

"Absolutely not."

***

Myrna lowered her V-Pad and glared at the accused. If she came back empty-handed, Waverly Nelson would be upset. The Lytoky needed a confession. Without one, the case could never advance to a Three-Strikes trial. Sexual Assault was only one of multiple charges her office had thrown at him, including Breaking and Entering, and Battery.

For the most heinous crime to stick, however, she needed a confession. Jordan's DNA did not match the samples taken from the victim, and he was already in Immigrations when the alleged crime took place. Hell, the victim didn't even identify him correctly, according to Myrna's sources. If the boy didn't confess, how could she possibly convict him?

TWENTY-SIX

The negotiations went quickly. Too quickly, in Paul's opinion. The minute President Buford arrived she agreed to drop all charges provided he release her daughter at once. He agreed, of course, but not without conditions. First, he wanted a full pardon on live TV for this and all his previous crimes. He also wanted an official escort back to New Canaan (complete with limousine, flags, and a parade), and a generous monthly stipend for the rest of his life. The woman had agreed so quickly, he regretted not asking for more.

What a pussy!

While he waited for the news crew to set up outside, he slicked back his hair and straightened the collar on his torn paisley shirt.

Too bad I used my sleeves last night to tie up the girl's wrists! he thought.

"Testing… One… Two…" he heard someone call over a bullhorn. "The crew is ready!" Paul ran to the bedroom's wall teleVISOR and flipped the unit on just as the words, "We interrupt this program to bring you the following important message…" was replacing the Emergency Broadcasting Tone.

While Paul watched, the screen blinked, and President Buford appeared. In the background, he saw the cabin and the front door where he had entered last night. He knelt before the screen to get a better look. She read from a prepared script granting him unconditional immunity, just as they had agreed, then looked up at the camera.

"I have upheld my end of the bargain," she said. "Are you ready to uphold yours?"

On National TV? he thought, as he turned to yank open the bedroom door. *You bet I am!*

***

Paul stepped into the cabin's front room only to find it empty. He frowned, ready to retreat back inside the bedroom, when he noticed a crowd of smiling reporters outside.

Now that's more like it! He strutted across the bear-skin rug and past the kitchenette.

Lieutenant Winters was surprisingly strong for a woman, he thought later. Just as he reached the front door, she pounced on him from behind, kneed him in the back, and yanked his arms back taut behind him. *She must have been hiding behind the kitchen counter!* he realized. Two other guards rushed in, he assumed from the bathroom, and cuffed him. He barely noticed the team of paramedics who ran past.

"Are you getting this?" he cried and strained his neck to address the gawking reporters outside. Someone kicked him hard in the jaw. When he rolled sideways, he saw the media dispersing.

"Wait! Where are you going?" he choked at them. "She promised me freedom; you heard her! The whole world heard her!"

With the lieutenant still holding him down, he watched as a tall woman with Captain insignia on her chest approached him.

"Where is she?" the Captain asked.

"Where's who?"

"Kat Buford, you monster! What did you do with her?"

He looked up, and his eyes widened as a paramedic handed the captain a blonde wig and pink paisley strips. His head twisted back to the bedroom and saw another paramedic stripping bloody sheet from the empty bed.

"No! She was there; honest! She must have run off while I slept!"

As the lieutenant yanked him to his feet, Paul felt his newfound taste of freedom slipping away.

"Tell me where she is!" she said.

"But I'm free!" he choked, his eyes wide in bewilderment. "You... she gave me her word!"

"President Buford isn't here yet!" she said. "She doesn't even know who you are!"

It was the last thing he heard before the lieutenant covered his head with a pillowcase.

TWENTY-SEVEN

Lieutenant Alex Winters had a sick feeling she was going to be in serious trouble before all this was over. The Lytoky Police had already escorted Kat's attacker off the Oasis in shackles, but Alex had remained behind to join in the search for the missing girl.

It was the least that she could do, she thought. *After all, I was the one who let that beast onto the island!*

Yesterday afternoon she had been away on a "personal errand" (aka ordering booze) during the man's Immigrations interview, so she hadn't been the one to approve him for transport. Even if she had, the man had a valid iris scan, so no one could be held accountable for that. Her friend, Private Saragusa, wasn't even in trouble for not holding him back last night due to his Tunnel reaction. Per procedure, male escorts who experienced distress going underground (just like the young man Alex had held back yesterday) were to be held overnight for observation unless they had been specifically requested by a paying customer. If they were scheduled to meet someone on the other side, all the rules were different. The Oasis patrons expected their escorts to be transported regardless of their experience. This was a customer-friendly operation, after all.

No, it wasn't until Captain Chad received that mysterious call this morning that Alex had started to sweat. She and her captain had been waiting for President Buford's jet to arrive when someone from Cis-Star had called in a panic. After Alex had confirmed the man's appearance last night, the woman on the Captain's VEE had cried out, "MA'AM help us! That's not Jordan!"

Apparently, Kat's attacker was an escaped rapist from Rock Island Prison whose iris scan and report had been switched with the senator's son. Alex had heard the woman direct Captain Chad to "get that monster out of that room at once, no matter what it takes!"

Chad had instantly gone into attack-mode after that. She ordered her IT personnel to rig up a Uniray message on the spot, with an actor playing Buford's part to deliver a fake Presidential Pardon and promise the man anything he wanted.

How could I have been so stupid? Alex thought now, as she moved along a narrow, abandoned path. *If only I had read his file, or at least read his goddamned NAME on the file, I would have known something was wrong! His file said he was Senator Danforth's son. Obviously, Danforth doesn't have a middle-aged son! I could have stopped that monster from setting foot on the Oasis! It's all my fault!*

She stepped over a fallen tree and heard a dry twig snap. She kept looking for tracks but had so far seen nothing but rhododendron and trees.

Other distant search party voices called out Kat's name, behind her, but they were all searching the blazed trails. The path Alex had chosen was animal-made, and unmarked. She knew the path well; it was the shortcut to the beach she had last walked with Robert. Just ahead, for instance, she knew there was a clearing—the one where she and Robert had first made love. As she got closer, she remembered the strong, earthy odor, and how contented she had been that night, bedded down in a sleeping bag with the man she had thought was her life-long mate.

Life-long my ass! she thought, trudging past. *MA'AM, I need a drink!*

She slapped her front jacket pocket. Empty. The flask was back in her cabin, or maybe the Jeep.

Fool! she scolded herself. *You knew what trail this was when you volunteered to search it. Did you really think you could forget?* She should have known better than to fall for Robert's lies, she told herself. Men aren't interested in love or family, she knew; all they care about is sex. Why else would he have run off in the middle of the night when he was done with her, she wondered. Why else would he have left her pregnant and alone?

Ancient history, she sniffed and started off again. *Doesn't matter now.*

But what about Kat? her conscience nagged at her. *It's your fault she's out here somewhere, hurt or dying! If you had followed procedure last night and verified Brown's eye scans instead of rushing through your chores, you would have discovered something was wrong. Amateur forgery: you should have caught that! You let an escaped convict onto the island—one incarcerated for RAPE, no less!—you should be ashamed of yourself!*

Alex wiped away a tear and kept walking.

And what about security? You shut down the cameras last night for your stupid Delivery, and now no one knows where the girl went. This is your fault!

Alex was crying now, blindly pushing through the brush, not paying attention to the scratches, or her steps.

How stupid could you be? You should have known that man was dangerous. No wonder Robert abandoned you. You even let them take your son!

Sudden sunlight flooded her face and reflected off her wet cheeks. She had exited the forest wall and was now standing on the beach, nearly hyperventilating from her angry sobs. She hadn't even known that she was crying. The waves rolled loudly, comfortingly, as she wiped her nose and cheeks. She closed her eyes, letting the sunlight work its healing magic. The heat felt good on her face.

I will make it right, she vowed. *I will!*

At last, she opened her eyes and squinted left. In the distance, she saw something lying on the sand where the forest met the beach. A log, perhaps? Seagulls were squatting near it. *Waiting?* She took a few tentative steps in that direction to get a better look, then broke into a run. There, in the sand, lay a crumpled girl—the one Alex had left behind at the cabin last night. Only, now her hair lay twisted in wet, matted clumps, and her pale bare arms, chest, and legs were crisscrossed with cuts and scratches. Her swollen lips were bloody, and both eyes were matted with dried blood.

Alex fell to her knees beside the still body, spattering more sand onto the girl's chafed skin, and listened for a pulse. An instant later, she collapsed over the girl as her own body shook with relief.

She's alive!

161

TWENTY-EIGHT

Kat regained consciousness just before take-off. She blinked up in quiet wonder to find herself wrapped in a blanket, with her head in her mother's lap. Her mom's chin seemed to be quivering as she stared outside her private jet's cabin window.

Is Mom crying?

As if in response, a teardrop landed on Kat's cheek.

"Mom?" she asked. Her voice came out weak, but her mother immediately smiled down and stroked her hair.

"It's okay, Sweetheart," she said. "I'm here! Everything's going to be all right."

Despite the smile, Kat thought her mother had never before looked so old or so sad. Kat tried sitting up, but a stabbing pain in her head and hip made her gasp. Along with the physical discomfort came memories from last night. *The cabin! The rug! His hands!*

"That man!" she cried.

"Shh now," said her mother, and instantly pulled her close and rocked her back and forth while someone else yelled for a medic. A few seconds later she felt a sharp sting on her arm.

Kat's movements felt instantly heavier, and she noted a tingling sensation start spreading from her chest to her head. Another tear from above trailed down her gritty cheek, and she felt her mother gently wiping it away. Unlike the hazy, humid terror inside her mind, her mother's fingers felt cold and real. Kat borrowed strength from their shocking coldness, and let the narcotics, and the jet's forward momentum, pull her away.

The Waves of Dissonance

***

Suddenly, just as the plane lifted off, her inner mind popped open. Like the loud "Coming Attractions!" reel in a previously quiet cinema, the booming voices in her head made her jump.

"I didn't do it, I tell you! I've never seen that woman before!"

Jordan? She tried opening her eyes, but her thick lids wouldn't budge. *Is that really you?* she wondered. *Am I dreaming?* She heard Jordan talking to someone, yelling, in fact, and realized he hadn't yet perceived she was there.

"I don't care if the victim identified me," he was saying. *"I didn't do it, and I won't confess!"* There was a lull in the conversation, and she felt him sensing her presence. *"Kat? Kat, is that you?"*

Jordan? Combined with the drugs, Jordan's voice felt like a hug from a long-lost friend. It made her feel happy. And sleepy.

"Kat! Where have you been?"

Having had the advantage of sensing him first, as well as having been heavily sedated, she sensed her thoughts were harder for him to read.

"What happened to you?" he asked her. *"Why did you disappear?"*

In the background in his world, she heard someone shouting. At him? At her? Her mind was swimming; she couldn't be sure. She felt a lock of hair being gently brushed off her face, and turned, automatically, toward the warmth of her mother's lap.

Everything's going to be okay, now, she thought, repeating her mother's words to Jordan as she nodded back to sleep.

TWENTY-NINE

"What do you mean he won't confess? He already has!" Waverly's words hung in the air as the District Attorney's on-screen image stared back.

"I know, I know," said Myrna Garcia. "But he refuses to make it formal."

"Well he can't just change his mind!" Waverly said. "What does he think this is? A game show?" She paced her office, aware that she was crossing onto and off the D.A.'s screen. She was still at her Boston satellite office and was impatient to leave. "Doesn't matter," she said at last, pausing abruptly. "We already have his confession from last night. Use that."

"We can't. The footage shows him being tortured, uh, I mean, interrogated. Believe me, it isn't a good visual."

Waverly sat down and tented her fingers under her chin.

"You're right, of course," she said. "We can't show the public that. It will only make him look pathetic." She had seen the recording earlier. To those with weaker minds, it might garner the boy sympathy.

"Ms. Nelson?" Myrna ventured, tentatively. "The boy was in Immigrations when the rape occurred, and the lab tests prove his innocence. With all due respect, I believe we should drop the charges and start searching for the real rapist. He could still be out there somewhere."

Waverly leaned toward her screen's camera and frowned.

"Are you questioning me, Counselor? Look here, I know who the real rapist is and believe me, he will pay. All men will! Right now, though, we have a crisis on our hands. Do you know who you are holding in that cell over there? That's Senator Danforth's son, New Canaan's virtual Heir-Apparent, and I am not going to waste this opportunity on a technicality. I'm depending on your help, Myrna. We must make an example of the boy. You don't want to let the Lytoky down, now, do you?"

"N- no. Of course not."

"Then believe me when I tell you this case will go to trial. I want Jordan Danforth convicted, and the only thing I want to hear from you is how you intend to do it!"

Myrna froze. Waverly could read her thoughts as easily as if she had implanted them. *What can I legally do besides let the boy go free?* Myrna's astonished face seemed to say.

"Listen, I need you to do whatever it takes to convict him," Waverly pushed harder.

"I- I don't think I can do that," Myrna said.

"Well, luckily I can!" In exasperation, she pulled up her Uniray program. Seems she would need to "suggest" more strongly to Myrna that she cooperate. Maybe this time she would tell her to plant evidence or change the test results.

"I don't have time for this!" she said and ground her teeth. "Kat needs me. I should be with her right now, not babysitting the help!"

To extract Brown quickly from the cabin and to preempt needless and time-consuming, negotiations, Waverly had told Captain Chad her captive's true identity and told her to extract him, pronto! She did not confide how she knew his name, however, so now she had some major damage control to settle.

And the faster I handle it, she thought, *the sooner I can be at my daughter's side!*

"How come I'm the only one around here who can get things done?" she fumed.

"Um. Pardon?" Myrna said.

Having forgotten the District Attorney's presence, Waverly looked up. Without a word, she quickly swiped that connection closed and resumed typing.

Stupid A-sensitives, she thought, recognizing that Myrna had not been receptive to any of her previous Adray programming. *To hell with her!*

This case will go to trial, and when I'm through, women everywhere will be demanding Danforth's blood!

THIRTY

It was an unexpected treat for Danforth to see the new Madam President groveling. All morning, he had been in a baffled daze wondering how he could have lost. *Didn't any women vote for me? What about the men? How could so many have gone over to the other side?* But now, Pat Buford was here on his screen with some crazy story about Katherine being hurt and her needing his help. None of it made sense. Over his desktop teleVISOR screen, Danforth studied his rival's face closely. She looked particularly old this morning.

Must be all that celebrating last night, he frowned.

"So, that's why the doctor requested her adoption records," she was saying.

Adoption records? The timing was awfully suspicious, he thought. Why would she want them now when she had never asked for them before? If this was some kind of ploy meant to further damage or humiliate him, she sure wasn't wasting any time.

"Sorry to hear about Katherine," he said. "But I'm not sure why I should help."

"Because you're the only one who knows how to obtain them, of course," she said.

"No, no. I understand why you came to me. I'm asking what's in it for me."

Buford's mouth opened slightly, then it closed. He liked it that he'd stunned her... for a moment, at least.

"Do it for her, Marshall," she said. "For old times' sake. It's your chance to be a hero, to show the world your compassionate side."

Good Lord, he thought. *She's exhausting every trick in the book. First, she tried begging, now she's appealing to my ego. Next, she'll probably try threatening me.*

Over the years, these two had clashed on every social issue imaginable. His distrust, by now, was nearly instinctual.

"They are keeping her sedated," Buford pressed on, "to help her injuries heal. But in the meantime, they need to know if she has any family history of mental illness."

Danforth whirled on her.

"Mental illness? Are you serious? Katherine isn't crazy; you just said she was attacked and bumped her head! If anything, she probably has a concussion! They should check for brain damage."

"They have," Buford nodded, "and luckily all her scans are fine." She paused, and acted like she was reluctant to say something, so he folded his arms and waited. After a heavy sigh, Buford continued. "She's hearing voices in her head, Marshall. The doctor mentioned possible schizophrenia."

"Bullshit!" he laughed. "Listen, I don't know what you're selling, Pat, but I'm not buying. Go make a fool out of some other fool!"

***

Pat Buford could not believe her ears. Was Marshall really going to sit there, spewing nonsense like an idiot, and refuse to help? How could he be so spiteful? She stared at him over the secure line from her makeshift office at the hospital and wondered how he had turned out this way.

She had answered all his questions about last night and this morning to the best of her ability, but she still didn't know all the details, herself. (She didn't know why Katherine had been at the Oasis in the first place, for instance, or why there had been some mix-up with her attacker's identity and why that mix-up was top-secret.) But she had to do something! Getting these medical records was the only constructive thing the doctor had suggested she do, so she was determined to get them... even if she had to beg. Or threaten.

"I'm warning you," she said. "The man who attacked her is one of yours, Marshall, so you had better take all of this seriously!" It felt good to raise her voice.

Danforth seemed unmoved. He licked his fingers and wiped them on his trousers. He had been eating a brownie while she talked, and now a dark smudge stood out above his upper lip.

"Assuming anything happened at all," he said, and shook his head thoughtfully, "how could this possibly be my fault? Or my problem?"

"His name is Paul Brown. Remember him? He was Number One on the so-called 'Pardon List' you kept threatening to release if you won. Maybe you let this man escape on purpose in retaliation for your loss."

"I did not!" His eyes widened.

"Doesn't matter. Who do you think the people will believe? It's quite a coincidence, don't you think?" She let him stew on that for a moment, then added, "Can you imagine what will happen to the person responsible for bringing back sexual violence into the Lytoky? If it's you, then MA'AM help us; it could start a war! Women will demand that New Canaan be abolished, or at least that men be pushed even farther west from the border. Your men don't want that. They'll distance themselves from you so fast you'll wish you'd never heard the name Paul Brown!"

She could see she finally had his full attention. His brownie smudge had begun to dissolve.

"Hmm... Paul Brown...." he said, his eyes darting back and forth in thought. "Yes, that name sounds vaguely familiar. No doubt it is public record I was going to pardon him if I won."

He paused, and she could almost see his mind percolating by the erratic movements of his eyes. When he spoke again, it was almost like watching a drowning man flailing to stay afloat.

"But I didn't win, did I? And I didn't pardon anyone or help anyone escape! Nobody can prove that! How could they? I wasn't there; I didn't do anything! Wait! I bet I know what happened! I bet she's not even hurt! You're probably making the whole thing up to discredit me!" He began talking slower now, having latched onto an idea. "That's it, isn't it? This was her first time, right? Ah! I can see by your face it's true! That explains everything! She was a virgin, and it hurt! I hear that's common the first time."

169

"How dare you!" Pat exploded.

"No!" Danforth roared. "How dare YOU! Come on, Patty; your string is showing! Everyone knows a woman can run faster with her skirt up than a man can with his pants down. If something happened, she must have wanted it to. The Oasis is a brothel, after all! You think I don't know? Why else was she there if she didn't want to get laid?"

"You misogynist bastard!" she spat between clenched teeth. "That attitude is precisely why we created the Lytoky—so that we don't have to live in fear. You blame the woman for being at the 'wrong' place at the 'wrong' time, but there should BE no wrong place! No wrong time! You preach that women are the 'evil temptress' in your god dammed Garden of Eden, so you men naturally think you're justified in treating women like objects. Why don't you teach your men to take responsibility for their actions, to act like civilized human beings instead of insinuating women must have 'asked for it' in some way? Rape is not a biological act; it's socially programmed! Rape-free societies have always existed when men and women are perceived as equals!"

Did Danforth just yawn? Unbelievable!

She stopped talking and felt her heartbeat pounding in her ears. She felt almost out of breath, as though she'd been running up a flight of stairs. She watched, incredulous, as he licked a chocolate smudge from under one nail.

"Are you done?" he said. "Listen, we're not on stage, and this isn't a campaign speech. Katherine will be okay; you said so, yourself. Besides, we both know you wouldn't even have a daughter if it weren't for me. So let's cut the bullshit. We both know what this is about: politics."

"What? No. Surely you don't believe that!"

"Like hell I don't," Danforth said, and leaned back in his chair. "You can't blame me for this. It wasn't until you declared yourself President that the 'Gloria-thing' happened... and now Katherine? It's all been happening on your watch, Sweetheart, so maybe it's a warning! Maybe my men are planning to revolt and to take back what's theirs. Face it, Patty, men are the stronger sex. We always win."

Pat glared at him. He had never called her Patty before today.

"Have you gone insane? I didn't 'declare' myself President, Marshall; I won, remember? This isn't a coup-attempt to oust you from office.

You're not IN office. Or haven't you noticed?" She took a deep breath, trying to return to mission.

"Look," she said, purposefully lowering her voice. "I was hoping it wouldn't come to this. I had hoped you would agree to do the right thing before I had to tell you the bad news, but you leave me no alternative. Your son, Jordan, was arrested last night in East St. Louis, and is a suspect in that 'Gloria-thing.' The trial begins today. You know what happens next."

Danforth's mouth snapped open. He studied her, then waved a meaty hand.

"Good try, Patty. Jordan is home, so you're lying! Besides, even if you had him, you couldn't keep him; he's my son. He'd have diplomatic immunity. I'd have him home by nightfall, and you know it!"

"You think so?" Pat said, feeling unwelcome malevolence stretch across her face in the guise of a smile. "You really think so? For your information, Jordan has been charged with rape: a capital offense. If he's convicted, he will die."

***

Danforth frowned and lowered his gaze. He smelled body odor and knew it must be his. He glanced out his office window, momentarily confounded, then back at her.

"Well, then what do you want from me?" he said.

"I already told you! I want Katherine's medical history. I need information on her parents, including their mental health."

"Or what?"

Pat sighed, but he could see her jaw muscles clenching. "Look, I know you're trying to act tough," she said, "but you must be worried about your son. Surely, his arrest is a mistake. I remember Jordan; he seemed like an okay kid. Right now, I need to concentrate on Katherine, but I promise to have someone investigate his case. Or better yet, come over and see him for yourself. I'm here in East St. Louis now. Maybe we could even meet and together figure something out."

"You must think I'm a fool! As soon as I step foot on Lytoky soil you'll probably trump up false charges against me, too! No, thank you! I'll contact Jordan from here!"

"But what about Katherine?"

"I'll send you the stupid files. They're redacted, anyway." He started to dismiss her, then blurted, "And don't you dare interfere with my transmission to Jordan!"

Good Lord, did I just give her an idea?

He hung up and glared out his office's floor-to-ceiling windows while he pondered his chin with his fingers. If he called into Lytoky territory—*to a Lytoky jail, no less!*—Pat would have access to his communications. *And to who knows what else?* he thought. *I can't let that happen!*

Then an idea surfaced.

Of course! he thought. *Marisa!* As Jordan's mother, she could cross the border without suspicion and without risking firewall contamination. *Problem solved.*

"There's more than one way to skin your teeth," he said as he placed the call to his wife.

THIRTY-ONE

From the witness stand, Dr. Taylor Bott sat facing the defendant. The boy's sun-bleached hair and young, handsome face made him look innocent enough, but Taylor wasn't fooled. She had seen his work up close.

At least there are bruises on his face, she thought. She hoped that meant Gloria had gotten in a few punches of her own. *Now it is up to me and the jury to finish off this wolf in sheep's clothing!*

Taylor had rushed here straight from the hospital about fifteen minutes ago, but already it felt like hours. The non-stop chatter over the P.A. system had been particularly draining in the antechamber outside the courtroom. Just like at the hospital, no one else seemed to hear the P.A. 'overspray,' as she called it. But unlike at the hospital, it was much louder. From the instant she had entered the municipal building until she hit the courtroom, itself, she felt as though she had stepped into a crowded, noisy restaurant, with nonstop words and phrases overlapping and drowning out all other thought.

Thankfully, here in the courtroom (as in the O.R. at the hospital) all was quiet.

As Taylor made her pledge to the New American emblem (a blue flag with a white, diagonal cross and red flame), she glared at the defendant.

I hope he gets the death penalty, she thought suddenly. *I'd like to watch him die.*

***

After the preliminary introductions, Taylor testified about Gloria's appearance and physical condition at the hospital last night. Gloria wasn't present (the court had allowed her to watch the proceedings from closed-circuit TV in another room since it caused her too much anxiety to be in the same room as the accused), so Taylor did not hold back. Under the prosecution's insistence, she shared each intimate detail of every medical test taken, and what it revealed. At the time, her only thought was for justice. (Later, when she heard her words repeated on the evening news, she felt sorry for the discomfort her testimony must have caused the victim, and was embarrassed by her own apparent callousness and how it looked as though she was enjoying herself on the stand.)

"The man who did this isn't human," she said at one point, offering her unsolicited opinion. "No sane person could do this to another! He must be an animal! He needs to be put down!"

The room exploded into cheers. It seemed the gathered crowd agreed with her.

"Order, order!" The judge pounded her gavel as the defense offered a half-hearted objection, but no one paid attention.

Later, when Myrna Garcia asked if the semen taken from the victim matched the defendant's DNA, Taylor offered her last words on the stand without hesitation.

"Yes," she lied. "It was an absolute match."

The courtroom rumbled quietly as Taylor's words sank in.

"Prosecution rests, Your Honor."

The judge called a five-minute recess and the bailiff hustled out the twelve-woman jury. Taylor stayed in the witness chair, temporarily forgotten and alone. Heads immediately bent in conversation at both counselors' tables. After a few minutes, Taylor decided to stretch her legs. She meandered over toward the jury box and to the door where the jurors had just disappeared.

Halfway there, she felt the faint, yet familiar buzz of uninvited words inside her mind. Unlike the broadcasts outside the courtroom, however, these words were clear and distinct. The phrase repeated and lingered in her brain like a medicinal aftertaste.

"YES. AN ABSOLUTE MATCH."

She turned and checked the others' reactions. The heads at the attorneys' tables were still bent, seemingly unaware, and everyone else in the courtroom seemed equally engrossed in their own conversations. Only her date, Detective Beverly Sparks, sat watching her with a curious—*or was that an accusatory?*—expression.

The door behind the jury box opened, releasing the bailiff, the jury, and a string of different phrases. The voice resonated with tuning-fork clarity.

"GUILTY!" it said. "FIND HIM GUILTY. WATCH HIM SUFFER AS HE DIES!"

Taylor stumbled back into the witness chair. When court resumed and Jordan's attorney spoke, Taylor barely looked up.

"No more questions for this witness, Your Honor."

On her way past the jury box, Taylor studied their collective faces. Even though the trial would go on for another four grueling hours, Taylor could see by their expressions it was already over.

THIRTY-TWO

By the time Kat came out of her drug-induced coma, the trial was nearly over. She had missed Dr. Bott's descriptions of Gloria's scarred vagina and the evidentiary exam results. She had even missed Gloria's emotional testimony and Jordan's prerecorded confession. What she did hear, as she slowly regained consciousness, was the voice of Myrna Garcia, the Lytoky's District Attorney.

"The Prosecution rests, Your Honor."

Hearing second-hand voices through Jordan's mind was not the same as hearing his thoughts. Foreign sounds and voices (those originating from outside Jordan's brain) were always filtered and distorted. For example, Kat loved listening to his mother, Marisa, but her voice didn't necessarily sound female. What came across, presumably by Jordan's own bias, held a touch of softness, as though defined by her character, itself. Recognizing voices this way was more powerful than in her direct world and made it seem almost as though she already knew them (or at least she knew how Jordan felt about them) with a single word.

Therefore, when Myrna Garcia spoke, Kat heard more than the crisp, blade-sharp tone of her voice. She felt the woman's anger and Jordan's mistrust. In contrast, the next voice she heard was so insipid it was almost like listening to waves. Even Jordan was having trouble paying attention.

"Your Honor, uh, I am going to prove beyond a shadow of a doubt that my client, uh-"

Kat frowned. Right now, millions of women were watching the trial over live TV, but even in her drowsy, near-dreaming state, she knew she

176

would not be one of them. After everything she had been through, she could not bear to see a man's face or to even think of Jordan as male.

In the background, she heard the public defender's speech wrapping up.

"Therefore, I would now like to call Senator Danforth's son to the stand."

With her eyes still closed, Kat held her breath and listened as Jordan was sworn in. She unconsciously balled her fists in an attempt to send him emotional support and was startled to feel an answering squeeze on her left hand.

"Katherine?" a voice beside her spoke. "Katherine, are you awake?"

A world of hospital-white caused her to squint when she opened her eyes. In the background, the trial continued in her head.

"State your name, for the record."

"Jordan Danforth."

"Let the record show that Jordan Danforth, and his alias, Paul Brown, are one and the same."

"So noted."

Her mother's eyes were puffy and bloodshot, but she smiled as she leaned over Kat's bed to kiss her forehead.

"Oh Katherine," she said. "I've been so worried! How do you feel?"

"I'm fine, Mom. Have you been here long?"

"Mr. Brown," said the public defender, calling Jordan by his official court name. *"Please tell us in your own words, of course, what happened when you came across the border last night."*

"Not long," her mother continued. The woman's grip was distracting. "I've been looking for your doctor but the nurse says she's out on a date. Can you believe that? At a time like this?"

In the background, Jordan's words were steady and strong.

"Yesterday, I crossed the border around ten and was immediately taken to Immigrations. I was there when the alleged crime took place."

"Objection! Your Honor, the Defense's own attorney acknowledged that a crime took place, so there's no cause to call it 'alleged.'"

"Anyway," said her mother, giving Kat's hand another squeeze, "I wanted to ask your doctor if I can take you home tomorrow. You'd like that, wouldn't you?"

"Yeah, Mom. That would be great."

"Sustained," came the judge's voice. *"The Court acknowledges that a crime was committed. The defendant is cautioned to keep his opinions to himself. Remember, young man, you are under oath, so answer the questions truthfully."*

Kat imagined the angry faces at his trial. Suddenly, she knew they would never listen, that they were going to find him guilty.

Tell them I was with you! she offered. *Tell them I can vouch for you!*

"No! You've been through enough already. Besides, they'd never believe me."

Just try! You have to do something! Tell them about our plans. Tell them about your father. Let me do it. I'll come there and testify!

"No!"

"No?" Kat heard he judge's voice thunder and realized Jordan must have mistakenly spoken to her out loud.

"Uh, no, Your Honor," he recovered. *"What I meant to say was, I told you the truth already. I was nowhere near the victim's house when the neighbors heard her screaming. I was already in custody at that time."*

"Liar! What about his confession?"

"Objection!"

"I was beaten to confess. They tortured me. At that point I would have said anything!"

"He's lying!"

"Order! Order! Ms. Garcia, is there something you would like to add?"

"Your Aunt Waverly stopped by earlier to see you," her mother's calm voice continued, not noticing Kat's shallow breathing. "I told her to check back later."

Kat threw off her blankets and grabbed her mother's arms.

"Mom! I need to be at Jordan's trial!"

Pat pulled back on the blankets.

"Nonsense, Dear. Lie back down now and relax. The doctor said you might get emotional. With all that adrenaline built up in your bloodstream, you're bound to feel agitated. You have to stop struggling, though, and relax so you can heal."

178

Kat surprised her mother by pushing her away and swinging her legs over the mattress' edge.

"You don't understand. He needs me!"

"We have a witness!" the District Attorney cried above the courtroom confusion. *"Your Honor, the victim identified him! Bailiff, play back the tape!"*

"Let me go, Mom! I have to testify! You don't understand. They're going to kill him if I don't!"

Feedback squealed the courtroom into silence, then Gloria's voice came over the loudspeakers.

"It was horrible! His eyes… they reminded me of a reptile's the way they looked at me."

"Describe him further, please?"

"Um… Blond hair… Muscular… Tan… Oh, and he had a twitch."

Kat sucked in her breath and froze.

"Katherine? Katherine dear, what's wrong?" Her mother, who had been struggling to keep her in the bed, now held her at arm's length. "Katherine?"

"Kat?"

Kat did not know what to say. Her skin stung, as though tiny shards of ice had suddenly pierced her flesh. She heard both Jordan and her mother calling her name but was unable to respond in words. Memories of last night, those she had tried to bury, came rushing back. Gloria's words shocked and confused her.

"He kept flicking his head, like to get his hair out of his eyes, but his hair was too short. It was some kind of nervous twitch, I suppose."

"I forgot about that," Kat said.

"WHAT?"

She felt Jordan's attention zeroing in on her as he put it all together. She could no longer hide what had happened. Jordan had deduced she was injured, of course, from the talk around her. He undoubtedly had heard about her blood loss, her injuries, and her concussion, but no one had mentioned assault. No one had ever questioned her the way they were grilling poor Gloria, so Kat had, so far, successfully hidden all memories of that monster deep inside.

"Forgot about what? Lie back, now. That's a good girl," said her mother, coaxing her back down gently. "I'll go get the nurse."

"How could I have forgotten?" Kat shuddered. She felt Jordan moaning. Now he was the one incapable of words.

"What's that, Dear?" her mother asked, pausing in the doorway. "Did you forget something?"

Kat remained silent. Her mother's brow furrowed, uncomprehending, and she came back to the bed.

"Are you okay?" she asked, bending over.

In the background, with his trial temporarily forgotten, Kat could sense Jordan waiting for her answer.

"The man at the Oasis," she spoke softly, without emotion. "I remember him twitching his head before he came at me."

"That bastard! I'll kill him!" she heard Jordan say, and then heard what sounded like a fist pound the witness stand.

Kat watched her mother's eyes as they widened in realization. "Oh Katherine," she said. "Oh, I'm so sorry!"

A few miles away, Jordan sank back against the witness chair.

"Oh Kat," he moaned. *"I shouldn't have pressured you to meet me. I'm so sorry."*

"It's not your fault," Kat said aloud to both her mother and to Jordan.

"Yes, it is," Jordan moaned.

"Oh, yes, it is," said her mother. "I should have been there for you."

In the background, Gloria's halted testimony continued over the courtroom speakers. *"Then he touched me... and..."*

"Stop it!" Kat moaned, covering her ears with both hands. Although the blow to the head on the coffee table last night had knocked her out, sparing her further assault and further injury except to her hip (where she'd fallen against the sofa), Gloria's words struck too close to home. She still remembered' that man's breath, and his hands. She felt violated and yet extremely lucky all at the same time. Everything Gloria experienced, Kat knew, could have happened to her.

"Stop it!" she heard a new voice wailing from inside the courtroom.

Gloria's prerecorded words throbbed and pulsated in her brain. *"...he pulled at my clothes, and then..."*

"Please make it stop!" Kat sobbed.

Inside the courtroom, she heard someone else begging the same thing.

***

Jordan listened in helpless silence as the bailiff clicked off the recording. The feeling of shock and bewilderment over what he had just learned made the scene around him surreal. He searched the room for the woman who had cried out. It was the same woman whose digitized voice had just sealed his conviction.

Gloria Chiang was on her knees, inside the doorway, sobbing. She evidently had just entered the courtroom and been shocked by her own previous testimony. He could only imagine the pain that memory must have caused her.

He also noted that no one in the courtroom moved to help her.

Jordan's testimony, strategically placed during prime-time programming, was clearly a ratings ploy. By now, the court knew about the iris scan mix-up, but since Jordan had entered the court system as "Paul Brown," he had been required to continue the proceedings under that name.

"Tom, Dick, or Harry.... who cares what we call him?" the District Attorney had argued off-screen during the preliminary proceedings when the public defender had objected to them using his alias. "As long as the public knows he's Danforth's son, the actual name on the file doesn't matter." The judge had agreed.

Portions of his previous confession (from last night) had already been allowed in as evidence. The jurors, gaping in horror, had watched the crime dramatically reenacted by actors on video while Jordan's pre-recorded voice narrated the scene.

"...I raped her. I tied her arms and legs together like a rodeo calf and left her there for dead..." It was a powerful image. Now, the jurors were studying Gloria. Her sobs filled the otherwise hushed courtroom and seemed to cement their conviction.

"Perhaps we could all use another recess," the judge finally decided.

Jordan hung his head as the Jurors scooted out. He was in no condition to argue.

THIRTY-THREE

Paul Brown's trial was held in Granite City, Illinois. Katherine was not present, nor was Gloria, Lieutenant Winters, or any other witness, for that matter. He sat alone inside a bare recording studio surrounded by three mirrored walls. He hoped that the mirrors were two-way glass, with someone back there watching. The fourth wall, behind him, was painted to resemble rich mahogany paneling, like in a real courtroom from his past.

The only furniture (besides his wobbly straight-backed chair), was the flimsy witness stand made of cardboard. Spying his reflection in the glass, he noticed the outer side looked like wood, but the corrugated, vertical cardboard ribs on the inside cheapened the whole experience for him.

When he had first awakened this afternoon, his hands had immediately flown to his broken nose. *Ouch!* That's when he remembered being kicked in the face this morning.

Did all that really happen? he wondered. It was still hard to believe. Just yesterday, he had been at the Rock. *Not the Ritz, mind you, but there were three squares a day and no one kicks you in the face… usually.* Now, he had broken ribs, an injured knee, a split lip and two broken front teeth. Not to mention the multiple bumps, bruises, and leg cramps from running around yesterday following the Voice.

And just what the hell was that about?

How had he felt compelled to follow the Voice's every direction? Not that he found anything it said distasteful, he recollected, but he liked to think he had more self-control than that. *Hell, that Gloria-chick wasn't even my type, for Christ sake! She was at least thirty!* He liked them young: like that other girl, in the cabin. *Now that was more like it!*

He shrugged. It bothered him that he hadn't been able to perform, there at the end, but that wasn't the Voice's fault. Nor was the fact that he had fallen asleep and gotten caught.

I'll leave all that out when I retell it to Leonard later, he thought.

He couldn't wait to see the look on the other prisoners' faces when he got back. He was glad the broads over here had finally stopped calling him Jordan Danforth and had started using his real name. If he had to go back to the Rock, he wanted full credit for his adventure.

Now they'll never call me Old Timer again, for sure!

Still, he was disappointed by the trial. He used to love the courtroom adrenaline. He fed off audience participation and got a rush from hearing their reaction. Even during his original trial, it had been a glorious and exciting trial.

Not like this, he sulked, looking around. Hopefully, at least, someone was behind that mirror watching him perform.

"Testing, one, two," came a voice over the loudspeaker. "Brown, can you hear us?"

He sucked in his stomach. Before he could answer, however, the Voice boomed in his head again. It was all-consuming, like at the Rock. Instinctively, he covered his ears, but just like last time, the blaring words were bearable. Through squinted lids, he spied a woman entering the room through a break in the mirrored wall. She had previously introduced herself in the deposition as his attorney. She was obviously unaffected by the Voice.

"Testing, one, two," came from the loudspeaker again.

"We hear you!" called the woman. "Let's do this."

"Okay then. In five, four, three…"

The lights intensified and the attorney stepped forward. He thought he spotted a listening device in her ear.

"Mr. Brown," she said, as though in the middle of a conversation, "perhaps you could start by telling us what happened last night in Fantasy Log Cabin #3."

Paul squinted at the attorney over the blaring words in his head. He hadn't heard everything she had said but he saw her expectant face and knew it must be his turn.

"Do I need to repeat the question, Mr. Brown?"

"N- n- no. I'm fine. I'm ready to tell you everything."

The attorney stepped back, and he looked directly at the camera as it zeroed in.

"Yesterday, I raped a woman," he began, repeating the Voice's first line. "I should be punished for it. I know it was a sin…"

He paused, then, and couldn't help adding a comment of his own.

"Well, maybe not a sin, exactly. I mean, where in the Bible does it say 'thou shalt not rape a woman'?" He counted off the commandments on his fingers, starting with his thumb. "'Thou shalt not commit adultery.' I'm not married, so I didn't commit that one! 'Thou shalt not lie, steal, or murder.'" Three more fingers down. "Nope; not those, either."

He wiggled his pinkie to continue when Myrna interrupted.

"We don't need a sermon, Mr. Brown. Why don't you just tell us what happened."

Paul shrugged and lowered his hands, giving the Voice time to readjust. Like a fish gasping for water, the next time Paul opened his mouth, he mindlessly repeated every word that flowed into his brain exactly as the Voice dictated.

THIRTY-FOUR

"Senator Danforth, any comments about the trial?"

"Do you feel responsible?"

"Are you going to resign?"

With nostrils flaring, Danforth pushed through the reporters. His great mass moved forward at an alarming speed considering his size, and the effort turned his face red. His white shirt was now damp in the armpits. He pumped his fists, as he had seen joggers do, and imagined himself going faster. Ahead of him, reporters scurried away at the last possible moment like sandpipers chasing waves.

By the time he reached the Info-Swirl's front plaza, the reporters had lost chase. Not because he outran them, he surmised with chagrin, but because the footage of him running was probably better from behind.

Only one reporter, Honey Campbell, waited for him at the storefront entranceway and held her ground. Before he could pull the door open, she squeezed in between him and the glass door and spoke—just loudly enough for only him to hear.

"Your son implicated you," she said. The words stopped him cold.

"He what?"

"He claimed you forced him to do it, that you brainwashed him. When this gets out, you're finished!"

Danforth tightened his thick fingers around the door's lever handle, debating whether to bench-press her out of the way, but he did not pull. Instead, he bent his sweaty face to hers.

"What do you want?"

***

Honey Campbell flinched. This was the closest she had been to a man in twenty years, but she needed to stay focused. Waverly Nelson had said she needed an interview, so Honey could not let her down.

Still, she couldn't help but recall the monster who had attacked her all those years ago at the Info-Swirl. Back then, she was only twenty years old and had gone there hoping to get an interview with the Info-Swirl's owner, Pearl Nelson. It was supposed to be Honey's big break into journalism. The MA'AM Revolution was just beginning, and she wanted to be a part of it. Instead, she had met the woman under far different circumstances—when the famous inventor had come to the hospital to offer her support after the attack.

"My company is taking action against abusive men," the kindly, older woman had said to her that day as she had patted Honey's hand. "We're creating a world where men can no longer hurt women like this. Join us in Salem when you're ready. Here's my personal number."

Honey always suspected that the world Pearl Nelson wanted to create (the Lytoky and the MA'AM Revolution, itself), was probably why she had been assassinated the following year, and the reason Pearl's granddaughter, Waverly, had eventually taken up the cause.

Honey understood the importance of this interview with Danforth. She believed in Man's hidden capacity for violence, how it was always lurking like a coiled snake ready to strike. Now, with Honey's help, Waverly was going to prove it. Most women in the Lytoky were already convinced, but the women out west needed a catalyst for change. Senator Danforth's son was going to be that catalyst.

"I want an exclusive interview!" she told him. "Agree right now or I'll share what Jordan said with the others." They both looked behind them and saw the other reporters unwinding their equipment and running toward them, having noticed the stand-off at the Info-Swirl door.

"Jordan is not my son!" Danforth said into Honey's ear.

"Then come on my show tomorrow and prove it. I'll interview you here at the Swirl: on your turf. What do you say?"

Danforth seemed to consider, then nodded. "Why not?" he winked, as if they had just made a dinner date. He yanked open the storefront door. Honey stepped clear just in time as the other reporters arrived, too late.

THIRTY-FIVE

As the judge called the trial back to order, Kat blinked at the dark teleVISOR hanging from a swing-arm on the hospital room wall, and decided she was finally ready to see Jordan's face.

I'm not afraid anymore, she thought, impulsively. *It's only a TV trial; it can't hurt me!* Besides, what if they executed him and this was her last chance to see him?

Her mother was down the hall consulting the nurses, so she had to move fast. While Jordan retook the stand and she heard the judge remind him he was still under oath, she turned on the overhead TV and held her breath. The courtroom scene looked exactly as she had imagined. The place was packed. Off to the right, she even thought she saw the back of her Aunt Waverly's bowed head; looking down as though she were playing on her VEE. Belatedly, Kat realized the court proceedings on screen were not in synch with the actual proceedings she could hear in her mind. On the teleVISOR screen, Jordan's previous testimony was only just beginning.

So much for live TV! she thought.

"Mr. Brown," his attorney began on screen. "Perhaps you can tell us, in your own words, of course, exactly what happened yesterday at 343 Plumb Street."

A moment later, before Kat had time to register the change in dialog, the camera zeroed in on the defendant's face.

"Yesterday," replied a familiar voice, "I raped a woman and I should be punished. I know it was a sin... Well, maybe not a sin exactly. I mean, where in the Bible...."

188

"Nooooooo!"

Kat felt her stomach revolt. She struggled with her covers but couldn't get untucked quickly enough. An instant later, her world went black.

***

They found her passed out on her side, caught up in her sheets and covered in her own vomit. On the teleVISOR above her, Paul Brown's face was confessing "Jordan's" sins.

THIRTY-SIX

Lieutenant Alex Winters had a nagging feeling that something else was wrong. Without access to last night's passengers' files, she had spent the entire trip back to Immigrations trying to piece together what she could recall in her head. Two thoughts kept resurfacing: who was Katherine *really* there to meet? And what had happened to the *real* Jordan Danforth?

By the time she arrived back at Immigrations, she thought she had figured it out.

Jordan must be that other young man who had experienced Tunnel Reaction last night! She had rather liked the serious young man she had interviewed, and had enjoyed watching him fight back with scripture of his own. She couldn't remember his name.

She went looking for him in Holding, where she had left him. When she couldn't find him, she went straight to the below-deck Disposition Officer, Private Saragusa.

"Where's the other 'remain-behind'?" Alex asked her. "You know, the blond kid with TRAAP syndrome?"

Saragusa barely looked up. She was busy printing out Boarding Passes for tonight's passengers. "Oh, you mean Paul Brown?"

Alex frowned. *Paul Brown? Yes, that sounded like the name the boy had given.*

"Didn't you hear?" Saragusa said, sounding astonished. "The Lytoky Police picked him up shortly after you pulled out. Turns out, your Mr. Brown was a naughty boy yesterday before coming here to us. He attacked a Cis-Star employee yesterday afternoon, can you believe it? It's all over the news."

"No, you must be mistaken," Alex said. "I'm talking about the kid I interrogated yesterday before my lunch break. The one who quoted bible verses? He was harmless."

"Yes, but you also thought that Robert was safe!" her friend's eyes seemed to say.

"Nope, the kid they arrested last night was named Brown; I'm sure of it. They collected him after an anonymous tip identified him by name. He fit the description perfectly."

"Which was…?"

Still semi-distracted by her check-in duties, Saragusa managed to keep up the conversation. "Someone tall, for one thing," she said. "And muscular and blond."

"That's all? That description matches my guy, too! Maybe they made a mistake."

"What do you mean, 'your' guy?"

When Alex didn't answer, Saragusa shrugged and continued. "No mistake," she said. "After the tip, I checked his iris scan, myself. Sure enough, he was flagged as an escapee from the Rock. He broke out yesterday during his own lunch break, so your timeline must be off. He couldn't have gotten here when you thought—unless you took a REALLY late lunch. You must be thinking of someone else"

Saragusa finally noticed Alex's face. "Oh! Right. The iris scan… Well, don't worry; since he never got on the train, it wasn't your mistake. It was a big group yesterday and everything was crazy. His iris-scan didn't flag an alert until just prior to the shuttle's departure. You would have caught it if you'd taken him on the shuttle. He's definitely the one."

Alex remained silent. It still didn't make sense.

The boy she left behind last night was certainly the real Jordan Danforth, she believed, and must be the one Kat had intended to meet. Brown must have somehow switched their iris scans so he could get away, but why had the boy agreed to the switch? Why hadn't someone else noticed the mistake? And why was he still in custody?

Saragusa tilted her head.

"You okay, Lieutenant? You don't look well."

"I'm fine," she said and turned away. She hated to lie to her friend while looking her in the eye. She hustled up the escalator and away from

191

her friend's curious stare. As she did, she tapped her lips, lost in thought, and wondered how the anonymous caller had known to ask for Brown by name. She could only think of one possible reason.

Someone is framing this innocent boy, she thought. *But why?*

THIRTY-SEVEN

"He'll be out shortly, Ms. Danforth," the guard said as she left.

To Marisa, the sterile Visitor's room looked more like an interrogations room than a place for her and Jordan to share some much-needed consolation time. She chose a chair facing the inner door (the one she presumed Jordan would enter) and rested her elbows on the table. A simple light hung overhead and reflected in the mirrored wall to her left.

The instant her husband had called with the news, she had paused only long enough to retrieve her purse and the family's VEE before heading out the door. As the only one in the family without a vehicle of her own, she had borrowed the groundskeeper's truck and driven it across the Mother Road Bridge. She left it running outside the East St. Louis Detention Center.

This was the first time she had been across the border since leaving Boston fourteen years ago. Now, waiting for Jordan to appear from the courtroom, she tried to prepare herself for the worst. Her son had been accused of rape, among other things. She knew it couldn't possibly be true, but would the Lytoky women believe her?

Probably not, considering he is Marshall Danforth's son. Hopefully, they won't convict him for that offense, alone!

Suddenly, a whoosh came from behind the closed Holding Room door. Ten seconds later, the door opened, and Marisa's hand flew to her mouth.

"Look what they've done to you!" she cried and tipped over her chair as she ran to her son.

The ankle chains slowed Jordan down. Wearing an orange jumpsuit, he cradled his left arm, which hung awkwardly in a sling. One eye was deep purple and swollen, but not shut, and his cheek had a bandage with what looked like stitches underneath. With her arms outstretched she paused, unsure where to touch him where it wouldn't cause him more pain.

"I can't even hug you!"

Jordan smiled and reached for her with his right hand. They stood clasping fingers until the guards closed the door. She guided her son to a chair and knelt beside him on the linoleum.

"Jordan?" she asked, looking up. "Are you okay?"

He looked at her and chuckled. After a beat, she also smiled at the absurdity of her question.

Then he wept. Her heart broke for him, and for herself. She reached for him and pulled his head gently to her shoulder as he sobbed. Jordan hugged her back with his good arm and sank into her warmth. On her knees, she rocked him—his body shuddering against hers—for the first time since his childhood.

It would be the last time she ever held her son.

THIRTY-EIGHT

"Thanks for a wonderful evening," Taylor said as the detective walked her to her apartment. "I had a really nice time."

"Did you?" Beverly asked. She was not so sure. Dinner had been a bust, in her opinion; her date had barely spoken the entire time.

"I know it doesn't seem like it," Taylor admitted, "but I did. I'm sorry I was so preoccupied, though."

"No need to apologize," Beverly said. "Well, good night!" She turned to go, but Taylor stopped her.

"Yes, I do need to apologize, and I need to explain. Want to come in?" She offered an embarrassed smile. "Please? I- I don't want to be alone."

Maybe tonight wasn't a total loss after all, Beverly thought, smiling back.

Inside Taylor's apartment was modern and clean.

"Make yourself at home," Taylor said once they were inside. "I'll go make some tea."

Beverly flipped on the TV then debated where to sit on the sofa. She did not want to appear too forward, but she wanted Taylor to know she was interested. Taylor had said she didn't want to be alone. *Did that mean she was finally ready to talk about the trial? Or that she wanted companionship? Did she just need a friend, or a lover?* Beverly wanted to be appropriately ready, either way.

As she pondered the pros and cons of edge-of-sofa versus middle, a familiar voice came from the teleVISOR screen. Today's earlier courtroom drama was being rebroadcast as a WLBC special edition.

Myrna Garcia, the Lytoky's District Attorney had just begun her cross-examination.

"Mr. Brown," Ms. Garcia said. "Perhaps you could tell us, in your own words, of course, exactly what happened in East St. Louis yesterday at 343 Plumb Street."

The scene shifted from the courtroom's wide-angled view to a narrower shot of a man's haggard face. Beverly frowned instantly. The man on screen was ugly and old. He was blond, had a receding hairline that exposed a scaly scalp, and his forehead was covered in age spots. This man was nothing like the handsome, young man she had seen in person.

"That isn't…" she said, frowning. In confusion, she started to call to Taylor, but stopped, not wanting to appear foolish. Many things about this trial had seemed odd. Maybe there was a simple explanation. *This is probably just some backstory footage I haven't seen before,* she thought. *Surely, the camera will soon shift to the defendant.*

"Isn't what?" Taylor asked, coming around the corner with a dishrag in her hand.

Beverly didn't answer but continued staring at the TV. The camera did not shift, and the more she stared, the more familiar the man seemed to be. It was as though her subconscious recognized him, even though her memory had not. She felt herself accepting him as the defendant despite what she had initially known to be true.

"Yesterday," said the man on the screen, "I raped a woman and I ought to be punished. I know it was a sin. Well, maybe not a sin, exactly…"

Behind her, Taylor gasped. Beverly turned and saw her date's mouth and eyes wide open. "Quick!" Taylor said. "Turn it off!"

Beverly complied at once. Still, they stood in awkward silence, unable to tear their gaze away from the now-blackened screen.

"That's not right," Taylor said at last. "That man isn't Danforth's son." She met Beverly's eyes, at last. "Or is he? I mean… I want to believe it's him, but… he's too old for one thing, right?"

Beverly didn't know what to say. Her own mind, at first, had known the image wasn't right, but she had a feeling that if Taylor hadn't insisted she turn off the unit when she did, she might have accepted him as Paul Brown by now.

It was time, she realized. Time to risk talking to Taylor about the Rebellion. She had once seen Taylor at a Statewide recruitment event, years ago, but she wasn't certain if Taylor had ever joined, or if she even remembered her.

In the silence that followed, the teapot whistled.

THIRTY-NINE

Marisa Danforth slumped against the elevator cab wall as though burdened by heavy luggage. Twenty years ago, when she and Danforth had toured the Info-Swirl together at its Grand Opening, it had been a happy day. Since then, she had only visited her husband's office two previous times in the entire three years he had been Senator. Her first had been right after he took office. The last had been about a week later, when she had walked in on him having sex with an aide.

So many years wasted in this pathetic marriage, she sighed now.

The elevator doors opened directly onto Danforth's penthouse office and revealed him sprawled on the sofa in his bathrobe, with two heaping plates of fried chicken balanced precariously on his knees. At the sight of her, he lowered a thigh and eyed her suspiciously.

"What are you doing here?" he said.

She didn't answer at first but trudged into the circular room and dropped her purse on a side table. Now that she was closer, she could see a glob of splattered chicken on his robe.

"I went to see our son," she said, and sank into a leather chair across from him. "Remember him? His trial was today, you know."

Danforth waved one slimy hand in the air as if to say, *"I know, I know,"* while his other hand fingered his next thigh. As usual, he was only eating the skin.

"That's okay," he said, in answer to a question she never posed. "You can stay. Make yourself at home." He swung an arm around the room as though to emphasize his generosity.

Is he being polite? she thought. *That's a first.*

"I'm actually glad you're here."

Glad I'm here?

The strange look in his eyes concerned her. At first, she mistook it for guilt or sorrow. Then she realized it was probably self-pity. Rumor had it that the Lytoky would soon come after him since Jordan had been convicted. She watched him take another bite and felt slightly nauseated. He always ate when he was stressed.

"So, how is Jordan?" he asked.

Marisa's next words spilled out much louder than she had intended, and staccato fast.

"About as well as can be expected for someone accused and convicted of a crime he didn't commit!" she said. Now that she had gotten started, she found she couldn't stop. "Seriously, Marshall, how did you think he would be? Not only has he been sentenced to die tomorrow, he's been abandoned by his father! How could you do that? How could you desert our son when he needs you the most? Not even you are that big of a coward!"

Danforth stared at her with a blank, almost lost expression.

"Geez, Risa," he said. "Shoot a man for asking, why don't ya?"

Marisa opened her mouth, flabbergasted. Her hands clenched and unclenched. Later, it occurred to her she should have known something was wrong; he had never before let her raise her voice to him. And he only called her Risa when he was feeling particularly contrite. Instead of responding with outrage, to her surprise, her husband smacked his lips and casually reached for a towel.

"Risa," he said, "you'd better sit back. I have something to tell you and you're not going to like it." He wiped his fingers and chuckled. "Actually, I'm kind of glad to get this off my chest. You know I never was good at keeping secrets."

Yes, Marisa agreed. Many nights he had shown up with lipstick on his collar or hotel chewing-gum wrappers with V-numbers on them in his pockets. He liked leaving her little clues. She suspected he did it because somehow it made her culpable if she knew about his affairs and said nothing. She could see from his expression he was simply bursting to reveal his latest secret.

"And this one has been driving me crazy!" he continued. "It's been, what, eighteen years?"

Marisa narrowed her eyes. She didn't like where this one was going. (Not that she ever did.)

"Jordan is not my son!" he blurted, and then grinned.

Marisa exhaled in relief. "No, Marshall," she said patiently, as if talking to a child. "Jordan is your son. I've never slept with another man."

"He's not yours, either, Silly! That's just it!" Danforth said, still grinning.

"Not my…" she blinked in bewilderment. "Excuse me?"

"Jordan is not our child. We had a little girl. I switched them at birth while you were out cold." And then, as if to explain everything, he added, "Honestly, 'Risa, you knew I only wanted sons. It's all your fault for having a daughter!"

DAY THREE

The Fray

"Shall we play the coward, then, and leave the hard knocks for our daughters, or shall we throw ourselves into the fray, bare our own shoulders to the blows, and thus bequeath to them a politically liberated womanhood?"

--Carrie Chapman Catt, The Crisis (delivered September 7, 1916)

DEPOSITION #20561110.003
(Continued)

I know what you must be thinking. How could I forsake one child in favor of another? People may argue there's a strong, emotional tie to a child they've raised, and for them, I'm sure that is true. But for me… in the end, I couldn't ignore my own blood. Blood is a powerful lure. It's instinctual. Primal. Immortal. Children carry our genes into the future. Without an heir, for instance, centuries from now who would ever know I existed? Who would know to care?

It's basic survival of the species, right?

Don't tell me you wouldn't have done the same!

FORTY

In the last moments before dawn, Lieutenant Alex Winters scrambled down her cabin's unlit back-porch steps and risked a glance over her shoulder. In the instant before the back door closed, she saw two LPs burst through the front door. In her haste, she missed the last porch step and nearly stumbled face first onto the hard-packed earth below. Luckily, another Lytoky Policeone was there to catch her.

"Let me go! Let me go!" she said, elbows flailing, but her captor held her tight. The badge in Alex's face identified the LP as Murphy, part of Captain Chad's inner circle.

"Easy now. Easy!" said Murphy. "No one's going to hurt you."

Just then, in direct contradiction to Murphy's statement, the two LPs from inside barreled through the cabin's back door, weapons drawn. One quick nod from Murphy, however, and they immediately stood down.

Alex stopped struggling. *At least they're not going to shoot me,* she thought. *At least not yet, anyway.* At this hour, only a few lights spilled from neighboring staff cabins. The morning air was still, and it smelled strongly of dew-moistened soil—Alex's favorite scent. When Murphy let her go, Alex steadied herself and mock-dusted her sleeves.

"Guess I lost my balance," she said.

"Happens all the time," said Murphy. "You ready now?"

Alex glanced between the three LPs and the woods behind the cabin.

"Don't even think about it, Winters. We don't want to hurt you. Like I explained before, someone at Headquarters wants a word, that's all."

"At this time of night?"

"Well, technically it's morning," Murphy said, and spread out a palm, as though asking Alex to dance. "Please. Allow me to escort you."

The other two LPs moved wordlessly down the steps until one stood at each elbow.

"Doesn't look like I have a choice."

Alex allowed them to lead her around front to an awaiting Jeep and eased into the front passenger seat. Murphy climbed behind the wheel. The other two hung back, as though surveying the woods with false nonchalance but they didn't fool her: they were poised in case she made a run for it. Sure enough, once the Jeep started moving, they climbed on board in back. As the Jeep's headlights cut through the quiet officer's camp, Alex reached into her front jacket pocket and fished out the small plastic card Murphy had presented to her earlier. She turned it over in her hand. The card was solid black on both sides except for the Cis-Star logo on front (a white cross with a red flame behind it) and a black reader strip down the side.

Ten minutes ago, when Murphy had first handed it through the front door, Alex had looked at it, dumbfounded. Still half-asleep and suffering another hangover, it had taken her a moment to realize it was a confidential dispatch. That's when Alex had snapped sharply awake. She had dressed quickly, peeking out occasionally through the curtains at the awaiting officers on her doorstep, and had slid the card into her V-cell's swipe device.

"Dear Lieutenant Winters," the encrypted message began. "A certain private matter has come to my attention regarding your personal activities. Report to my office at once." It was signed, simply, "Captain."

A certain private matter? she thought now, tapping her thumbs on her thighs as the Jeep swayed around a curve. *How much does the Captain know? Had she discovered my alcohol-trade with the Rebellion? My blatant disregard for the island's security protocol and occasional treasonous comments? Or maybe the new President blames me for what had happened to her daughter and they are going to court-martial me for transporting a known rapist to the Oasis!*

Captain Chad's note was marked urgent, yet she had taken the time to have it hand-delivered? It didn't make sense.

And why send the Lytoky Police? her mind raced. *Why three of them?*

She glanced at the passing dark foliage. If she leapt now, she doubted Murphy could stop her, but where would she go? She was on an island, after all.

From the Jeep's side mirror, she noticed the back-seat guards watching her closely, their weapons on their laps. One nodded when they made eye contact. It was a slow, deliberate motion that to Alex looked more like a dare than a salutation.

***

With Murphy in the lead and the other two LPs close behind, Alex entered the Oasis Headquarters and approached the Captain's office. Once there, Murphy knocked twice and stepped aside to let Alex pass.

Captain Chad had her back to the door, so Alex had an instant to survey the room, looking for possible escape. Though on the ground level and facing the woods, she knew the windows had motion-sensor alarms. Alex had overseen their installation, herself, during her early days on the island. Their activation would alert the whole compound. There was not even a potential weapon in sight. The Captain's walls were uncharacteristically bare, and her desk was empty except for a single sheet of paper. Even the built-in shelves, which normally held pictures of Chad's wife, Emily, were empty.

"Good morning, Lieutenant," Chad said as she turned. "What took you so long?"

Alex did not know how to respond. Barely thirty minutes had passed since Murphy first appeared at her door, and they certainly had not stopped for coffee along the way. If she didn't know her captain better, she would have sworn the woman was toying with her.

"We don't have much time," Chad continued, and motioned for Alex to take a seat. "The compound will soon be awake, and I don't want anyone knowing you were here."

Alex bounced her right knee nervously. *Why not?* she wondered. *If they are going to arrest me, why keep it on the QT?*

She followed Chad's gaze to the parchment on her desk—to its rows of clumsy, handwritten text—and craned her neck to get a better look. No one wrote letters by hand anymore. They hadn't taught hand lettering in school for decades.

Who would waste time drawing out words (much less a whole page of them!) when it was easier and quicker to dictate to text?

"Do you know what this is?" Chad asked, and drummed a thumb on the parchment.

Alex leaned forward, trying to buy a little time, and pretended to notice the page for the first time. "A letter?"

Captain Chad looked up. There was something new in her expression. Was it sorrow? Impatience? Anger? Alex couldn't be sure.

"You're right, of course, Lieutenant. It's a letter… addressed to you."

"To me?" Alex looked down again, genuinely intrigued this time. "Who would write to me?"

"That's what I want to discuss." Chad settled back in her chair and took the letter with her, so Alex sat back, as well. "Let me start by asking you a question, Lieutenant. Are you happy here with us?"

Alex started to answer with the obligatory, *"Oh, yes Ma'am, of course I am!"* donkeyshit, but stopped herself. She felt the first stirrings of anger, and instead of answering, she folded her arms across her chest. *If they're going to arrest me anyway,* she reasoned, *why should I have to answer such a personal question?*

Chad nodded and set the letter aside. "Emily was right. She commented once that ever since you lost your baby, you haven't been the same."

Alex closed her eyes and winced. Her jaw muscles clenched painfully.

"What was his name, again? Oh, yes… Bobby. Of course!"

Alex groaned. She had started drinking to deaden these memories. Why was the Captain being so cruel? Alex slouched in her seat and patted her left shirt pocket, out of habit.

"I'm not saying this to hurt you, Dear. It's just that we never really talked about it, did we?"

Dear? Since when did the Captain call anyone Dear? she wondered.

"No, Captain. We didn't."

"I apologize. I'm sure it was difficult for you, losing him like that, and all, but…."

"That's enough!" Alex said. She had been prepared to accept a reprimand, or to even be arrested if that's what they had in mind, but she was not going to sit here and listen to Captain Chad, of all people, discuss Bobby. She leaned forward.

"Let's set the record straight," she said. "I didn't lose him, Captain. Losing implies I misplaced him somewhere, or that he vanished into THIN FUCKING AIR! But that's not what happened, and you know it. I didn't lose him; you took him!"

"Settle down, now. I didn't mean to-" Chad was finally the one to appear off balance. "I was only following procedure, doing what's best for the Lytoky!"

"I'm sick of hearing about what's best for the Lytoky!" Alex responded. "He wasn't evil. He couldn't have hurt anyone. He was just a little boy!"

"Exactly! A boy. And boys grow into men. His very presence here would have disrupted our whole society. It's the whole reason we don't allow natural conception anymore."

"Look around you, Captain; we're on an island filled with men, or haven't you noticed? He wouldn't have upset anything; he was my son! You had no right to take him!"

"And you had no right to mess around with Robert and get pregnant!"

"What?" Alex's mouth dropped open. "How do you know about Robert?"

Captain Chad pinched the bridge of her nose and let out an exaggerated sigh. Then she motioned to the letter on the desk. "He just told me," she said. "I had no idea the two of you were… whatever you were… or are."

Alex followed her gaze to the paper, past the neat lines of upside-down lettering, and focused on the words at the bottom, "Love, Robert."

Robert?

Alex searched Chad's face, and saw tears in the older woman's eyes. After Chad handed over the letter at last, Alex barely noticed that she stood and left the room, allowing Alex the courtesy of digesting Robert's news in private.

Alex held the fragile parchment as though cradling a butterfly.

***

My Darling Alexandra, the letter began.

How do I begin to tell you about the last ten months of pain, and joy? Pain from missing you. And joy from learning about our son.

I know you must be shocked, and possibly angry, to be hearing from me after all this time, but please let me assure you, I did not abandon you. I was relocated that night without warning and I've been trying to get word to you ever since. Unfortunately, it wasn't safe until now.

There's so much to tell you! But not in a letter. I'll explain everything in person, but until then please trust me. Tomorrow, the three of us will be together: you, Bobby, and me. That's right, my darling, tomorrow! (Or today, depending on when you receive this letter.)

Things are going to happen quickly now, so please be prepared and follow your Captain's instructions. Above all, please know I never stopped loving you. I hope you can find it in your heart to forgive me. I love you!

Love,

Robert

***

Alex read the letter twice and drank in every word. Her memories of him (buried by years of anger, bewilderment, and confusion) resurfaced instantly. She remembered, without the pang of bitterness this time, how they had fallen in love. How his humor and easy manner had intrigued her during the many nights she spent transporting him back and forth to his Fantasy Cabin, and how she had begun to question the stories she had always heard about men.

"Believe what you know to be true, not what you hear others say," he had told her once as they sat on the beach together. "The Lytoky and New Canaan are both brainwashing their people. Don't get caught up in their lies and propaganda. Believe in what you experience, not other people's opinions and feelings. Believe in this!"

Then he had kissed her. It was their first kiss. Over the next several weeks, Robert spoke more about love, freedom, and his friends in the Rebellion—a relatively small band (both men and women) unaffected by the governments' mind control. He spoke about their mission with such enthusiasm that Alex began to identify with them, as well. They mostly lived in the Gamma states, he had explained, but not all. Some, like him, traveled between New Canaan and the Lytoky, trying to infiltrate the mind-control source.

"We know it originates with Cis-Star," he explained, "but we don't have anyone on the inside yet."

He explained that by living on the Oasis (where the special O-rays were only directed at the men), Alex had remained relatively free from the "outside" mind-altering suggestions.

"And the fact that you hear the Infirmary's messages (while the other guards don't) must mean you have some other natural immunity to their wavelengths we haven't yet discovered!" he said. "It's extremely exciting! You have no idea how much we need you! How much I need you," he added, with a kiss.

Alex remembered feeling so proud and special that last night, as she leaned back in his arms on the front porch of Fantasy Log Cabin #3 to watch the stars.

"You understand what I'm fighting for, don't you?" he asked her. "The Rebellion must win! We have to destroy the O-rays, the Adrays, and Cis-Star's VEE technology before it's too late! If New Canaan and the Lytoky go to war, innocent people on both sides will die."

Alex had nodded. At that moment, she was ready to fight by his side, and would have done anything he said. But the next morning, Robert disappeared. That's when she began second-guessing his intentions, and had started hating herself for being so gullible.

Now, with his letter in hand, she didn't know what to believe.

FORTY-ONE

Danforth snorted and fumbled for his glasses. Per the wall-mounted digital, it was just after four o'clock in the morning. *Damn that racket!* he thought. *I'll never get to sleep!*

Every few months, the Info-Swirl's exterior window-washing contractor circled the building. This morning, their equipment was staged directly below his balcony. The crew couldn't—*wouldn't?*—work at night (they had some lame excuse about safety and the Union) so there was always a platform protruding from his building. It reminded him of a glob of mascara on an otherwise attractive woman's eyelash. Usually, the padded platforms were merely unsightly, but this morning the wind was banging them around in a loud beat, out-of-tempo. He huffed in exasperation and rolled onto his back. His Penthouse office suite had a mini apartment in the back, complete with a king-size bed.

He stared up at the ceiling. For the last hour, he'd been unable to stop remembering events he hadn't thought about in years… like that nonsense with Jordan. He hadn't meant to tell Marisa he had switched him at birth; it just slipped out. With every bite of chicken, the words kept flowing. Before he knew it, he had confessed everything.

It felt good to get it out, though, he thought. *What a relief!*

Since then, other random haunts had resurfaced; like how he had watched Jordan being born. That day, Danforth knew he shouldn't have been watching a complete stranger give birth, but he couldn't help himself. They had wheeled the pregnant girl in right next to his wife.

What else was I supposed to do?

The whole ordeal had been fascinating. The two deliveries couldn't have been more different. Marisa had been given an epidural, so her contractions were more controlled, and she struggled in near silence. The teenager, however, screamed and cussed—her eyes wide with terror and pain. Her passion had enthralled him.

The girl's son, Jordan, came first. His fat little hands and feet kicked furiously, and he turned red the instant he screamed.

What a fighter!

The doctor barely had time to check the lad and lay him aside before moving over to help Katherine out. Compared to the boy, his daughter seemed small and quiet, just like her mother. She barely made a sound. In fact, she almost looked blue. Without an assistant, the doctor quickly thumped Katherine's tiny chest until she started breathing, then set her beside Jordan to assist Marisa with the afterbirth that had started tearing inside her. The doctor's pager kept ringing the entire time. Finally, a nurse rushed in and explained the doctor was needed for an emergency down the hall. With Marisa somewhat under control, the doctor and nurse ran out the door, leaving Danforth essentially in charge.

The boy's mother, whom he noted was no more than a child, herself, was covered in sweat. She kept looking around and over her shoulder, weak and confused. That's when he realized neither mother had yet seen her infant or been told if it was a boy or a girl. There hadn't been time.

Danforth studied the naked babies side by side. In that moment, as he looked at the boy, he felt what every new father must feel: amazement, affection, and the sudden urge to protect him.

What kind of life will this boy have with a teenage whore for a mother and the MA'AM Revolution taking hold? he thought. *He won't stand a chance!*

His former Chaplain, Reverend Pat Buford, had once confided she had tried to adopt, but the agencies had claimed she was too old. She had recently become Senator of Massachusetts.

Imagine how grateful she would be if I helped her adopt, he thought. *Besides, in the newly forming Lytoky, any daughter of hers will eventually have power, prestige, and fame. What father wouldn't want that for his child?*

He had to move fast. By the time the nurse returned, he had already scrolled the baby's gender in each woman's respective chart and had placed the boy on Marisa's chest. Still groggy from the epidural, she had cooed to him instinctively.

"I will not say this again!" he purposefully bellowed at the nurse. "Get that whore and her little runt out of here! I paid for a private room, and that's what I intend to have!"

As expected, the nurse first glanced at both charts, then she wheeled out the teenage girl. She came back a few minutes later for their daughter and took Katherine to the nursery. Danforth finally began to relax. To ease his conscience later, he said good-bye to her in private in the nursery. He even changed the infant into the frilly pink outfit Marisa had packed, and had patted her awkwardly as he had carried her out of the nursery.

That part had been easy. The duty nurse, it turned out, was far behind on her rent. For a sizeable fee, she had agreed to look the other way while he took the child. (Since he had ensured her the teen would sign the adoption papers, they agreed the nurse's risk was reasonably small.)

After a few quick calls, Katherine had been in the senator's arms that very day.

He never looked back. For a while, he even pretended the whole thing was a dream—that OF COURSE Jordan was his biological son. It hadn't even fazed him when he saw the two toddlers together at the airport years later, when he and Marisa had fled Boston.

Back then, he was too concerned with his reputation and career plans to think twice about Katherine. With the burgeoning MA'AM Revolution, he had nearly been caught off guard and, like a general who refused to withdraw his troops when he could, he had almost waited too long to evacuate Boston.

A few years later, when he saw Katherine on Buford's TV show, he couldn't help feeling mildly jealous. The plucky kid in Buford's arms had green eyes, like Marisa, and even when she glowered at the woman, after being disciplined on screen, he could tell that the two of them already shared an intimacy he and Jordan lacked. He had thought about taking her back, but he knew that was impossible. Buford and Marisa would both publicly skewer him if he admitted what he'd done.

By the time Waverly Nelson came to him with her Uniray machine, he already had an eating disorder. His new political party, New Canaan, was gaining momentum in St. Louis and his responsibilities were growing… but so was his waist. He suspected it was his guilt that prompted him to started adopting other boys, but nothing seemed to work. His appetite continued to grow.

He wasn't the only one with a problem, though, he knew.

As Katherine grew and the Adrays took off, Rev. Buford seemed to change, as well. Her focus shifted more toward politics than to administering the poor. She took her message on the road, and left Katherine behind on most trips. Eventually, she put the girl in boarding school.

Several times, he had considered reaching out and telling Katherine the truth, but what purpose would it serve? Both he and Buford were household names in their respective states by then, so their children's switched births would have been front-page news. He might have even gone to jail. He had supposed the Adrays could have influenced his New Canaan followers to support him, but with so much tension already between their two sides, he couldn't have risked it, or Buford's wrath.

Danforth rolled onto his side again. Today he had an interview with that hot reporter, Honey Campbell. *That's where I'll set the record straight!* he decided.

Since he had already lost the election, and Jordan's arrest would soon be public knowledge, what more did he have to lose? He decided it was time to tell the truth. He would claim Katherine as his own at last and get the truth out in the open. The Lytoky already adored the girl, so maybe once they learned she was his blood, they would love him, too.

Who knows… Maybe one day they'll all thank me for reuniting the Lytoky and New Canaan!

FORTY-TWO

Pat started her day, as she had every morning Katherine was sick or in pain, sitting by her daughter's bedside. Only this time, there were no skinned knees to kiss, no fevered brows to cool, and nothing to do but sit and wait.

And worry.

Katherine was still asleep (either from the drugs or from her head trauma, Pat could not be sure which), yet she still called out for Jordan.

Jordan?

Her daughter's Imaginary Friend had first appeared the day Danforth and his family left Boston. Katherine was only four years old back then, and the MA'AM revolution was still gaining momentum. Men were scurrying west like cockroaches. She had taken Katherine with her to the crowded airport to see the Danforths off. While she and Marisa were saying their good-byes, Danforth had brooded nearby, supposedly watching the children. Even so, Pat had kept a close eye on them.

Katherine and Jordan had instantly connected. They reached for each other, grinning and mirroring each other's outstretched palms as though separated by a sheet of glass. Travelers shuttled past and adult voices barked overhead, but the two seemed oddly at peace inside the eye of their own storm.

Just as Pat and Marisa were hugging good-bye, Katherine had yelped. When Pat turned back, Katherine was standing there with her little hands on her hips and studying the crowd as though someone had goosed her. Pat recognized the posture. Even at that young age, Katherine didn't like being surprised. Jordan was doing the same thing. Both looked more insulted than hurt. Katherine later said it felt as though someone had pinched her.

Danforth had reacted as though it were Katherine's fault. He snatched up his son and offered Pat a curt "good day." Over his shoulder, Jordan raised a hand in silent farewell as Katherine cried and mirrored his farewell gesture. Danforth never slowed or looked back.

Katherine started talking to herself during the ride home from the airport. From the rear-view mirror, Pat watched the girl carrying on a full one-sided conversation from the comfort of her car seat. Pat recalled distinctly hearing the name Jordan. At first, she thought it was cute, but a little sad. After all, he was probably the last male she would ever see in person.

Now, as Pat glanced at her sleeping daughter, she realized Jordan was not so imaginary after all. Worse yet, somehow the boy had gotten inside her daughter's mind. Pat had never before felt so helpless or so scared.

A hand landed gently on her shoulder from behind. She turned to see Waverly Nelson, her good friend and work associate, holding out a large cup of peppermint tea and a dry-cleaning bag.

"Sorry to startle you, but I thought you could use a break. Here, take this and let me sit with her awhile. The nurse gave me Katherine's skari, too. Looks like they cleaned it for her."

Pat wiped at her eyes. "Thanks, I'll put it in the closet. I don't want to leave her, though. I want to be here when she wakes up."

Waverly patted her shoulder, a little less gently this time, and scolded her softly. "You've been here all night, and it shows. What you need is a few hours' sleep and a shower. The nurses set up an on-call room for you right down the hall. Why don't you stretch your legs? I'll stay with Kat while you rest. The last thing she needs is to see you like this."

Pat grimaced, and reached for Waverly's hand, still on her shoulder. Her friend was right, of course; Pat was so fatigued that even this small act of kindness had made her eyes sting. She nodded, resolutely, and felt herself giving in. Arthritic knees popped as she stood.

"Alright. But promise me you'll call the instant she wakes up."

"I promise."

***

Buford was barely twenty steps down the hall before Waverly took Kat's hand in hers and bent over the bed. "Kat," she whispered loudly, "Kat, can you hear me?" Kat moaned, but did not stir. "Kat, it's me, Aunt Waverly! Wake up!"

Still no response.

Disappointed, Waverly scooted Pat's still-warm chair closer to the bed and sat. She rubbed Kat's hand lightly against her cheek and gazed at the young girl's sleeping face. She looked so peaceful.

What better time to practice my speech? she thought and took a deep breath. *Here goes nothing!*

"Kat," she whispered. "I'm your mother! Your REAL mother." Kat turned her face toward her, as though in response, but she still did not wake up.

"Where do I begin?" Waverly continued, and knit her brows in concentration. "Should I start by telling you how I found you? How I broke into the Boston adoption registry and traced you back to Buford? (It took some digging; my name wasn't even listed in your file, but Danforth was the point of contact, so I knew it was you.) Or should I start by telling you how I knew you were my daughter the instant I saw your precious face?"

She smiled and stroked Kat's limp hand. The girl twitched slightly, and her forehead wrinkled.

"You were such a beautiful child. I barely caught a glimpse of you the day you were born, of course, but years later, when I saw you at the airport, you were exactly how I'd imagined."

She dropped her gaze and fell silent, remembering the effort she had gone through to identify Kat. Though the adoption registry led her to Buford, Waverly wanted to be sure. Cis-Star had already perfected the Adrays by then, and the Uniray prototype was still in its infancy. The plan was to target specific DNA. As Cis-Star's president and C.E.O. (having inherited the company from her grandmother), Waverly had access to all the labs and technology, and had daily briefings from each department head. She took great interest in their work.

216

On the theory that her offspring would have half her DNA, she calibrated the Unirays' neurotransmitter frequency according to her own dopamine fingerprint and took the prototype out for the day. The unit was surprisingly compact.

Her timing was perfect. She followed Buford to the airport and waited until the girl was finally unattended. Then, she tested Kat's reaction.

"When I saw that Danforth and Buford were friends, I didn't need further proof, but I hid behind a column and forwarded you the very first message from the portable device, "QUICK! TURN AROUND!" You jumped like you'd been shocked. That's when I knew for sure it was you."

She trailed off for a moment.

"I've waited a long time to tell you this, Kat! (Too long, perhaps, but there were things I had to accomplish first.) I hope you understand." She smiled down at the sleeping girl's face, feeling closer than ever to the daughter she had not yet claimed. "Oh, of course you'll understand. We were both raised by older women. We have that in common, too."

In a slow, painful monologue, Waverly told Kat her tale, beginning with her mother's funeral. Practicing the whole story as Kat slept, she revealed more than she had intended, but it felt good to get it out. When she got to the part about the Adrays, and how easily she had fooled both Danforth and Buford, she smiled and rested her elbows on the mattress.

"He was so excited about the Adrays he almost wet his pants. Imagine what he'd have done if he knew about the Unirays! Or that I'd already been using them on him for a full year by then."

She recounted how she had obtained his dopamine signature from his ophthalmologist the year before, and how she had tuned the Unirays to his exact brain-wave frequency to send him undetectable verbal pulses. Like a conductor, she had orchestrated his every action since.

"Don't get me wrong," she added. "I didn't make him do anything against his will. I merely gave him the encouraging nudges that he needed. He already felt superior to others, so when I convinced him he was a natural leader, the notion naturally appealed to him. Luckily, he is so repulsive he was the perfect Bad Example. By now, thanks to my years of programming, women everywhere associate the word MAN with Senator Danforth. The original plan was to also tie the word DANFORTH to Paul Brown's face. I had everything set up to exchange the two men's identities (at least on camera) and to influence New Canaan to turn on him. I was looking forward to watching his face the moment he realized his followers had betrayed him. It was to be the ultimate retribution. But then his son came along! Jordan's arrest was an unexpected bonus."

Waverly felt herself getting excited as she explained.

"Someone as evil as Paul Brown, with his smug attitude and small, lizard-like eyes, was easy to label a Monster." She explained how thanks to his ugly face, systematically interchanged with the name DANFORTH via concentrated Adrays programming, it had been easy to force the two images together. Transferring her plans from the Senator to his son, however, had taken a great deal of last-minute scrambling.

"But it was worth it, don't you see? Having him watch his own son die is going to be even more fulfilling. I couldn't have planned it better, myself.

"Except for you being hurt, of course," she added. At the unwelcome thought, Waverly looked down and rubbed the scars on the top of her head. "I didn't mean for that to happen. I didn't know you would be at the Oasis."

It wasn't my fault! she wanted to say, but it sounded weak and pathetic, even to a sleeping audience. She wasn't used to justifying her actions, even to herself.

"Regardless, now the names Brown and Danforth are practically synonymous. Women are incensed beyond mere indignation, Kat! They are finally ready to strike back! Soon, everyone (even the men in New Canaan) will start calling for Danforth's blood… literally and figuratively. After that, I will program the men to turn on each other."

She studied Kat's frowning face and sighed.

"I'm sorry you had to see that man's face again, Sweetheart, but I had to switch the trials, don't you see? It took a lot of last-minute scrambling to deal with the mixed-up identities, but it was worth the added effort. Believe me, Kat. In time, your sacrifice will prove worthwhile. After today, no man will ever hurt you again. I promise."

Kat's eyelids twitched and Waverly smiled. It wouldn't be long until the girl would be awake and she could tell the story again. *For real, this time!*

FORTY-THREE

Alex started talking the moment Captain Chad reentered the office. "He didn't leave me! He loves me!"

"I know."

"How did you...? How did he...? Did you know that we...?" Alex didn't know where to begin. Chad sat on the edge of her desk and nodded gravely.

"Listen. We don't have much time, and there's a lot to say. Some will be difficult to hear, so let me get this out before you ask questions, okay?" She paused and took a deep breath. "Robert is my son."

Alex's jaw sagged open as the older woman told her tale. Fifteen years ago, while stationed in Salem, Caroline Chad had embraced the MA'AM revolution. With heterosexual marriages becoming increasingly unpopular, the tension between her and her then-husband became untenable. Chad, therefore, was not surprised when Robert's father called it quits, and moved west, taking their son of seventeen with him.

"At the time, for some reason, I was actually glad to see them go. Although now, for the life of me, I can't remember why. It seems unconscionable I didn't fight for my family, for my son."

Over the years, Chad had kept track of her boy. Without her supervisor's permission, she had watched him graduate high school valedictorian via special satellite feed. She followed him as he earned his doctorate in Political Science from Notre Dame, and when he got hired on as an intern with the Indiana state senate.

"Two years ago, however, at the age of thirty, Robert disappeared. Imagine my surprise when he showed up here, at the Oasis. I couldn't believe he recognized me after all these years, and that he had forgiven me. Turns out, he had come here to use me, to advance the Rebellion's cause. It's amazing how easily he played me.

Determined to save him from the degradation of performing sexual favors for random Lytoky dignitaries, Chad had made the hasty decision to disengage the O-rays for his visit. Apparently, that's exactly what the Rebellion had anticipated. With the security systems off-line, they had covertly besieged the resort and orchestrated four high-ranking Rebellion Escorts' escape.

"And here I thought I was the clever one," Chad said. "I had his assignments redirected to me at Fantasy Log Cabin #3 where I'd meet him every evening for dinner. Sometimes Emily would join us. He never once mentioned the Rebellion. Or you."

Alex glanced down, trying to look guilty, but failed. She was still too thrilled with Robert's letter to look convincing.

"I suppose you knew he was with the Rebellion?" Chad asked. Alex glanced up and then back down. "I thought so."

"I didn't at first," Alex said, feeling compelled for some reason to explain. "But, yes, after a while he told me. We were supposed to leave together when his time was up. But then-"

"Then he left without you."

Alex nodded.

"I'm afraid that was my fault. I sent him away, you see. I didn't know about you, of course. All I knew was that I couldn't let him go through the Motel's Debriefing. Not after finding him again! I couldn't stand for them to tinker with his brain and wipe out his memory. I wanted him to remember me; is that so wrong?"

Chad sighed, and then continued.

"Since I still didn't know about his Rebellion involvement, I had Murphy escort him out west to the Gamma States—to a place Emily had researched. In the rush, I didn't even get a chance to tell him good-bye, myself. Once he was gone, it was too dangerous to contact him again. I never knew about his involvement with you until I received that letter last night, and another one for me. Finally, everything made sense: your depression, your drinking, your negligence to your duties… and, of course, your pregnancy.

"Even though you claimed to have met someone in New Canaan during a recruitment trip, I always suspected you had been with an Escort. I must confess, though, I never dreamed it was Robert."

"Where is Bobby?" Alex asked. "Where's my little boy?"

"He's on his way to meet Robert. His foster family is taking him to the airport. I had to pull a lot of favors to make that happen, believe me."

Alex didn't know what to say. Did the Captain expect a Thank you? For what? For returning the child she had taken away in the first place?

"Anyway, Emily and I are leaving today as soon as you are safely off the Oasis. We're already packed, as you can see." Her arm indicated the empty office. "We're tired of all the secrecy and brainwashing. We're going west, to join Robert and the Rebellion. Maybe there, I can clear my conscience."

She reached for Alex's hand, which Alex automatically withdrew.

"I knew losing your child was devastating to you, but I- I didn't know he was my grandson. I followed procedure and gave him to New Canaan. It's part of our agreement to turn over any male children resulting from border crossings. I believed in what I was doing, Alex. A boy? Here? It wouldn't have worked. Or so I thought. Now, I'm not so sure. I know I can never make it up to you, but please know I am deeply sorry. I hope one day you can forgive me."

Was that a tear in her Captain's eye?

Alex sat in stunned silence. She had never thought Captain Chad capable of emotion. It was surreal thinking of her as Robert's mother, as her son's grandmother, and quite probably her future mother-in-law. After another moment's hesitation, she reached across the desk and awkwardly squeezed the Captain's hand. It was weird, like kissing a sister.

"Of course I forgive you," she said, faking a smile.

After all, the worst is over now, right? she thought.

***

Twenty minutes later, armed with the Rebellion's secret location and the knowledge that Robert loved her, Alex left the Oasis for the very last time.

"Don't forget…" Chad had reminded her, as Alex was leaving her office.

"I know," Alex said. "If I see him first, I'll tell Robert you love him."

FORTY-FOUR

Pat's makeshift bedroom was comfortable enough, but it was not "right next door" as Waverly had suggested. *It wasn't even on the same floor, for MA'AM sake!*

With an angry scowl, she rolled over, and punched the pillow down. Instant gratification followed, so she struck the pillow again. Then again. And again. *How DARE that man hurt my daughter!* she thought, each time. Finally, anger turned to tears and she used the same pillow to smother her hiccupping sobs.

From the moment she had first held Katherine as an infant, she had vowed to protect her. She spent years building thelytokies all over the east so that things like this could never happen. She had put men like Brown in prison, and had even executed some of them—all to keep her daughter safe. So many hours spent lecturing Katherine about Man's inherent evilness…. For what? Instead of enjoying the haven Pat's efforts had created, her daughter had not only ignored her warnings, she had rushed headlong into the enemy's arms. Literally.

Where did I go wrong? she wondered. *Was I too stringent? Too lenient? Too absent? Or too hovering?*

She hadn't been around much since becoming Senator, and certainly not as much as she would have liked. But ever since Katherine turned thirteen, the girl seemed to sulk whenever they were together, anyway. Pat knew teenage daughters and their mothers tended to clash, but Katherine was so quiet, so introspective, and so good otherwise, that Pat thought the phase would soon pass.

Now, she knew she had waited too long.

If only I had been home more often, maybe she wouldn't have felt compelled to sneak away.

A hundred unwelcome memories came thrusting to the surface—each intent on reminding her of missed, or ignored, clues. Just last week, she recalled, Katherine had specifically asked her about the Oasis.

"Are the stories true, Mom? Do men and women really meet there on purpose? What's it like? Have you been there?"

On her way out the door, Pat had scoffed and waved a hand, brushing off her daughter's queries as though Katherine were being ridiculous, but in reality, she hadn't known what to say. Yes, she had been to the Oasis, but only to oversee the facilities, not as a Guest. She knew what happened there, and knew it provided her constituents a necessary release. But after everything she had told her daughter about the horrors of Man, how could she possibly tell her that some women still craved them? That no matter how badly men treated them, some women couldn't get enough?

For numerous reasons, the Oasis was the Lytoky's pressure valve. It appeased the few women who wouldn't otherwise be satisfied living in an all-female society, and it helped keep the peace. It was a drug… a fix that her administration doled out like a sympathetic dealer. The Oasis fed this addiction in a controlled, safe environment, by letting women have their fantasy vacations, and then going back home to lead ordinary, productive lives.

Long ago, Pat had decided it was worth the expense and the trouble (not to mention the hypocrisy) to keep her constituents sated, but how could she have explained that to her teenage daughter? The truth would have only piqued Katherine's curiosity further. Half-truths would have led to more questions, and Pat knew her explanations would have fallen short. Worse yet, they would have come out completely wrong and the two would have undoubtedly argued.

Only now did Pat realized that by not talking openly (about the Oasis, or anything important, for that matter), she had discouraged Katherine from opening up. Mentioning it that day must have been hard for Katherine. She had clearly wanted to talk.

Maybe she had wanted me to talk her out of going!

Pat wiped at her eyes. Her guilt wasn't helping, she knew. Maybe watching something on TV would make her relax and get some needed sleep. She activated the wall unit and pulled up a nature program. On screen, it showed a clan of hyenas surrounding a lioness and two cubs. Greatly outnumbered, the lioness growled and swiped, sprinting back and forth, as the scavengers slowly closed in. They took turns nipping at the helpless cubs each time their mother's back was turned. They seemed to be gauging her reaction time.

"Will she fight to the death? Or to exhaustion?" asked the program's narrator. "She can't carry them both away to safety. To save one cub, she will have to abandon the other and leave it exposed. What will she do? Which one will she save? And why? Stay tuned for the thrilling conclusion…"

***

Across the border, Marisa Danforth turned off the Nature Channel just as a hyena sank her teeth into one lion cub's tiny neck. She glanced at her VEE's clock feature and winced. She needed to get some sleep. Every time she tried, though, she kept replaying her husband's words, "Jordan is not our son. We had a little girl."

At first, Marisa thought that losing the election had made him lose his mind. What he was saying couldn't be true.

"Oh come now!" he had said playfully, after licking his greasy fingers. "Surely, you suspected."

That's absurd! she thought now. *He put Jordan in my arms and told me he was mine! Why would I have questioned he was mine? I know he's done despicable things—Lord only knows how many women he's brought here to his Penthouse office suite, for example—but I never dreamed he would abandon his own child! What kind of monster does that?*

And yet, a certain memory niggled at her subconscious.

A few years ago, when he had deposited yet another infant boy in her lap, she had finally spoken up.

"No!" she had told him. "I refuse to raise any more of your bastards! I'll let this one starve; I swear I will! With all these children in the house, I barely have time for my own son!"

That's when Danforth had winked, seemingly amused, and had made a puzzling remark.

"Oh, Risa. I wouldn't get too hung up on which sons are biologically yours and which ones aren't. Jordan is as much your son as that infant there in your arms."

At the time, she believed he was speaking metaphorically... that all the boys were hers. Now, if she were to believe her husband's late-night confession, that wasn't the case at all. Jordan was not her son. At least, not biologically.

Last night, she had watched her husband in shock and disbelief. Between mouthfuls of Neapolitan ice cream (he had finished the chicken and moved on to dessert by then), he described the day their daughter was born.

"She was a scrawny, sickly-looking girl, at that," he had added, as though that explained everything.

How easily he forgot the reason I went into premature labor in the first place, she thought, remembering their argument that day over comments he had made in public about other women. *I was only seven months pregnant, after all, and we almost lost the baby! Yet all he remembers is being disappointed he had a daughter instead of a son? Incredible!*

She never told him they had been expecting a girl. She had seen the sonograms, of course, but she hadn't told him. *In time, he'll come around,* she had reasoned. *He'll fall in love with a little girl and maybe even change his views on women once he sees life through a daughter's eyes.*

She was surprised, therefore, not only that Jordan was male, but that he was so large and healthy. He didn't appear premature at all.

Guess that's why the doctor warned me never to trust a sonogram 100%, she had thought at the time.

Marshall had claimed he had been a large baby, himself, so until last night Marisa counted herself lucky she hadn't carried full term. Now, she didn't know what to believe.

"You never knew the difference," Danforth explained, twirling his ice cream spoon in the air. "Besides, I knew someone looking to adopt. You'll never guess who it was!"

But, of course, by then she had figured it out. She'd always known it was too great a coincidence that Pat Buford had adopted a daughter the exact same age as Jordan. But she had assumed the teen who had given birth next to her that day had abandoned her baby, and that Marshall had simply facilitated the adoption. She never dreamed he had switched the two children and given Pat THEIR child.

A myriad of conflicting thoughts filled Marisa's sleepless night.

That bastard!

No, it can't be true!

I had a little girl?

Can it be that Katherine, the girl I was cursing just yesterday, is really my long-lost daughter?

***

Gloria Chiang hit the alarm's snooze button for the fourth time this morning and sighed. Although she had lain awake nearly all night, the hotel clock's pre-set alarm started going off at six a.m. and she hadn't found the energy to find the off button. Finally, in exasperation she gave the cord an angry yank and pulled it from the wall.

Add it to my bill!

She eased back into her chair and watched the sunrise alone.

I wish Dale were here, she thought, sullenly.

She hadn't spoken with her husband in two days—not since she'd been formally admitted to her private hospital room after the attack. That night, after the tests were over and the kindly Dr. Taylor had assured her the baby was okay, Gloria had called him. She had broken her VEE during the attack, so she had pirated her hospital room's teleVISOR unit to call him from her Cis-Star account. She had wanted to see his reaction when she told him they were pregnant, but she never got the chance. Instead, she saw his eyes immediately change from his normal, good-natured 'Glad to see you' look to round-eyed horror at the sight of her.

"What happened?" he had demanded before she could even say a word.

His expression had surprised her. That's when she realized her mistake. She had been so excited to tell him about the baby that she had momentarily forgotten the attack. She hadn't considered the reality of explaining her bruises to him, and what (and who) had caused them. The ER doctor had given her a sedative that night, so maybe that had accounted for her blocking out the memory at that instant. But once Dale was on the screen and she was suddenly faced with his reaction, she hadn't known what to say.

"Are you okay? What happened?" he repeated.

"I—I fell down some stairs," she lied. "I'm in the hospital; but there's no broken bones. I'm okay now."

Later that night, when she had checked in again, his message had been frantic. He said he had heard on the news that a woman at her address had been assaulted.

"Was that you?" he asked. "What's going on? Why didn't you tell me?"

After that, she saw where his video messages had arrived every ten minutes, but she had avoided opening them. She couldn't handle the look in his eyes. (Not again!) At last, he had texted to say he'd been detained trying to cross the border and been sent home.

"THE WHOLE BORDER IS CLOSED!" he'd concluded. "PLEASE TELL ME YOU'RE OKAY!"

Gloria knew he had a right to know what had happened; she just couldn't be the one to tell him. How could she? How could she even begin to tell the man she loved that another man had violated her?

Sitting here now, a few days later, she realized she'd been selfish. He deserved to know, and it was time to tell him. She finally felt strong enough to deal with his anger, his grief, and his pain.

She approached the hotel's teleVISOR unit on the wall. It was meant for broadcasting only, but Cis-Star had taught her to improvise. She searched the room, and the complimentary hygiene package the hotel had provided, until she found what she needed. Using the end of a toothbrush as a screwdriver, she carefully pried off the monitor's side panel and started tinkering with its controls.

As she worked, her stomach growled. Although she knew it was only hunger, she moved her hand instinctively to her abdomen.

"I'm right here," she cooed softly. "Don't worry; Dad and I will protect you. And Dr. Bott, too!"

Dr. Bott had discharged her yesterday for the trial on the condition she return for more observation. When Gloria had expressed concern about going back (the Uni-Lifers would no-doubt target her baby for termination as soon as they found out it was a hetero pregnancy, she had explained,) Dr. Bott had assured her she would keep her baby a secret.

That meant the only other person who knew about the baby was Waverly Nelson.

And "the Voice," don't forget!

Ah yes. The Voice had appeared in her head during the lineup, and again while she was on the stand. It always seemed to show up when she was the most upset, and it promised to help her keep her baby if she testified against Paul Brown.

Gloria wasn't a fool. She knew the voice was a Uniray message from Waverly—or at the very least from someone inside Cis-Star whom Waverly trusted. No one else knew she was pregnant. Gloria wasn't sure why Waverly was sending her messages this way, or why she was linking her testimony with keeping her baby, but she had assumed her boss had a reason, and guessed maybe it was more expeditious than calling or coming to visit. Regardless, Gloria had done as Waverly's Voice had demanded, and had testified against Paul Brown.

Now it's time for Waverly's Voice to come through for me! she thought. *It's time for her to help me keep my baby!*

Wavery had never called or visited her after the attack, nor had she sent flowers. In fact, Gloria realized now, it was while she'd been waiting for Waverly's call—just as Waverly had directed—when that monster had attacked her.

Odd that Waverly never called then, either.

Suddenly, Gloria stopped tinkering with the teleVISOR and slumped into her chair. A cold chill spread up her spine as she considered perhaps Waverly wasn't her friend, after all.

FORTY-FIVE

As usual, the express return shuttle traveled nonstop from the airport back to Immigrations. Onboard, Alex felt as though she were strapped to a cannonball. The train, traveling at well over two hundred miles per hour on the magnetic track system, roared through the tunnel's smooth barrel darkness. She leaned back and tried to relax.

This morning, she was escorting three female guests and two male Escorts back to Immigrations. Since the men had already been debriefed back at the Oasis, it was customary for all the passengers to ride together. It helped normalize the return. Since the car only seated eight, eavesdropping was inevitable.

From the train's rear seat, she watched the show with disinterest. Three rows up, two females were chatting excitedly about their experience on the island.

"You'll never believe what my Escort did next!" one breathless guest was saying. They weren't supposed to talk about their experiences off the island… especially not in front of other men, but Alex only shrugged.

Who am I to stop them? she thought.

The third woman, in contrast, had chosen a seat next to an Escort, and had started up a conversation. Alex knew her well.

Beth Edgewood was an Oasis recruiter. They called her the Spider. It was easy to see why. Her job was to entice the desirable Escorts back. To wrap them in her spell, so to speak. Alex watched with begrudging admiration as Beth coyishly tucked her shoulder-length hair behind one ear and flirted openly.

Poor sap, Alex thought.

Beth's latest prey was young and handsome, and totally unaware. He had probably traveled east originally on a dare. Now, he would never get away. By the time they reached East St. Louis, Beth would convince him to sneak back across the Mother Road for a secret rendezvous. Only, instead of meeting Beth, her victim would be arrested for Illegal Immigrations and would be subjected to another three-month sentence. Debriefing would follow. He would forget, and the whole thing would start again.

Alex marveled at Man's willingness to be manipulated. It seemed that even without the O-rays' influence, men were helpless against a pretty face. Thanks to Debriefing and the Spider's encouragement, this man, like so many others before him, had already forgotten the past tortuous hours in the Roach Motel, the numerous old hags he had been forced to entertain, and the daily emotional abuse he had received from the guards. Even when he returned home, assuming he ever did, he wouldn't warn the others. Assuming he remembered the details, how could he admit what he'd endured? Bondage and male sex trafficking were not things men discussed openly.

Beth giggled, rubbed against the Escort's leg, and whispered something in his ear.

He'll be back, alright, Alex mused. *At least I won't be here to see it.*

As the tunnel's lights whizzed by, she hugged herself in anticipation. By the time this boy came back, she would be long gone, tucked safely in Robert's arms.

With any luck, she would never see this place again.

FORTY-SIX

How could all these hospital floors look alike? Pat wondered. Having given up on sleep twenty minutes ago, she had started making her way back to Katherine's room, but was helplessly lost. There wasn't a nurse in sight. It made her recall an old Twilight Zone episode, where every hallway led to nowhere.

How did Waverly convince me to leave in the first place? she wondered.

Her shoes clicked on the seamless vinyl as she turned another corner. Every step felt heavier than the last.

Had the election really been just two days ago? The celebration seemed so distant and unimportant now.

Her Transition Team had been leaving her messages, but had otherwise left her alone, as requested. Unlike pre-Plague Presidential elections, which occurred every four years and became official after a January inauguration, the shift in power these days was nearly instantaneous. This was possible because candidates now had to announce their potential cabinet while still on the campaign trail—a result of previous appointment surprises and past "lame duck" inefficiencies. Therefore, her team was already onboard when her President-elect status changed overnight to that of Madam President.

Due to President Sotomayor's sudden passing, and Pat's personal emergency, the former Gamma state VP agreed to maintain status quo until Pat was ready to govern. The important thing was perception, anyway, they all agreed. The public didn't know about Katherine's situation, and they never would. A few sound bites and some previously-recorded Holos would tide the public over until Katherine healed and Pat began making public appearances again.

Ah. This is it!

Finally, she recognized the nurse's station outside Katherine's room. As soon as she opened the heavy door, she saw Waverly leaning over the bed and roughly shaking Katherine's shoulders.

"Kat! Wake Up! Wake up!"

The desperation in Waverly's voice brought Pat instantly awake. Her throat caught, and her heart seemed to tighten. Waverly's next words, however, snapped her out of her daze.

"Kat! Who told you the testimonies were switched? Where did you hear about Jordan?"

Pat staggered backward in relief. Apparently, Waverly was not shaking Katherine back from the dead.

"Stop it!" Pat roared, and startled Waverly into stepping back. "What are you doing? She's on medication to make her sleep!"

"Sh- she was talking!"

Pat had never before seen Waverly so frazzled. Her expression seemed almost frantic. Regardless, Pat brushed past her and surveyed Katherine with a practiced, motherly eye.

"It's okay, Sweetheart. Momma's here."

Katherine turned in her sleep toward her mother's voice and moaned. Pat heard her moaning. It sounded like, "… innocent… help him!"

Waverly peered over Pat's shoulder. "See?" she said. "We need to wake her up and-"

"Hush!" Pat said to Waverly and bent to stroke her daughter's hair. She patted the wet bangs aside and kissed Katherine's forehead gently. "No one is going to hurt Jordan, Sweetheart. I promise. Everything will be okay."

Only then did Katherine visibly relax.

✳✳✳

Once her daughter was peaceful again, Pat whirled on her friend.

"What the hell was that all about?" she whispered. "The doctor said to keep her calm!"

Waverly sulked like a willful child. For the first time, Pat noticed how young she looked, how immature.

"I know what I'm doing," Waverly said.

"Like hell you do! Waverly, when you have a child of your own, you can jeopardize her health all you want. Until then, leave my daughter alone." The flash of anger in Waverly's eyes surprised her, but her own annoyance kept her going. "And what was Katherine talking about? Did you really switch the confessions?"

Pat had not watched or read the news in two days—relying, instead, on her Cabinet to call in case of a National Emergency but to otherwise leave her alone—so she was one of the few who had failed to see the confessional broadcast.

"Of course I switched them!" Waverly said. "By now, Brown's face (with the caption, DANFORTH'S SON) is on every screen in the Lytoky. You have to admit that showing the public Brown's ugly face is better than showing them Jordan's! What better way to hammer our point home?"

OUR point?

"So Brown attacked them both? We should let the court know! Jordan can go free and-"

"Too late. It's over."

"Over?"

"Results came in last night."

From Waverly's smug air, Pat could tell the results were not favorable for Jordan. She wondered how they had gotten enough votes so quickly. For a trial and a Results Show to start and conclude on the same day was unprecedented. Usually, the sponsors dragged the verdict out for at least a week... sometimes two. Someone must have been very anxious (and very prepared), to have already proceeded to the Sentencing show.

"Why are you looking at me like that?" Waverly asked. "Danforth's son stood trial, didn't he? There's no law anymore that says we have to wait. Swift Justice, remember? It's on our national emblem. His lawyer agreed to a speedy trial and the jury found him guilty. End of story."

"Yes, but what about the Adrays?" asked Pat.

"What about them?"

234

Pat stared at her friend. The woman suddenly seemed like a stranger to her.

"Did you program them to influence the jury?" Waverly looked away and didn't answer. "What about the voting public? Did you influence them, as well?" When Waverly still didn't respond, Pat threw up her hands in exasperation. "Katherine is in love with him, you know."

Waverly rolled her eyes. "How could she be in love? She's only eighteen, for MA'AM sake!"

Pat had wondered that, as well. *How could anyone love a man? Still...*

"I don't know. Maybe after all these years, she's just gotten used to him."

"What do you mean, 'all these years'?"

Pat sighed. "It's a long story."

"Tell me."

Against her better judgment, Pat explained what she had learned about her daughter's telepathic friend over the last twenty-four hours. Katherine's outbursts had revealed that the two of them had been communicating since they were children, and that they had planned to meet at the Oasis.

"They apparently lost contact when he descended into the tunnels. She was still expecting him when that animal arrived!" she concluded.

"So THAT'S what happened!" Waverly said, looking distracted. "When did she say they regained contact?"

"Just as we were leaving the island. By then, Jordan's trial had already begun. She could hear Gloria's testimony."

"What do you mean she could hear it? Through Jordan?" Waverly's eyes darted back and forth, then she suddenly grasped her President's arm. "Does that mean Jordan hears what Kat hears, too?"

Pat contemplated the question with disinterest. "I guess so."

"Even when she sleeps? What about now? Can he hear what we're saying right now?"

Pat disengaged herself from Waverly's grip. "Waverly, I really don't know; but probably. It would make sense, wouldn't it?"

Waverly's face seemed stricken. She took one last look at Katherine then turned for the door. Pat followed, puzzled, but Waverly was already pushing through the stairwell door by the time Pat peered into the hallway.

FORTY-SEVEN

"Senator Danforth! Over here!"

The cry came from a set technician in the Info-Swirl's lobby. In the past two hours, the *Today Show's* crew had transformed his first-floor lobby into an impromptu studio. Danforth hardly recognized the place except for the New American emblem on the wall behind the reception desk, which now doubled as the backdrop for their interview.

Danforth, who had been skulking by the water cooler, looked up. The technician motioned him forward with one hand and patted the overstuffed black and white lobby sofa with her other. Heat from the makeshift stage lighting hit him the instant he stepped onto the set.

"You'll sit here," the technician said. She spoke in choppy sentences, constantly moving her attention between him and her notes. "Yeah, here on the sofa. The show's about to begin, so we need to hurry. Campbell will sit here, in the chair next to you. I'll bring you coffee in a second. Decaf okay? It's all we brought."

Danforth nodded. He wanted something stronger, but since they hadn't thought to ask earlier, and since he couldn't find his own assistant, decaf would have to do. Left alone with the sofa, he tested it before easing back—*Good, no creaks!*—and watched the news crew hustling in preparation.

With only minutes to spare, Honey Campbell emerged from behind a dressing curtain. Make-up artists, news personnel, and scriptwriters followed her. Danforth immediately sucked in his stomach and fidgeted with his tie. Under the brilliant overhead lights, he noted she was even more beautiful than yesterday's encounter, as if that were possible.

She must be over forty by now, he thought, *but she certainly doesn't look it.*

True to her name, she had honey-colored skin and golden hair that fell in lovely waves around her face. He had spent countless hours daydreaming about her over the years. He never wondered why her *Today Show* program was available in New Canaan, when all the other Lytoky channels were scrambled. She was the only female news reporter he knew. Maybe that's why he didn't think of her as 'one of them.'

I would have granted her an interview even if she hadn't threatened to expose me, he thought.

The set technician zipped by with his coffee.

"You ready?" she asked.

"You bet," he said, and he meant it. He couldn't wait to set the record straight.

Honey sat on the sofa beside him and smiled. In return, he gave her an awkward, toothy grin.

"Places people! Forty seconds and we're live!"

This announcement came from the onstage director. She tested the lights, nodded to Honey, and then turned to Danforth.

"Oh my goodness! Somebody get this man a towel! He's sweating like a pig!"

Her words cut and made him sweat even more as she turned and spat additional directions offstage.

"Makeup! Pat him down. Wardrobe! New shirt. Lights! Add a filter. You there! Find a fan and turn it on him. Thirty seconds, people!"

Hands came from every direction. They tugged at his jacket, mopped his forehead, and powdered his face and chest. Danforth panicked, suddenly certain the broadcast would begin with him in his undershirt.

He glanced at Honey, but she graciously ignored him as they worked. She straightened her jacket and calmly tapped her mike as the director called out.

"In five… four… three… two… one. Live!"

The camera's light blinked on, but for a moment, Danforth didn't breathe. His suit jacket was back on, but a false shirtfront had been hastily tacked into place underneath. Every sweat droplet had been patted dry or covered by thick, flesh-colored powder. He offered a flustered smile to the camera, grateful the viewers had missed the pre-show chaos.

"Good Morning," Honey began. "This is Honey Campbell, coming to you live…"

FORTY-EIGHT

Waverly tapped her foot on the concrete floor as the guards brought the prisoner forward. He walked stiffly, but unassisted. His face looked as though he had been on the losing end of some street-gang brawl. She wondered if they had virtually cut off his testicles, or only burned them. She had left the details of the interrogation to the guards since she didn't like to micro-manage.

He studied her as the guards stepped away. The look disturbed her. She had expected a rebellious teenager full of rage and indignation. And why not? Over the last two days he had been arrested, falsely accused, and beaten. He had been found guilty in a mock trial any moron could tell was rigged *(as long as they weren't under the Adrays influence, that is)*, and had been sentenced to die tomorrow. He should be throwing a tantrum.

Lord knows his daddy would.

Instead, Jordan stood before her with clear, thoughtful eyes that resembled resignation.

"Let me introduce myself," she began.

"No need. I can guess who you are. You're Waverly Nelson."

"Then you're probably wondering why I'm here."

"Not really. I've been expecting you."

His confidence was throwing her off.

"Then you are undoubtedly aware I can help you."

"I'm aware that you can. But I doubt that you will."

Waverly walked around him, circling close. "Well, several people have testified against you. They claim you are dangerous and deserve to die for your crimes. Why should I help you?"

240

No answer.

"Kat says you're innocent. She claims you two are telepathic and that she was "with" you when Gloria was attacked. Is that true? Answer me, dammit! Tell me if you can hear her and if she can hear you!"

Still no response.

"Are you just going to stand there, or what?" she said.

This is maddening. The whole reason I called ahead to transfer him back underground was to block his communications with Kat. If he won't talk, how can I be certain it worked?

"Is Kat right? Are you innocent?" Her voice echoed slightly against the tunnel's metal walls. "Why won't you tell me you were framed? That you're innocent? Or that you've been falsely accused?"

"Because you know that already," he spoke at last.

Waverly appraised him sharply.

"Are you aware that your father has forsaken you? He is not going to help. If you cooperate with me and tell the press he brainwashed you into attacking Gloria, I can set you free. It's him I want, not you. With one word from me, I can make all this disappear. I have the power to either spare your life or end it."

"You won't kill me," Jordan said.

Waverly smiled and leaned forward to sneer in his face.

"Is that what you believe? You think that because you know Kat you know me? Well, my young friend, I have killed men like you before, and I won't hesitate to do it again. 'You can't make an omelet without breaking a few eggs.' Isn't that what your Dad always says? I'm quite prepared to break you to exterminate the rest."

"Will that make your pain go away?"

Waverly drew back sharply.

"I knew it! You DID overhear me at Kat's bedside!"

"I know you think your mother never loved you, and that you want to punish men for what my father did to you. But you must realize revenge won't make it better. It won't take your pain away."

"I'm not doing this for me, you fool! I'm doing it for Kat!"

"Kat doesn't want this! You freed a rapist in order to start a war, and because of that, she was assaulted. Then you switched our trials—totally manipulating public opinion. You think Kat wanted any of that? If you do, you don't know her at all."

"I know more than you! You're just a boy!"

"Healing starts from within. Kat will get over this in time because she's strong, not because you declare war on men. She wouldn't want you to do this; I know it. I also know that if you were my mother, I wouldn't want you to be harboring so much hate. It's unhealthy."

Who does this kid think he is? she thought. Her heart was pounding in her ears.

"Look, don't concern yourself with me, boy. You're the one in trouble."

"Then tell me why you did it. Why did you have that woman attacked?"

"Oh? Something you don't know?" She smiled indulgently. "For your information, Gloria was practically begging for me to make her an example! She represents compliance with New Canaan. She reads their propaganda and sleeps with the enemy; what more do you need? Now, women are more determined than ever to follow my commands and strike out! It's the only way for them to make sense of it all and to believe in a just world."

"But this isn't justice."

"Son, justice is in the eye of the controller. And today, that's me."

"Then do what you will, but let it stop with me." He raised his chin in defiance and offered, "But I want you to know that I forgive you."

FORTY-NINE

The first thing Kat noticed when she regained consciousness this time was the sound of absolute silence. Jordan was gone. Again. Vivid memories from the last time he had disappeared—*The Clouds! The Dragon! The Rug!*—resurfaced.

She struggled with her sheets, but before she could slip into full-blown panic, she detected a whiff of her mother's Channel No. 5. Sure enough, her mother was asleep in a chair against the wall. Her face was almost gray in this light, and she had swollen bags under her eyes.

The last few days had not been easy on anyone, Kat realized. She chastised herself for being so stupid. Her mom was right; men were monsters.

Even Jordan?

She squeezed her eyes shut and tried to block out that last, unwelcomed thought. Without Jordan in her head, her mind had filled with doubt.

No, she finally decided. *None of this is Jordan's fault. If I had gone west, like he had first proposed, none of this would have happened. No one cared about women crossing into New Canaan. It would have all been totally legal.*

It was almost laughable how afraid she had been back then to enter a world of men. Much safer, she had thought, to meet him in the Lytoky.

Suddenly, Kat opened her eyes. *I'm tired of being afraid!* she thought. Setting her jaw, she looked above her at the dead teleVISOR—the one that had earlier shocked her with her attacker's face. Quietly, so as not to disturb her mother, she located a pair of ear buds from the side tray table and took a steadying breath. Five seconds later, half-expecting to see Brown's face again, she turned the unit on.

***

Honey Campbell's smiling face stared toward the main camera.

"Good Morning. This is Honey Campbell coming to you live from New Canaan. Joining us today is Senator Marshall Danforth, who has graciously invited us here to the Info-Swirl for an unrehearsed interview."

Honey turned and faced him.

"Good morning, Senator."

"Good morning, Honey." Danforth liked the way her name felt in his mouth.

"Senator Danforth, I'll get right to the point. Women all across the Lytoky are petitioning for your resignation. Some are even calling for your arrest. They say that since your son committed such a heinous crime, you are responsible for his actions and should, therefore, be held accountable."

"Hogwash!" Danforth said. "I am not responsible. If anything, they should applaud me for raising the boy to begin with. Besides, I'm not even convinced a crime was committed. I'm not saying Ms. Chiang is a liar, but someone should look into her story."

"I see. Well, the fact remains that your son was tried and found guilty, and is-"

"Found guilty by whom? A bunch of lesbians? I'm not surprised they took her side."

That barely fazed the reporter. "Regardless, New Canaan parents are held responsible if their children skip school. This is a significantly more egregious than skipping school, don't you agree? So since you sired such aggressive DNA, some are saying you should be held accountable. What do you have to say about that?"

Danforth smiled for the first time since arriving on set.

"Glad you brought that up, Honey. It is time I set the record straight." He turned and stared into the camera. "Jordan is not my son. I adopted him eighteen years ago, and he's been nothing but trouble ever since."

He was disappointed he hadn't heard Honey react, but he imagined everyone else watching from home had gasped. He smiled into the blinking camera in an attempt to connect with the viewers.

"Let me tell you a story, about ol' King Solomon, the wisest man in the Bible," he started.

"Wiser than Jesus?"

Danforth scowled at Honey's interruption, then trained his smile back to the camera.

Too bad they couldn't edit that part out, he thought.

"As I was saying, Solomon was so wise that people came to him to settle disputes. One day, a guard brought him an infant boy and two prostitutes. Each woman claimed the boy was hers, so Solomon instructed a soldier to give each woman a half. When the soldier drew his sword, however, one woman intervened. She said she'd rather see the other woman raise her son than to see him cut in two.

"So guess what King Solomon did?" he winked at the cameras. "He gave that woman the child. The moral? He who saves a child is a hero. I am like Solomon, you see. I saved Jordan from his whoring mother, so I should be honored, not accused."

"But in the story," Honey said, "wasn't it the child's mother who saved the boy from death, not Solomon?"

Danforth gave the reporter a patronizing smile. "No, Honey. It was King Solomon's wisdom. If it weren't for him, the child would have been put to death."

"But the child's life wouldn't have been in danger if it weren't for King Solomon. He ordered the child cut in half."

"Yes, but the other woman claimed-"

"King Solomon wasn't the father. It wasn't his blood in the child's veins. Your situation (even if what you claim is true) is nothing like the story you described. Your argument makes no sense."

Honey was pushing now, and Danforth didn't like it. *Pretty face or not, she ought to learn her place!* He scowled dangerously.

"You're missing my point. I saved Jordan's life by adopting him, but I couldn't save his soul. His mother's crime gene was too strong. I came here today to assure everyone I cannot be held responsible for what Jordan did since he is not my biological son. I am willing to make the ultimate sacrifice for the good of society by not interfering with his execution. Like the story of Abraham and Isaac, I'm willing to sacrifice my son for-"

"You're abandoning your own son?" Honey interrupted, not giving him the chance to compare himself with another biblical figure.

"It's his genes that are defective, not his upbringing. Anyone can see that! Clearly, I am not responsible."

"What about the story's moral?" Honey asked.

Danforth looked at her blankly. "What do you mean?"

"'He who saves a child is a hero.' Isn't that what you said? If you're washing your hands of him, doesn't that make you a coward? A villain?"

Danforth mopped his upper lip.

"No; you're still not getting it!" he said. "Jordan is not my son. He's not a child at all, for Christ's sake. He's eighteen! If he were still a child, he would be worth saving. Now that he's an adult, he's on his own. In New Canaan, we love our children, whether in uterine or newborn. Once they grow up, though, they need to pull their weight."

"You sound more like the 'other' woman," Honey countered. "The one who didn't care whether the child lived or died."

He was losing his patience. If they weren't on live TV, he would have told her to keep her mouth shut. At the very least, he would have walked out. She had totally ruined his speech.

"Why have you cut ties with your son, Senator? Rape doesn't even count as a crime in Missouri. You could have demanded we extradite him for a trial among his peers. You didn't, though. Why not?"

"Because I want to show how fair I am. How I love the world so much I am willing to sacrifice my own begotten son-."

"Your son?"

Too late, he realized his mistake. He could almost hear the triumph in her voice.

"Senator Danforth, I believe you are trying to manipulate our audience into thinking you are wise and fair. You are comparing yourself to God and Solomon. You want us to feel sorry for you for sacrificing your son, when you just announced he is not your son. Which is it?"

"But he's not, I tell you! I am not Jordan's father!"

He sat in stunned silence as his words echoed on set.

What the hell is going on? The interview was not supposed to go like this.

He had preapproved a specific list of questions for today's interview, but Honey had not asked a single one. After he finished the story of King Solomon, Honey was supposed to say, "You went out of your way to save a helpless child? That's very admirable of you, Senator."

I had a daughter! he wanted to yell. *Katherine Buford is mine! I switched her and Jordan at birth!* but he realized this was not the time to reveal his second bombshell. Honey wasn't taking him seriously, and she didn't deserve to get a scoop like this. Not from him! Not after the way she had dismissed him!

I'll announce it some other way, he thought as he squinted into the lights.

He heard Honey wrapping up, then she began reading a Promo for the program's second half.

"Stay tuned. Right after the weather, we'll recap yesterday's trial and show you outtakes from the confession before we cut to the execution pre-coverage. Thank you, Senator Danforth, for your entertaining story. I'm sure our viewers found it amusing."

Danforth did not respond.

First someone hacks into my Pardon List, then Jordan gets arrested. Now this? What else could go wrong? he thought.

***

Kat watched in disbelief as Senator Danforth denounced his son.

Is he serious? she thought, *or has he gone mad?*

She'd never seen Jordan's father, of course—the Lytoky didn't allow minors to watch New Canaan networks—but he'd looked exactly as she'd imagined. With sweat running down his temples in powdery, fake-tan streaks, and his shirt's half-collar sticking up on both sides, the man on screen had certainly appeared absurd.

But why was he condemning Jordan, and Jordan's mother? Kat had "lived" inside that home for years and never heard mention of his father adopting Jordan. Was he saying that Marisa had slept with someone else? Who? What did he mean by Crime Gene? It didn't make any sense.

And Jordan being 'nothing but trouble?' she thought. *Come on! I know better.*

Until now, she hadn't believed the Lytoky would really go through with an execution. She figured Jordan's father would protect him. Instead, the senator had not only abandoned him, he had practically accused him! Making a hasty decision, Kat threw off her blankets and sat up. Blood rushed from her head and she swooned, but she knew what she had to do.

FIFTY

"Sorry I took so long."

Dr. Taylor Bott entered Gloria's exam room, still studying her VEE, and halted when she saw the dismantled teleVISOR. All the other units down the hall were playing the *Today Show,* but by the looks of it, this one had just blinked onto the Cis-Star Info-net homepage menu.

"Hey, how did you--?" she quickly shut the door and came closer to the screen.

Seemingly startled, Gloria dropped her makeshift tools (a paper clip and a ballpoint pen's metal spring) and skitted off the counter.

"I didn't break it; honest!" she said. "I was just talking with my husband. I'll put it back together! It's easy."

At Dr. Bott's quizzical expression, Gloria explained that the public address unit on the wall was meant to transmit one-way broadcasts, not two-way conversations, so she had plundered through boxes of swabs and utensils until she found what she needed: a flat-edged tongue depressor. Using it as a screwdriver, she had pried off the monitor's side motherboard and had tinkered with its controls.

"You can do that?" Tylor asked her.

Gloria shrugged. "I'm a communications engineer. I work at Cis-Star Technologies, remember?"

Taylor stepped forward as though to inspect Gloria's work. The woman would make an excellent asset for the Rebellion, she knew.

But can she be trusted?

The Rebellion had previously rejected the idea of recruiting her because of her high-ranking job in Cis-Star. It had always seemed too risky. Now, perhaps things had changed. Taylor tapped her VEE thoughtfully against her thigh.

"Like I was saying, I'm sorry it took me so long, but I was unable to get you onto the Partho-lab registry."

Gloria visibly slumped.

"Someone tipped off the Unisex Family Planning Commission that you were denied artificial fertilization on the morning of your attack, so you've been flagged. I wish you had told me. Now they'll be watching. When they find out you're pregnant…"

Gloria's eyes widened and Taylor raised her hand to offset the objections.

"Don't worry; I haven't told them. But, of course, they will find out. Gloria, listen to me. You are not alone. There are others like you who believe in desegregation. We've been trying to stop Cis-Star from brainwashing the public, and to regain the right to choose. We call ourselves the Rebellion. Some are even heterosexuals, like yourself. We need someone with your skills and credentials to disrupt Cis-Star's frequencies." She noticed a flicker of indecision in the other woman's eyes.

"Gloria, we can help each other. Let me explain what we can do for you.…"

FIFTY-ONE

Alex had time to kill once she left Immigrations. Her flight to meet Robert wasn't for three more hours so, feeling nostalgic, she stopped at her favorite coffee shop for an early lunch. While seated at the counter, which doubled as a flat-screen TV encased in a waterproof seal, she moved her iced-coffee glass and wiped condensation from Honey Campbell's face.

The *Today Show* was in its last half hour. The meteorologist had just finished her forecast for clear skies and more unseasonably warm temperatures this afternoon.

"Perfect weather for a midday execution!" she concluded.

"There you have it, folks," Honey took over. "Don't miss today's great event! For those who couldn't get stadium tickets, the live broadcast airs at noon. Join us prior for the preshow recap that-" She stopped, suddenly, and Alex saw her eyes drift to the right. "Uh, please stand by," she said. "We're having technical difficulties."

"No!" a voice called from off-screen. "I have something to say! Danforth lied; Jordan is innocent! I want to set the record straight!"

The camera panned to the right where a young woman in a white skari was pushing her way past the makeshift barricade and a small crowd of onlookers. The woman stepped forward and the camera zoomed in.

"Here's your sandwich, Lieutenant," said the waiter, Jean, as she placed a platter on the teleVISOR counter. "Glad to have you back. I was just telling the girls.... Hey, what's wrong?"

Alex had shoved the plate aside.

"That's Kat Buford!" Alex said, mostly to herself. "What's she doing there?"

Jean peered at the countertop's screen, upside down for her. "Hmm. That's odd," she agreed. "They're filming in New Canaan today. I wonder why she's there. Want more coffee?"

The camera spun back to Honey. Her smile seemed perplexed.

"Ladies and Gentlemen, as we continue our Special Broadcast here at the Info-Swirl, we have an unexpected treat! President Buford's daughter is here with us now in person. This may be the first time she has stepped foot in New Canaan, but both sides of the border have seen her face before. How are you, today, Kat?"

When the lone camera shifted again to Kat, she refused Honey's offer to sit. She appeared to be waiting for the camera's close-up.

"She looks nervous," Jean said, resting a hip on the counter to watch.

"Those of you in the Lytoky know me," Kat said, speaking directly to the camera. "You've watched me grow up my entire life and you know I have nothing to hide. I'm here to tell you that Senator Danforth lied. His son, Jordan, is innocent, and I can prove it."

The camera jolted, and a rustling sound came from off-screen.

"I know for a fact that Jordan was in custody before Gloria was attacked," Kat continued. "Jordan is my age, but the man they're showing you is middle-aged. That's not Jordan! Someone switched his testimony with a man who also attacked me two days ago! Ask anyone who was there at the trial, or who works at Immigrations, and they will confirm it. Jordan is only eighteen and he did not commit this crime!"

Jean shifted her weight to glance down at Alex. "You work at Immigrations; right, Lieutenant?"

Alex ignored her and moved her sandwich platter even farther away.

"Jordan is innocent!" Kat continued. "You have to believe me!"

Suddenly, both Honey and Kat looked beyond the camera—to something happening off-screen—and Kat hastily backed up. In that moment, an Info-Swirl Security Guard rushed forward.

"Look out!" cried Honey, an instant too late.

"Oh no!" cried Jean and pointed to beside Alex's plate. "He got her!"

The officer pinned Kat's arms behind her back and started pulling her away. The camera followed.

"Look around you!" Kat yelled. "Turn off your TVs and start thinking for yourselves! The people in charge of this trial are lying to you! Jordan is innocent, I tell you!"

Alex nearly toppled her stool as she stood and swiped her wrist-VEE over the counter's check-out square. A corresponding beep acknowledge her payment.

"Hey, Lieutenant! Don't you want your soy sandwich?" Jean called.

"Sorry, Jean," Alex replied over her shoulder. "Not hungry!"

FIFTY-TWO

Beverly fished the vibrating V-cell from her left breast pocket and stared at the tiny screen. Taylor was calling from her private line. Since this was the first time they had spoken since last night, she paused in indecision. Should she answer with "Good morning, Beautiful!" *Too forward?* Or maybe her usual, "Detective Sparks speaking!" But that seemed too formal.

"Hello?" she finally answered.

"Beverly!" Taylor said excitedly. "I need to see you!"

"Ok. Give me a sec and I'll project," she said and moved toward her office, where she'd left her Holo-enabled laptop.

"No!" Taylor responded. "Don't plug in. I don't want this out on the Net. Just listen."

The detective had already reached her office, so she sat on the edge of her desk and tried to hold her V-cell screen steady.

She might not want to see me life-sized, she thought, *but I like looking at her, even if it is only on a two-inch, two-dimensional screen.*

"What's up?" she asked.

Taylor glanced around before continuing. "I can't tell you here. Meet me at my place in twenty minutes, okay?"

Beverly checked the time and shrugged.

"Sure, okay."

Does this mean maybe last night wasn't so bad, after all? she wondered. After the trial fiasco in her apartment, their evening had ended in strained silence. Even though Taylor had asked her in for tea, they had both been so confused by what they had seen on the screen that Beverly had not expected a second date.

"What's this about?" she added, trying to keep Taylor on the line.

The doctor shot her a dirty look as if to say, "I just told you I can't talk!" and Beverly grinned. "Give me a clue at least?" she asked.

Taylor seemed to consider her next words carefully.

"Someone is in trouble," she said, "and he needs our help."

He?

Beverly was suddenly grateful Taylor couldn't see her face life-sized, after all. The open-mouthed stare was not attractive on her, she suspected. Taylor must have understood the unspoken question because she nodded back silently.

"Twenty minutes?" Taylor asked.

"I'll be there."

She slipped her V-cell back into her pocket and was startled to see a visitor, wearing khaki, standing in her doorway.

Don't be a dolt, she chastised herself silently. *No one overheard your conversation. You're being paranoid.*

She noted the stranger's rank by her uniform's lapel.

"May I help you, Lieutenant?"

"You the detective covering the Chiang case?" the soldier asked. She had a crisp, no-nonsense tone and a slight southern accent.

Beverly smiled and motioned to a chair beside her desk.

"I am. What can I do for you?"

The lieutenant closed the door and sat down.

"My name is Alex Winters," she said. "I have some information, but you first have to agree to keep this confidential."

"Can't do that," Beverly said. "If you give me evidence regarding a case, I'm obliged by law to act on it. Or, at the very least, to report it."

"Oh, I can guarantee you that none of your superiors will want you to act on this."

Beverly was intrigued, but not persuaded. She had seen that expression before; the woman was obviously struggling over whether or not to get involved.

"Tell you what, Lieutenant," she said, taking her own seat behind her desk and checking her wrist-VEE. "You tell me what you know, and together we'll decide what to do about it. Okay?"

Probably nothing important, anyway, Beverly reasoned. Besides, she only had twenty minutes.

Alex paused, then pulled her chair closer and spread her elbows on Beverly's desk. Playing along, Beverly mirrored her actions. After hearing the lieutenant's next words, however, Beverly abruptly sat back. She now understood the woman's trepidation.

"Jordan Danforth is innocent," the lieutenant whispered. "And I can prove it."

FIFTY-THREE

Kat's jail cell looked similar to those she had seen on TV. A single cot was attached to the concrete-block wall, and a metal table and two chairs had been bolted to the floor. She inspected the sink. It worked, but the liquid running out was brown and smelled foul. The toilet was even worse. The door seemed solid metal, except for a square view-window.

From down the hall came the sound of laughter: male, of course.

Although the head jailor here had introduced himself as Sergeant Pendry, everyone they passed in the station had called him Big Steve. Kat could see why. His neck was easily twice as thick as any she had ever seen, and his arms and chest bulged beneath his uniform. He had ducked when he had entered the precinct during her processing.

Kat stared up at his ugly face in open defiance, and decided her mother was right: all men were hideous after all!

Big Steve noticed her staring.

"What's the matter?" he grinned. "Never seen a man before?"

His liverwurst breath made her nose wrinkle, and that caused Big Steve to laugh. He slapped the front counter where her uniformed Intake Officer was still typing.

"Look at that, Ernest. We're making the young lady sick."

Ernest continued his work without looking up.

"Come on," Steve said. "I'll take you down, myself." He reached for her elbow, but at his touch, Kat instinctively snatched her arm away and raised her fists like she'd learned in kickboxing class.

"No!" she yelled, instinctively.

The precinct fell silent as the other officers turned to watch. Her heartbeat was the loudest sound she heard until Big Steve cleared his throat.

"Everything's ok here," he said. She wasn't sure if he was speaking that last to her or his fellow officers.

Kat moved out her elbows ever-so-slightly and tightened her fists. Big Steve seemed to consider her posture, and chuckled. As the other officers returned to their duties, he bent his face toward hers and spoke with surprising gentleness.

"Better come with me, now, Miss. No one's gonna hurt you on my watch. I promise."

After a moment's hesitation and a glance around the room, Kat slowly lowered her arms. This time, the giant didn't touch her as he ushered her through an oversized steel door. As it shut behind them, Kat grew alarmed again, but Big Steve led her forward.

"It's unfortunate that they couldn't take you to the Ladies Jail," he said. "Apparently, that one's full."

Big Steve whistled cheerfully as they walked past numerous individual cells. The men inside looked up when they saw her, and a few stood and approached the bars. It reminded her of wild predators smelling fresh blood. At the end, they took a sharp right and repeated the routine down another corridor. She noticed an open cell ahead and steeled herself, but Big Steve kept going. Several turns later—*How does he keep from getting lost? It's like a maze in here!*—and they crossed into a noticeably older part of the building. It was quiet here, and the cells in this wing had no bars, only steel doors, painted grey. At the first, Big Steve stopped and pulled out an old-fashioned key ring from his belt.

"See, I told you no one would harm you," he said, and stepped aside.

Kat peered inside the empty room and felt her eyes sting with relief.

"Thank you," she said, and wiped back a tear.

"No worries. I'll be back to check on you later," he said as he locked her in.

His whistling resumed as he walked away. It was an unfamiliar tune, but comforting. Before long, all was silent. She carefully eased back onto the brittle, bare cot and tried not to let it touch her skin as she crab-walked her way back against the wall. There, she hugged her knees to her chest.

It was in this position that her thoughts slipped back to her hospital escape. Being careful not to disturb her sleeping mother, she had quietly searched for her clothes. The rest had been easy. With her mother's VEE, which she found resting on the nightstand, she had used the family account to program a border pass, much like she had secured a flight to the Oasis. A half hour later, she crossed the Border Bridge on foot. The streets had been surprisingly empty at that hour, so the journey's ease had belied the potentially dangerous consequences. It was only another few minutes before she had entered the Info-Swirl lobby and interrupted the *Today Show's* filming.

As she studied the rough, concrete-block walls, she wondered about those consequences and hoped she would find the courage to face them.

***

Footsteps approached outside her cell, and Kat felt goosebumps prick her arms. When the hydraulic hinges released, the first face to appear in her doorway was her jailor, Big Steve. He surveyed the room in a sweeping glance and gave her a reassuring nod.

"You have a visitor," he said, and stepped aside.

Behind him, a tall, overweight man in a three-piece powder-blue suit was wiping his face with a blue handkerchief. Kat recognized him at once from the TV interview.

"Whew! That's quite a hike, isn't it?" the man said, as he clapped Big Steve on the back and tucked the handkerchief into his front coat pocket, being careful to fluff out the corners so they showed. He walked straight inside and eased himself onto one of the bolted-down chairs. "Why'd you hide her way back here?" he added. "Something wrong with the new wing?"

"No, Sir. It's just a little crowded over there, is all."

"This wing's under renovation, though, right?"

"Starts Monday."

Senator Danforth shrugged. With his knees and belly pressed against the tiny table, it reminded her of a grown-up attending a child's tea party.

"Guess you know what you're doing," he said. "I'll take it from here, Pendry. You're dismissed."

Big Steve and Kat shared a wary glance.

"But Sir," the jailor said, "it's protocol for me to stay."

"Sergeant, seriously? Look at her; she can't hurt me." When the man still didn't move, Danforth added more sternly, "I'm afraid I must insist. I need privacy."

While Danforth returned his attention to Kat, Big Steve backed outside. He directed his next words to the senator, but his eyes never trailed from Kat's.

"Holler if you need me," he said. "I'll be right down the hall."

He left the door open. She heard his keys jingling as he went.

"Young lady," Danforth began. "Do you know who I am?"

Kat took a seat across from him but didn't answer. She knew from past experiences (through Jordan) that when Danforth was feeling particularly chatty there was no reason to interrupt.

"Well, of course you do," he continued. "Who doesn't? You've been in the Lytoky, but not underground, for goodness sake! And from that little stunt you pulled at the Info-Swirl, I take it you saw my interview with Honey this morning."

Kat crossed her arms.

"You seem to know a lot, but you obviously don't know everything. For instance, did you know that I'm your-"

He paused, and smiled widely, apparently enjoying what he thought was suspense. Jordan's dad always did like to drag out his stories. Back home (back at Jordan's home that is), he did it all the time. He would make Jordan and his brothers stand at attention and then pause, dramatically, to let his fabricated tension grow.

"Wait for it; wait for it!" she and Jordan would laugh while they waited in exasperation.

"No," Danforth said. "Perhaps I should put it differently. How's this: Do you remember when you were born? No, of course you don't; but I do! I was there! I helped bring you into this world… in more ways than one." He chuckled.

Kat tilted her head and frowned. She didn't like where this conversation was going.

"A long time ago," he continued, "I had the opportunity to be of some assistance to President Buford. You see, my wife had just given birth… to a girl. As luck would have it, another child was born that day… a boy. I ended up raising the boy. Can you guess what happened to the girl?"

Kat's eyelids tightened. She felt her pulse quicken and her skin growing suddenly cold.

"Come on, Kat. You're a smart girl; don't you get it? You are my daughter! I gave you to Buford, and I kept Jordan!"

Her mind was in turmoil. *No, that can't be true!*

"But don't worry. All that is over; I'm here now to claim you and to bring you home with me. I'll set the record straight, and you and I will turn things around. Better late than sorry, right?"

Kat didn't move. The man's cliché was wrong, and his delivery tactless, but there was no chance she had misheard him.

He smiled indulgently. "I bet you're wondering why I now choose you, my biological daughter, over Jordan, the boy I raised. You're too young to understand this, Katherine, but it's a natural instinct. Don't believe me? You're looking at me like I'm despicable, but President Buford is just like me. Given the chance, she would turn on you in a heartbeat if she had a biological child."

Kat couldn't stand it any longer.

"Liar! Mom is nothing like you. You know nothing about family, loyalty, or love."

"She speaks! Excellent! For a moment there, I thought the cat had your goat!"

Kat felt lightheaded and realized she had been holding her breath. Luckily, his botched cliché helped snap her out of her shock.

"You mean 'your tongue,'" she said.

"What's that, Dear?"

"'The cat had your tongue;' that's how the saying goes." At his blank expression, Kat sneered. "What? Doesn't anyone ever correct you?"

Now it was his turn to scowl. His round cheeks, still a patchy pink from his long walk to her cell, turned even darker.

"Whatever."

"Oh, that's right," she said, feeling a mild sense of control for the first time in days. "That's the whole reason I'm here, isn't it? I publicly challenged your attempts to frame Jordan, and you don't like being corrected, so you made up that story. Admit it! You're a liar and a selfish tyrant. If Jordan didn't need your help to get a stay of execution, I'd say he was better off without you!"

The Senator leaned forward. "Regardless, Jordan is without me. You think I don't see what Buford is doing? She plans to exterminate all the men, but I'm not going to let her."

He paused, and then sat back.

"That's where you come in! Once people accept that you're my daughter, and they see you thriving in New Canaan, they will forget this gender war nonsense and-"

"Are you insane?" Kat jumped to her feet "I'm not staying here! As soon as Mom learns what you've done, she will destroy you, and I'll help her!"

She smelled his cologne mixed with sweat as he, too, worked his way out of his too-small chair and stood, towering over her.

"Well, like it or not, you are my daughter and you belong to me! DNA tests will prove it. You are my blood, and there's nothing that old crone can do about it!"

"Holding me hostage won't help you overthrow the Lytoky! No matter how many children you kidnap or how many sons you sacrifice, you are finished! I'll see to it that mom has YOU executed!"

"Young lady!" he bellowed. "Someone should have taught you manners a long time ago! Women don't talk to men like that in New Canaan!"

"Well, maybe they should! What are you going to do about it? Wash my mouth out with soap? Hold my head under water? Whip me until I bleed? That's how you teach your children obedience, isn't it?"

She flinched as his hand reared back to slap her, but instead, his hand hung in midair.

"How- how do you know all that? Who have you been talking to?"

"I know everything!" she shouted, squaring off to him again. "I know what it's like to be your child, to have your arms strapped to a whipping post and lose consciousness from the pain. You will have to kill me before I ever call you Father."

"So be it!" His hand curled into a fist. He was between her and the door, she noticed. There was nowhere for her to run.

"Hey! Everything okay in here?"

At the sound of Sgt Pendry's voice, Senator Danforth spun like an unbalanced top. In Big Steve's hands was a large baton.

"I heard yelling," the officer continued. "Came to make sure no one was hurt." His eyes darted once to Kat, then back to the senator.

"I'm fine!" Danforth snapped. "Get out of my way." He pushed past the taller man, then turned back to Kat. "I already issued a statement. By now, everyone knows you're my daughter. I can keep you here forever if I want. You just think about that!"

He turned to Big Steve and added. "Keep an eye on her. No visitors!"

Kat listened to his receding footsteps but knew he wouldn't get far without his escort. She reached for the cot, beside her, and sank on trembling legs.

"Thank you!" she mouthed to Big Steve.

"No matter to me one way or another," he said and shrugged. "Just doing my job." He half-turned, then glanced back. "You take care now, Miss. Holler if you need me."

Kat watched the cell door close and a random thought occurred to her. *Perhaps Big Steve was not so ugly, after all.*

FIFTY-FOUR

Not knowing where else to turn, Pat left the hospital and went to question Jordan, thinking maybe he would know how to locate Katherine.

Her new security detail met her in the hospital lobby (having been directed previously to stand down) and escorted her the short distance to the East St. Louis Detention Center, less than five minutes away. She doubted Katherine knew Jordan was so close. Pat certainly hadn't told her, and it was unlikely Jordan knew, himself, since the tunnels frequently disoriented those unfamiliar with them. Still, she hoped Jordan could help her find her daughter.

While walking toward the Jail's Security desk, Pat heard a disturbance down the hall. Two guards had a woman by the upper arms and were forcefully dragging her toward the exit. Pat's eyes widened in recognition.

Marisa was no longer the beautiful, carefree woman she remembered. When Danforth and his family had first moved to Missouri fourteen years ago, Pat had noticed that his wife had silky brown locks and a delicate figure. She had always conducted herself with a kind of inner strength and grace that Pat found admirable—especially considering who she had married. But today, that presence was missing. Her brittle hair had escaped its bun and flailed wildly as she struggled. Her pale face had aged prematurely, and mascara tears had left dark lines down her face.

"Where have you taken him?" Marisa was yelling. "I have the right to know! He's my son, dammit! Isn't it enough you're going to kill him? Don't deny me this last chance to see him!"

Pat had to be nudged by her own security detail to pass through the turnstile gate, now cleared for her to enter. She thanked the wide-eyed prison Security Guard, then motioned with her head.

"What's that all about?"

"Prisoner's been moved," came the reply, "but the woman's been complaining for hours."

"Moved where?"

"Uh. Not sure."

Pat watched Marisa raise her right hand and clutch at the air. It reminded her of a day, long ago, when Jordan had made the exact same gesture: the day he and Katherine had parted at the airport.

"Wait!" Pat called, raising her own outstretched palm to get the guards' attention. "Where are you taking this woman?"

The guards stopped when they saw her, and their mouths fell open. The result was what Pat recognized as hero-worship. (She had observed it many times before over the years whenever people recognized her.) The guards tried to salute, but they couldn't without releasing their charge.

"Pat!" Marisa cried, struggling anew. "You have to help me save Jordan!"

"Madam President," said the guard to her right. "Sorry if she's disturbing you. We're escorting this woman outside. We've explained to her that the prisoner's been moved and we don't know where he is, but she keeps getting back in and insisting we let her see him."

"Pat!" Marisa broke in. "Marshall claims Jordan isn't my son! He claims he switched him at birth... with Kat! Now they'll execute Jordan for sure! You have to help me save him before it's too late!"

Pat squinted in confusion. *He switched them at birth? Jordan and Kat...?*

She hesitated for only a second, then sharply addressed the guards. "Find us a secure room. Now! I need to talk with this woman in private."

What is Danforth up to? she thought. She had always feared that her daughter's biological parents would surface someday... *But Marshall and Marisa? Preposterous!*

She studied Marisa carefully now. The younger woman was several inches taller than herself. Pat wondered, suddenly, how fourteen years had passed without a word between them. That day at the airport, they had promised to keep in touch but, it turned out, neither of them did. At first, Pat hadn't even noticed. Both had toddlers, after all. Pat was busy revamping her TV series to include Katherine, and she assumed Marisa was equally busy settling into her new home in New Canaan. As time went on, however, Pat got the feeling Marisa was avoiding her. She never returned Pat's messages, and the few times she got through, Danforth was the only one who answered. His excuses ("She's too tired to talk," or "too busy to come to the teleVISOR") sounded contrived and insincere. After a while, it seemed, there was no friendship left to salvage.

Pat wondered, now, if Danforth had purposely kept them apart (them and the children) by telling lies on both sides.

The guards led them past the exit (their previous destination) to a small conference room in the back.

"No do me a favor," Pat ordered the guards. "Find Lieutenant Alex Winters and bring her to me, Pronto! She's an Oasis Transport Officer. She should be next door, in Immigrations."

The guards nodded and closed the door. *The Lieutenant found Katherine once,* she thought. *Surely, she can do it again!*

Alone at last, Marisa grasped Pat's hands, not wasting time on pleasantries.

"Pat, don't let them execute Jordan!"

"I won't, but first tell me everything Marshall said about Katherine. And please don't tell me you think it's true!"

Marisa took a deep breath and explained what Danforth had said last night. Likewise, Pat shared about Kat—about the Oasis, the attack, and the doctor's concerns over her mental state.

"When I woke up a half hour ago and found her gone, I worried what she might do," Pat admitted. "She's as desperate as you are to prove Jordan's innocence."

When the door swung open, an out-of-breath Lieutenant Winters rushed in, looking disheveled. Before Pat could even ask for her help, the officer began.

"I know where Kat is," she said. "But first, there's something you both need to know…. Jordan is in trouble!"

FIFTY-FIVE

"Never say all men are useless," her grandmother once told her. "It only shows your ignorance. Some men are quite tolerable. Others, entertaining. The rest might seem useless, of course, but remember this, Little Wave: every splinter serves a purpose."

This off-handed remark—made one summer, decades ago while Waverly sat perched on a stool in her grandmother's lab—came back, fittingly enough, as Waverly strolled through her former lab at Cis-Star Technologies. Back then, her grandmother hadn't even looked up. She had flung out the statement so casually Waverly doubted the woman had even remembered making the statement later. But Waverly never forgot. She remembered everything her grandmother had taught her.

"Besides," the older woman had continued, winking over her bifocals, "people learn better from bad examples."

Waverly smiled, now, and glanced around the Yardstick's empty lab—closed today, in honor of the execution. She ran her fingers over a random counter, enjoying the feel of hard, cold granite. Each abandoned microprocessor or accessory she touched made her feel more grounded; it felt like coming home. She had spent ten years in this lab (during summers and on weekends after school) and had absorbed a myriad of such "pearls of wisdom." This was also where she had studied for physics, learned how to solder a motherboard, and recorded her first electromagnetic wavelength in a stimulated brain.

Before her death, nineteen years ago, Pearl Nelson had been touted "the most brilliant mind in modern-day science." As a renowned entrepreneur and humanitarian, she had previously won the Nobel Prize for her efforts during the Plague War, and had been chosen *Time's* Woman of the Year. Some had encouraged her to run for President during that initial New American election, but she had refused.

"I preferred working behind the scenes," she had once confided to Waverly with a wink. "Besides, how else could I have founded the MA'AM Revolution?"

Her grandmother's early role in MA'AM was their little secret. The organization's early mission had been to stop the Plague's terrorists by creating a system for reporting all suspicious or malicious behavior via her women's networking site.

"We didn't intend to target American male behavior," Pearl had explained with a grin. "But you have to admit, it was a great side effect!"

They had both laughed at that one.

Waverly remembered feeling so special during those private talks. She would listen for hours while they worked side-by-side and would clap her hands in delight every time her grandmother shared something new, or something secret. That was how Waverly knew the Adrays had something to do with MA'AM's success, too.

The public knew about the Adrays, of course, but only as an entertainment feature. No one knew how they really worked, or their early covert use during the plague war. Even now, Waverly trusted only a handful of employees with that knowledge, and contrary to what Danforth believed, he was not one of them. Even Buford only had a vague idea. Waverly had briefed both of them, of course, but neither understood what really went on here in the Yardstick. The same was true of most of the Cis-Star personnel she employed.

Since all Adrays programming originated from the Cis-Star's main server, her techs distributed them via special relay stations—either to the east or the west (depending on the topic's slant), and sometimes to both. From Waverly's private office, she could override them all, with the exception of the Unirays, which could only be programmed from each individual mobile device, itself.

The original Uniray prototype (the one she had first used on Danforth, and then on Kat, years later, at the airport) had a range of only fifty feet and had to be calibrated to a specific individual. Since then, her team had increased its range to roughly five miles, similar to the Adrays frequencies, and could influence specific groups that shared DNA characteristics, like to all males who shared a thrill-seeker gene.

Unirays could be transmitted from one cell tower to the next, but since Pearl had once warned her against "holding all her eggs in one basket," Waverly refused to house the program on the Cis-Star's main server.

Waverly left the lab, now, and its memories, and punched in her private elevator code on her VEE. Her penthouse office, above, although not as fancy as Danforth's, was on the 77th floor and aligned perfectly with the Info-Swirl's curving peak and the secret Cis-Star Relay station buried there above Danforth's office. From there, she had a clear view of the Info-Swirl, where Danforth was no doubt standing on his balcony, staring forlornly back across the river still reeling from his devastating loss and wondering why she hadn't called.

As the elevator doors slid opened, she flicked opened her ladybug pendant's VEE to make what she thought of as a "game-day adjustment." Her personal virtual screen appeared, and her favorite words, "DANFORTH'S BLOOD..." preceded her into the empty cab. She programmed her adjustments as the elevator ascended.

Finally! she thought. *Danforth will understand what it's like to lose a child.*

Last night, right on schedule, Waverly had compelled Danforth to start telling the truth. Although she hadn't yet been able to watch his interview with Honey (all outside cell transmissions were blocked in the lab), she knew the reporter had taken care of him. Honey was a professional, and one of Waverly's most trusted associates.

The Lytoky's women, having been bombarded by the relentless message, "DANFORTH'S BLOOD MUST DIE," for the last several hours, would soon start demanding retribution. Strong emotions, like hate, were always easy targets, she knew. Given an outlet, the public responded every time. Her grandmother had told her how similar past presidential elections had been fueled, and won, on similar techniques, even before the Adrays' invention.

She could hardly wait to see the look in Danforth's eyes when he realized what she had done to him, and why. She could almost picture the confrontation.

"Hello Danforth," she would say. "Remember me?"

269

He would be confused at first because of course he knew her; she was his friend and advisor, Waverly Nelson.

"Wrong!" she would say. "My name is Waverly Lancaster. My mother, Irene, attended your First Calvary Baptist Church, in Boston, and committed suicide. You officiated at her funeral but wouldn't let her be buried there. Remember now?"

At that point, his forehead would wrinkle as he tried to recall, but, of course, that wouldn't be enough. She was sure there had been many such funerals he hadn't bothered to remember. "You took away my baby and called me a whore!" she would say. She knew it would take him a moment to register, and that was okay. She would wait. As the memory slowly resurfaced, she would finally get to witness his actual Moment of Revelation.

"That's right!" she would say. "I'm Kat's mother!"

After that, she would explain how she had been manipulating his every thought for the last fourteen years, and how she had used his arrogance to nearly annihilate the very religion he claimed to hold so dear. Then, he would grovel. She pictured him pleading for forgiveness, and her laughing in his face. After that, if there really was a God in Heaven, she would finally have her revenge.

She flicked her VEE closed, then back open in anticipation.

"How would we learn without bad examples, indeed, Grandma?" she said aloud. "See? I listened! Too bad Kat doesn't yet know the truth."

Times like this made her grandmother's absence even more pronounced. She wished they could have shared this victory together. Without an accomplice, it was difficult to fully enjoy the fruits of her masterpiece. She certainly couldn't share this with Gloria. With everything orchestrated to a delicate balance, she didn't even fully trust Honey Campbell. As a reporter, it might prove too hard to resist such a scoop.

Just as the doors opened onto her penthouse suite, her wrist VEE vibrated. With a flick of her hand, the words "BREAKING NEWS!" appeared. Waverly glanced at the summary that followed, then she stopped mid-stride.

"KAT BUFORD ARRESTED AT THE INFO-SWIRL TODAY. BEING HELD AT ST. LOUIS JAIL UNTIL A TRIAL CAN BE…"

"What?" Waverly cried out loud. *"No! Kat can't be in New Canaan when the war breaks out!"*
She immediately turned and punched the elevator button back down.

***

Ten minutes later, Waverly was running through East St. Louis' crowded streets.

On a typical day, she could have walked from the Yardstick to the border bridge in twenty minutes or less. But this was no ordinary day. The streets were already crowded with pedestrians gathered for the execution. Even the main roads were blocked to traffic. Everyone in the Lytoky, it seemed, had gathered to witness the event live over the mega screens set up throughout the plaza. The scene reminded her of her grandmother's stories about New Years' Eve celebrations at Times Square.

Waverly pushed off a curb and fought against the incoming tide. Women immigrants were storming the border and streaming onto Lytoky soil—taking refuge in their eastern sisters' arms. She, alone, it appeared, was traveling west, to New Canaan. In her haste to get to Kat, she barely even registered the thrill of her creation: her war had at last begun.

FIFTY-SIX

"Hurry!" a gruff voice called from the darkness. "Follow me!"

Kat opened her eyes and squinted. Smoke instantly stung her eyes, and she felt burning in her lungs. She could hear an alarm, but it sounded far away.

"The Jail's on fire! We have to get out! Now!"

Kat recognized Big Steve's voice and fumbled her outstretched arms toward the sound. One hand was immediately engulfed in his enormous mitt, and she gasped as he yanked her out into the smoky passageway.

"What happened?"

"No time to explain! Move!"

He practically dragged her down the corridor. When they turned left at an intersection, she glanced right and saw the far end glowing hazy orange from what she realized must be the new wing's emergency lighting. Scrambling guards strobed in the blinking light as though outlines in a surreal battle scene. They yelled over the sound of spewing water and a loud automated voice announcing there was a FIRE IN THE BUILDING. PLEASE EXIT NOW.

"Come on!" Steve said.

He led her away from the new wing and cut down an even darker corridor. They were both coughing now.

An explosion sounded behind them, followed by angry shouts of confusion. Kat jumped and tried to look back, but Big Steve squeezed her hand and pulled.

"Don't worry. I've got you."

A few seconds later, Kat felt herself pushed outside. Her free hand rose to shield her eyes, but Big Steve held fast to the other. Around her, the outside world was swirling in screams, sirens, and more distant gunfire.

"What's happening?" she yelled.

"New Canaan's gone crazy! Senator Danforth ordered your execution! (Some sort of retaliation for his son's sentence!) Rumor has it, he's going to soon announce you are his daughter and claim this is his sacrifice!"

"He what?"

Kat's mouth fell open and she stared at him in disbelief.

No! Surely he wouldn't! she thought.

The old jail's emergency exit had deposited them into a wide, empty alley. As her eyes still struggled to adjust, she saw moving figures stampeding past at both ends. Toward the east, the Info-Swirl rose high above the fray.

"There's a riot brewing out front," he said, "so don't go that way! They're out for blood. Make for the border!" He nodded toward the Info-Swirl, and the Mother Road Bridge, beyond.

Kat blinked and noticed that Big Steve was injured. He had a deep gash below one cheek, and his right shoulder was bleeding. The bloody limb hung close to his body, unsupported. She looked down at his other arm, and the big hand in hers, and finally understood.

"You set the fire, didn't you?" she said. "You went against your own people in order to save me. Why?"

He shrugged, though it caused him obvious pain. "Seemed like the Christian thing to do," he said. "They weren't going to give you a fair trial." He looked away as if that explained everything.

"It will take them a while to realize you're gone," he added. "I'm the only one who knew where you were, and although the new wing is fireproof, they'll need to clear the smoke before they come looking for you."

He opened his fingers, at last.

"Now, get on home where you belong, Miss. I'll take care of things here."

"Thank you," she said. When she reached up to kiss him good-bye on the cheek, she felt his head turn sharply away. She followed his gaze to three big men entering the alley from behind her. Three women followed, wearing tight miniskirts and black lace stockings. One wore a short, red trench coat on top.

Obviously not a Lytokian. Kat thought.

"What have we got here, boys?" said the blond man in the middle. "Hey Charlie, isn't that the new President's daughter? The one we saw on the news?"

"Oh yeah," said the man to his right. "I remember that tight little skari!"

The pack laughed and moved closer.

"Well, then…" said the first. "Why not have a little fun?"

"Go!" Big Steve whispered, and pushed Kat away. When she reached back for him, he whirled on her. "Don't stick around here trying to help," he said. "That will only distract me and get us both hurt. Believe me; I know what I'm doing. I come out here all the time. As soon as you're around that corner, I'm ducking back inside the jail. So, the sooner you go the better. Now, scoot!"

He pushed her away again.

Kat glanced down the alley toward the Info-Swirl, and back to the three angry men. They were advancing slowly. If she didn't leave soon, she would never get away.

She gave one last, wide-eyed look at Steve, who winked his good-bye, then she ran. Her bare feet made soft, slapping noises, but were barely audible over the growing din at the alley's mouth ahead. Right before she reached the end, she turned back. Big Steve had thrown a massive punch with his left hand (the gentle hand that had led her out of danger) and had knocked the blond man down. She saw Steve hesitate and glance toward her, so she tore her gaze away and ran into the frenzied crowd.

***

Behind her, Big Steve threw another punch, but this time his intended target ducked. The man named Charlie threw a counterpunch just as the grounded blond dusted off his knees and came at Steve from behind. Together, they slammed the guard against the jail's exterior block wall while the third man pinned his good arm.

The blond man stepped back and let his two comrades take over. That's when he drew a small revolver from his belt.

"Say yer prayers, woman lover!" he shouted as he aimed.

***

Amid the bustling crowd, Kat thought she heard a gunshot sound from behind her. She started back, but the crowd (men and women, alike) pressed her forward. Some were running for the Mother Road Bridge and others were running for the Info-Swirl. From this side of town, it was all the same direction.

Behind her, in an unnamed alley behind the St. Louis Jail, a blond-haired man shoved a gun into his waistband and followed his friends back into the street from the direction they had come. They left behind a security guard slumped against a flush-mounted, unmarked exit. There wasn't even a handle on the door.

FIFTY-SEVEN

Pat forced on a tight-lipped smile as the Emergency Broadcasting Tone slowly faded. The shrill, initial blast had left her feeling uneasy. She wondered if Marisa had gotten through to Katherine yet. Back at the jail, Pat had at first planned to go west to get Katherine, herself, until Lieutenant Winters had insisted there wasn't time.

"If we're going to save Jordan, we have to act now!" Alex had said.

Still, Pat had hesitated. She had wanted to call Danforth, Waverly, and even the St. Louis Jail, if she had to, but Marisa had stepped forward.

"I'll go to the jail," she promised. "I'll stay with Kat and protect her. Don't worry; I'm certain she'll be fine. Marshall would never hurt her; she's his own flesh and blood, remember?"

You fool! Pat had wanted to scream. *Which child do you think he'll protect? The boy he previously chose over his own flesh and blood, or the girl he abandoned once, already?*

In the end, however, she realized Katherine would want her to help Jordan. Kat would be safe enough for now, she had decided. Marisa would protect her and bring her home.

A movement beside the blinking camera caught the President's eye. The set director had lowered her arm.

"And… we're live!" she called.

Pat cleared her throat.

"My people," she began. "At this very moment, an innocent man is scheduled to die. I need your help to stop his execution.

"According to the ninety-first amendment, I have the right to pardon any Three-Strikes criminal whom the people vote to acquit. So, please stop what you are doing and log onto the Lytoky webpage to sign the petition to save Jordan Danforth. The petition will be active for the next thirty minutes (until the execution), or until we have the requisite thirty percent participation to make it official. An innocent man's life is in your hands. Please help me do the right thing. Thank you for your attention."

Pat glanced left and caught a nodding Lieutenant Winters disappear behind a screen. As agreed, the lieutenant was going to keep watch over Jordan while Myrna Garcia (the Lytoky's District Attorney) was to file an emergency appeal. Together, they were all determined to save the boy.

FIFTY-EIGHT

Taylor escaped the teeming crowds and squeezed, unnoticed, inside the Yardstick's marble lobby. The thick, steel doors clicked shut behind her with disturbing finality, and seemed to suddenly encase her in silence. Outside, East St. Louis' streets were filling with rioters. Some wore buttons and carried banners proclaiming DANFORTH'S CHILD MUST DIE in large block letters. Taylor had never before seen such frenzied madness.

It's as if the whole town became possessed overnight! she thought.

She and Beverly had exchanged information earlier in the day after Beverly had brought with her an anxious Transport Officer. The whole time Alex had spoken, Beverly had held Taylor's hand. Ever since, Taylor's heart hadn't stopped racing.

"I knew yesterday that Jordan was innocent," Alex had told them. "He was in custody when Gloria was attacked. I even figured out that his retina scan had been switched; but I was determined to not get involved until I saw Kat on TV. I guess I should have done something sooner."

The woman had looked down uncomfortably, but Taylor and Beverly shared a knowing look.

"We did the same thing," Taylor explained to Alex. "We weren't going to get involved, either, even though we knew better. The trial-results propaganda from last night almost convinced us that man was Jordan, but something didn't feel right. Luckily, we had each other to overcome the Adrays' influence."

"It sounds like someone's using O-rays," Alex said, and then described the Oasis' Infirmary. "Only, now they're using them on women, too?"

Taylor nodded at Beverly. "Gloria told me Cis-Star is using something similar on us," she said. "On all of us! That's why I wanted to meet. She confirmed that some people, such as myself, hear actual voices over the PA systems, but for most people it registers only at the subconscious level. And here I always thought I was immune to them... until the trial, that is."

Beverly squeezed her hand.

"Anyway, according to Gloria, Waverly Nelson has been brainwashing the public using Cis-Star's public broadcasting systems, both in the Lytoky and New Canaan. Gloria believes she wants to incite another Civil War, but this time it's a war between the sexes. She wants to destroy all the men!"

"We can't let that happen!" Alex said. "I have a little boy, and-"

Beverly had squeezed Taylor's hand again before vowing to Alex, "We won't."

That had been nearly twenty minutes ago. Since then, Alex and Beverly had gone off to try to get Jordan help, and Taylor had been tasked with turning off the Adrays.

Too bad Gloria couldn't turn the damn things off, herself, Taylor thought now, patting her wrist-VEE self-consciously, where Gloria's passwords were stored.

But, of course, they had agreed the poor woman had been through enough. She was needed in the courtroom for the appeal, and after that she was going home... to her husband. Taylor couldn't blame her.

Taylor's hands shook. If someone caught her breaking in to Cis-Star Headquarters, the punishment would be severe. Still, what choice did she have? Only a few people knew what was really going on. She couldn't just sit back and watch this injustice without at least trying to help.

Could she?

She ran through the front lobby. A gaggle of older women were pecking around the information desk, looking for free handouts and taking an air-conditioned break from the noise outside, but none seemed to notice her. They were too excited about the execution.

A V-Pad, with the message "Museum Closed for Execution" had been propped on the Registration Desk. A stick-figure cartoon danced below the bright red words and a hangman's noose swung beside it. Every few seconds a big red arrow pointed at the cartoon and the words DANFORTH'S SON appeared.

The first elevator bank was labeled EXPRESS ELEVATORS – FLOORS 51-77. The doors were open, but Gloria had forgotten to give her the elevator code, so Taylor couldn't make them work. Gloria had said the Cis-Star's server was in the penthouse (on the 77th floor), and she had described precisely how to dismantle the latest program.

But how am I supposed to get there without the elevators? she thought angrily. *Fly?*

Looking around in frustration, she found another set of elevators labeled, FLOORS 11-50. The ride up was quick. On the 50th floor, a lone internal elevator awaited her and appeared to connect all the 'Adray Division' floors, from what she could tell. Once she reached the 67th floor, however, there were no more connecting elevators.

She noticed an Emergency Exit stairwell to her right and pulled the door open, expecting an alarm.

Oh shit.

There was no alarm, but the stairwell inside wound its way up and seemed to go farther than what Taylor could see. She took a deep breath, checked her VEE, and plunged up the first flight. There wasn't much time. In order to eliminate the Adrays programming before the execution, she needed to climb 10 floors in less than twenty minutes.

She had heard President Buford's Emergency Broadcast on her way to the building, asking for Jordan's pardon, but with Cis-Star so blatantly working against him, Jordan didn't stand a chance. Taylor needed to shut the system down, and fast. Gritting her teeth, she rounded the second flight, and hoped Alex was having better luck with her mission.

If she and President Buford failed, she knew, Alex might be Jordan's last hope.

FIFTY-NINE

By the time Waverly made her way across the Mother Road Bridge, the St. Louis demonstrators had packed the New Canaan streets, as well. Inside the jail's front lobby, she smelled smoke. The power was out, and sunlight filtered through the storefront windows in hazy, horizontal slits. Reporters crowded the reception desk, all asking questions at once.

"Calm down everyone!" yelled the officer behind the front counter. "It's only a minor fire, nothing more! Everything is under control." He held up his empty palms as though to prove he had nothing to hide.

"But Ernest," asked one reporter, who obviously knew him by name. "What about the rumors? They say one of your guards started the fire in protest over Senator Danforth's decision to execute Kat Buford. Is that true?"

What?

Waverly elbowed her way to the front and flashed her Cis-Star credentials.

"Is Kat alright?" she demanded, but the officer ignored her.

"What's going on back there, Ernest?" someone else asked, from behind. "Is the jail under siege, or what?"

"Gentlemen," Ernest pleaded from behind the counter. "And Lady," he added, finally acknowledging her. "I don't know where you all have heard such nonsense, but really, there's nothing to-"

Just then, an explosion came from behind him. Waverly and the others were thrown to the floor. Several gunshots sounded from the jail's inner depths, but after a moment, all went quiet.

"What do you say now, Ernest?" someone asked in the momentary stillness. Several others snickered nervously and began disentangling themselves from the rubble, and from each other.

"Ernest?"

No answer. Dust and smoke swirled overhead.

"He's dead!" another voice called out.

Waverly looked up and saw the man's neck had been pinched to the counter by a large metal shard. Frantic voices came from behind the now-splintered inner security door.

"She's gone!" someone yelled. "Kat Buford escaped!"

Waverly pushed off those around her and raced back toward the main entrance. Once outside, she headed east. There, only six blocks away, was the towering Info-Swirl. For the second time today, Waverly Nelson began to run.

***

They came within arm's length of each other: Kat, running for the bridge with thousands of others; and Waverly, pushing her way toward the Info-Swirl.

If not for two other bodies sandwiched between them, they would have easily spotted each other. Instead, when Waverly stepped up onto the Info-Swirl curb, Kat sped past and out of her life forever.

***

At first, Kat thought it strange that so many Lytoky women were returning home from New Canaan, then she realized these were New Canaan refugees racing toward freedom. Since the guards had abandoned their check-point posts, women previously forbidden to leave (by their husbands, fathers, or brothers) were making a run for the border.

Once she hit the bridge, she heard her name over the public broadcasting speakers. Every twenty feet, she heard it again.

"BREAKING NEWS! KAT BUFORD IS ACTUALLY SENATOR DANFORTH'S LONG-LOST DAUGHTER!"

She kept running. Once safely across the Mother Road Bridge, the atmosphere instantly changed. The crowd's desperation seemed to morph into Mardi-Gras-like euphoria. On this side, there were already women marching and chanting, and holding up signs and banners. It became difficult to move. Kat pushed her way back toward the hospital and merged with those celebrating in the street.

In Kat's haste to make her way back to the hospital—the only place she knew to look for her mother—she stumbled into a woman wearing a red trench coat. Kat instantly recognized her from New Canaan, from the alley behind the jail. The woman in red recognized her, as well.

"Hey, look!" she yelled and pointed a freshly painted nail. "It's Kat Buford! The one on the news! She's really Danforth's daughter!"

Heads turned, and those nearby stopped chanting.

"Danforth's daughter?" she heard someone murmur.

A placard turned in her direction as more women from New Canaan crowded close. The words on the sign, "DANFORTH'S BLOOD!" now seemed to hover above the throng.

Kat surveyed her surroundings. Here by the river, the streets were narrow and shadowed by skyscrapers. A news helicopter hovered nearby, overhead. She felt women pressing in. Those from behind tried to get a better look. Those already close had hatred in their eyes. Another sign on a stick, "DANFORTH'S BLOOD MUST DIE!" seemed to float overhead like a helium balloon.

Red Trench Coat repeated the words, as though reading the sign.

"Danforth's blood must die," she said.

Kat looked in horror at the nodding faces, and she took a step backward into someone else's chest. Too late: she was surrounded. The hyenas were closing in.

"Danforth's daughter...." the chanting began.

"No, wait! You know me; I'm Kat! I'm Pat Buford's daughter!"

Someone yanked her ponytail back, hard. At the same time, she felt pain in her shin as someone kicked her. She fell to her knees on cobblestones as the mob, above, descended.

SIXTY

Taylor lifted a weary leg up another step.

Only one more flight to go. Thank goodness! she thought.

Sweat already drenched her white silk blouse, and a stitch in her side contracted, slowing her down. Still, she climbed. She checked her VEE and gritted her teeth. Precious minutes were ticking away. The execution would start in less than three minutes; she had to press on. No time for pain. She had to stop the Adrays.

At the next landing, her left calf cramped into an agonizing spasm. She glanced up, as if willing the penthouse landing to come to her, and, grabbing the handrail, yanked herself upward.

SIXTY-ONE

President Buford waited by the massive teleVISOR screen for the petition's final tallies to register. The telethon-like broadcast had been set up here at the East St. Louis Courthouse lobby so she could be close to the action and watch Myrna Garcia file the appeal.

"Yes, Your Honor," said Myrna on-screen, standing beside Gloria Chiang, whose back was to the camera.

"I want to hear from the victim, herself," the judge said, looking down over her bifocals at the victim. "Ms. Chiang, are you aware that if you change your testimony now, you could be found in contempt of court and charged with perjury?"

The image on screen changed to Gloria's swollen, bruised face. Pat had to strain to hear the answer.

"I am," Gloria said. "But I realize, now, I have to do this. I couldn't face him before, but if this man is innocent...." she trailed off and looked down.

The judge took off her glasses. "This is an unusual request," she said, tenting her fingers. After a moment, she leaned back. "Okay, tell you what... since you never saw the defendant, let's bring him in now. If he's not the right one, I'll release him and dismiss all charges. If he is the one, the execution will proceed as planned. Fair enough, Counselor?"

Myrna Garcia nodded. "Yes, Your Honor. Thank you!"

The judge motioned to the bailiff. "Is the defendant still in the building?"

285

"He is, Your Honor. They've been holding him below ground in preparation for the event. It will just take a moment." She pulled out her V-Cell and turned her back to the camera.

As Pat watched, Myrna reach out and squeezed Gloria's hand.

***

"Hurry up!"

Lieutenant Winters yanked the cell door open. It clanged loudly against the bars and she saw Jordan wince. He sat up slowly and rubbed at his eyes.

"Hey, don't I know you?" he said.

"I was your intake officer back at Immigrations. You need to come with me if you want to live!"

"What's happening?" he asked.

"You'll see, Kid. Let's go!"

***

While the viewers at home waited, the President made one last pitch for Jordan's release.

"This can't be right," she said to the screen, then turned to the camera. "So far, it looks like only a small percentage of you have logged in, but there's still time! If you're at one of the celebration parties, stop what you're doing and sign the petition now! We must save an innocent life. Here, let me walk you through the petition."

With a large swipe, she minimized the projected tally scores to picture-in-picture, placed it beside that of the small courtroom scene, and exchanged the main image with the Lytoky's default website.

"See? Click on the special PETITION tab, here at the top. On the petition, there's even a photo so you can-" Pat's breath caught. There, beside the name "Jordan Danforth," was the leering man who had attacked her daughter.

A scream sounded from inside the courtroom. The main screen view automatically reverted to the action inside, where Gloria Chiang was sobbing into Myrna's shoulder and pointing.

"That's him! That's the monster! That's Jordan Danforth!"

The judge pounded her gavel. On screen, Gloria's subtitled words for the hearing impaired lingered: "THAT'S JORDAN DANFORTH!"

The words splayed in large text below Paul Brown's smiling face as he waved to the cameras.

SIXTY-TWO

High above the St. Louis chaos, two old acquaintances came face to face.

"Waverly! So glad you're here; I was hoping you'd come! I just broadcast an announcement!"

Marshall Danforth had been staring at his computer, but when she stepped out from the elevator, he stood to greet her.

"Where is Kat?" she demanded.

Although she had managed to catch her breath during the elevator-ride up to his office the rage and adrenalin made her voice shake. Just as she had entered his express elevator, her wrist-VEE had pinged a "BREAKING NEWS" report again, but the signal had died the moment the doors had closed. She had seen the earlier one about Danforth calling for Kat's execution, so she had ridden all 77 floors in anguish and couldn't wait another minute pretending nonchalance.

Danforth didn't seem to notice, however. He twirled a hand in the air and turned back to gaze triumphantly out his penthouse windows toward the river.

"Oh, she escaped," he said. "There was a little misunderstanding among the guards, and someone let her go. Don't worry; she'll turn up!"

Waverly felt relief flush through her, and she turned away so he couldn't see her reaction.

"I wasn't really going to execute her, you know," he said playfully, as though telling her something in confidence. "That was just a ploy to get Buford's attention. What's good for the gander will cook your goose, you know!"

Waverly shook her head and turned to face him again. She wondered if she would miss Danforth's botched clichés.

"So, what are you going to do now?" she asked.

"Isn't it obvious?"

He pointed a thumb over his shoulder at a monitor on the wall. It showed the congested city, as seen from a closed-circuit camera apparently mounted above the front lobby doors, below. Crowds were chanting an indiscernible catchphrase that was getting louder. Sometimes, the word "Danforth" escaped above the fray like the lone voice from the pre-plague story, *Horton Hears a Who*.

"Have you seen what's going on out there? Come look!"

He opened the balcony door in a rush, like a child wanting to brag on his many Christmas presents, and ushered her outside. Out there, he swept out a palm and indicated the city below. His enormous chest expanded another two inches as he took a satisfying breath. There were throngs of people in the streets for as far as Waverly could see.

"You see that?" he called out happily. "It's better than I could have imagined! My men are armed and ready! They're going to storm the Mother Road Bridge and take back what's theirs!"

"They're going to fight unarmed women and children?"

"Unarmed my ass! Come on, Waverly! You know women have their own ways of fighting back! Besides, liberal feminists are treacherous and deceitful. Hardly innocent!"

She stepped in front of him to block his view. She was shorter than him, so she waited until he looked down and made eye contact.

"You couldn't wipe your own ass," she said sternly, no longer concealing her contempt.

"Wha- what?" he stammered. The look on Danforth's face was priceless.

"You heard me. My women are armed with the one thing you can never possess… intelligence."

Danforth turned red and stepped closer. He towered over her. From the look on his face, though, she could tell he was more confused than angry. She knew a part of him was waiting for the punch line—for her to explain it was only a joke and that she was sorry. She gave him a second to wrap his brain around the sudden change in their dynamics, and to realize that his once-trusted advisor had now turned on him. When she spoke again, each word came out thick, like delicious venom.

"You think I would let you destroy the Lytoky after all the hard work I've done? I've been waiting for this day for eighteen years. No one down there is planning to follow you, Marshall; they're here to destroy you. They may once have felt threatened by the Lytoky and what it stands for, but after years of careful manipulation, most have learned to accept it. Why do you think Buford won the presidency? I've been controlling this election from the start. You were just too stupid to notice."

"That's enough, young lady!" Danforth punctuated his roar by pointing a finger in her face.

On screen, the chanting crowds were getting louder. *They are finally coming for him!* she thought.

"Try and stop me, you pig!"

He reared back. By now, his face was so red that, for an instant she feared he would have a heart attack and ruin all her fun. But, of course, he didn't strike. Instead, he stood there, with his impotent palm suspended high above his head, and gaped down at her with wide, dumbfounded eyes. His stance's resemblance to *the Awakening* statue gave her an unexpected rush. She had imagined this exact moment—had dreamed about it, in fact—for eighteen years. It was everything she had hoped for.

In frustration, Danforth lowered his arm and stomped past her to the balcony rail, where he slammed that same fist, repeatedly, against it. The outward-sloping glass, below the railing, trembled. She thought she heard a splinter, but still he pounded.

"Listen to the crowd!" she yelled, pointing back to the monitor inside. "Don't you hear what your men are saying? They are coming for you!"

His fist paused and he listened. Sure enough, one chant, "Danforth's blood!" was now clearly identifiable above the on-screen din. His fingers turned white as he strained against her programming.

"That's right," she said. "Go ahead! Try to hurt me; you can't. Feels like you're caught in a trap, doesn't it? As of this morning, thanks to my Adrays, no man can physically harm a woman... especially you. Face it, Marshall; you're finished. When your men storm the border, they'll be unable to lift a finger against my army."

"No!" He spun to face her, but stood there, limp and powerless. Waverly knew it was time to finish him off.

"Remember the day Kat was born?" she said.

"Y- yes," he said, looking freshly confused. "What does that have to do with anything?"

"Remember what you said to her mother?" When Danforth merely frowned, Waverly continued. "Let me refresh your memory. You said, 'You are unfit, by the standards of any good, decent Christian, to raise an innocent child.' Then you suggested she pray to God for her soul before it's too late. Remember now?"

A fog of incomprehension still shrouded Danforth's face. Waverly stepped forward and raised her chin to him.

"I was that woman," she said. "It was my baby you stole and gave to Buford. And believe me; I prayed! I prayed that one day I'd watch you fall off that pompous pedestal of yours and start begging for your own misguided soul."

Danforth turned away and stared out over the city. She pressed in even closer beside him so she wouldn't miss his expression as she continued.

"I programmed Brown's escape and led him to Gloria... Me! Because of your idiotic public support for that monster, I knew my women would cry out for your blood. But now, thanks to Jordan, my women don't trust ANY of you men—not even the young, good-looking ones—so they are willing and ready to exterminate all of you!

"Oh, don't look so horrified. You won't be around to see it. Your men will destroy you long before that happens. They believe this is all your fault, so they've turned on you. Finally, your God has answered my prayers!"

She followed his gaze over the balcony's edge at the advancing mob, far below.

"You know the best part?" she continued. "You made this possible. Without your incessant sermons about intolerance and hate, neither side would have been outraged enough to fight. Now, everyone is out for your blood. Literally!" She laughed a little at that. "You, and all your offspring."

She turned back to him and waited. She had expected him to pound his fist again, or to grovel. Instead, an unsettling grin flitted across his moist lips, and his eyes widened, making him look slightly maniacal. For a moment, she worried she had pushed him too far.

"Well, Waverly…" he said slowly as he turned to face her at last.

She braced herself for the words she knew were coming.

"I am sorry…"

Finally! She closed her eyes to savor the moment.

"I'm sorry," he repeated, "to be the one to tell you this, but there is something you need to know before you go and destroy ALL the men."

SIXTY-THREE

Pat gaped in horror at the failed petition, now closed. Her Lytoky women, it turned out, did not want her to pardon Jordan Danforth.

"But he's not the real rapist!" she wanted to tell them. *The man they see is Paul Brown!* She had forgotten the two men's identities had remained switched for the trial. Apparently, no one had ever switched them back.

She looked at the courtroom scene. The judge was pounding her gavel, Gloria was weeping, and Myrna, the District Attorney, was trying to object. Pat knew there would be no further appeal.

She turned to face the cameras. The public expected her concurrence. She thought of her daughter, and of her Presidential vows—taken just two days ago—and slumped against the big screen behind her. The back of her head rested on Brown's enlarged identification photo.

"I'm sorry," she said. "I wash my hands of this execution. You have chosen 'Jordan Danforth' to die; so be it."

SIXTY-FOUR

Kat knelt with her head pulled back and arms stretched taut. Someone spit in her face and the mob laughed. Hands above her pushed, tore at her skari wrapping, and clawed at her hair. Tears ran down her face, and for a moment, her throat caught. All around her, the angry mob was chanting.

"Danforth's blood must die! Execute Danforth's child!"

In desperation, Kat clasped her fingers together as she silently began to pray.

***

Jordan and Alex rounded an underground corner where they stumbled into two LPs guarding the subway platform.

"Where are you going?" they asked Alex. "This man is scheduled for execution!"

"I was told to take him to the Oasis," she explained. She stepped forward and presented her V-Cell credentials.

When the first officer reached for the supposed orders, Alex caught her hand, wrenched it behind her back, and grabbed for her gun. Immediately, the other LP drew her weapon, but Alex shot first. Then she elbowed the first guard in the nose.

"Move!" she yelled to Jordan.

Jordan, still in handcuffs, crouched low as shots came from behind. Then he ran ahead toward the awaiting shuttle. A bullet grazed his upper arm an instant before he heard the shot. He turned and saw Alex racing toward him, with three more LP's in pursuit.

Jordan and Alex were only six feet from the train's open doorway when gunfire erupted. It sounded like exploding popcorn kernels. Alex faltered, falling against Jordan, and they both went down. Jordan looked up and saw the subway's doors beginning to close.

***

Through tear-filled eyes, Kat beheld her attackers. Their small pupils and hideous sneers made them look inhuman. Behind them, loomed East St. Louis' Cis-Star Yardstick tower.

"Danforth's blood must die!" the women chanted as they beat her.

Suddenly, a squeal thundered overhead and made her attackers look up. At first, Kat thought it was a voice from the heavens, but then she realized it was from a bullhorn.

"Stop! Don't hurt her!" said the voice, as the helicopter began its descent. "You are all under arrest! Move back!"

Shots were fired above the crowd, and the people dispersed.

"Kat! Can you stand?" came the loud voice.

She tried but couldn't. Her legs were too numb from the hard cobblestones, and her right ankle was sprained. She braced herself as gale-force winds slammed her flat against the ground. When the Cis-Star helicopter's skids touched down, a woman's face appeared. She immediately leapt and ran to Kat's side, crouching low. The older woman's troubled face looked somehow familiar.

"Marisa?"

Her birthmother nodded quizzically, but she didn't ask how she knew.

"Yes, it's me! I heard you'd escaped. Come on!"

Marisa reached for her and glanced anxiously at the crowd, who stood watching from thirty feet away, like hyenas watching for a sign of weakness. Underneath the helicopter's whirling blades Kat heard them resume their rumbling chant, "Shed the Blood of Man…"

"Hurry!"

Marisa dipped to wrap Kat's arm over one shoulder and hoisted her up. Kat's legs felt like rubber. The rush of blood made her swoon and stagger backward, nearly taking Marisa with her, but the older woman tightened her jaw and took a lurching step forward.

Around them, the hyenas were closing in.

"What about Jordan?" Kat asked.

She had doubted Marisa would hear her, but the woman answered with a grunt. "Buford is taking care of Jordan; don't worry! Come on! Let's get you out of here!"

They were almost to the door when Kat saw the pilot pointing furtively behind them. Leaning on her mother for support, Kat reached for a soldier's hand inside the helicopter.

Suddenly, a near-sonic blast exploded above them. It shook the ground, and both Kat and Marisa cupped their ears. A woman's voice—it sounded like her Aunt Waverly's voice—followed the tone, calling the people back.

"DANFORTH'S BLOOD MUST DIE!" it said. "EXECUTE DANFORTH'S CHILD!"

Kat squinted up. The words were streaming from the Yardstick's exterior speakers. They overlapped and repeated, growing faster and louder until the crowd returned to its previous fighting frenzy. Arms grabbed at her again, and she fought back. Instants later, just as she was certain they had her, she felt herself falling. She heard someone calling her name.

"Kat!"

SIXTY-FIVE

From Waverly Nelson's workstation high above East St. Louis' cobblestone plaza, Taylor heard a distraction below. It sounded like a helicopter.

Focus! she told herself. *Keep your eyes on the screen; pretend you're in surgery!* She knew if her eyes wavered for a full second, the screen would turn off and she would have to reboot.

Five minutes ago, after climbing the last flight, she had entered through the unlocked door and logged onto Waverly's computer. Following Gloria's detailed instructions, she had found what she was looking for in a file named ADRAYS, but couldn't activate the program.

Wait a minute. What's that?

Then her gaze fell on a tab labeled AUDIBLE OPTION. The instant she chose it, however, a loud boom came from the speakers outside, followed by the words, "DANFORTH'S BLOOD MUST DIE! EXECUTE DANFORTH'S CHILD!"

The building trembled. Taylor instinctively covered her ears. A second later, when she hastily reopened her eyes, the screen had already gone dead.

SIXTY-SIX

A strong wind buffeted them as Danforth casually leaned against the Info-Swirl's balcony rail and considered the woman he had, until now, considered a friend. "I remember you," he said. "You were that young prostitute who gave birth next to Marisa!"

Ah! Here it comes, Waverly thought. *Soon he'll be down on his knees begging my forgiveness.*

"I remember that day distinctly," he continued. That feral look was still in his eyes. "Marisa gave birth that day, too, as you will recall. She was a scrawny little thing."

Waverly frowned. *Is he saying that Marisa was scrawny?* She didn't understand, but at least he was spilling his guts, as she had programmed.

"This may surprise you," he continued, "but I had been hoping for a son. You can imagine my disappointment, then, when it turned out Marisa had a girl. I mean, really! What could I do with a daughter back then? A man like me needs a son to carry on the family name! Anyway, as luck would have it, a plump, healthy boy had just been born—literally before my very eyes! How's that for divine intervention?"

Waverly had glanced away in thought halfway through his little speech. Danforth must have seen her confusion.

"That's right; Jordan is your son! I switched them at birth! I announced everything just a few minutes ago to New Canaan on my public broadcast. Didn't you get it? I guess not, by the look on your face."

Is he actually enjoying himself? she wondered.

298

"Well, then, in that case," he continued, standing erect again in a gesture of mock formality, "let me be the first to congratulate you. Surprise! You had a boy!"

Waverly's shoulders sagged, momentarily perplexed, as she rubbed at her head thoughtfully.

In the stillness that followed, they heard a loud boom from across the river. It sounded like a mass notification beacon. A second later, Danforth's desk teleVISOR clicked on. Through the open balcony doorway behind her, she heard its Emergency Broadcasting Tone, and then Honey Campbell's voice excitedly reporting. Her words reverberated on the close-circuit monitor, as well, since the Broadcast was also playing on the street speakers, below, and therefore on the penthouse office wall monitor. It created a surreal, echo-effect.

"Attention, please! As we have been reporting all morning, Jordan Danforth's execution is about to begin. The President's request for a pardon has failed, and so has the court's unusual appeal. Jordan Danforth has just arrived and is being strapped onto a gurney. Looks like he was already sedated, some, because he was moving very slowly. Above the blindfold, we can see his sun-bleached hair. The doctors are ready. Any minute now, the countdown will begin."

"No!" Waverly whispered, startled by her own sudden concern.

"In related news," Honey continued, "Kat Buford, who was just recently identified by Senator Danforth as his long-lost biological daughter, is currently being mobbed in East St. Louis. We take you live to the scene, where it appears a Cis-Star helicopter is attempting to lift off!"

"That's right, Honey!" another reporter's voice chimed in, apparently from a second helicopter providing the footage. "Kat is trying to get inside, but the crowd keeps pulling her back. It's hard to see what's happening, but-. Oh my! Now the mob is going for the chopper! They are climbing onto the running boards and… No, wait! The chopper is safe. She jumped out! It's taking off without her! Oh! I've never witnessed anything like this before! The crowd has totally engulfed her!"

"No!" Waverly cried, and staggered back against the rail.

The roar from the wall-mounted monitor was also growing louder. Per the announcer, the crowd below had broken through the Info-Swirl's front doors and would soon breach the inner doors to Danforth's express elevator cab.

Waverly looked up at Danforth. Her first thought was that he resembled a bleating sheep next up for slaughter. His eyes were wide, and perspiration covered his upper lip and forehead. His face was blotchier than she'd ever seen it.

"Sorry to interrupt," Honey's voice echoed again. "We will continue to show the East St. Louis footage in split-screen view, but right now, you can witness the execution on the right side of your screen. The countdown has begun. In Ten... Nine..."

Waverly turned to face the TV. Helpless to form coherent words, her mind went back to all those years spent planning.

I had a little boy? she thought. *Jordan is my son? How can any of this be true?*

"Eight... Seven... Six..."

She remembered Jordan's last words to her, "I forgive you," and felt her knees weaken. She stepped back once, and her back was to the balcony rail.

Oh God! What have I done?

"Five... Four..."

Her heart went out to both children—to her stolen, infant son, and to the girl she'd always thought of as her own—and to the damage she had caused them both.

Oh, I'm so sorry!

Just then, from inside the office the elevator made a ding and the doors slid opened, revealing at least a dozen men.

"Danforth's blood must die!" they chanted as they rushed out as though in a daze.

"Three... Two... One."

Suddenly, Danforth collapsed against her. Both his hands clutched at his heart and he gasped. His eyes rose to the heavens as his full weight pinned her against the outward-sloping balcony glass railing. She saw in his face what she had so ardently sought; astonishment, fear, and pain. His wet lips opened into a perfect, rounded "O." She waited for the feeling of satisfaction, but nothing came. She was completely devoid of emotion.

The massive, cracked pane held for only an instant. Like careless skaters splayed out on thin ice, she and Danforth froze in morose anticipation. Just before the glass gave way, splintering into a thousand, falling pieces, Waverly felt oddly at peace for the first time in over nineteen years, since her grandmother had died. Her all-consuming hatred had, at last, vanished.

She wondered if Jordan had truly forgiven her, like he had said. He had been tortured, both mentally and physically—*All because of me!*—yet before his execution, her son had been able to forgive.

Why hadn't I?

When the glass finally gave way, it was like being in a slow-motion Adray film. She saw Danforth reach out a flailing arms for a handhold, and felt his thick fingers encircle her arm. There was no time to squirm away. Like *the Awakening* statue in D.C., Danforth was falling, hurtling toward the next spiraling level 250 feet down, and he was taking her with him.

For a moment, it felt like she was flying.

DAYS LATER

The Revelation

"Rarely do we find men who willingly engage in hard, solid thinking. There is an almost universal quest for easy answers and half-baked solutions. Nothing pains some people more than having to think."

-Martin Luther King, Jr.

DEPOSITION #20561110.004
(Continued from Previous Deposition)

That fall should have killed me. Instead, it probably saved my life. My own people had intended to kill me. I saw it in their eyes as they rushed off the elevator and chanted their slogans. One man even grabbed my desk teleVISOR screen, undoubtedly planning to crush in my skull. When the glass finally broke and the crowd watched us fall, I guess they assumed we were both dead.

They were half-right.

By the time they realized I was still alive, suspended by a window-washer platform three floors down, they had apparently come to their senses. I woke up here, in St Elizabeth's hospital in East St. Louis—of all places— under Dr. Bott's care. I guess Buford didn't think I was safe in New Canaan.

Doc says it will take me three months to learn to walk again. That's nothing; it took me three days just to learn the truth. Seemed like an eternity.

When Buford came to visit that day, she was the last person I expected to see. Our conversation was stilted, at first.

"You look different," she said.

"I've lost weight."

"It's not that."

Her words were unsettling. Was she mocking me? Or could she tell I had changed? True, I had only been in the hospital a few days, and I had already lost fifteen pounds, but I guess that's not what she meant. Maybe self-torment leaves a mark. Alone in my hospital bed all that time without visitors or outside news must have transformed me.

Anyway, when she finally told me what she had come there to say, all I could do was stare at her.

"Marshall, they're alive," she said. "Both of them."

How could she be so cruel? I thought.

Then she explained. The real rapist was dead: executed, as the public had demanded whether they knew it or not. The public's appetite for vengeance was sated with Paul Brown's death, and my son—I guess I will always think of him as my son—was safe.

Even so, according to Buford, Jordan had barely escaped with his life. Amid gunfire, he had dragged a Transport Lieutenant into the shuttle's train just as the doors were beginning to close. After that, the Rebellion had helped them both find refuge. (Buford wouldn't tell me where. Odd they still consider me a threat, but who could blame them after everything I've done?)

Finally, she told me about Katherine, my daughter—the girl who could always turn my head, albeit usually away from her.

"The helicopter didn't take off without her," Buford explained. "She was safe inside. It was Marisa who jumped. Marisa sacrificed herself to save her daughter."

That's when I started to cry.

I have to admit they were tears of relief. Not over Katherine, per se. I had already accepted her death, so news of her safety hadn't really affected me yet. No, as crazy as it sounds, I was relieved to know Marisa hadn't forsaken me. For days, I had awaited her confrontation.

When she hadn't come, I had imagined the worst. To me, the worst had been her indifference, not her demise.

Then Buford did the unthinkable. She patted my shoulder.

"Don't beat yourself up too much, Marshall," she said. "You weren't yourself. We were all under Waverly's control. She targeted you first, and hard, then she went after me. It's not your fault."

I looked at her in amazement. That's when I knew the war between us was over, and that she was telling me the truth about the Adrays being destroyed.

Someone, she had explained, had rebooted Cis-Star's server and disrupted all outgoing messages by sending wavelengths out-of-phase with the original frequency.

"It's called Destructive Interference," Buford had explained, and I believe her.

Why do I believe her? It's simple! If the Adrays were still working, she wouldn't have been so kind.

Unfortunately, though, I know the truth: I chose my fate long before Waverly's frequencies. I deserved what I got.

I cannot explain why I felt entitled to switch the children. At the time, I told myself girls belonged in the east and boys in the west, but that's not it. Truth is... I didn't want a daughter. There; I admit it! I turned away from her in disgust because I was selfish. I watched her grow up from afar and never looked back until I saw her years later. Even then, I didn't feel guilty... only jealous. Jealous that she and Buford seemed so happy.

It's no secret Jordan and I never bonded. Lord knows it was my own fault. I guess I felt he had too much of his mother in him, and for that I could never forgive him... not that he needed my forgiveness.

Anyway, now you know my story and you know that Waverly's fall was an accident. I didn't push her, as some have claimed, and I didn't mean for this to happen. I am guilty of many things, but not that. I can't wait to publish my memoirs and to show the public how much I've changed.

---End of Senator Marshall Danforth's official testimony

EPILOGUE

After taping the Senator's deposition regarding the accidental death of Waverly Nelson, Detective Beverly Sparks turned off her V-Corder and left Danforth's hospital room.

He does look different, she admitted.

With a sunken eye socket and multiple broken bones, including his nose and both ankles, it was hard to look at the man without seeing metal, gauze, or bruising. The scar above his right ear, from the secret implant Dr. Bott had installed, was still oozing through the bandage. Beverly knew he had been given a pacemaker as well, and that he probably faced open-heart surgery soon if he didn't change his diet. With everything he had been through over the last few days, including impeachment proceedings and multiple surgeries, he looked appropriately pathetic, but the Rebellion wasn't fooled. They knew he was still a threat. He had all but admitted it in his deposition.

His blog (or memoir, he called it, which he claimed would document his healing process) was just the beginning. Before long, he would once again start having notions of grandeur. So, the Rebellion had taken action. Thanks to the Uniray chip Gloria had provided (a Cis-Star prototype, apparently), which was now imbedded in Danforth's temple, they would keep Danforth's thoughts in line.

"Like Waverly always said," Gloria had smiled when she handed over the tiny package, "keep your friends close and your enemies on close-circuit TV!"

It had been good to see Gloria smiling, Beverly had thought.

Now, as Beverly entered a private on-call room down the hall from the Senator, she watched Dr. Bott instantly hop off a cot and rush over.

"Did you get it?" she asked, excitedly.

"You bet. The case can now be officially closed."

"And what about the implant?"

Beverly bent and kissed Taylor behind her left ear.

"He bought every word. He's convinced the Adrays were destroyed."

"Let's go tell Alex and the others!"

Beverly held Taylor in place and kissed her lower on the throat. Then she moved lower still. Taylor giggled. Around her neck, a small, hand-held ladybug-shaped device hummed benignly from a chain. With Beverly's ear by the device (and moving lower with every kiss), she imagined she could hear the faint program still emanating from within.

"THE ADRAYS WERE DESTROYED; THAT'S WHY BUFORD WAS SO KIND..."

"Alex and Robert can wait," Beverly murmured, moving lower still. "Captain Chad is busy reintroducing them to Bobby, so there's no rush."

Taylor arched her neck and let out a delighted sigh. "Mmmm," she responded. "This will definitely take more than a minute."

Beverly chuckled. "Aren't you glad I'm not a man?" she said.

***

A heavy fog settled over the coastal dock as two weary bodies embraced. The older woman, standing a head shorter than the other, stepped back and surveyed her daughter at arm's length. Beyond her, an awaiting ship swayed gently.

"You're sure you won't stay?" Pat asked. The two smiled, reading each other's thoughts by the tears in their eyes. "I didn't think so." She sighed, and then added, "I'm glad you stayed for Marisa's funeral, though, and for Waverly's."

"I still can't believe Marisa died for me," Kat said, lowering her eyes.

"I can," Pat said, and reached out to tuck a stray wisp of brown hair behind her daughter's ear. Kat caught her hand and pressed it to her cheek. After a moment, both turned and walked, arm-in-arm, toward the boat's metal gangplank.

"I know it sounds funny because I just learned she was my biological mother," Kat said, "but after all these years hearing Marisa's voice in my head, through Jordan, I miss her, you know? It's like I grew up with two mothers, all along, and never realized it." She glanced up, as though belatedly afraid she had hurt her mother's feelings, but Pat only smiled.

"Actually, you had three."

Katherine winced, and after a moment nodded her head. "You're right of course. I guess, in her own way, Aunt Waverly thought she was looking out for me, too."

"I wonder what King Solomon would have said about that?"

"I think he would have said I was lucky to be loved by so many," Kat said. A large tear fell to her cheek and they hugged. The cruiser rocked in the mist. Its engine giving off a faint smell of diesel that mixed with the salt sea air. Another moment passed.

"I wish I could go with you," Pat said at last.

"No, you don't," Kat said. Pat couldn't help noticing the lack of childish jealousy that had always seemed to surface whenever they used to talk about Pat's public duties. "We've discussed this already, and your people need you. They're like children who need to learn how to think again. And…" she smiled, "I happen to know from personal experience you're pretty good with kids."

A horn sounded.

"It's not too late to change your mind," her mother reminded her one last time. "I mean, Jordan is-" She couldn't utter the rest.

"Jordan is male!" she wanted to say. "How can you be sure you're in love with him?"

The idea of interacting with MEN was still offensive to her, and the thought of Katherine going off to be with one felt wrong. Prejudice couldn't change overnight, she realized, but she had committed to trying.

"Mom, I have to go to him, don't you see? It doesn't matter that he's male. He's not the enemy. He's not like his father!" That thought made Kat pause. "I mean, he's not like MY father." She sighed heavily. "It's still so weird to think of him as my father."

The ship's horn blew again, then, and the two women embraced a final time. The tide wouldn't wait.

***

On board, Kat waited until her mother's waving figure on the dock was out of sight, then she turned toward the horizon. The salty breeze stung her cheeks. Ahead of her, there was no trace of land, nor her adventures yet to come. Still, she could sense it out there. She inhaled slowly.

She and Jordan had not yet regained their telepathic abilities, but she liked to believe he was equally impatient for their reunion.

Though no one could confirm why their communications hadn't resumed, a Cis-Star technician had theorized that Kat and Jordan's original connection must have been a Unirays' side effect from when Waverly had first targeted them as children.

"That's the thing with prototypes," had come the tech's best guess. "Must have been really strong. We have no idea what future side effects might be."

Kat feared the severed link might be permanent.

Not that it matters now, she realized.

She could feel Jordan's presence far deeper than where he had once only touched her mind. Now, she knew he was in her heart. And this time, she vowed, nothing would keep them apart.

THE END

Made in the USA
Columbia, SC
16 November 2020